Love and Liquidation

A CHOREOGRAPHED COUP

JASON WRENCH

A Choreographed Coup
ISBN # 978-1-80250-757-7
©Copyright Jason Wrench 2024
Cover Art by Kelly Martin ©Copyright April 2024
Interior text design by Claire Siemaszkiewicz
Pride Publishing

A
CHOREOGRAPHED
COUP

Dedication

This book is dedicated to my Ninja Rebels, whose insightful critiques have been the sharpening stone to my pen. Your honesty and camaraderie were invaluable in this journey. Additionally, I dedicate this work to my students, who fill each day with inspiration. Your curiosity and zest for learning are the sparks that ignite my creativity.

Acknowledgements

First, I want to express my profound gratitude to the exceptional team at Pride Publishing Family, specifically Claire Siemaszkiewicz, Rebecca Scott and Jamie Rose. Their collective efforts and dedication are truly remarkable, and I am privileged to be a part of this dynamic team. Second, my sincere thanks go to my fellow Ninja Writers, whose consistent encouragement fuels my creativity and keeps me writing. Last, I must acknowledge my colleagues, family and friends, who continually inspire me with their actions and words.

Chapter One

Blayne

Blayne gave himself one last look in the mirror. *I look like an idiot*, he thought. His boyfriend, Ethan Bond — one of the five members of the pop group ZERO — had assured him that the outfit was perfect for a concert. It was a white T-shirt under a black T-shirt, black skinny jeans rolled up at the ankles and white tennis shoes without socks. To complete the look, he also had a black lambskin leather jacket, accented with navy-blue satin lining. "I look like I should be a model." In Blayne's mind, that idea was not exactly reassuring. He applied some pomade to his hands and worked it through his short, blond hair until it was tamed to his liking.

There was a buzz from his left. He glanced at a text message on his iPhone screen.

Driver will be there in five minutes.

"The driver will be here in five minutes," he announced to the small group of friends in his apartment living room. He grabbed his favorite cologne, gave a quick spritz and walked through the fragrant mist before pocketing his wallet, keys and cell phone. Coat in hand, he left his bedroom.

"It's about time," Kira remarked as he emerged. "I thought I'd have to rescue you." She paused for a second and let out a low whistle. "Look at you, all grown up." She pantomimed wiping a tear from her eye.

"That's it, I'm changing," Blayne declared.

"Why?" Kira asked.

Blayne gestured to his outfit. "It's not me."

"Wow, Mr. Dickenson, you look almost hot," Jamie Reich teased from the couch. The sixteen-year-old had short, green spiky hair and wore a cast on his arm, a remnant from an attack a month earlier. The bullies had turned into violent sexual predators and were now behind bars. And while Blayne didn't wish harm on anyone, he hoped the trio would experience a fraction of the fear and torment they'd put Jamie through.

"And, Blayne," Dr. Madeline Reich, Jamie's mother, said, "you look devilishly handsome. I'm sure you'll stand out tonight."

"Thanks," Blayne replied, letting the corner of his lip creep up as he averted his gaze. Blayne was in love. It had only been a little over a month since he had finally met his now-boyfriend, Ethan, but they had been pretty much inseparable ever since someone tried to blow up Ethan, shot Blayne then tried to kill them both, along with Kira, all for a fucking cell phone. And no one seemed to know what had been so fucking important on Ethan's phone that it cost hundreds of lives.

Honk, honk. The sound was right outside his front door. "I guess that's our cue." He took a deep breath through his nose and let it out as the rest gathered themselves, stood and headed toward the door. Kira opened it, and Jamie and Madeline followed as Blayne took up the rear. The last thing he did was enter his security code into the keypad next to the door, a recent addition to his apartment. The security panel was a 'gift' from Ethan's manager and a complete security upgrade after 'the incident', as the band had called everything that had happened.

"Door is armed," a robotic voice chirped as Blayne shut it behind him. He walked out into the parking lot and found Zahava Peretz standing next to the open door of the black SUV.

"Ethan told me he had arranged transportation. He hadn't told me it would be you, Zahava." The woman wore a black suit, white shirt and a black tie. He couldn't see her eyes behind the dark sunglasses.

"I was available. They don't need all four of us for a simple security detail at the venue."

Ms. Z. was one of four bodyguards hired by Ethan's band for their protection. While the other three bodyguards always seemed more stand-offish, Zahava had been friendly to Blayne from the start. Blayne knew little about her. She was in her late twenties or early thirties and had worked for the Israeli Institute for Intelligence and Special Operations before an injury had forced her into early retirement. Somehow, Ron Hightower, the band's manager, was given her information, and Zahava had been flown to the States and never left. She was technically a dual citizen, born on the East Coast before her parents moved to Israel.

Blayne heard the door shut behind him as he sat down and reached for the seatbelt. A moment later, the driver's side door opened, and Ms. Z. climbed in. Without checking on her charges in the back, her eyes were already scanning the road.

"ETA is approximately thirty-five minutes," she said, but Blayne didn't think she was talking to them. The SUV headed out of the apartment parking lot and headed to the Toyota Center for the ZERO concert.

He listened to idle chitchat around him, leaned his head back and closed his eyes. Immediately, Ethan's face, with his boyish features, brown hair and blue eyes, filled his mind, the image of Ethan smiling. Of course, Blayne immediately remembered all the other things Ethan's lips had done to him the previous night. Ethan may not have been the most experienced lover Blayne ever had, but Ethan made up for his lack of experience with a willingness to satisfy Blayne that was unparalleled. Ethan wanted to try everything with him. Since Ethan had come home with Blayne after the attack, he'd been like a kid in a sexual candy store. Millions of fans worldwide may have wanted Ethan, but only Blayne got to be with him – got to touch Ethan, got to taste Ethan, got to feel what it was like to be inside Ethan. Blayne's crotch stiffened against the skinny jeans as he remembered the night before. Ethan's nipples, like Blayne's own, were hardwired directly to his cock. Play with those while stroking or blowing him, and the ultimate climax would blow them away.

Blayne felt the SUV exit the interstate. He looked out of the front window and saw the Toyota Center looming ahead in the late afternoon sun. The SUV drove past the outer parking lots that would soon be filled with cars, trucks and SUVs, all there to see his boyfriend perform. They could watch him, but only Blayne got to have him.

The SUV drove around the outer perimeter of the Toyota Center before heading south on Jackson, then west on Bell. The SUV pulled into the Tundra Parking Garage next to the arena. It slowly crept up to the third story before stopping near the sky bridge that would take them to the Center.

Ms. Z. parked the SUV in the middle of the garage and turned to them. "Make sure you keep this around your neck." Ms. Z. handed Blayne a stack of security badges and lanyards. "These are your all-access passes to the facility." Blayne wore a lanyard around his neck and handed the others theirs. "I'm going to let you out here. You're going to cross the sky bridge. When they scan you in on the other side, see Meghan, the Event Services Coordinator for the Center. She'll take you to the green room, where you can wait for the band until they're ready." Ms. Z. turned to Blayne. "Don't be surprised if Ethan's PA comes to drag you back to his dressing room. He's been worried all afternoon that something would go wrong with getting you here on time."

With that, Ms. Z. exited the vehicle and came around to open the door for Blayne, Kira, Jamie and Madeline. Blayne finally shrugged into the leather coat. He glimpsed himself in the glass bridge while the group started crossing as Ms. Z. drove away. Ahead, they could see ticket people already poised with their scanners. There was no one else on the bridge but them at this early hour, but a few people who worked there were milling around ahead.

"It's a shame Alan couldn't join us this evening," Blayne told Madeline. Madeline had been quietly dating the Pennington University Vice Provost for a while.

"Surprisingly, pop concerts just aren't his thing. He'd much rather hang back and chill at a wine bar or take in some jazz at a back-alley bar in New Orleans," Madeline said.

Her collar had flopped up when she'd put the concert lanyard around her neck. Jamie noticed and immediately reached over to fix it.

"Please have your passes ready," a ticket taker said as they approached the arena side of the bridge.

"We're supposed to be meeting Meghan," Blayne said.

"Ah yes," the woman said as she scanned their badges. "The guests. We were told you'd be here shortly. Let me call Meghan." The woman pulled a walkie-talkie from her belt and said, "Meghan, it's Sharice at the Tundra Entrance with the VIPs. Again, the VIPs have arrived."

A squawking sound came over the radio that Blayne couldn't make out, but Sharice said, "Ms. Flores said she'd be here momentarily. You can go stand over there." She motioned to a side lobby next to the glass that overhung Bell Street. Blayne looked down at traffic passing underneath.

"Good afternoon. You must be the friends of ZERO," a voice cut through the silence.

Blayne turned to look at the businesswoman walking toward the group. She wore a gray pantsuit. Her shoulder-length black hair had light brown highlights that popped in the foyer lighting.

"Blayne Dickenson." He extended his hand to greet the woman, who freely took it and shook it. "And with me are Kira Strickland and Madeline and Jamie Reich."

"Meghan Flores," the woman said, turning and shaking everyone's hand. "Welcome to the Toyota Center. Please ask me or anyone on my staff if you need anything while visiting us. If they can't help you, they'll find me. Are we all here?"

Kira answered. "Another one of our party will show up later —"

"Yes, Special Agent Sarah Murphy," Meghan cut in. "I'll ensure she is ushered into the greenroom as soon as she arrives." Then, without skipping a beat, she spun on her heels, all six inches. "Follow me." Meghan Flores started walking through the arena without waiting to see if anyone would follow.

She walked the group around for almost thirty minutes as a tour guide. "We broke ground in 2001 and opened in 2003."

"Have you been here this whole time?" Madeline asked.

"No. I joined the team in 2015. Before moving back to Houston, I worked at the Toyota Arena in Ontario, California, in guest relations and event management."

"How many seats does this place have?" Jamie asked. The group stood in one of the many social clubs with amazing views of the arena inside.

"The arena sits eighteen-thousand, three-hundred guests on game days, and we can seat about nineteen-thousand guests for concerts."

"There are going to be nineteen-thousand people here tonight?" Jamie asked, the shock in his voice clear.

Blayne walked over to the railing and stared into the arena.

"No," Megan answered. "Tonight's concert only uses about two-hundred and seventy of the full three-hundred-and-sixty degrees. The band's layout doesn't enable concertgoers to sit behind the stage. I think we're expecting some fourteen-thousand visitors tonight."

Blayne looked down across the arena at the stage on the other end. Behind it was a giant wall of monitors. Images flashed across the giant screens. The crew scurried back and forth on the floor like ants. He marveled at how so many people seemed to know exactly what they were doing and how their small part fit into the larger picture of a multi-million-dollar concert.

"Mr. Dickenson?"

The sound of his name snapped him out of his wonderment.

"Yes?" The words were out of his mouth more by instinct than anything else.

"It's time to head down to the green room," Meghan said.

Blayne smiled and started following the group. Meghan led them out of the club area to an escalator down to the stadium floor. She passed a few checkpoints, and everyone was summarily let through as they followed their guide, who continued to rattle off facts about the facility.

They walked through an entryway and right onto the floor of the Toyota Center. Blayne paused just for a moment to take in the arena's size. He'd been inside a large arena before but never a professional one.

"And it only cost us about two-hundred-and-thirty-five million dollars," Kira mumbled from his left.

"Imagine what the city could have done with those funds."

"You're right, Ms. Strickland. The citizens of Houston made a substantial investment in the Toyota Center when they voted to increase the sales tax by zero-point-one percent. But it was an investment. For example, we held a UFC event several years ago estimated to have had an economic impact of twenty-five million dollars. Half of that was in direct spending by the organization and our out-of-town visitors. That one event garnered almost a half-million in direct tax revenue for the city. People only often hear about the initial investments in these facilities. Still, they rarely hear the full story about how these facilities pay for themselves over time."

"Mm-hmm," Kira responded, clearly not wholly buying the argument.

Meghan had clearly dealt with skeptics before, because she smiled and led the group through the arena floor to a side tunnel area to the left of the stage. For the first time, Blayne saw heavy amounts of security. Blayne recognized Mr. J. talking with security personnel Blayne didn't recognize. At six-five, with three-hundred pounds of solid muscle and a bald head that glinted in the stadium lights, Mr. J. stood out like a giant security beacon. Of course, Mr. J. wore his sunglasses. Blayne had seen none of the ZERO security team without sunglasses…ever.

The group was led through a metal detector, and their bags were checked by security personnel. In a few minutes, they entered the part of the arena that was more business than entertainment. The gray concrete walls had a few decorative items adorning them, reminding you that the arena was the home of the

Houston Rockets. Still, it was mostly plain gray industrial walling.

"Here you go," Meghan said, opening the door to a room. "The band will be with you when they finish getting ready. You probably have" — she glanced down at her watch — "at least thirty minutes. So please, enjoy the buffet." She gestured to the tables of steel chafers. Caterers immediately began unrolling the tops of the dishes and the smell of food entered the room. "And if you need to use the facilities" — she gestured toward a hallway at the other end of the room — "they're right down there."

With that, she spun on her heels and left the group, who were now outnumbered by attendants and caterers to serve them.

"So, this is how the other half lives," Madeline commented. "I hate to admit this, but getting used to this kind of treatment wouldn't take me long."

Chapter Two

Ethan

He stood center stage, his chest heaving up and down from the choreography he'd just finished executing for the third time that day.

"Thank you," a voice over the intercom said in heavily accented English. After almost two months of working on this concert, Ethan's nightmares were filled with a combination of Ji Chu-young's and Sally Higgins' voices. The concert director and the choreographer made a dynamic duo, who strove for perfection. "That will be all," Chu-young's voice said.

"Dancers, stick around for notes," Higgins yelled from somewhere in the back.

"Oh, thank God," Zach said from Ethan's left. "I thought they were going to have us rerun it."

"You and me both, brother. You and me both," Orr chimed in.

Ric just let out a sigh before bending at the waist.

"Yeah," Ethan chimed in. "This is worse than two-a-days when I was in high school. At least high school football coaches had parents to answer to if we died of heat exhaustion."

The four slowly exited the stage to the right and headed down the staircase. Ethan's personal assistant was waiting at the bottom of the stairs. He hadn't believed he needed a PA, but both Ron Hightower, the band's manager, and Dan Rawlins, the band's producer, had insisted he get one after the events in New Orleans and Houston the previous month.

His PA, Lucas Andrade, had been born in Brazil before his family had immigrated to the US when he was two. Lucas had graduated from high school in his mid-teens. He finished college the spring before at the University of Houston at the ripe old age of twenty. Lucas was objectively attractive, but he seemed oblivious. He had the whole 'hot-gay-nerd' vibe going on and ran Ethan's life better than ever.

"I just got the update. Blayne and his friends should be here in under thirty minutes. You need to shower and get ready. You have maybe ninety minutes before you need to be in the green room for the official meet-and-greet," Lucas read from his tablet PC.

"When Blayne gets here…"

"Yes?" Lucas said, looking up at Ethan.

"Can you bring him to my dressing room?"

Lucas used his stylus to make a note on his screen. "How long do you need with him in private?"

"Wow, when you say it like that—"

"I don't mean it. Well…err…if that's what you want—"

"Calm down. Blayne and I won't hook-up in the dressing room."

"Good. Because you wouldn't have time to take another shower," Lucas said dryly.

"What if we just did it in the shower?" Ethan joked.

Lucas looked up to the left for a second before quirking his head. "I guess that could work. Should I pencil that in?"

"I was joking," Ethan said, widening his eyes. From his right, he heard Rick snickering.

"Oh?" Lucas responded.

"I think I can find my way to the dressing room from here," Ethan said. "Take a break."

"It's not time for a break," Lucas responded. "I'll go respond to interview requests and other emails."

"You do that," Ethan said before he took off down the tunnel to the dressing rooms.

Ethan heard feet jogging to catch up to him. He was about to spin and yell "*What?*" when Ric's voice cut through the silence, "I love your little robot. He's so much fun to watch."

"Lucas is not a robot. He's just…efficient."

Ric quirked an eyebrow but said nothing. They walked in amiable silence until they hit their dressing rooms.

"Well, since I'm not meeting up with my boyfriend," Ric said, "I'm going to take a power nap. Tell Blayne I said hi. And if you two decide to have sex in the shower, keep it down."

Ethan was about to respond, but Ric opened the door to his dressing room and darted inside, leaving Ethan's jaw still open as he tried to find a retort. Ethan opened the door and went inside his dressing room. He walked over to the vanity slash desk and grabbed his charging cell phone. There was a single text.

Have fun tonight. Tell Blayne I send my love. Wish I could be there.
Stephanie

Stephanie Anne Mitchell was Ethan's best friend. And after she'd lost all her possessions in an explosion the previous month, Ethan had done everything in his power to help her get her life back together. He'd hired her the best lawyer he could find to help her navigate the insurance process. The insurance company claimed that the explosion was an act of terrorism. Since her policy didn't explicitly cover terrorism, they tried to deny her claim. Her lawyer argued that since her coverage provided protection against property and personal belongings being damaged because of explosions, fires and smoke, her policy did indeed cover what happened to Stephanie.

For his part, Ethan had been putting her up in an old mansion turned into a bed-and-breakfast in the Garden District until everything could be straightened out. He typed out his response.

Thanks. Excited to have Blayne see the concert. I still can't believe he's never been to a real concert.
E

With the single text sent, he stripped out of his sweaty rehearsal clothes and headed into the shower. Ethan let the warm water flow from the spout sticking out of the tiled wall.

He'd spent a lot of time in dressing room showers over the past several years. This one wasn't the largest, but it wasn't the smallest. *The showerhead would hit Blayne mid-chest.* The mental image of Blayne's chest caused Ethan to smile. He loved to lay his head on Blayne's chest and wrap his arm around his torso as they drifted off to sleep. The sound of Blayne's heartbeat was his personal white noise machine. Ethan absently started stroking himself, remembering the amazing sex they'd had the night before. He imagined what it would be like for Blayne to spin him around and have sex with him in the shower. Ethan hadn't taken Blayne yet, but the thought of it caused him to moan slightly.

"Mr. Bond?" a voice yelled over the shower, bringing Ethan out of his bliss.

"Yes? I'm kind of busy, Lucas." *In more ways than one.* Lucas was barely out of college, but he was already keeping track of Ethan's life better than Ethan ever had.

"I'm sorry to interrupt your shower, but I needed to review your revised schedule with you."

"Okay."

Lucas began rattling off everything Ethan had to do before and after the concert. Ethan only half-listened to the guy deliver his itinerary in clipped, almost military precision. He finished rinsing the soap from his body before stepping out of the shower. There was a stack of towels on a shelf near the shower, so he reached over, grabbed the top one and started drying his hair. He didn't want it too dry because the stylist team would be by to fix his hair and apply his makeup. Thankfully, the makeup would be applied after the meet-and-greet, before he went on stage. He wasn't exactly that white, but the stage lights would drown out his facial features if he had none on.

With his hair and body dry, he wrapped a towel around his waist and returned to his dressing room.

Lucas was still talking and hadn't even noticed Ethan, so he cleared his throat.

"Oh," Lucas said, his eyes leaving his tablet long enough to glance at Ethan. Lucas' eyes grew three sizes, and his jaw practically hit the ground. Ethan wanted to laugh but kept a straight face, opting to lean against the doorframe to the bathroom. Lucas gulped and tried to keep a neutral face, which caused Ethan to smile at the young man. "Well, umm...I...uhh."

"You should probably leave now."

"Yes, exactly." Lucas spun on his heels and headed to the door. "And uhh...Mr. Bond, your guests have arrived. I'll bring Mr. Dickenson back to your dressing room in about ten minutes. They're still being given a tour of the facility."

Lucas left the room. Ethan imagined Lucas leaning on the other side of the door, fanning himself. Ethan didn't consider himself vain, but he knew he was hot. You don't succeed in the world of boy bands if you aren't attractive. As much as he hated to admit it, half the band's success was that they were all crazy photogenic. The cameras loved them. Ethan had a love-hate relationship with the cameras.

He slipped the towel from his hips and hung it on the bathroom door handle. Standing stark naked, he lifted his hands over his head and stretched. He walked over to the dressing room door and locked it before heading to his suitcase. He pulled out a pair of Alessandro Cattaneo boxer briefs. They were a black square cut that provided enough support for his goods without being bulky. Ethan unrolled his yoga mat and set about doing a simple warm-up routine. He started in the lotus position, closed his eyes and focused on breathing for a few minutes. He then ran through a basic yoga sequence that stretched all his major muscle groups. His goal wasn't to exercise, just to limber up for the night's performance.

He was just finishing the routine when there was a knock at his door, as someone tried the doorknob and found it locked. "Just a second," Ethan yelled as he stood and walked over. "Who is it?"

"It's Lucas. I have Mr. Dickenson with me."

Ethan unlocked the door, opened it and poked his head around the corner. Blayne stood behind Lucas, dressed in the outfit Ethan had picked out for him the night before. He said nothing. He just reached out, grabbed the front of Blayne's T-shirt and pulled him into the dressing room.

"You have twenty —"

The door shut behind Blayne as Ethan pinned his boyfriend against the closed door, and they aggressively kissed. Pulling away, he said, "God, I've missed you."

Blayne stood there, looking down at Ethan, and smiled. "Well, I've missed you, too." Blayne reached up, put one hand on Ethan's chest and pushed him away slightly. "And while I'd love nothing more than to rip those boxers off your body and have my way with you, you have fans that are amassing in the green room."

"You're no fun," Ethan replied, putting on his best puppy-dog eyes.

"Down, boy," Blayne said. "Get ready. Like Lucas said, you have a few minutes before the stylists barge through that door."

Ethan sighed and leaned in for one more kiss before turning to the hanging rack where his clothes were. Blayne looked over at the stand.

"How many outfits do you need?"

"We have six costume changes in this concert."

"Six?"

"Yep. But I'm not even getting into my first costume yet. I must put on my meet-and-greet outfit."

"You have a meet-and-greet outfit?"

"Doesn't everyone?"

Blayne rolled his eyes as he sat down on the dressing room couch. He stretched his long arm across the back.

"God, you look fucking amazing," Ethan said, fighting the urge to straddle Blayne and lay on a barrage of kisses.

"It's growing on me. I admit, I wasn't so sure about this. But I've received enough compliments already that I'm rethinking my fashion sense."

"You had a fashion sense?" Ethan joked.

"Bitch."

"Yes, but I'm *your* bitch." Ethan rolled on a pair of socks before shimmying into his skinny jeans.

"I can practically tell your religion, those things are so tight."

"You can see my religion any time you want, baby."

Blayne licked his lips before biting on his lower one suggestively. "I can't wait to reacquaint myself with your religion after the concert."

"Tease." Ethan was putting on his T-shirt when there was another knock on the door. "Come in."

The door opened, and a team of three stylists walked into the room.

"Mr. Dickenson, if you'd come with me," Lucas said, following the stylists into the room. "I'll take you back to your friends."

"Does he have to go?" Ethan said, already sitting in a chair in front of the vanity as one stylist plugged in a hairdryer.

"Yes," Lucas said flatly. "The stylists need to do their jobs."

Ethan wanted to whine but knew better. Despite how easy it was to fluster Lucas, he had a spine of steel regarding Ethan's schedule.

"I'll see you shortly," Blayne said, who was already standing up from the sofa, ready to follow Lucas out.

Chapter Three

Blayne

Blayne looked back one last time as he exited the dressing room. He still couldn't believe this was the life he was living. Inside, Blayne was still a small-town gay boy from West Texas. Now, he was dating one of the biggest names in music. Part of him wanted to pinch himself to see if he'd wake up from this fantastic dream.

"So, how long have you two known each other?" Lucas asked as they started walking through the tunnel system back to the greenroom.

"Not too long," Blayne said in a noncommittal way. Outside of Blayne's friendship circle and the inner circle of ZERO, no one else knew the actual nature of Ethan and Blayne's relationship. Blayne assumed that Lucas had put two and two together and reached the correct conclusion. Ethan believed Lucas was utterly clueless and wanted his PA to stay that way, even though he'd admitted to Blayne that he loved messing with the poor kid.

"Did you hear he was listed as one of the most eligible bachelors in one of those teen magazines?" Lucas asked, eyeing Blayne for a reaction.

"Well, I'm sure Ethan will be officially taken off the dating market one day. But until then, we don't want to break too many young girls'…and boys' hearts, do we? With Orr's engagement announcement the past month, I don't think the world's teen population could handle another disappointment this soon."

Up ahead, a custodian pushed a cart through the tunnel. The woman turned and looked at Blayne for a fraction of a second before turning down another tunnel. "It's her." He'd recognize those glaring eyes anywhere. It was the eyes from his nightmares. Without thinking, he bounded down the hallway after the woman. *Is she here to finish the job?* He reached the intersection where the custodian had turned…and there was nothing. He listened and didn't even hear a cart being pushed. Nothing was echoing in the concrete and tiled hallway.

"Are you okay?" Lucas gasped out. Blayne looked down at the young guy, who was panting.

"I thought I saw someone," Blayne admitted. "Must have been a trick of my eyes." Even as the words came out of his mouth, Blayne wasn't sure if he believed them.

* * * *

Dr. Hennigan

The Constitutional Liberation Army were minor players as far as extremist groups went in the US. Still, the chance to take out some of the leadership of the National Democratic Party of Germany was just too enticing to miss the opportunity. When they heard that a small contingent of the CLA's leadership would meet with thugs from the far-right NDP, they decided to liquidate the leadership of both groups, hoping the vacuum would cause enough instability in both to sideline them.

Her two best operatives, Denzili and Richardson, were already in place when she arrived at the Toyota Center. Hennigan had slipped in with the loading crew, which was easy. They'd gotten full-access badges from an inside source, so the three had complete access to the facility. She looked like any other personnel working for the arena in her gray coveralls. She passed through the metal security detectors with zero problems.

"I'm inside," Dr. Hennigan said.

"Good," a voice responded in her ear. "I can see your location. You'll go down to the third door on your left and open it. You'll find a cleaning cart with your supplies."

Dr. Hennigan walked down the hallway and followed the instructions. She opened the door and slipped inside. Sure enough, the cart was waiting for her. Inside, she found a coyote beige-colored bag. It looked like an oversized attaché case, but she unzipped it to find what she needed for this evening's operation, a modified B&T SPR300 Pro rifle. At only one-hundred-and-twenty-one decibels, the .300 caliber ammunition wouldn't be heard firing over the concert sounds. The gun was perfect for this type of job because it was as close to silent as a high-powered rifle got. She inspected the firearm, putting it together before pulling it apart.

She put the bag back into the cart before exiting into the hallway. "Ms. Wilson, I'm heading to staging point one."

"You are a go," Ms. Wilson responded in her earpiece.

Dr. Hennigan pushed the cart through the maze of tunnels toward one of the elevator bays marked for staff only. She heard voices coming from her left. She swiveled her head. *Fuck.* She pushed through the intersection. "Ms. Wilson, I just saw Blayne Dickenson. I think he recognized me. I need an escape route…fast."

"How did he recognize you? He never saw your face."

"I don't know."

"Straight ahead, take the first turnoff on the right. It's thirty feet ahead of you. You'll then go another twenty feet to a secondary hall on the left. The third room down is a security room with keycard access."

Hennigan followed Ms. Wilson's instructions and barely got into the first hallway before she heard Blayne's feet hit the intersection. She didn't wait to see if he would pursue her. She kept going, keeping the cart as quiet as possible until she was safely behind the security door.

"How did that happen? How did we not have eyes on him?"

"He was in Bond's dressing room. He must have left. There's a blind spot in the security feed in that section."

"Why didn't we install a camera there?" Hennigan questioned.

"Nothing on the itinerary we hacked had Mr. Bond and Mr. Dickenson rendezvousing until the green room. You would have been in your position before that happened."

"Dammit," Hennigan said. This operation began to feel like the clusterfuck that started in New Orleans. *What about these two men keeps royally screwing up my plans?*

"I now have Dickenson on a security feed heading toward the green room. He did not pursue," Ms. Wilson let Hennigan know.

Hennigan pushed her cart back into the hall and made it safely to the perch she'd picked out for the evening's operation. Now, she simply had to lie in wait.

"Ms. Wilson, is everyone in position?"

"Yes. All is a go."

* * * *

Blayne

Blayne was already questioning his sanity. Admittedly, it wasn't the first time he'd seen the no-name, no-face woman over the last month. But those eyes... Those dark pits had been soulless as they'd pointed the gun at Ethan. He hadn't gotten as good of a look at them as Ethan had. Ethan had yelled for Blayne to run, but he still heard the woman's voice as she calmly instructed Ethan, "*I wouldn't move if I were you,*" as Blayne had run for his life.

"What's wrong?" Kira said, eyeing her friend warily as he entered the green room.

"Nothing, I'm sure it was nothing."

"I seriously doubt it's nothing. What happened? Did that boy do something—?"

"No, no, nothing like that. Besides, we didn't have time to do anything salacious," he said, trying to use a bit of bad humor.

"Oka-ay," Kira said, drawing out the word to ensure he knew she saw right through his bullshit.

"I thought I saw her."

"Who?"

"*Her,*" he said emphatically.

"Oh." Kira's eyes flashed. Blayne couldn't tell if shock, fear or anger crossed her face, but Kira masked her emotions as quickly as they had flared. "And?"

"I'm sure it was nothing. There was a custodian with a cart, but I swear it was her eyes."

"Blayne," Kira said, drawing out his name a little, "this isn't exactly the first time you've seen ghosts."

"I know. I know. I bet it was nothing. My mind played a trick on me."

"And the custodian?"

"Never saw her again. She was gone by the time I got to where I'd seen her."

"That is curious," Kira said, with a slight tilt of her head and an eyebrow furrow.

"Not that curious. There are so many passages down here. It's like a maze. She could have crawled and turned a corner before I'd gotten to her."

Kira smiled and brought him in for a hug before she pushed him away gently. "Yeah, we are *so* not huggers," Blayne said.

"No, we're not. Let's pretend that didn't happen."

"Kira," a woman's voice said.

Blayne looked over to find Special Agent Sarah Murphy walking up to them. She was wearing an outfit that was similar to Blayne's. She wore skintight black jeans, boots and a black leather jacket over a white T-shirt. Where Blayne's outfit looked like he'd stepped out of the pages of a fashion magazine, Agent Murphy looked like she was auditioning for the role of Sarah Connor in the next *Terminator* movie.

She reached out and brought Kira in for a hug before kissing her on the lips. Blayne averted his eyes to give the women a moment alone.

"How was your day?" Kira asked as she broke away.

"Not too bad. Busted a small drug ring that was using Houston Intercontinental to smuggle drugs from South America. We did all the work, ATF conducted the takedown and took all the credit for the cameras."

"That sucks," Kira said.

"It is what it is," Sarah responded.

Sarah had transferred to the Emerald City, what people called the Houston FBI field office because it was made of green glass that made it stand out like a sore thumb. The local field office had fumbled the ball, so Sarah had been asked to step into the Chief of the Houston office while the FBI made long-term plans. Almost immediately, Kira and Sarah had started dating.

"So, have you seen Ethan?" Sarah asked, bringing Blayne into their conversation.

"Yes. I just got back from hanging out in his dressing room."

"And?" Kira asked mischievously.

"And nothing," Blayne responded. "I was a good boy and didn't ravish him in his dressing room. Trust me, he wanted me to. He was only wearing his underwear when I walked in, and he proceeded to—"

"Eww," Kira joked, scrunching up her face. "I shouldn't have asked."

Sarah laughed. "You two."

"Us two what?" Kira said, making googly eyes at her girlfriend.

"You're too much." Sarah leaned in and kissed Kira. "In a good way."

"Where are Jamie and Madeline?" Sarah asked.

"One of the band's assistants agreed to show Jamie and Madeline one of the merch kiosks. I can only imagine how much stuff Jamie will return with," Kira said.

"What kind of merch do they have?" Sarah asked.

"Oh, trust me," Blayne cut in. "You name it, and they have it—T-shirts, caps, bumper stickers, albums, jackets, sweatshirts, sweatpants, underwear, shoes... You can be decked out from head to toe in ZERO merchandise."

"Underwear?" Sarah asked.

"Oh yeah. They even have a ZERO thong you can buy," Kira joked.

"You may think you're joking, but they actually sell them," Blayne said. "I should rephrase that. The band doesn't sell them, but they are available online from some websites breaking copyright laws and putting the band on a whole range of...let's just say interesting items and toys."

"So basically, if you weren't already fucking ZERO, you could get fucked by ZERO?" Kira asked.

"Eww... I *so* didn't need to know that," Sarah said.

"I'm more surprised their attorneys haven't had them taken down," Kira admitted.

"It's apparently like Whac-A-Mole. You get one site taken down, and ten others pop up to replace it. And that's not even including the do-it-yourself crowd that makes items and sells them online on global marketplaces," Blayne said.

"Wow, you've become well-versed in ZERO's business practices over the last month," Kira said. "I'm impressed."

"I'm almost finished with my doctorate, and knowing a little about global commerce is what impresses you?" Blayne asked. "I feel like I should be offended." He gave her a playful wink.

"Whatever," Kira responded with an exaggerated eye roll.

"But anyway, I've heard a lot of one-sided conversations between Blayne, the guys and the management company over the last month. I've learned a little about running a multi-million-dollar corporation. Who would have guessed boy bands were such a huge global enterprise?"

"Almost anyone who pays attention to pop culture," Kira joked.

"Excuse me," a loud voice cut through the room. Blayne turned and found Meghan Flores, the Toyota Center's Event Services Coordinator, standing in the entryway to the greenroom. "ZERO are on their way here. If you want to get a photograph with the band before the show, please line up." She gestured to where a photographer stood waiting in front of a backdrop with the band's logo. "Once your picture is taken, you'll be given an access code to the band's website, where you can download your pictures tomorrow."

She said something else, but the room erupted into applause as Zach, Ethan, Ric and Orr entered. Blayne hadn't realized how many people were in the greenroom until the deafening applause.

People immediately started jockeying for the opportunity to take pictures with the band. Blayne looked over at Jamie, who looked in awe at seeing his favorite band standing in the same room with him.

"Don't worry, Jamie," Blayne said. "Ethan promised we could take selfies with the band after the concert. I promise you'll get more one-on-one time with them than anyone else in here." The look of pure excitement that crossed Jamie's face made all the madness around them totally worth it.

"Mr. Dickenson," Lucas said, appearing out of nowhere. "Whenever you're ready, I'll happily take you and your friends to your seats."

"Oh, thanks, Lucas. I think we're ready." Blayne turned and looked at his small group. "Ready to head up?" The group nodded in agreement. Jamie practically jumped and squealed with excitement. "Lead the way."

Lucas headed out of the greenroom, followed by the group. Blayne tried to wave goodbye to Ethan, but he was so engrossed in taking pictures. *Oh well, I'll see him later.*

Blayne was glad they had Lucas ushering them through the tunnels, because he had no idea where they were. There was a turn to the left followed by a straightaway, then a turn to the right followed by another right. *Dear God, this place is a labyrinth.* In minutes, the group exited the Tundra Tunnel right at the base of stage right. Blayne nodded at Ms. Z. and Mr. J., who stood on either side of the entrance to the backstage area. He guessed Ms. A. and Mr. S. were doing the same on the other side.

Lucas led them up a flight of stairs to the right and quickly found their seats. Ethan had asked if the group wanted ground seats, but they had opted for something that gave them a better view of the entire stage.

"If you need anything during the concert, just ask one of the arena attendants. They can get ahold of Ms. Flores, who can contact me." Lucas then turned to Blayne. "Actually, you really should have my cell number. And honestly, I should probably have yours." Lucas reached out his hand expectantly. Blayne reached into his pocket and handed over his phone. Lucas hit a series of buttons. Blayne was awed by how quickly Lucas' fingers flew over the screen. "There you go. I've programmed my contact information and texted my phone, so I'll have your info." With that, Lucas spun on his heels and headed back down the stairs.

"He's…different," Kira said, leaning in close.

Blayne wiggled in his chair to access his pocket as he slipped the phone back inside. He stopped, pulled it out and put it in airplane mode before returning it.

"He means well," Blayne said, but his voice tilted upward, making it sound more like a question than a statement.

"Ladies and gentlemen, welcome to the Toyota Center!" a voice blared over the speakers. "Welcome to the stage, Riley Neon." There was polite applause as a middle-aged woman walked out on stage, waving her hands enthusiastically.

"Who's that?" Jamie asked.

"Oh, wow," Sarah said. "I had such a crush on her when I was younger."

"She was a pop singer from the early nineties, long before you were born," Kira informed Jamie.

"Oh, so, like in the prehistoric era?" Jamie replied with a smirk.

"Watch it, kid," Sarah said, leaning forward to give Jamie the stink eye.

The group laughed as the track to Riley Neon's most famous song, *Summer Forever*, started playing. "*In a world of Discmans and neon lights, we were young, wild, dancing through the night,*" the former pop star sang.

Blayne had grown up primarily on contemporary Christian music, so his knowledge of pop music was severely limited. Sure, he'd heard the song on one of the oldies stations before, but he didn't know the lyrics. On the other hand, Sarah clearly knew every word, because she was singing along with the music.

"*Summer forever, we're catching the twilight. Living in the rhythm, feeling so right,*" the chorus started. Three backup dancers joined Riley Neon on stage, and the group executed choreography while she stood stage center and kept singing.

Blayne leaned back in his chair and let the pop anthem pour over him.

Chapter Four

Dr. Hennigan

Dr. Hennigan was not a fan of crowds, so she was glad she wasn't down in the throngs. She could see nearly everyone she wanted to see using her high-powered scope from her perch in a skybox. She swiveled the scope to find the locations she'd marked earlier. Finding seating arrangements hadn't been challenging for a techie at The Foundation. *These ticketing companies need to up their security game.*

She pointed her scope toward the stage, then off to the left. She found Blayne Dickenson and Kira Strickland sitting alongside a woman and her teenage son. Dr. Hennigan focused the scope on the seat next to Kira and noticed a dressed-down Agent Sarah Murphy.

The lights in the arena suddenly dimmed as a voice boomed over the speaker system, welcoming them to the Toyota Center and the launch of ZERO's North American tour. *"The use of photography, videography and cell phones to capture any part of this event is strictly prohibited by law. Violators will be removed from the concert and could be banned from the venue permanently. Get on your feet, put your hands together and let's hear some noise for Zach, Ethan, Ric and Orr...ZERO, live in concert!"*

Dr. Hennigan turned on the night scope, so she could see in the dark. A loud, blaring orchestration started. Even though Dr. Hennigan wasn't familiar with the music, the fans clearly were. There was a loud, drawn-out note. Then the band was shot up on stage from underneath as the first musical number started. The frenzied motion on stage split people's attention until one band member sang a solo. She could hear the music, but the words were muffled from her perch. She wasn't sure if that resulted from her being so far away from the stage or if that's what pop music sounded like these days.

After listening to three songs, the real reason Dr. Hennigan was there appeared. In another skybox, she saw the lights pop on. A group of five security guards and two dignitaries entered the room. The Foundation had been alerted that the heads of the National Democratic Party of Germany and the Constitutional Liberation Army, a domestic terrorism organization, would use the cover of the concert to meet.

"Denzili, Richardson, on my mark," Dr. Hennigan said into her communication device. "You are cleared to liquidate."

* * * *

Ethan

The third song in their set was the title song from their first album, *Dog Days*. After the speed of the first two songs, Ethan was glad this song didn't have crazy choreography. Sure, the entire song was scripted from beginning to end, but it allowed him to catch his breath after the marathons of the first two high energy songs in the set.

"*The rhythm of summer, in every phrase, we're living it up, in the dog days.*" The harmonies came so easily to Ethan. Admittedly, he'd lost count of how many times he'd sung these lyrics. The tempo changed, and the group started in on the chorus, "*Dog days, living free and wild, like a child, let's get beguiled.*"

Ethan and the other guys stood center stage. Most of the stage lights swiveled to focus on Orr, who had the next verse. With his perfectly pitched tenor voice, Orr sang, "*Fire up the grill, let's have some fun. With friends and laughter, the day's just begun.*" Off stage left, Ethan caught something glittering in the arena. It looked like metallic confetti falling on one section. *What the fuck?*

Ethan traced up to find the source of the glitter, still maintaining his choreography. He long ago admitted it felt like his body went on autopilot when a concert started. All the rehearsing turned to muscle memory. He often let his mind wander. Ethan's eyes widened. A light emanated from one of the luxury suites on the second tier. *Holy shit, that was glass?* Time seemed to slow, and the crowd's din softened into a distant murmur as more eyes turned to trace a trail of shimmering shards falling on the section below.

An icy shiver of shock and fear raced down Ethan's spine, his heart pounding against his ribs like a desperate, trapped animal. He was rooted to the spot, staring at the horrific spectacle before his eyes. Ric bumped into him. He shot Ethan a '*what the hell?*' look.

Everything seemed to freeze as Zac and Orr realized something was wrong.

A body hurtled through the broken window, tumbling into the open air. Ethan's breath hitched. Silence descended upon the arena. A collective gasp of thousands of spectators hung suspended as the body descended into the crowd below.

The band stood frozen on stage in the glaring lights. The music continued, but the vocals had stopped.

Then the screaming started.

* * * *

Dr. Hennigan

"What the fuck?" Dr. Hennigan stared at the shattered glass where she'd just sent a bullet. *The glass shouldn't have shattered outward like that.* "Richardson? Denzili? What was that?" No response. "Ms. Wilson?" Nothing.

A body flew out of the suite and into the crowd below. She didn't know what had happened, but something was terribly wrong. She left the gun where it lay. It was new and unmarked, so there was no way it could be traced back to The Foundation.

The Foundation had protocols for situations like this. She needed to get out of the building and go to ground until she could contact the Mesa Juamenes Complex. Thankfully, Ms. Wilson had drawn up three different escape routes in case of an emergency. She ran through the lobby area to a side door and pushed it open. It didn't budge. She tried again.

The chaos from the arena could be heard in the background. While the concertgoers had stared in horror at a flying body, she'd sprung into action, so she was seconds ahead of the onslaught of concertgoers looking for a way out.

She turned around and headed to her second exfiltration point. This door opened, and she walked down the stairs. At the bottom, there was a small lobby and an emergency door. The emergency door was alarmed, but she wasn't worried about setting it off with the chaos building in the arena.

She exited the stairwell then paused for a second before swiftly walking across the lobby. The emergency exit was just a few feet away.

"Good to see you, Phillipa."

Hennigan glanced toward the woman's voice and found a woman clad in black standing with a gun leveled at her. She barely had a chance to move before the woman pulled the trigger.

The sharp pain of the bullet piercing her body caused a blinding flash of pain, but the adrenaline set in, and she barreled through the emergency door. The other woman was moments behind her. Dr. Hennigan darted into traffic and ran.

* * * *

Blayne

Blayne was on his feet one second, and the next, he was face down on the concrete with someone in a black coat lying on top of him. He hadn't even realized Ms. Z. was hovering in their section, watching over them.

He twisted his head to see Ms. Z. with her gun out. She tried to say something over the loud chaos around them. She got a disgruntled look, removed the earpiece and let it flop over her shoulder. He looked over to check on everyone else. Kira, Jamie and Madeline had all crashed to the floor in the stands beside him. Sarah crouched with her service gun pulled out, too. *Where did she even keep that thing?*

Ms. Z. reached down, grabbed the back of his shirt, and yelled, "Up. We need to move you to a secure location."

Before Blayne even registered what had happened, he was on his feet. Ms. Z. half dragged, half led the group down the concrete stairs to the arena floor. Blayne stared at the section where concertgoers were covered in glass, scrambling away from what looked to be a body splayed across the seats. He looked toward the light from the suite.

The faces of what had been cheery concertgoers now painted a horrifying tableau of shock, confusion and terror. Eyes, wide as dinner plates, glistened with unshed tears or flickered with the reflective glow of the stage lights. *Why hasn't someone turned on the arena lights yet?* Most either crouched behind their chairs or stood in a look of disbelief, as if the minds behind those eyes were frantically trying to reconcile the joyous concert atmosphere with the grim reality that had just imposed itself. Armed with flashlights, ushers were screaming over the chaos, directing people out of the arena. Others were using their cell phones to shine lights. A voice over the loudspeaker began saying, "*Please stay calm. Arena personnel will guide you to the nearest emergency exit,*" on repeat.

Despite it all, Blayne was impressed with how quickly the arena staff immediately implemented their crisis management plan.

No ushers were directing people to the left of the main stage, where Ms. Z. led their group. As they approached, Mr. J. looked at them and yelled. "Coms are down. Something is interfering with all communications in the building that are not hardwired into the arena."

"Say that again," Sarah asked. She had been trailing the group, almost like covering their rear from a sneak attack.

"There is a communications blackout. Something is jamming our signals."

"That explains why I couldn't get anything over my earpiece," Ms. Z. said. "Let me get them to the greenroom," she said, gesturing to the group, "then I'll be back."

"Great. I left Ms. A. in the greenroom. Mr. S. is on the other side of the stage, coordinating evacuation efforts with the local security personnel and the arena staff."

"Has anyone checked the suite?" Sarah asked.

"Not yet," Mr. J. said. "I was focused on getting people out of here and locking down the band. We were waiting for the Houston Police Department to get here."

"I'm going up there," Sarah said.

"Sarah," Kira said, "is that wise? What if there is someone up there waiting?"

Sarah turned to look at Kira. "Don't worry. I won't take any unnecessary chances." She then turned to Mr. J. "Any chance you have a spare bulletproof vest lying around?"

The corner of Mr. J.'s mouth quirked ever so slightly. "I'm sure there's one around here somewhere." He then looked at Ms. Z. "Get the rest of them out of here."

With that, Ms. Z. ushered the group through the Tundra Tunnel and into the arena's bowels. Periodically, guards were stationed in the underground area. Every time the group walked by security, the guards nodded at Ms. Z.

They entered the greenroom to find the ZERO family standing in shock. Blayne ran over to Ethan, who immediately wrapped his arms around him.

"I was so scared," Ethan said. "No one could tell me what was happening or whether you and your friends were safe."

"Something is interfering with their communications." Blayne took a moment to inspect Ethan. He looked fine, maybe a bit disheveled, but he didn't look like he'd been injured. "Are you okay? Was anyone on stage hurt?"

"We're fine. What about you?"

"We were on the opposite side of the arena from the body. Other than being tackled to the ground by Ms. Z., we're all fine."

"Yeah, Zahava has amazingly quick reflexes. I've been on the receiving end of one of her tackles before."

A throat clearing to their left caused them to break apart. Lucas stood there with his tablet PC in hand. Now that Blayne and Ethan had separated, he gave them a quick nod and walked away.

"What was that about?" Ethan asked.

"He's worried about your image as the American heartthrob."

"Yeah, but everyone in here is family."

"True, but you're the same man who doesn't think Lucas realizes we're dating. Trust me, he knows."

"Not this again." Ethan rolled his eyes. "He's clueless."

Blayne was about to say something when there was a loud whistle.

"Thank you," Megan Flores said, nodding to Ms. A., who had apparently been the whistler. "As you know, something is interfering with cell phones right now. Even our walkie-talkies aren't working."

"That's because the same jamming technology that's taken out cell phones interferes with signal transmission and reception of walkie-talkies," Ms. A. said in her clipped Indian accent.

Flores gave Ms. A. a polite nod. "I don't know much right now. But I'm happy to answer any questions I can."

The barrage of questions was immediate. Unfortunately, Ms. Flores didn't have many answers.

"No, we don't know how many people were injured."

"No, we don't know who the man was who dove into the crowd."

"No, we don't know if this was an accident or a crime."

Blane leaned against Ethan as the questions went on for a few minutes. He leaned his head down to Ethan's ear. "How are you holding up?"

"I'm shook. This is all way too familiar," he admitted.

"Tell me about it."

The next couple of hours flew by in a haze. The group was questioned by the local police when they got there. Then the FBI and the ATF showed up and had their own questions. Eventually, the group was informed that the arena was secure and had been thoroughly swept for other devices. By this time, it was almost two in the morning. Everyone had a weary look.

Jamie had curled up on the ground at some point and fallen asleep using his mother's lap as a pillow. Kira had stared at her phone every other minute until cell service was returned. The FBI had found the signal-jamming device and safely disabled it.

"Are you ready to go home?" Ethan asked Blayne when they were given permission to leave.

"I thought you'd never ask."

* * * *

Dr. Hennigan

She needed to find a way out of there. She ducked down periodically to see if she was being pursued. At least once, Dr. Hennigan had seen the dark-clad figure, but thankfully, the figure had never found her to finish the job.

She made her way to one of the large parking lots and searched for a car she could open easily. Some modern vehicles were impossible to break into. Still, some had known glitches that made them easy to hot-wire with a cell phone. She found the car she was looking for. She pulled out her burner phone and the charging cable in her back pocket. The door lock clicked. Slipping inside the car, she was met with the faint smell of old leather and a hint of gasoline. Hunching down in the driver's seat, she winced at the pain in her side. She pulled off her coat and bundled it against the wound. Then she stripped her belt from her pants and used it to tighten the material against her injury. *This isn't good.* Her heart beat a steady rhythm against her rib cage. The glow from the parking lot lamps barely illuminated the car's interior, casting long, mysterious shadows that danced on the dashboard.

She revealed the car's steering column using the burner phone's flashlight. She removed a small, flathead screwdriver from her pocket with a practiced hand. Long ago, she'd learned to travel with a multipurpose tool, because you never knew when you'd need one. Unscrewing the lower part of the steering column, she exposed the jumble of wires beneath, then located the cluster of cables she needed. She stripped the rubber insulation on the red and brown wires with surgical precision.

She twisted the red ignition and brown starter wires' exposed ends together before focusing on the white battery wire. She stripped it and carefully held the exposed part to the twisted pair.

The car rumbled to life. She untwisted the brown starter wire from the cluster, leaving only the battery and ignition wires connected, ensuring the vehicle remained running.

She quickly checked her surroundings, adjusted the rearview mirror and backed out of the parking space.

"Ms. Wilson?" she said, hoping her comms were working. She'd forgotten to check back in during the heat of her escape.

There was silence. She pulled out the phone and called the direct line. She got a busy signal. *That shouldn't happen.*

"Denzili? Richardson?" she said into her comms, hoping she would still be linked to them via their satellite. No one responded.

She stopped at a red light. A sharp pain in her side caused her to grunt as she held her foot against the brake pedal. *I need somewhere safe.* She ran through the list of possible safe houses. She dismissed the idea of using any known property of The Foundation. Something was wrong. She wasn't sure what was going on, but she knew there was a serious problem.

An idea popped into her head. *That's just insane enough it might work.* The light turned green, and she pointed her car to the Houston suburbs.

Chapter Five

Ethan

Ethan curled up next to Blayne on the back seat of the SUV. Kira sat in the passenger seat next to Ms. Z. Madeline leaned her head against the window. Ethan couldn't see Jamie, so he presumed the young guy was curled up on the seat next to his mother.

"Penny for your thoughts?" Blayne asked.

"I think I'm still in shock. I can't believe they wouldn't give us answers before we left," Ethan admitted. "From the look on Sarah's face, I swear she wasn't telling us everything."

"I'm pretty sure she wasn't telling us everything, Ethan. She's an FBI agent. They're not known for their openness and willingness to share information with the public."

"I guess...I just thought... God, we are the public, aren't we?" Ethan ran his hand through his hair before pinching the bridge of his nose. "I just... I can't seem to put into words what it is I'm thinking. We just saw something happen...again. Let's face it. With what happened last month, we're still seeing conspiracies around every corner."

"It's okay. Our minds mess with us after trauma. I swear I saw the woman's eyes today. Can you believe that? I think I recognized a pair of eyes. What's the likelihood of that happening? I searched for it online once we had cell service again, and facial recognition is based first on someone's eyes, then their mouth and nose. I doubt I could pick a pair of eyes from a lineup. In my head, her eyes are these giant black soulless pits."

"You know, Dr. Secada warned us about this. She said that fear and hypervigilance, along with anxiety, depression and PTSD, are all things we can expect," Ethan said. Sarah had helped Blayne and Ethan find a clinical psychologist with a low-level security clearance at Pennington University for the couple to talk with, which is how they'd ended up sitting in Dr. Esperanza Secada's office several times a week.

"I know. I know. It's just… Our lives were returning to normal." Blayne looked at Ethan and smiled. "Well, a *new* normal."

"Me too, babe. Me too." The SUV pulled to a stop. Ethan looked out of the front window and realized they'd already made it back to Blayne's apartment. "Wow, that was fast."

"The lack of traffic at this time of night helped," Blayne said, stifling a yawn. "Excuse me." He shook his head and wiped his eyes.

"I'm with you. I just want to crawl into bed and pass out. I just hope I can sleep."

"Well, if you can't, I'm sure we can think of something to tire ourselves out," Blayne said suggestively.

"Oh, come on," Jamie complained, sitting up before them. "Is that all you two think about?"

"I was talking about watching old episodes of *I Love Lucy* on the television."

"Uh-huh, a likely story. What's next? You're going to convince me you two are looking into purchasing two beds?" Jamie asked.

"He's a cheeky one," Ethan said.

"How did I get so lucky?" Madeline asked before she tousled Jamie's hair. "Stop messing with them, dear. Let's get you home and into bed."

"Yes, Mom," Jamie said in a half-patronizing, half-yawning manner. Madeline swatted him gently on the side of his ear.

"None of that lip."

Ms. Z. opened the side door, and Jamie practically bounced out of the SUV, suddenly filled with a new reservoir of energy.

"God, youth is wasted on the young," Blayne said.

"Oh yes, because you are so ancient," Madeline said, rolling her eyes in the vehicle's interior light. Madeline scooched over to the door. Ms. Z. reached out a hand and helped the woman out. "Thank you," Madeline said.

Blayne was up next. With his tall body, he practically bent in half to get out of the back seat to the door. Ethan didn't mind because it gave him a nice shot of Blayne's gorgeous ass. He reached out and swatted it with the back of his hand.

"Watch it," Blayne said. "Children can see."

Ethan followed suit, and their group stood outside in the crisp autumn air. They said their goodbyes and gave each other quick hugs.

"Should I perform a security sweep?" Ms. Z. said through an almost imperceptible yawn.

"Nah," Blayne replied. "We have the new security system, so I'm not worried." Blayne pulled up the app on his phone and showed Ms. Z. that it still indicated the alarm was set and the place was secure.

Ms. Z. nodded once before getting back into the SUV.

Next up was Kira.

"You're being awfully quiet," Blayne said as the taillights faded into the distance.

"I got a text from Sarah. They recovered several bodies."

"Really?" Blayne said.

"So, this wasn't an accident," Ethan added.

"Definitely not," Kira replied. "And it's weird. Three of the bodies, including the one who took mosh diving to a new level, were members of a domestic terrorist group, while the other four belong to a far-right German paramilitary group."

Ethan let out a low whistle. "Seven bodies? Fuck."

"Sarah doesn't think there's a connection to what happened last month. The working hypothesis is that these two groups used the cover of the concert to meet, something went wrong and the groups killed each other."

"You got all that from a text?" Blayne asked.

"I'm extrapolating a bit," Kira admitted. She handed Blayne her phone. Ethan leaned next to him to read the message as well.

Looks like our domestic terrorists had issues with German dicks bent on bringing fascism back. The groups wiped each other out. Doesn't seem like last month at all.

"Well, that's at least somewhat reassuring," Ethan admitted. "At least we're dealing with different blood-thirsty crazies this time. God knows, we were growing bored with the last set."

"Tell me about it," Kira agreed. "On the plus side, it seems like this had nothing to do with you. You can sleep well tonight, knowing no one is after you again."

"That's both reassuring and not reassuring," Blayne said. "I'm way too tired to deal with this shit. I'm going to bed."

"Me too." Kira hugged Blayne before giving Ethan a pat on the shoulder. "I'll call you two tomorrow afternoon to check in on you and see how you're holding up."

Kira walked over to her vehicle before he and Blayne turned and headed toward the apartment's front door. Blayne pulled out his key and inserted it into the lock. He opened the door, walked inside and punched in the security code. "*Door has been disabled*," a robotic voice chimed in.

Ethan flipped the switch and headed into the living room.

A woman sat on the sofa with a gun leveled at him.

* * * *

Blayne

Blayne was physically and emotionally exhausted. All he wanted to do was climb into bed with Ethan and pass out. He finished disabling to arm.

"*Door has been disabled*," a robotic voice chimed in.

Ethan went around him. The light from the living flooded the small hallway as Blayne closed the door. He turned. Ethan stood motionless.

"What's wrong, babe?" Blayne asked.

"Why don't you ask Mr. Dickenson to join us?" a female voice asked.

Blayne would have recognized that voice anywhere. It was a chilling tone that had infiltrated his nightmares for weeks. Every syllable was an icy finger tracing along his spine, igniting a cold sweat upon his brow. He experienced an overwhelming urge to fling open the door and dive into the refuge of the night beyond, but that would leave Ethan alone with her. As much as terror gnawed at his courage, pressing him to bolt and save himself, he wouldn't do that to Ethan. With his last shred of resolve, Blayne steeled himself.

"Ethan, honey, I didn't know we were expecting company?" His feet moved beneath him. Somehow, his brain let his feet move, despite his fear.

Blayne came up behind Ethan, who was still standing statue still. Sitting on their sofa, pointing a gun at them, was the woman.

"Please, join me," she said with a motion to the kitchen table between the sofa and the small kitchen. "I need your help."

Ethan laughed, even as his feet did as she had commanded. "You...need *our* help? You've got to be fucking kidding me."

Blayne followed Ethan to the table.

"Please remove your cell phones, place them in the middle of the table and keep your hands where I can see them. I would like to keep this...civilized."

Ethan made a garbled sound. Blayne guessed Ethan was finally realizing how dire things were. A woman who led an army of assassin mercenaries was pointing a gun at them. *This is not the time to oppose her.* They both slipped their phones onto the table and kept their hands in plain view.

"Thank you," she said, casually placing the gun on her leg. "Let me reassure you. I am not here to cause either of you harm. We have stringent protocols for that. We do not kill without strictly defined orders, our lives are in danger and killing is our only way out. Besides, as I said, I need your help. You see" — she motioned to her side — "I ran into a minor hiccup this evening and got myself shot."

"That was you, then?" Ethan questioned. "You caused the mayhem at the concert?"

"Yes and no," she intoned. "Yes, I was there for a job. And before you ask" — she held up a hand — "this job did not involve anyone you know. The leaders of — "

"A domestic terrorist organization was meeting with Nazi terrorists from Germany," Ethan interrupted.

"I see… I guess Agent Murphy has already started putting some pieces together. Agent Murphy and Kira Strickland make an interesting couple. I admit, I hadn't seen that coming."

Blayne's mouth started speaking before his mind put the thoughts together, "How do you — ?"

"I've kept tabs on everyone involved in that regrettable business last month. I apologize for the unfortunate mistakes that were made."

"Mistakes?" Ethan spat out. "You assassinated my lover, blew up my best friend's house and shot Blayne."

"Sometimes you do regrettable things for the greater good. And in the spirit of openness, I also blew up a plane to kill you."

"You *what*?" Ethan stared at the woman, his eyes wide and his mouth open.

"The Peregrine Airlines Flight from New Orleans you were supposed to be on... That wasn't an accident." Dr. Hennigan gave a little shrug before continuing. "I don't expect you to understand. But I did what I thought was in the world's best interests — blowing up one plane versus the damage that could have been done. You may not understand, but the four-hundred lives lost that day were a drop in the bucket of the damage that would have been done if your cell phone had ended up in the wrong hands."

"How very utilitarian of you," Blayne said.

"Yes. And if you had all the facts, I'm sure you would agree that our actions were perfectly justified. Even Jeremy Bentham or his intellectual successor John Stuart Mill would agree that my actions were for the greater good."

"Whose greater good? Yours? And who gets to decide what's 'in the greater good'?" Blayne asked rapid fire.

"You always have been the questioning type, Mr. Dickenson. Even your earliest report cards described you as inquisitive—"

"You just dropped that in there on purpose to show how high and mighty you are."

"Maybe," the woman said with a smile. "But my point was made." She moved to adjust herself on the sofa and winced.

"How bad is it?" Ethan asked, clearly picking up on the grimace.

"I wouldn't be here if it was good. As I said, before we started discussing moral philosophy, I need your help. I need medical attention, and it's not like I can go to the hospital. The woman who shot me knows she shot me, so they'll be looking."

"Why did you come here?" Blayne asked. "We're not exactly doctors."

"True. But you two have proven yourselves to be quite resourceful. And besides, this was the last place someone would look for me. Tonight's exploits show a hole in my organization's security."

"And why should we ever help you?" Ethan asked before Blayne could.

"Because you want answers, and I'm the only one who can give them to you. And in exchange for helping me, I'll give them to you. I'll also inform you why we're here and the threat this imposes. Trust me… What you know — or at least think you know — is but a speck of sand in the Sahara."

"What do we even call you?" Ethan questioned.

"You can all me Dr. Hennigan."

"You? A doctor?" Ethan barked out a laugh. "Physician, heal thyself and all that —"

"Yes, no, all the above." Dr. Hennigan looked at Blayne. "Truly, I don't see what you see in him. But then I don't understand why someone with your IQ would waste their time with this…dotard."

"I wouldn't turn to insults if you really want us to help you," Blayne replied, his eyes narrowed. "And answers would be nice, but they could just as easily come out in a court trial."

"You think I would make it to trial? I wouldn't make it to the county jail. I would be rescued or killed long before I could speak to anyone of consequence. And besides, tonight was part of why I'm back in this godforsaken city. A much larger operation is in the works, and I'm here to stop it. If I die or go to jail, I won't be able to do that. If that happens, the blood will be on *your* hands."

"You're lying," Ethan spat.

"Maybe so. But do you want to take the chance that I'm not?" She gasped as her eyes rolled into the back of her head and she slumped against the couch.

Blayne was out of his seat and grabbed the gun from her limp hand.

"Is she?" Ethan asked.

Blayne put his hand on her neck and looked for a pulse. It wasn't strong, but he wasn't entirely sure what a strong pulse should feel like.

Ethan had his cell phone in his hand.

"Who are you calling?" Blayne asked.

"Nine-one-one."

"Should we?"

"Of course we should."

"She promised us answers."

"She took down a plane full of innocent people to kill me. I don't think I'd like the answers she has," Ethan said. "This is like a puzzle to you — and you love puzzles — but this woman is dangerous. We can't trust her. We should use our favorite ride-hailing app, order a car and spend the night in a hotel. Let her bleed out on the sofa. We can find her dead body tomorrow."

"Yeah, she's already bleeding out," Blayne said, gesturing to the red spot under Dr. Hennigan.

"I can call Mr. J. He'll know what to do."

"Or we can handle this like the adults we are." Ethan was clearly not swayed, so Blayne switched tactics. "She said she knew about another threat. If we don't save her, what if more people die and we could have stopped it?"

"Let the police pry it out of her. That's not our job. You're a graduate student. I'm a pop star. We are not the Hardy Boys."

"True, but we have found ourselves in this situation. Are we not obligated to try?"

Blayne could tell the second the wind let out of Ethan's sails. "You will *not* let this go, are you?"

"I don't think we can. This may be our one shot to get answers and save many lives."

"Fuck it! What do we do?"

"We find a surgeon."

Chapter Six

Ethan

Blayne put the gun down as he grabbed his phone off the kitchen table and immediately started flying his fingers across the screen. Ethan paced. He had placed his cell phone in his pocket. Every few seconds, he had the urge to dial either nine-one-one or Mr. J. and wash his hands of this. *Sure, Blayne would be mad at me, but we'd be alive. And this woman, this Dr. Hennigan, would be out of our hair forever*. But he didn't do it. He couldn't betray Blayne like that. And a part of Ethan was just as curious as Blayne about the answers Dr. Hennigan offered.

"I got a surgeon," Blayne said, coming up behind him. Blayne wrapped his arms around Ethan and kissed him gently on the neck. "It's going to be okay."

"None of this is okay. I hope you realize that."

"I do. And I know you disagree with not calling someone for help. I just have a hunch that we're making the right decision."

"A hunch? You know who else had a hunch? Quasimodo. And he died in the end."

"True, but he was holding on to his dear love, Esmerelda."

"I'm letting you know now," Ethan said with zero emotion. "I will not let myself starve to death clutching your lifeless body."

Blayne's lip quirked, a hint of a smile.

"What?" Ethan asked.

"I never knew you were a fan of Victor Hugo."

"Well, Mr. Dickenson, you still don't know a lot about me. And it so happens that I wrote a paper on Quasi as an undergrad. Don't forget, I have a degree in business. So, there's more to this body than a pretty face. I do have a brain."

"That you do." Blayne wrapped his arms around Ethan's lower back and leaned down to kiss him before pulling away. "That you do."

There was a knock on the door. Ethan's head swiveled and his heartbeat sped.

"That would be the good doctor making a house call."

Blayne let go of Ethan and walked over to the front door.

"Arthur, so glad you could join us."

"How could I turn down a threesome with you and Ethan?" Dr. Arnold Giest-Mueler said as he entered. "I mean, it's not every day that one gets this opportunity."

"And unfortunately, that opportunity isn't today either," Blayne said. Ethan had been blocking the view of Dr. Hennigan, so he stepped to the side. "We need your help."

"What the hell?" Arnold said as he rushed to Dr. Hennigan's side. "What's going on?"

"She was shot," Ethan said.

"By you?"

"We found her like this."

"Who is she?" Arnold was already laying her down and inspecting the wound. He found the belt holding the blood-soaked material to Dr. Hennigan's side.

"As for who she is," Blayne said, "you'd be better off not knowing."

Arnold had his cell phone in hand and was dialing.

"We can't let you do that," Ethan said. He'd walked over to the kitchen table and had picked up the gun, which he now held pointing toward the ground. He wasn't threatening the doctor directly but hoped the gun did the trick. The doctor's eyes grew like saucers. He spun on Blayne.

"Explain."

Blayne gave him a much-abbreviated version of events. Ethan set the gun back on the table and paced.

"And that's why I tricked you into coming over."

"With my medical bag?"

"How did he get you to bring the bag?" Ethan asked.

"He told me you wanted to play doctor," Arnold said, nodding in Blayne's direction. "Here's what I need."

The apartment was consumed by a tense silence as Arnold prepared to operate on the kitchen table, which now served as a makeshift operating table for the wounded Dr. Hennigan. Blayne had run through the house, getting the items requested by Arnold.

Ethan had set about boiling water to sterilize items as Arnold prepped for the impromptu surgery. When everything was ready, Arnold removed the belt supporting Dr. Hennigan's soaked bandage. He made quick work of the rest of her clothes.

"Blayne, point the flashlight here," Arnold barked.

Blayne didn't hesitate and held the flashlight at the wound to give the doctor a better view of the injury. "It's not as bad as I feared,"

Blayne

Arnold looked up from Dr. Hennigan's body, meeting the anxious gazes of Blayne and Ethan. He explained, "She's been shot in the lower left quadrant of her abdomen near the hip. I could stop the internal bleeding, but it was precarious. She's one lucky person."

Ethan swallowed. His eyes flicked to the unconscious body, then back to Arnold. "Lucky?" he asked, skepticism entering his voice.

Dr. Muller nodded. "Trust me... An inch in either direction, she would have bled out, and there would have been nothing I could have done to help her. So yes, in this case, she's lucky. The bullet took a less destructive path. Instead of penetrating the abdominal cavity and damaging internal organs, it hit her pelvic bone, deflecting through muscle and fat tissue before exiting near her lower back."

Blayne shifted, his knuckles white around the flashlight he continued to hold. "She's going to be okay?"

Arnold paused. "The wound is serious, and there's significant blood loss. But her vital signs are stable, so no major arteries were hit. That's the positive news. She's not out of the woods yet. And she's going to need blood. Without a transfusion, I doubt she'll make it through the night. She's just lost too much blood."

Ethan looked at Dr. Hennigan, her blood painting a stark contrast against the kitchen table. He turned to Arnold. "I'm a universal donor."

Blayne shot Ethan a look of surprise. Ethan's voice held steady. His eyes reflected a quiet resolve.

"All right," Arnold said, nodding at Ethan. "Blayne, I need you to gather a few things while I prep Ethan."

Blayne nodded, ready to follow instructions.

"I need a clean, thin plastic tube—something like a straw or, better, a drip irrigation tube, if you have it for houseplants. I also need rubber bands."

Blayne moved quickly to rummage through the kitchen. In a cabinet, he found a pack of new, transparent straws he'd purchased for a party he'd thrown over the summer. In the junk drawer, he found the rubber bands he'd been collecting. He handed the items off to Arnold.

"Good," Muller said, taking the items. Arnold pulled an alcohol swab from his bag to sterilize Ethan's arm and the area around Hennigan's wound. He used the straws and rubber bands to create a makeshift tourniquet on Ethan's arm, tightening it just enough to make the veins stand out.

Arnold inserted a needle into Dr. Hennigan's arm. Blayne was surprised the makeshift blood transfusion even worked. The blood flowed from Ethan to Hennigan. It wasn't perfect, it wasn't pretty, but it worked.

Arnold monitored the transfusion closely, adjusting the rubber bands when needed to regulate blood flow.

"You don't need to hold the flashlight anymore, Blayne. It's gonna be a while. Might as well pull up a chair."

Blayne sat down and grabbed hold of Ethan's free hand. Ethan's eyes flicked to Blayne's face. Blayne smiled, doing his best to reassure Ethan that everything would be perfectly fine. It was the only assurance Blayne could offer. Ethan was saving a life, even if it was *her* life.

It was a couple of hours before Arnold pronounced the transfusion successful. As Arnold pulled the needle out of Ethan's arm, Blayne let out a breath.

"Ethan, I need to make sure you understand what comes next. Under the best of circumstances, donating blood takes a toll on your body." Arnold's gaze steadied on Ethan's. "First, you need to eat something. Blayne," Arnold said, turning to him, "do you have raisins or almonds? They're both rich in iron, which Ethan needs right now."

"Yeah, I have some trail mix packs that have. Would that work?" Blayne stood and was already making his way into the kitchen.

"Perfect. Trail mix will also have sugar, which we must regulate. And water" — he turned and locked eyes with Ethan—"lots and lots of water. You must stay hydrated. And don't be surprised if you feel lightheaded or dizzy. Your body adjusts to the sudden decrease in blood volume, so don't try to stand fast for a bit. Also, it's common for you to be tired and a little weaker than normal. And again, it's important to rest and keep yourself hydrated." Arnold gave Ethan a small, encouraging smile. "You're young and in excellent shape, so you're resilient. Your body is already replenishing the lost blood cells, but it takes time. But your body will take four to six weeks to return to normal completely. In the meantime, take care of yourself." He then rattled off a list of potential side effects.

Blayne handed Ethan a bottle of water and trail mix. "Can I get you anything?" he asked Arnold.

"Any chance I can clean up and get something else to wear?" Arnold asked, gesturing down to the blood-stained clothes he'd entered with.

"Of course, I can put those in the laundry for you."

"Give him a pair of my shorts," Ethan said. "I think we're closer in size than you are to Paul Bunyan over there."

"I'm not a giant," Blayne said without looking back as he headed into his bedroom. He ruffled through Ethan's stuff before pulling out a pair of shorts, grabbed a ZERO T-shirt and walked back into the living room where Arnold and Ethan were talking.

"Here you go," Blayne said as he handed Arnold the clothes. "Do you remember where the bathroom is?"

"I think I can find it," Arnold said with a tired smile.

When Blayne heard the guest bedroom open, he turned to Ethan. "Now what?"

"We wait," Ethan said.

* * * *

Agent Murphy

It was three in the morning, and they were still processing the scene at the arena. It immediately became an interdepartmental pissing match between the Houston Police Department, the ATF and the FBI. She had half expected the NSA and CIA to swoop in just for the hell of it.

As interim Special Agent in Charge over the Emerald City, she was still woefully under-equipped to handle this bureaucratic political bullshit. The phone rang in her pocket. Part of her wanted to throw the blasted thing across the arena and see if she could make a basket. The phone had been going off the hook with reporters and politicians, all trying to get the scoop on what was happening. She kept referring them to the Public Affairs Office in Washington, DC, which wouldn't be open until nine a.m.

She looked at the number. *Fuck!*

"Special Agent Sarah Murphy. How can I help you, Director?"

"Murphy, what the hell is going on in Houston? I'm getting complaints from the President's office that no one will talk to them. They even said you referred them to the Public Affairs Office?"

"I might have, sir," she winced, waiting for the blowback.

There was a chuckle on the other end of the line. "Good for you. Sometimes you gotta put those politicians in their place."

"I wish I could say it was on purpose, sir, but it wasn't. My phone has been ringing off the hook with people trying to weasel information out of me. I've gone to autopilot."

"I remember my first high-profile case as the Chief of the St. Louis Office. It was a sniper killing people on the interstate. Everyone was panicking, and people didn't want to go anywhere. The press was crawling up my ass. When one reporter asked for a scoop, I sarcastically told him it was aliens — the outer space kind, not the illegal immigrant kind. Anyway, he printed that shit. Then I had to make a public statement

Jason Wrench

that it wasn't aliens. I got reamed out by the director at the time for opening my mouth. Thankfully, we caught the guy two days later, and everyone forgot about aliens."

"That's quite the story, sir."

"I can tell you're tired, Agent Murphy."

"Sorry, sir. It's been a long night. This was supposed to have been a fun time, and it turned into a horror show followed by a political circus."

"That explains what it feels like anytime I get hauled in front of Congress for questioning." He let out a loud breath. "So, what can I tell the President when he wakes up in a few hours?"

"Here's what we know so far… We have six bodies. Two of the bodies belonged to members of the paramilitary group known as the Constitutional Liberation Army. The FBI has kept track of them for a while, but they were minor players and didn't register high on the threat level. The other three were high-ranking officials of the far-right National Democratic Party in Germany. Although nothing officially ties them together with the German Chancellor, there are rumors that the NDP helped him get elected."

"Be careful of rumors, Agent."

"Yes, sir."

"But the rumors are accurate, from what I've read. Although the NDP differs from the Chancellor's German Values Party, their underlying ideology is more similar than not. Basically, the NDP does what the Values Party cannot get away with."

"I see."

"Don't be surprised if you find representatives from the German Embassy calling you in the morning. Refer them to the State Department. And dear God, don't tell them anything I've told you here."

"Yes, sir."

"And, Agent?"

"Yes, sir?"

"Get some sleep. Hand off the scene to the people under you. You'll have a long day tomorrow, so there's no reason to burn yourself out tonight."

And with that, the call disconnected.

"Hey, partner," Agent Benjamin Harper said as he approached her. He was dressed in the usual FBI coat and cap, his shield on one hip and holster on the other. "Who was that?"

"Director Steele."

"Good old Steelwork, himself? Look at you, moving up in the world."

"And I keep dragging your ass along with me. What do you have for me?"

"We found three sniper rifles."

"Huh?" Sarah's mind was trying to catch up. "The glass exploded inward, not outward?"

"You are correct. The forensic tech removed one .300 caliber slug from one victim. Their wound pattern differed from the others, which is what caused it to stand out."

"Take me."

Benjamin led Sarah through the maze until they were at the first one. She looked down at the gun, still perched on the edge. The suite in question was clearly visible. They then visited the second and third ones.

"These are definitely sniper nests," Sarah said, mostly to herself.

"That was my initial assessment," Harper agreed.

"Were the snipers backup? And if so, whose side were they on?" Sarah walked around the area, taking it in. "I want to get all surveillance footage of these areas, including the hallways outside. I'm hoping a camera caught something."

"Yes, sir," Harper said. "Anything else?"

"Yeah, tell Agents Callahan and McCoy they will be left here to close shop. They can come in late tomorrow and file their reports. The rest of us will have a busy day tomorrow, so we might as well get some sleep. And before you argue, that came from the director. He warned me this will turn into a political shit show in the morning."

Harper left her in the sniper's nest. Sarah motioned for one of the FBI techs who was standing by. The agent came over and quickly started dismantling and tagging the evidence.

What am I missing?

Chapter Seven

Ethan

Ethan got a few hours of sleep. He lay curled next to Blayne, his arm wrapped around him. Despite losing a lot of blood, he'd still woke up with a raging hard-on. His was the type of hard-on that shot up his stomach instead of straight out, ready to poke someone in the eye. He'd seen enough porn in his life to know that dicks came in all sizes, shapes and colors. His was slightly above average. Blayne was not exactly average. The first time Ethan had seen Blayne's dick, he thought, *Where the hell is that supposed to go?* ran through his head. He was afraid it would feel like he was being impaled by an actual eggplant or he would get lockjaw, because he wasn't sure his mouth opened that wide. "No wonder Arnold jumped to attention and ran over here last night."

"Someone's happy to be awake this morning?" a groggy voice said from in front of him.

"Sorry… It has a mind of its own," Ethan joked.

"Uh-huh," Blayne said as he rolled over to face Ethan. Ethan reached out, grabbed the back of Blayne's head and drew him in for a kiss. He wasn't surprised to find said eggplant poking him in the stomach. "I'm apparently not the only one."

"I wonder if a lot of babies get made because of morning wood?"

"Where did that come from?"

"Just popped into my head. I can see many straights waking up just like this and the next thing you know, it's slipped inside, and a new human enters the world nine months later."

"How romantic," Ethan said sarcastically.

"I'm always romantic," Blayne said as he nudged his cock against Ethan a couple of times.

"God, I'm horny," Ethan admitted. "But…"

"But we have Arnold and a guest lying out there. And besides, you heard the doctor last night. You shouldn't do anything physically exerting for a couple of days."

"You know Chu-young and Higgins are going to have my hide when they hear about this."

"Well, your director and choreographer will have to wait a few days while you recuperate. And if they come here mad, we'll sic our pet assassin on them — assuming she's awake by then."

"How long do you think she'll stay here?" Ethan asked.

"Arnold says she will probably be stable enough to transport in a few days. Hopefully, she'll know where to hide and lick her wounds, and we can pretend this never happened."

Ethan let out a sigh. "Until then —"

"Until then, we keep going. You'll call in sick. Tell the band what you need to tell them. I would limit harboring a known terrorist and fugitive thing, but you can tell them you're ill and I'm taking care of you."

"And you?"

"I have to teach."

"So, you're going to leave me here with…them?"

"Honestly, I think you're safer here than anywhere else right now."

Ethan rolled onto his back and laid his other forearm across his eyes. "Can this get any more fucked up?"

"Don't ask that question," Blayne chastised. "Destiny is always poised to offer a response you may not like." Blayne hitched up on his elbow to look down at Ethan. "For now, we make the best of an unpleasant situation. And I, for one, have an idea on how to do that."

Ethan's arm dropped from his head as Blayne lowered his head and started sucking on his right nipple. Blayne used his hand to trace around the outline of his cock through his shorts.

"Now, lay back and let Dr. Dickenson take care of you. You're not supposed to do anything active, so let me do all the work."

Blayne reached over and tweaked Ethan's other nipple, rolling it between his fingers, varying the amount of pressure, which only seemed to cause the rest of the blood in Ethan's body to race for his cock. Thankfully, he wasn't getting lightheaded.

By the time Blayne freed Ethan's cock from his shorts, there was already pre-cum around the head of his dick. Blayne lay between Ethan's legs and licked the cum as he traced the cockhead with his tongue. It took every ounce of control Ethan had not to moan in ecstasy, but he didn't feel like putting on a show for their guests. When Blayne took Ethan down his throat, he was already on the verge of busting.

"I'm gonna co—"

The whispered words hadn't even escaped his lips before he came down Blayne's throat. Blayne didn't hesitate. He applied more pressure with his lips and drained him. Blayne finished between Ethan's legs and looked up at him, a satisfied look crossing his face.

"My turn," he said as he lay down next to Ethan. "And before you ask. Just lie next to me. I just need to feel you beside me."

Blayne reached over to his side of the bed and grabbed the bottle of lube sitting on top of the dresser. He squeezed out just enough to make his hand glide down his dick but not so much that it didn't provide friction.

Ethan lay on his side, pulled Blayne's face toward his and began kissing his boyfriend. He cupped the side of Blayne's face and stroked his cheek with his thumb. Ethan licked down the side of Blayne's throat as he leaned his head backward. Then, just as Blayne had done before him, he latched his teeth onto Blayne's nipple and teased it. Ethan felt the change in Blayne's breathing seconds before thick rivulets of cum coated both.

Instead of rolling back onto the sheets, he just lay on Blayne's chest. Blayne's cum seeped into his side.

Ethan could have lain like that forever.

Blayne had other ideas. "Shower?"

"I'm not ready to get up," Ethan grumbled next to Blayne's chest.

"My class is in two hours. Besides, I've already missed a lot this semester."

"You were shot."

"I still missed class. One of the other graduate students covered for me last time. I can't do that again unless they can all come see the bullet wound this time."

Ethan groaned but rolled off Blayne onto the side of the bed. He stood up to find Blayne on his feet, trying to keep the cum from running onto the carpet.

"Geez! I didn't realize I'd come this much."

"You didn't feel it because half of it was on my back," Ethan joked, and turned his back so Blayne could see his handiwork.

They made their way into the shower. Despite everything that had happened over the last twelve hours, both men had smiles on their faces.

* * * *

Blayne

Blayne ran his hand through his hair, adding enough product to tame the blond locks on his head. He had opted for a wool blue check tweed vest with gold lining over a plain rust twill button-down shirt with a dark pair of jeans. His walnut-colored wingtip Oxfords completed the look. With one last look in the mirror, he shrugged. It was another one of Ethan's attempts at modernizing his wardrobe. Blayne was more comfortable with the ill-fitting clothing he picked up at big box stores and the mall, but his new wardrobe was growing on him. Even his students noticed and started complimenting him on his style choices.

He left the bedroom. At some point in the night, the woman had been moved to the couch. Ethan sat at the kitchen table, drinking a cup of coffee and conversing with Arnold.

"How's our patient?" Blayne asked.

"She's stable," Arnold said, turning his head to look at Blayne. "Damn." He drew out the word. "God, you look gorgeous."

"Don't get any ideas there, Doc," Ethan said with a smile. "That's my boyfriend you're ogling."

"Maybe so, but I had him before you knew him."

"Eww," Blayne said. "I'm not a piece of meat, you two."

"Where are you off to?" Arnold asked.

"I have to teach."

"What about…her?" he asked, cocking his head toward the woman.

"If I don't show up to class, I think that will cause more problems. I need to keep up the pretenses."

"And what about Ethan? Doesn't he have to keep up the pretenses?"

"As for me," Ethan replied, "the band is kind of in a holding pattern. I got a text from my producer earlier. As the investigation continues, the arena is still off-limits, so we have the day off. Our concert tonight was canceled. They haven't said it yet, but I'm guessing the other four nights will also be canceled. Then we'll pack it up and head to our next stop on the tour."

"Where's the tour heading next?" Arnold asked before taking a sip of coffee.

"Washington, DC."

Blayne walked into the kitchen, grabbed a mug and poured a cup of coffee. He turned to the fridge and took out the milk. "Almost out of milk. I'll buy some on my way home." He poured just a dab of milk into the cup. It wasn't enough to change the black color to tan, but enough to take the biting edge off the dark roast. He sat at the table with the other two men.

"So, will you two tell me what this is about?" Arnold asked.

"We told you last—" Blayne started.

"You told me some of it. I know you left out details. If you want me to keep this silent, you must give me one damn good reason."

Blayne took a breath and looked at his watch. He had an hour before he had to be in class. This would have to be quick. He spent the next fifteen minutes diving into everything. Periodically, Ethan would jump in to fill in some blanks to get Arnold caught up.

"And so, we got home last night and found Dr. Hennigan—that's what she called herself—on our couch," Blayne said.

"Somehow, she bypassed Blayne's new state-of-the-art security system. Still pissed about that," Ethan grumbled.

"But who is she?" Arnold asked.

"Your guess is as good as ours. From what we've put together, she's protected by some people high in the US government."

"Whoa, you're telling me that plane explosion in New Orleans last month wasn't an accident?" Arnold questioned.

"Yeah," Ethan started, "I guess we glossed over that one. That woman over there blew up a plane to kill me and destroy my cell phone."

"Why on earth would you have me save her life?"

"She hinted that something bigger was coming, and we couldn't stop if she died. So, we decided…" Blayne looked at Ethan, who tilted his head sideways, furrowing his brow. "Okay, I decided that saving her life to stop something bad from happening was more important than putting her behind bars, which is where she clearly belongs."

"Why not let the police handle it?"

"That's what I said," Ethan grumbled.

"She said the police wouldn't get a chance to question her. She'd either be rescued or dead before they could interrogate her. And from everything we've seen about her and whoever she works for, I didn't think she was lying. There's more at work here than any of us understand. And the only one with those answers is lying unconscious on my couch."

The three sat in silence for a moment. Arnold let out a low whistle. "What the hell have you gotten me into?"

"I wish I knew," Blayne admitted. He glanced down at his watch. "Damn, I have to be in class in thirty minutes." He stood up, took his empty coffee mug to the sink and rinsed it out before setting it inside. He kissed Ethan on the top of the head, said goodbye to Arnold and headed to class.

* * * *

Agent Murphy

Sarah sat in the Emerald City's sensitive compartmented information facility — SCIF — staring at a group of FBI agents and members of other law enforcement bodies around the country.

"Agent Murphy, what can you tell us about the groups?" Director Steele asked.

Sarah shuffled the papers in front of her. The director had sent her an email earlier that day to put together a dossier on both groups for this meeting.

"The National Democratic Party of Germany, or NPD, was founded in 1964 as a far-right political party but failed to gain significant traction. That changed in the late 1980s following the fall of the Berlin Wall." She went into detail about the origin of the group and its past and current leadership structure. She explained that the group turned toward a hardline, well-organized and militant force espousing a mix of extreme nationalism, xenophobia and a belief in German racial superiority. "Today, we're not sure who runs the movement. We have heard rumblings of someone known only as *Der Führer*, but we cannot know if this person is real or a part of mythology."

After the quick presentation, there were several questions, and Murphy did her best to answer what was lobbed her way. Thankfully, a young woman from the NSA who specialized in threat analysis and far-right groups filled in a lot of the blanks that Sarah couldn't.

"And what about this Constitutional Liberation Army?"

"Honestly, sir, we'd heard grumblings of this organization, but no one considered them any threat. This is the first time this group has done anything violent or has associated with more militant groups."

"Why do you think they escalated?" a woman from the NSA asked.

"I don't know. Here's what we do know. The Constitutional Liberation Army—CLA—was founded in the early 2000s and is a group rooted in the belief that the US government has strayed from the Constitution's original intent, infringing upon citizens' rights. From our intel about this group, we know they believe that liberal ideology is the primary culprit behind America's perceived decline. The CLA views themselves as patriotic defenders of traditional American values, advocating for radical measures against the government. However, none of their rhetoric has been overtly violent."

"Well, yesterday that clearly changed," a man from one agency quipped. Sarah couldn't remember which agency this guy was from, but she ignored him.

"The group was founded by a former Marine named John Black, who seems to have been radicalized during his time in the military. He completed three tours in Afghanistan and another four or five as an independent contractor. His previous employer wasn't what I would call forthcoming with the information about his employment record."

"Who was his previous employer?"

"GreyGuard. I have a call into their CEO, Nathaniel Greaves, but have been stonewalled by their lawyers."

"Have someone in the Office of the General Counsel pressure Greaves. If that doesn't work, we'll contact the DOJ and see if they can help," Steele said.

Murphy waited to see if anyone else would jump in. When no one did, she continued. "As for the CLA, the group originally crossed our radar following the 2008 financial crisis. The group held several rallies in New Mexico and Texas where they protested the, and I quote, *'corrupt and bloated nature of the federal government.'* Then they kind of went off the radar. They rose to prominence again after the 2016 presidential election. They apparently saw former President Trump as a political ally, so they became more active and vocal. This was when rumblings within the group for armed resistance started. Although there were rumblings, nothing ever happened. A threat assessment was conducted in 2022 by the FBI, DHS, ATF and NSA, but they were not deemed homegrown violent extremists—HVEs."

"Excuse me," a woman from an agency Murphy couldn't remember cut in. "How does the FBI categorize HVEs?"

"Let me handle that one, Agent Murphy," Director Steele said. "HVEs are defined by the FBI in conjunction with DHS as domestic terrorists engaging or planning unlawful acts of violence. These acts intimidate civilian populations or influence domestic policy. These groups are *not* associated with another country. Sadly, HVEs are completely ours."

There was a pause after the director finished. Hearing no other questions or comments, Murphy finished her presentation. "More recently, the CLA has supported secessionist movements in states like Texas and New Mexico, hoping to establish a Constitution-abiding nation. The original leadership parted ways with the organization. We're unsure why. Right now, we have no idea who the current leadership is. And until yesterday, none of our agencies were tracking them."

The group sat around for another forty-five minutes discussing directions for the new task force. Unfortunately, Murphy was appointed as the head of the new group. She was already stretched thin overseeing the Emerald City, so this new task force was poised to send her over the edge.

"Thank you," Director Steele said, as the meeting finally ended. "I look forward to robust interagency cooperation as we address the immediate situation." With that, members of the forum started disappearing from Murphy's screen. Murphy was about to sign off herself when Director Steele asked her to stay on.

When Steel and Murphy were the last two on the conference call, Director Steele said, "Congratulations on making it through your first interagency review. These meetings are fraught with politics. You handled yourself well today. Leadership suits you."

"Thank you, Director. I won't lie. I was a nervous wreck coming into this today. I wasn't sure what would happen."

"Thankfully, everyone seemed to be on their best behavior. Don't expect it to last. If something goes wrong, the finger-pointing and blame game will start. Right now, everyone was caught by surprise. We really need to get a handle on this fast. Any resources you need, just let me know. I want you to coordinate with the Albuquerque, Dallas and Oklahoma City field offices. We know this group is based in West Texas, so those three field offices create a triangle around that area. Hopefully, someone in one of those field offices will have better intel."

"Yes, Director. I'll contact them once I finish this call."

"Keep me in the loop. I expect at least daily updates. If there are any significant developments, I need to know immediately."

With that, the director left the meeting, and Murphy was alone in the SCIF, wondering what step to take first.

Chapter Eight

Ethan

Shortly after Blayne went to Pennington to teach, Arnold informed Ethan that he had to head to the hospital. Arnold had a spare pair of scrubs in his car, so he went out and got them before taking a quick shower. Of course, Arnold had asked Ethan if he wanted to join him. Still, Ethan informed the cheeky surgeon that he'd already taken a shower with one man that morning and was perfectly clean. Arnold hadn't said anything in return but had cocked an eyebrow and smiled.

Before leaving, Arnold gave Ethan specific instructions on what to do when the patient awoke. Ethan had a lot of other words for her, and 'patient' was not on the list. With Arnold out of the apartment, Ethan took to pacing. He kept the woman's gun in his pocket and didn't take an eye off her except when he inevitably had to go to the bathroom. Even then, when he returned, he held the gun out in front of him like a scared victim in a horror film right before whatever creature pounced and ate them for dinner.

"God, this is ridiculous," Ethan muttered to himself.

He sat at the kitchen table with another cup of coffee. He glanced down at his watch, and it was a little past one. Blayne would be back around three-thirty, so he had to wait until then. He pulled out his cell phone. He desperately wanted to call his security team or Stephanie, but the last thing he wanted to do was violate Blayne's trust or drag anyone else into this mess.

"Well, I guess I'm not dead," a voice grumbled from the couch.

"Don't move," Ethan said, fumbling to pick up the gun and hold it at the woman as she pushed herself into a sitting position. She winced. She turned her head and looked at Ethan.

"Put that thing down. The last thing we want is for you to shoot me accidentally. One bullet wound a week is my limit." She lifted the T-shirt to inspect the wound. She peeled back the corner of the dressing and stared at the stitching. "Good work. Clearly not something you or Blayne did. Who'd you find to patch me up?"

Ethan stared at the woman. His right hand holding the gun was visibly shaking, so he braced it with his left. "You don't need to know."

"Let me guess...Dr. Arnold Giest-Mueler." Ethan faltered for a second, letting the gun dip toward the table. "Ethan, dear, I told you last night... I assume it was last night—"

"It was."

"So, how long have I been out?"

"About ten hours."

"Fuck. I need to get moving."

"You're not going anywhere—at least not until Blayne gets back. You promised us answers. That's the only reason you're still alive. Trust me... I voted to let you bleed out on the couch."

"Thankfully, Blayne is the more logical one. You two make an impressive pair. He's all brain, and you're all heart."

"You know nothing about us."

"Don't I?"

She dove into the biography of each of them. Ethan was amazed at the detail she knew about their lives. She knew about things no one else did.

"Then there was the time when Blayne and his friends hid behind a fence and threw snowballs at passing cars. It's a good thing they ran when they hit the police car. That officer would have ruined all their lives forever. As for you, the only remotely criminal behavior I've found on you was the one incident when you were drunk and ran your car into the private school's playground. Thankfully, your manager acted quickly and made a huge donation to the school on your behalf so they wouldn't press charges. You also upgraded their equipment. The police never knew it was you because the security footage was conveniently lost."

"No one knows about that. Not even anyone in the band..."

"There's always a trail when you dig hard enough. One of the security personnel kept the footage. I can only guess that he planned on using it to blackmail you one day." Ethan let out a garbled choke. "Don't worry. That man's computer crashed, and his cloud backup had several missing files, including that one."

"So now you're going to blackmail me?"

"Ethan, dear—"

"Stop calling me that."

"Ethan?"

"Dear. I'm not your 'dear' anything."

The woman made a *tsk*ing sound. "And just when we were becoming such good friends." She drew her face into an exaggerated pout. She moved on the couch and winced as she twisted her torso.

"You need to take one every six hours for pain." Ethan tossed her a bottle of pills Arnold had left.

She grabbed the bottle out of the air and winced at the sudden motion. She looked down at the label. "Not even the good stuff."

"Yeah, well...it's hard to get the good stuff when you're not supposed to be here."

"Can I get some water?"

Ethan eyed her warily before standing. He backed his way into the kitchen, holding the gun at her. He opened the fridge and reached in to grab a bottle of water. The second he took his eyes off her, she sprung off the couch, over the kitchen table and stood before Ethan. She jabbed her palm into his chest. He stumbled backward into the sink. The gun slipped from his hand. She kicked the fridge door shut and snatched the gun out of the air. Ethan closed his eyes, waiting to hear the gunshot. When it didn't, he opened one eye. The woman stood before him, her arms crossed, holding the gun with one hand.

"Honestly, I would have done it already if I had wanted you dead. Get that through your thick skull." She turned around, walked into the living room and picked up the pills before coming back into the kitchen and grabbing the bottle of water that had fallen to the floor.

Ethan stood leaning against the sink, staring in shock. "How'd you —?"

"Ethan, dear,…oh, sorry about that. Old habits and all." She sat at the table, popped open the pill bottle and swallowed a couple of pills before opening the water. "Ethan, you must know by now that I have a skill set you can't possibly understand. I've been groomed my entire life for my job. You grew up in a world where you could flourish and decide your path. Call it child prodigy development. My skill set involves protecting this country and its values at all costs. Anyone or anything deemed a threat is liquidated. That's our fancy term for killing or destroying someone or something. I don't kill indiscriminately."

Ethan pushed himself away from the sink and sat across from her at the kitchen table. "You act like you're high and mighty, but you killed Cynthia and Daniel, blew up an airplane, blew up Stephanie's house and shot Blayne, not to mention all the injuries you caused in that damn shootout of yours."

She sat there in silence for a moment. She lifted the water bottle to her lips, then sat the bottle down without taking her eyes off Ethan. Just her unblinking stare was enough to cause Ethan to glance down at the table.

She let out a quick breath. "Cynthia was the target. Daniel was collateral damage. We had no intelligence that he was there. The plane was brought down because it was deemed the fastest way to ensure your phone was destroyed. You ran off to meet Blayne, which was unexpected. Stephanie's phone also contained the same data leak from my organization. Blayne was a pure accident. He had your cell phone. We had no idea you two were conducting your own end run around the paparazzi, which was genius in its own way."

"What was so important that you killed hundreds of people?"

"A highly detailed list of our operatives, both domestic and international. Cynthia Dunning was one of ours. She and an unknown accomplice had hacked into our system, which should have been impossible. If that data got into the wrong hands, it would topple governments and possibly lead to several international conflicts. So, you see, Ethan, stopping that data was paramount for the security of our nation and the world."

Ethan sat back in his chair as a large, booming laugh burst deep within him. His entire body shook. His chest heaved as he threw his head back, and a loud, open-mouthed guffaw echoed through the room.

When he settled, the woman looked at him. "Are you done?"

"You expect me to believe that bullshit? I'm sorry, but that's the most insane thing I've ever heard."

"And yet it's all true. I have no reason to lie to you, Mr. Bond." She drew out Ethan's surname in a way that made the hair on the back of Ethan's neck rise.

Dr. Hennigan

Dr. Hennigan narrowed her eyes at Ethan. She'd just told him more than she'd told anyone outside of The Foundation in her entire life. She wondered if she'd made the right decision to be honest with him. He could prove nothing she'd said, so The Foundation was still secure.

"As I said last night, none of what happened last month was personal."

Ethan let out a short, dismissive laugh. The sound hung in the air, a simple message of his skepticism. Dr. Hennigan waited for Ethan, playing another one of their staring contests. She wouldn't blink. Ethan clearly wanted to act all strong and tough. Dr. Hennigan had stared down men much more intimidating and dangerous than this boy could ever hope to be. He averted his eyes.

"Who *are* you people?"

"Well, that's something I cannot delve into. But, suffice it to say, we're the good…ish guys. We do things the federal government can't or won't do."

"So, you're like the CIA or something?"

"Oh, the CIA wishes they had our resources and moral flexibility. No, we don't have those kinds of constraints. We operate…independently."

"And who died and made you judge and jury?"

"Lots of people. Some you've heard of. Others went to their graves unknown by society. If we do our jobs right, no one knows we lurk in the shadows."

Dr. Hennigan stared at Ethan, her gaze soft and laced with gentle condescension. Her smile was warm but pitying. Although outwardly attempting to be kind, she put on an expression that communicated her belief that Ethan was naïve about how things worked in the world.

"Now what?" Ethan asked.

"Well, before I finish telling you everything I promised to tell you, we should wait for Blayne to get home. Unfortunately, the information I promised you two last night involves him."

"What?" Ethan gasped. "Is he in danger?"

"Calm down, Ethan." She clicked her manicured nails on the table. "He's in no immediate danger. But people he cares about could be vulnerable if the Constitutional Liberation Army isn't stopped."

* * * *

Blayne

Blayne tried to get the class back on track, but his students peppered him with questions about the concert. They didn't seem to know he was dating Ethan, but his students were bright enough to realize he was at least friends with Ethan after he had been shot.

"Mr. Dickenson, come on. Tell us what happened?" Emma Davis asked. "My followers want the inside scoop."

Emma's social media profile had shot up after she'd uploaded photos of Blayne the previous month. He'd concocted a plan with Ethan to dress like him to confuse the paparazzi. Thankfully, the scheme worked…a little too well, since it led to him getting shot. His students didn't know the entire story. They didn't know even a tiny portion of what had happened, and Blayne intended to keep it that way.

"There's not much to tell. You've seen the news."

"Yes, but your boy…Ethan Bond," Emma corrected herself. Blayne had known Emma was smarter than she let on. She portrayed herself as a bit of an airhead as an influencer, but Blayne knew it was an act.

"Ms. Davis, this isn't the time or the place to discuss this, anyway. We have compositions to evaluate. So, find your peer-editing team and trade papers. If you forgot to bring a hard copy of the paper, there's the door. Go print it now." Two students got up and left.

Blayne tried not to let his frustration show, so he plastered on a smile. He spent the next hour walking around the room, working with each group. Some groups were clearly stronger than others. He caught several mistakes as he looked over students' shoulders. By the time class was over, he was looking forward to going home. Then he remembered what was waiting for him there and groaned inwardly. In the normalcy of teaching, he'd forgotten what awaited in his apartment. His classroom had always been a safe place to escape, where he could leave his troubles at the door.

He was packing up his materials on the front table when Emma approached. He glanced up and did his best not to frown.

"Yes, Ms. Davis?"

"I will not ask you about last night. I promise."

"Great. How can I help you, then?"

"Are you okay?" she asked, a genuine look of concern washing over her face. "After last month and last night, I don't see how you're not curled up in a little ball somewhere. I know I'd be."

"I'm fine," he said, drawing a tight smile. "Thank you for asking."

"How's Ethan handling it?"

"He's fine, too," Blayne said, with a bit more trepidation.

"I promise, this is totally off the record."

"We're both fine. Sure, last night brought back memories, but we're adults and can soldier on with the best of them."

Emma nodded her head and walked out of the room. Blayne let out a huff as he finished putting stuff in his bag. There was a soft knock at his door. He looked up to see Dr. Esperanza Secada, the FBI-approved psychologist, standing at the entrance to his classroom.

"Got a minute?" Dr. Secada asked.

"For you" — he glanced down at his smartwatch — "I have ten. But I need to get home soon."

"Ethan's waiting for you there?"

"Yes, he stayed at my apartment today."

"I saw the news," she said, letting the intent hang in the air.

"I'm fine," Blayne said. She cocked her head, narrowing her eyes. "Really, I'm fine. Everyone keeps asking me how I'm doing. I'm okay. I must get back to my place. Ethan is taking this harder than I am."

"How so?"

"It was his concert that was interrupted by that mess. It's been a rough month for ZERO between canceling dates last month and this."

"Well, if you need anything, you know where to find me."

Blayne could tell that Dr. Secada didn't believe a word he'd said about being fine, but she would not push him if he didn't want to talk — and he really didn't want to talk. He was half afraid that everything would come rolling out of his mouth if he started. He slung his bag over his shoulder.

"I'll see you at your regular time?" Dr. Secada asked as they exited the classroom.

"Of course," Blayne said and tried to offer a genuine smile, but he was sure it came off as more cocky than genuine. As he left the Akokisas Lecture Center, he let out a breath he hadn't realized he'd been holding. He wasn't sure how long he could keep up the pretense of everything being okay.

He walked north, passing Gonzales Hall on his right and the Hale School of Education, recently renamed to honor the first Black teacher in Texas to win Teacher of the Year. The fall air was crisp but not too cold. The temperature was in the mid-seventies, so he didn't need a coat yet. He waved at a few people he knew from a distance but was thankful none of them tried to talk to him. He just wanted to get home.

He was almost at the northern edge of the main campus when someone came up beside him and threw her arm around him. Something metal poked into his back.

"Where is she?"

Chapter Nine

Agent Murphy

Murphy had decided she hated reports. She detested reading them, abhorred writing them and loathed making others read them. She sat at her keyboard, flying her fingers over the keys, the buttons making the *click-clack* sound as she depressed them while writing her mid-afternoon update for Director Steele. This update would be handed off to President Jeffery Barnes. How did she know the report would be passed on to the President by the Director? She'd found out the hard way when the White House Chief of Staff, Sepi Amin, had called to ream her out for 'opining' in the morning report. Apparently, the President didn't like to read...ever. So, his reports had to be easily digestible and short.

"I'm sorry," Murphy had told the Chief of Staff. "I didn't realize my report would make it to the President's desk."

"Assume everything makes it to the President's desk, Agent," the White House Chief of Staff had drawled out the word "agent" like it was a curse word, as though Murphy were gum on the bottom of her thousand-dollar high heels that she couldn't scrape off.

"I understand, sir," Murphy had responded. "Is there a preferred character limit?"

"Don't get glib with me," was the response before Murphy had been hung up on.

By mid-afternoon, Murphy had talked to the Special Agents in Charge of both Oklahoma City and Dallas. Both had welcomed her into the club of being yelled at and summarily dismissed by the White House.

"I heard you had your first run-in with Sepi today," the Special Agent in Charge of Dallas had said. "That woman is a bunch of contradictions rolled up in one tightly wound package. She reminds me of a snapping turtle. They may look all cute and innocent, but don't get too close. They're fast and will snap your finger off."

Murphy wasn't sure if the statement was supposed to be misogynistic or just a bad metaphor. She had opted to let it fly by her. Working for the FBI, she'd learned that many 'good old boy' tendencies still existed in the Bureau. Most men didn't mean to demean women in power, but it happened regularly. Murphy had been someone who called every guy out for every microaggression early in her career. Still, she realized she hadn't wanted a career in Human Resources, so she'd learned to pick her battles. Sadly, to become part of the club, she'd had to make a few concessions along the way and hold her tongue.

The Special Agent in Charge of Dallas jabbered about nothing, so Murphy finally stopped him before he put his foot firmly in his mouth. "What can you tell me about writing for the President?"

"K.I.S.S. Him. Keep. It. Stupidly. Simple. Aim for writing for a high school student with a moderate understanding of the government's workings, then dumb it down until a fifth grader could understand it."

"You're kidding."

"I wish I was. He's a moron. He may be all tan with good hair, good looks and white teeth, but there's nothing going on behind his blue eyes. Trust me. I'm amazed he knows where he is half the time. Remember when he couldn't remember his own senator during the televised debate?"

"Who doesn't? It was one of those moments that gave comedians fodder for a week."

"Yeah, that's not even the dumbest thing I've heard come out of his mouth. But he's our President. God help us all."

Once Murphy finished talking with the Special Agent in Charge of Oklahoma City, she quickly realized the Dallas agent was probably being kind.

"I sat there, giving my first briefing about the race riot in Oklahoma City after the police officer was acquitted." The agent was referring to a national case where a police officer in Oklahoma City had shot an unarmed Black eight-year-old boy in the back. The White officer's only defense was, "I felt threatened." It had been the first major political shit show of the Barnes Administration. "President Barnes informed me, and I quote, '*I thought all that prejudice stuff was over.*' I sat there, stupefied. I'm an openly gay conservative FBI agent. I was like, *what the fuck*?"

"What did you say?"

"I informed him that all forms of prejudice were still alive and well in our country, and this verdict showed the ideological and racial divisions that ran deep in some Southern states. Amin called me up after that briefing and threatened to have me fired if I ever said something like that again in the President's presence."

Murphy hadn't been sure how to respond to that revelation. "Is he naïve or just woefully ignorant?"

"I think the sky in his personal world is full of rainbows—not the gay kind, mind you—and puppy dogs and dancing theme park characters. And I voted for him and will probably do it again in the next election."

"How can you support him knowing what you know?" The words had been out of Murphy's mouth before she could stop them.

"Better him than the other guy in the last election. Besides, he's a figurehead. I'm not worried about him making any of the decisions. Everyone in DC knows the White House is run by Sepi Amin and the First Lady. Now, if you want to meet a woman with a scary high IQ and ambition to match it, talk to Cleo Barnes. She's the real puppet master. Actually, *don't* talk to her. She comes off all down-homey and Southern sweet with her Kentucky-schtick, but that woman is the genuine power in that couple. And the best part is, her husband doesn't have a clue. If you ever get a call from her office, don't respond. Call the Director and let his office know."

"Why?" Murphy had asked.

"Because she's downright scary. She's all smiles and Holly Homemaker for the American Press, but nothing in the White House happens without her knowledge and approval."

"I hate my job," Murphy muttered.

"Trust me, I get it," the OKC Agent in Charge responded. "None of us get into the FBI hoping to claw our way up to the top politically. Sadly, some of us rise. We're just doing our job to the best of our abilities, and then bam, you're in a position of power, and the DC vultures circle."

Murphy finished typing the revised memo for the President explaining what the FBI and other agencies had pooled together about the active shooting incident in the arena. She'd been warned not to use the phrases 'domestic terrorists' or 'far-right German party' because it would hurt the President's feelings. Her first draft of the revised report had simply stated, "*Bad guys killed other bad guys. Good guys are clueless,*" but she had deleted the sentences and followed a more traditional report format, even if it was dumbed down to the best of her ability.

The rapping sound on her office door frame startled her. She turned to her left to see who it was. Agent Harper stood at the door, his forehead wrinkled.

"That bad?" he asked.

"You have no idea. I've been on the phone with OKC and Dallas getting read-in on navigating the political trappings of this position."

"Ouch! I'd rather be in a firefight in the Sudan than dodging DC's political snipers."

"Some days I'd have to agree with you." Murphy finally pressed send and sat back in her chair.

"How are things with the arena?" Harper asked after a moment of silence. "Anything I can do to help?"

"We're just waiting for more information," she replied. "At least the shooters are all dead, so we don't have to hunt them down. It's just a matter of sifting through all the evidence now."

"Well, if you need me for anything, you know where to find me."

"Thanks, Harper," she said, offering him a small smile.

As Harper left the room, Murphy leaned back in her chair, staring blankly at her computer screen. She was left with a lot to ponder — political intrigues, presidential ignorance and the puppet strings that were pulled by the First Lady. All these factors made the already grueling work of handling crisis situations even more difficult. The politics of it all seemed more challenging than the actual crisis management. She hoped she was up for the task.

* * * *

Blayne

Blayne's first instinct was to turn around. Still, he had a sneaking suspicion he'd be dead, or at least knocked out, if he tried, and he had no desire to deal with either of those situations today.

"Who are you?" He stopped in his tracks as he asked the question.

"Keep moving." As if the demand wasn't enough for Blayne to start walking again, there was a little nudge from what he assumed was the muzzle of a gun pressed into his back. "I'll ask you one more time. Where is she?"

"I'll keep walking, but I need to know who you are seeking. If you're looking for my mother, I'm guessing she's at home in Plainview. I can't guarantee she's there. She could just as easily be at her church doing something 'for God'," he said in the best imitation of his mother's West Texas twang. His parents might live in West Texas now, but his mother had grown up in Southeast Texas, in Beaumont, near the Louisiana border, so her accent always was a bit different compared to other West Texans, who had an accent all their own. "Or are you looking for my grandmother? My mom's mother is in a cemetery in the Galveston area. But my dad's mom? She's alive and well, retired in—"

"Corpus Christi," the woman replied. "I know."

"You and your people seem to know a lot of things. I take it you've lost someone?" There was a swat across the back of his head—not enough to make him stumble, but strong enough to let him know she wasn't messing around. In the distance, Blayne could see the Dream Bean. "I'm heading for coffee. Would you like coffee? My treat."

"Oh, for heaven's sake," the voice behind him said. "Don't make me kill you."

Blayne considered it briefly and tested a hypothesis based on something Dr. Hennigan had said. "Your organization has stringent protocols for killing someone. Correct?" There was a grunt of surprise behind him, but Blayne acknowledged it. "Well, since you don't have an order to kill me and I'm not a threat, I'm going to go in, order two coffees, then we can sit down and converse like two civilized people."

"Don't make me shoot you again." For added emphasis, she grabbed him around his upper arm and placed pressure on his still-healing wound. Blayne winced, but he didn't make a sound. He was glad the woman couldn't see his face.

"Ahh, so you were the sniper?" *What the hell am I doing? If I tell her outright where Dr. Hennigan is, am I dead? If I keep her talking, am I dead?* He just kept walking, taking long strides. One of the nice things about being so tall was that most people needed to take two steps to keep up with one of his, so he could hear the woman moving quickly behind him to keep up. He could smell the fresh coffee roasting in the back about fifty yards from the Dream Bean.

The woman slipped in beside him and wrapped her arm around his back while poking him in the side of his stomach. "What do you think you're doing?" The woman jabbed him in the side a little more with each word.

"I figure you're a friend or you're a foe. If you're a friend, we'll sit down, have coffee and we can talk. If you're a foe, I'm dead if I talk and dead if I don't. So, why would I talk? And if you're really the woman who tried to shoot me last month, then I'm guessing you're more in the friend than the foe category. Besides, if you shoot me right now, enough people are milling around that you'll be seen, which is something I don't think you want."

"There is a third option."

"And what is that?"

"I'm neither friend nor foe, but I'll still happily shoot you in the back. In fact, the larger the crowd is, the better. I shoot you in the back, scream for help and escape during the ensuing panic. It's always easier to escape when people are scared and rarely remember who screamed first. Sure, they'll know it was a woman, but that's usually all they know. Memories are unreliable after a traumatic experience."

They climbed the stairs to the outside patio in front of the coffee shop.

"So, what can I get you?" Blayne asked, looking at the woman who was no longer holding a gun to his side. He wasn't sure what he expected the woman to look like, but the woman standing next to him wasn't it. She was slender and came up just past his shoulder. She had brown eyes that matched the color of her short hair. The first thought that came to his head was 'androgynous'. The woman wore an ill-fitted suit coat. She could easily have been mistaken for a teenage boy if not for the glint of makeup she had on.

"Coffee, nothing in it. And suppose you talk to anyone other than the barista. In that case, I'm putting a bullet in that person first, followed by you and a couple of extra people in here, just for good measure."

The look on her face told Blayne everything he needed to know. She'd follow up on that threat and not lose any sleep.

Blayne reached out and opened the door before waving the woman in ahead of him. "I think not. I can hold my own door," she said, cocking her head.

Blayne shrugged and walked in, not bothering to see if the woman grabbed the glass door after he'd let go. He walked over to the counter and found one of his students working.

"Hey, Mr. Dickenson," Todd Rice started as Blayne approached. "What can I get for you today?"

"Two tall coffees. One black and the other with half-and-half."

"Easy enough." Todd turned his back to Blayne, grabbed two paper cups and started pouring from the commercial coffee maker on the shelf. "Sorry I missed class today. I got stuck here on a double shift when one of my coworkers didn't show up. She didn't even bother calling in to let us know she wouldn't make it."

"It happens," Blayne replied absently. He leaned against the counter to keep one eye on Todd and another on the woman, who stood near the front door. She had positioned herself so she could easily see outside while keeping track of everything inside the coffee shop. Blayne knew little about the world she lived in, but he had a sneaking suspicion she was quite good. The woman was very unassuming. If he'd had to draw a picture of who he thought shot him, this wouldn't have been the person. The woman had been exotic in his head, a cross between an Amazonian and a Mossad agent.

"Here you go, sir," Todd said as he returned with the coffees. "The one with the stick has the half-and-half."

"How much?" Blayne asked as Todd rang up the order. After a quick exchange of money, Blayne stepped away from the counter.

"I forgot to ask. Did I miss anything?" Todd called after him.

Blayne looked at the woman, who was now clearly staring at him. He turned back toward Todd. For the first time since he'd gotten to the counter, Blayne couldn't see the woman, even though he knew her eyes were burrowing a hole in his back. He took a deep breath. "Honestly, Todd, both of my classes today are in slightly different places. I would email one of your peers. I really can't talk. I have business I need to attend to now."

"The creepy girl hanging out near the front door?" Todd asked in a low voice.

She does stand out a bit here. "Yep. She's another graduate student. We're working on a class project ourselves," Blayne lied. Todd just gave him a weird look. Thankfully, another customer stepped up to the counter, so Blayne made his getaway. He didn't wait. He exited the coffee shop, headed over to the exact table where he'd been shot and sat down.

The woman was there instantaneously, sitting down.

"The coffee without the stick is yours," he said. "And dress a little less conspicuously. My student spotted you immediately as someone who didn't quite belong."

"Exactly. And if you ask him in thirty minutes to describe me, he'll say I had short hair and dark features or looked like someone who was a witch or emo. He may even think I'm a young man."

Blayne picked up his coffee and sipped.

"I don't dress like this everywhere I go. Trust me. If I slip out of this into a brightly flowered shirt with red hair, I could walk back into the coffee shop and flirt with the clueless boy, and he'd never be the wiser. That's the beauty of dress. Dress is like a stereotype, and that's what people remember, the stereotype. I could go back in and shoot up the place, and all that kid would remember was 'the emo girl who came with Blayne.' And we both know what kind of a dead end that would be for any investigator."

They stared at each other momentarily, neither saying a word. Blayne finally asked the most obvious question. "Why should I trust you?"

"You're not dead. We both know you would be if I really wanted to hurt you. Besides, I'm nothing if not bluntly honest. I don't do subterfuge very well. As my boss likes to put it, *'You're a beautifully blunt instrument.'*"

"Tell me something only we would know," Blayne said. He wasn't sure what he was looking for, but he figured the question could provide interesting answers, no matter what she said.

"Last month, at the Emerald City, you and your friends ran behind a building and thought you were safe from the firefight around you. I had you in my scope the entire time. Our job that day was to retrieve your boyfriend's cell phone, not kill anyone. If we had wanted to take out your entire convoy, we would have. We were armed to the teeth, and your FBI escort was caught woefully unaware. How's that for something only *we* would know?"

Blayne sat there for a second, replaying that dreadful day's events. As much as he hated admitting it, she was right. The FBI had been caught unaware and unprepared.

"Oh, and we left once my boss put a bullet in the cell phone. Again, we had a single aim that day."

"Why not just take out the convoy?"

"Easy. Some things are harder to cover up."

"You covered up blowing up an airplane."

"She told you about that?"

Fuck! It was the first time Blayne had slipped and admitted to any conversation with Dr. Hennigan. "Yes," he said, realizing there was no reason to deny it.

The woman nodded her head. "Yes. You'd be surprised at how easy the coverup of the Peregrine flight was. We had operatives within the NTSB who replaced the black box when it was found. With that, it wasn't hard to spin the tale of an accident. Taking out a convoy of FBI agents would have been harder to explain away. Even if we misdirected and led them toward a different target, there would be people who wouldn't let it go — your friend, Agent Sarah Murphy, for example. She's smart."

"Won't they still come after you? I mean, you attacked them?"

"Sure. They're looking for us as we speak. And we know Agent Murphy hasn't let it go. *But* since no one was killed at the scene, it will eventually be placed on the back burner. And if anyone gets too close, we have methods to handle such situations."

"Blayne?" a voice called. Blayne looked to see Kira walking up the steps to the Dream Bean. "Kind of surprised to see you here. I figured you'd be at home." Kira looked at the woman at the table before turning back to him. "With your houseguest."

"I had to teach."

"And who is your friend?" Kira said, eyeing the woman warily.

"I'm Caroline. I'm one of Mr. Dickenson's English students," the woman said in a bubbly voice that sounded nothing like the cold-blooded killer he'd just been discussing the mass murder of innocents with.

Kira glanced at Blayne sideways, almost as if asking, *'Why are you having coffee with a student?'*

"I stopped by to grab a drink on the way home, and…" — he paused for a second, trying to remember the name the woman had just used — "Caroline, here, bumped into me and asked about her paper."

"Yep, I'm writing an essay on Emily Brontë's *Wuthering Heights*, or Ellis Bell's if you use her original pen name. I'm interested in the sexist underpinnings of the use of pseudonyms by the Brontë sisters. But Mr. Dickenson said I should focus on a specific text, so I went with my favorite."

"Well, I'm sure you're in expert hands," Kira said. "Wish I could talk longer, but I'm picking up a coffee before heading off to a deposition." She turned to Blayne. "I'll call you this evening. I have a few updates about last night."

"Great. I should be home all evening," Blayne said with a smile he hoped would appear genuine.

Kira turned to the woman. "It was nice to meet you, Caroline. Good luck with your paper. Blayne's love of the Brontë sisters will serve you well on your assignment."

"He's already been such an immense help. His extensive knowledge on the subject has helped me focus."

"I'm glad to hear it." Kira turned to Blayne. "I'll call once I'm out of the deposition. I should be done around seven."

"Talk to you then," Blayne replied. With that, Kira turned and headed into the Dream Bean. When the door closed, Blayne turned back to gape at the woman. "I take it you know your Brontë literature?"

"I was an English Lit major in college. Well, I double majored in that with Gender and Sexuality Studies."

"Deadly and educated," Blayne said as he absently stirred the stick in his coffee before taking a drink. "I guess we better get out of here before we run into anyone else?"

"I take it you trust me?"

"Not at all," Blayne admitted. "But I don't think you intend Dr. Hennigan harm, and it's not like you haven't figured out I know where she is, so there's no point in delaying the inevitable, is there?"

They grabbed their coffees, stood, pushed in their chairs and left the Dream Bean.

Chapter Ten

Ethan

Ethan sat on the couch, half watching the news and half watching Dr. Hennigan seated on the other end. She was in remarkably good shape, considering she just had a bullet removed from her.

"When is your boyfriend supposed to get back?" Dr. Hennigan asked.

"Anytime now," Ethan said. He glanced down at his watch. "Actually, he's a bit later than normal." He turned and looked at Dr. Hennigan. "Don't worry. That means nothing. Students regularly question him, so he's often forty-five minutes to an hour past when he's *supposed* to get home."

"*Good afternoon, America. This is Tika Downs. We're broadcasting live from the Real Time News Network's Main Studio in New Orleans. This evening has several brilliant shows being brought to you worldwide via the RTN Network. A complete listing of all shows can be found on our website at www.rtn.media.*" She twisted herself on the swivel stool to look into a different camera. *"Our top news story this afternoon is the terrorist attack last night in Houston, Texas."* A screen appeared over Tika's left shoulder with an image of the arena. *"For the latest updates on this unfolding tragedy, we turn to Stephen McNeil, who is on the ground in Houston."* The picture of a redheaded reporter with a close-cropped beard filled the station. From Ethan's vantage point, the guy looked like a slick used car salesman. *"Stephen, what is the latest from Houston?"*

"Thank you, Tika. The tragedy last night caught the attention of all Houstonians and Americans. Last night's terrorist attack was just the latest setback in the boy-band ZERO's North American tour, which has been riddled with problems from the explosion of Peregrine Flight 923, the plane the band was supposed to be flying, to the attempted assassination of one of its members, Ethan Bond. People are already questioning the safety of attending their concerts."

A few interviews with witnesses from the night before filled the screen. McNeil had clearly coached the interviewees into saying they were scared and wouldn't be attending ZERO's concerts any time in the future, even though most of the people McNeil interviewed weren't even in the right demographic for one of their concerts.

"As of right now, the FBI and ATF have yet to release a statement to the press," McNeil continued. *"In an exclusive video obtained by RTN, we can show the RTN viewers the devastating moments. The video we're about to show is unsuitable for audience members of all ages, so viewer discretion is advised."*

The TV studio hadn't even waited for a heartbeat to pass before the video played. Ethan watched in horror as the events from last night played out again. It was a different vantage point from the one he had on stage, but the events didn't change. The glass shattering was still followed by the man flying out of the window. From this angle, it was clear that someone inside the room had helped the man. Someone in all black had run toward the man and shoved him out.

"Well, now we know how that happened," Ethan mumbled.

"You didn't think the man leaped, did you?" Hennigan asked, the corner of her lip curling upward in a smirk. She grabbed the remote and muted the television as the rest of the segment played on.

"Of course, I didn't. I'm not an idiot. But it's one thing to realize someone threw him out of the room and another to see it happen."

"I'm more curious about the person who shot the video," Hennigan said. "How was this person's cell phone recording that window when it shattered?"

"Coincidence?" Ethan said, but his voice clarified that he didn't even believe that.

"I don't believe in coincidences. I'll have Ms. Wils…" Her voice trailed off.

Ethan turned his head fully to stare at Dr. Hennigan. She gave him a sideways glance and rolled her eyes. Ethan noticed the moment she told him what she was thinking. "An associate of mine has been out of contact since the incident. She's my go-to for research and when I need eyes in the sky. I don't know what's happening there, but something is wrong. I don't enjoy being out-of-pocket like this."

"Maybe she's busy?" Ethan suggested.

"No. It doesn't work like that." She paused momentarily, clearly trying to figure out how to phrase what she would say next. "She's my person. I don't want to say she's at my beck and call, but she's always available when I need her. And I lost touch with her last night when things went sideways. I'm worried."

"Honey, I'm home," Blayne called from the front door. "And I brought a guest."

As Blayne walked in, Hennigan immediately reached for her gun and leveled it at the entryway. His hands were up. Ethan could tell someone was behind him, but he couldn't see who the person was since Blayne blocked the view.

"Lower your weapon," Hennigan said.

"You first," a woman's voice echoed.

"Denzili?"

"In the flesh." A short woman stepped from behind Blayne. The woman called Denzili immediately put the gun she had held in a holster on her side. Hennigan didn't follow suit as she continued to eye the woman, the lines of suspicion creased her forehead. "It's just me," Denzili finally said.

"Blayne?" Ethan asked as the standoff continued.

"I'm fine," he said, not moving from the woman's side. "If she wanted to kill me, she could have done it hundreds of times."

"You trust her?" Ethan asked Dr. Hennigan.

"I wouldn't exactly say that I trust her," Hennigan said. "No offense." Denzili shrugged but didn't take her eyes off Hennigan. "But I don't believe she's here to hurt anyone," Hennigan finally said, as she lowered the gun. "Ethan, meet Denzili...one of my associates?"

"The one you haven't heard from?" Ethan asked.

"A different one. When I go out into the field, I have two associates who work directly with me. Denzili is half of that team." She turned and looked at the other woman and asked, "Have you heard from Richardson?"

"No. I scoped out all the pre-arranged safe houses. They were all under surveillance."

"Why did you seek out Mr. Dickenson?" Hennigan asked.

"I thought, where is the last place on earth you'd go? So, I tracked Mr. Dickenson down on campus and gave it a shot."

Hennigan gave a single approving nod.

"Can I put my bag in my bedroom?" Blayne asked, nodding at the attaché case slung over his shoulder. "It's getting heavy."

"Sure," Hennigan replied. Blayne started walking toward his bedroom, and Denzili followed.

"Leave the man alone," Hennigan chastised. "If either of these two men wanted to harm us, they could have let me die last night."

"You trust them?" Denzili asked. The skepticism was clear in her voice and the look she gave Dr. Hennigan.

"Trust is a tough word to define," Hennigan said. "I don't trust anyone. But I don't think these two men have the desire to cause you or me harm at this juncture."

Blayne opened the door to the bedroom. Denzili walked over to the kitchen table, grabbed one chair and dragged it into the living room area before swiveling it around, facing the back of the chair as she sat. The three sat in silence, waiting for Blayne to come back.

The toilet flushed in the bedroom, followed by the sound of Blayne washing his hands. Blayne joined the group and asked, "What did I miss?"

Dr. Hennigan

Hennigan gestured for Blayne to grab one of the kitchen chairs and join the rest of them in the living area. Blayne had just sat down when there was a soft click toward the front door. Denzili silently got out of her chair and positioned herself next to the entryway as Kira marched into the apartment with a small gun pointed at Dr. Hennigan.

"What the actual fuck?" Kira said, as she took in the scene before her. "Who are — ?"

The words weren't even out of Kira's mouth before Denzili reached out, disarmed Kira and disassembled the woman's gun into five parts. Denzili strode over to the kitchen table and deposited the pieces. "Cute toy, by the way." Denzili picked up the cartridge and slipped the bullets out. "I'm going to keep these. Don't want anyone to get accidentally hurt, do we?"

"You're…" Kira said in disbelief, leaving the words hanging in the air.

"Yes, I guess introductions are in order, Ms. Strickland," Dr. Hennigan said with a warm smile that didn't meet her eyes. "You can call me Dr. Hennigan, and this is my associate Denzili." She gestured to the other woman, who had returned to her chair. "Please, pull up a chair and join the group." Then, almost as an afterthought, she added, "And before you even think about dialing the cell phone in your pocket, please be a dear and put it on the table with the pieces of your weapon. After last night, everyone's just a little jumpy."

Hennigan made a swooping gesture with her gun toward the table. Kira went over to the kitchen table, pulled out her cell phone and set it down with the remnants of her gun. She grabbed a chair and pulled it next to Blayne.

"How'd you know?" Denzili asked when Kira was settled.

"How'd I know what?"

"You knew I wasn't a student of Blayne here. How'd you know?"

"Brontë," Kira said, a satisfied smile crossed her face. The other woman didn't respond, so Kira finished her thought. "You said you were writing an essay on Emily Brontë's *Wuthering Heights* and that Blayne was helping you. First, the writing class Blayne teaches isn't literature-based, so why you would write a literary treatise in that class is beyond me. Second, this guy is the last person on the planet you would want to seek help with a paper about *Wuthering Heights*." She gestured with her thumb in Blayne's direction. "Victorian Gothic literature is simply not his specialization. I doubt he's even read the book — or any of Brontë's books, for that matter."

"It's true," Blayne admitted. "The only classic I truly ever loved was *Great Expectations*. There was something about Miss Havisham that I found so intriguing to this day."

"Hmm," was the only response Denzili gave.

"Well, that was fun," Dr. Hennigan said, breaking into the conversation. "That was an excellent lesson for everyone about the joys of espionage. Now, as for why we're here." She turned to Kira and said, "I guess we should catch you up." Dr. Hennigan disclosed the events of last night, along with the information she'd previously provided Blayne and Ethan. She also told Blayne about the conversation she'd had with Ethan earlier. As she wound down, she asked, "Any questions?" like a college professor nearing the end of a lecture.

"So, you're not here to kill us?" Kira asked.

Dr. Hennigan rolled her eyes. "For the last time, if I wanted any of you dead, I would have done that already. Keep trying me like this and I just might change my mind."

"Well, it's not for lack of trying," Blayne said under his breath.

Dr. Hennigan chuckled. "You do have us there. Denzili and I had a bear of a time trying to kill Ethan last month." She turned and looked at Ethan. "For the record, I'm glad you're alive. I've even become somewhat of a fan. ZERO is on my exercise playlist. And don't worry. I always legally download my music."

"You realize how crazy that sounds, right?" Blayne asked. "I mean. You run around the country killing people—"

"World," Hennigan said.

"Huh?" Blayne questioned.

"You said we run around the *country* killing people. We do it globally when necessary." Blayne looked confused, so Hennigan added, "Since we're being open and honest here, I just want to ensure the record is correct."

Blayne scrunched up his brow. "Okay... As I said, you run around the world killing people but insist on legally downloading music. You don't see the cognitive dissonance here?"

"My dear boy... Oops, sorry. I hope you don't mind me using the word 'dear.' I know Ethan has an issue with it, so I promised not to call him that anymore." She paused for a second, waiting for a response from

Blayne. When none came, she continued. "You see us as being outside the law. That's your first mistake. We exist in a bureaucratic gray area. Will the United States acknowledge our existence or have anything to do with us openly? Of course not. Will the US rely on our special ability to work outside the traditional confines of the Constitution to ensure US interests are protected? Every day. The Foundation is as important to the security of this country as any branch of the military or federal agency. We do what's necessary by making the hard decisions no one else wants to make or wants to be held responsible for making. Are there times when we regret what must be done? Of course. That doesn't mean I lose sleep at night over our decisions."

"You realize you sound like one of those militia groups, don't you?" Kira said.

Hennigan made a scoffing noise. "That's a great transition—and the reason we're back in Houston. We received intelligence that the National Democratic Party of Germany was on US soil to meet with a group of homegrown violent extremists known as the Constitutional Liberation Army. The CLA wasn't even a blip on our radar, because they had done nothing."

"Well, that sure changed last night," Kira quipped.

"You are most definitely correct. Something has changed within the CLA. They decided to up their profile out of nowhere. And here is where you come in." She gestured to Blayne. "We have intelligence that Pennington University is on the CLA's hate list. We weren't taking it too seriously, but after last night—"

"And let's face it," Denzili cut in, "if this group wants to make a name for itself, they're off to a good start. These groups tend to 'up their game', so to speak. The next attack will be bigger."

"Which is why an attack on Pennington University is highly likely at this point."

"But you don't know this for sure?" Blayne asked.

"In our world, you rarely know things for sure. And since I'm out of contact with…" — there was a hesitation as she searched for the right word — "my office," she finally decided. "I'm not sure how the intelligence has changed. Currently, we're flying completely without a safety net and little information. All I know is that I was targeted last night. Very few people know who I am and what I do."

"Why are you telling us?" Ethan asked.

"Because I must trust someone. And right now, the people in this room are some of the most honest people I know. You can act all strong and fearless" — she stared Blayne in the eyes — "but I know that you're still suffering from the post-traumatic stress from last month, which I apologize for inflicting. I don't apologize for our methods, but I am sorry it had to be you."

"What do you need us for?" Blayne asked. "It's not like we're superspies or anything. We're average people just trying to live our lives."

"Well, besides the help you provided me last night, we need to work together to stop whatever is going to happen. And because of the current communication blackout with my office, we must do this the old-fashioned way. Before the advances in technology, my organization regularly worked with people in the public during extraordinary circumstances. This is another one of those times."

The group spent the better part of the next hour hashing out the details they had. Sadly, they didn't exactly have much to go on. At some point, Ethan got up and made coffee for the group. Blayne had grabbed a stack of legal pads from his home office in the main bedroom, and the group had sketched out all the information they had.

Blayne's pocket buzzed. Blayne looked at Dr. Hannigan as if asking permission to pull it out. Hennigan nodded.

"Area code nine-one-five? Where's that?"

"El Paso," Hennigan said. "What's the number?"

Blayne read it off.

"Answer it," Hennigan replied. "And put it on speaker."

Blayne did as instructed. "Hello?"

"Mr. Blayne Dickenson?" a woman's voice said over the phone.

"Yes…"

"Ms. Wilson!" Hennigan exclaimed. "What in the hell is going on?"

Chapter Eleven

Ms. Wilson
Twenty-four hours earlier

The announcer's voice fed through Ms. Wilson's earbud, "...put your hands together, and let's hear some noise for Zach, Ethan, Ric and Orr...ZERO, live in concert!"

"Dear God, Phillipa, how can you listen to that nonsense? I'm switching to channel two."

With a flick of her fingers across her tablet, the noise from the concert disappeared, and a team of agents appeared on her screen, escorting a recently rescued royal from Saudi Arabia back to his family. Sadly, if the kidnapped royal had been his sister, as the terrorist group had originally intended, the Saudi Royal Family wouldn't have been as likely to negotiate. The Foundation had been called in through back channels to handle the negotiation and retrieval. The princeling didn't look any worse for wear. He was still confused by the group of five women dressed all in black who had swooped in, taken out the terrorists holding him hostage then dragged his ass kicking and screaming to safety. One problem Ms. Wilson commonly faced when dealing with these ridiculous patriarchal monarchs was their underestimation of women's capabilities. Sure, on average, women may not have the same muscle mass as men, but that didn't mean they couldn't be just as skilled and deadly as their male counterparts.

"The money has been transferred. You are free to return the Prince Amir bin Lu'ayy Al-Saad." She paused for a second before switching to a different channel before speaking again in crisp Arabic. *"'tama al'iifraj ean al'amir 'amir bin luayi alsaeda, wasawf taqum wasayil alnaql altaabieat lana bi'iisalih 'iilaa almakan almutafaq ealayh fi ghudun khams daqayiqi, yurjaa min alharas almalakii 'an yakhudh mawqieah liaistiqbalihi,"* she said in a polite, but officious voice—Prince Amir bin Lu'ayy Al-Saad has been released. Our transportation will deliver him to the agreed-upon location in five minutes. Please have the Royal Guard in place.

She listened to the response from the Saudi Arabian officials as she switched channels. "Alpha, Bravo, anything I need to know?"

"Alpha here, the room is still dark," Richardson replied.

"Bravo. Nothing to report," Denzili said.

"laqad kan min dawaei sururi taqdim almusaeadat alyawm lilmamlakat alearabiat alsaeudiati," she spoke into her headset—It's been a pleasure helping the Kingdom of Saudi Arabia today. There was a momentary burst of chatter as the Prince's guard escorted him from the helicopter. They had chosen the Sir Abu Nair Airport for the handover. One of the Abu Dhabi Islands, it was roughly fifty nautical miles from both Abu Dhabi and Dubai. The Saudis were flying from their Embassy in

Abu Dhabi, so her team was flying in and out of Dubai. Of course, neither the United Arab Emirates nor the Saudi Arabians knew with which flag The Foundation was most closely aligned.

"*As-Salaam-Alaikum*," a voice said. 'Peace be unto you.'

Ms. Wilson wasn't entirely sure, but she thought it might have been the king thanking her. "*Wa-Alaikum-Salaam*," she replied. 'And unto you peace.'

She watched the monitor as the helicopter lifted off the ground.

"ETA to Dubai, twenty-five minutes to touch down," the pilot said.

"The Mesa Juamenes Complex is signing off," Ms. Wilson said. She pulled up the interior cameras at the Toyota Center in Houston and started flipping through.

She had access to the arena's internal security system. Furthermore, each team member had placed a small camera in their nests so she could see their vantage points as well. She was flipping through the feed when the light in the arena suite turned on.

"Team Leader, this is The Complex. We are a go."

"Denzili, Richardson, on my mark," Dr. Hennigan said. "You are cleared to liquidate."

Ms. Wilson rolled her eyes. "What's the point of using code names if Phillipa never uses them?" she asked herself.

Something flashed on her screen, and the video feed disappeared. She walked over to her desktop and tried to find out what was going on. She made it halfway through the room when suddenly everything went black.

She tapped her tablet to provide her light. It wasn't the first time they'd had a power outage at The

Complex. It's difficult to get massive amounts of electrical power to a hidden facility in the middle of a valley surrounded by mountains. The backup generator would kick in within thirty seconds, so she used the tablet to light her way.

In the dimly lit office, cracks of gunfire shattered the silence. The rapid succession of gunshots was not near her, but from the direction they were heading, she had seconds before they would be outside her door. She dropped the tablet and ran to the main entrance of this part of The Complex. She hit the glass case with her elbow and pulled on the black handle inside. Immediately, three inches of armored steel dropped from a place in the ceiling, barricading the door from anyone trying to get in. The manual blast doors had been one of her suggestions a few decades ago—a last deterrent to slow down someone if they attempted to invade The Complex. Between the steel door and the steel reinforced walls, she now stood in the dark in a bomb-proof cage.

The backup generator kicked on, and Ms. Wilson hurried to her desktop, immediately pulling up the internal surveillance feed.

"You've got to be kidding me." A ragtag group of what looked like ranchers playing military had infiltrated The Complex. Underneath their body armor, their cowboy boots stuck out like sore things. "We've been invaded by Nickle-Dicked Rednecks!"

In the excitement, Ms. Wilson had temporarily forgotten the op she was running. She looked for where she'd dropped her tablet, strode over and picked it up. She pulled up the feed for Houston. Nothing happened. "Team leader, can you hear me?" she said into her earpiece as she poked at the screen. Only then did she realize the Wi-Fi network wasn't showing on her tablet. She walked over to her desk and logged into the wired system, but she still wasn't connected. She picked up the phone on her desk. There was no dial tone.

She scrolled through the internal surveillance she had access to, knowing that those were hardwired differently, so one couldn't simply turn off the system unless they knew the location of each camera individually. It was a little failsafe she'd built into the system long before she started working for the youngest Hennigan. Speaking of the Hennigans, Ms. Wilson checked the video feeds from Deborah's and Sarah's offices. Sarah was the Chairwoman of The Foundation. She was also Phillipa's grandmother. Deborah was Phillipa's mother and next in line to chair The Foundation. No one knew she'd installed these cameras. They were a device of her own design and were never found during the daily security sweeps. She pulled up the images and found both women secure in their offices — Deborah pacing, Sarah was simply reading a book. Admittedly, the older Hennigan had seen more over the years than anyone in The Foundation could imagine. She'd propped up royalty and torn down nations. She looked more like an editor for a New York fashion magazine than one of the world's most powerful and deadly women.

"Glad I don't have to worry about those two." She pulled up the other internal feed. Ms. Wilson was shocked by the carnage she found around The Complex. Ms. Wilson had worried that the place had become too relaxed in their assumption of invulnerability. "I should have seen this coming." There was pounding at her door, followed by bullets ricocheting off the steel back into the hall. There was a yelp as someone was hit by one of their own stray bullets.

She pulled up the feed to the hall. A man in dirty cowboy boots lay in a pool of blood as another man tried to help him. *One down*, Ms. Wilson thought. *Now, how to get rid of the other?* She steepled her hands under her chin as she spun in her office chair to face the large, empty television monitor that took up the back wall of her office.

She took stock of the facts. Their backup diesel could run The Complex for approximately one hundred and twenty hours. After that, their security systems would stop working. She had four days to topple the coup.

She had an old computer in the corner that hadn't been plugged into an electrical socket in years. She pulled the plastic cover off the computer and plugged it in. On a shelf nearby, she drew the box of floppy disks she had held on to. She flipped through the box, finding the one she needed. She took a deep breath and pressed the power button, filling the area with the whirring sound of the internal metal mechanisms. *I forgot how loud these things were.* She waited for it to boot up before typing in the command line to run the old computer-aided design program from the early nineteen-eighties. The whizzing and buzzing noises from the disk drive filled her with a feeling of nostalgia. "Ahh, the good old days." She waited for the program to boot. When it did, she loaded in the Mesa Juamenes Complex's original blueprints. A lot had changed since these were drawn and input into the system, but there were secrets only she had access to.

She spent the next few hours drinking coffee from her coffee pot, snacking on meal replacement bars and searching for the blueprints. "There," she said when she finally found what she sought. "Well, I'm going to have to get a little creative. And I hope Phillipa doesn't mind getting a new carpet in her office." She searched their offices and labs for the tools she'd need before creating a hole in Phillipa's office. A little acid, some creative chiseling and Ms. Wilson had made a hole that would lead her between the floors. She would have to be careful, but it would lead her to a ventilation duct in a maintenance closet. She'd drawn a map on spare paper and was ready to shimmy her way through the systems. Her short stature was ideal for the first time in a long time.

* * * *

After crawling on her stomach through the crawl space, she had made it into the ductwork, armed only with a penlight and a screwdriver. The mapped-out path had taken her almost forty-five minutes. The room below her was pitch black. She listened above, waiting to hear any movement below her. When she was finally satisfied, she showed her light around the room. It was small but empty of any humans. She unscrewed the grate in the ductwork before quietly dropping to the ground in the room. She spent several minutes taking stock of what she had to work with there. To her delight, she found a box cutter and several cleaning supplies. There was even protective gear. She smiled to herself, realizing the fun concoctions she could create with these. She found two chemicals she'd hoped to find, oxalic acid and trichloroisocyanuric acid. "These shouldn't even be stored in the same closet," she muttered. "I'll have to put an end to that once this is over."

She set about preparing herself, and within minutes, she opened the door to the closet and peeked her head out. The hall was empty. She heard clopping noises on the marble tiles. She closed the door just enough to watch a group of three guys in those blasted cowboy boots walking through the halls. They'd taken off their masks. They looked like a bunch of good old boys out playing army. None of them held themselves like they had real military training. When the walking subsided, she slid out. She placed the chemicals in a mop bucket and prayed the wheels wouldn't squeak.

Ms. Wilson headed into the hallway and went to the T-intersection connected with the armory. She knew they couldn't get in without someone in senior leadership, so the room would be locked up tight. Two guards were standing in the hall. *This should be easy*. She mixed the chemicals, waited for them to turn into a gas, and kicked the mop bucket down the hall.

"What the—?" before he started coughing.

She waited just a second before dashing madly toward the men. The protective gear helped her see while the other men rubbed at their stinging eyes. She held her breath as she slid under one man, severing his femoral artery with the box cutter. As he crumpled to the ground, she used him as a steppingstone to launch herself at the second man, driving the screwdriver through his eye and into his brain. She spun around and finished the first one, slicing through his trachea just below the larynx to stop him from screaming. All-in-all, the entire ordeal took less than thirty seconds. The first man attempted to grab her, but she knew he only had two minutes left to live. She kicked his hand away, walked up to the keypad, entered her code and let the device scan her iris. There was a whirring sound as the locks on the door disengaged. She opened the door and slipped inside.

The lights flickered to life. She found three women braced for battle at the other end of the room.

"What are you three doing in here?" Ms. Wilson asked in her authoritative voice. She recognized the recruits. She'd started their training a month ago.

"We were checking out weapons for training when the lockdown happened, Ms. Wilson," a petite blonde woman said. Ms. Wilson tried to remember. *A senator's wife?*

"What's going on out there?" asked a bulky brunette. Ms. Wilson remembered this one, a former Marine.

The third was an ordinary housewife that no one thought would last as long as she had. Ms. Wilson smiled at the memory.

She turned to the housewife. "I'm glad to see you are still with us. I've been rooting for you. You remind me so much of myself. When I went through training, no one believed I would last to the end, either." The woman nodded once. "Well, let's get out there and do some damage, shall we?"

She had the three women arm themselves, and they spent the next twenty minutes discussing specific military tactics. "Remember... You are now the insurgency. Use all the insurgency tactics you've learned. Do *not* play military. The only rules of engagement are don't die and don't kill one of our own, unless necessary. At the same time, don't trust anyone roaming the halls. Someone let these people in. Until we know who it was, assume everyone you run into is an assailant."

"You're out roaming the halls?" the Marine asked.

"Yes, but I'm one of the good guys," Ms. Wilson said flippantly. "If I'd wanted you dead, you'd be dead."

She looked the three women over. They weren't exactly ready for this, but they were about to be tried by fire. It would have to do for now.

"You three do some damage."

"What are you going to do?" the housewife asked.

"I need to call in the cavalry."

With that, they slipped open the door. Immediately, gunfire erupted. Two women took an isosceles stance while the third dropped to her knee and set up counterfire. The gunmen at the end of the hall dropped in seconds. *Like shooting fish in a barrel.* Ms. Wilson slipped the other direction. She now needed to get to the backup generator room — one of only two places in the entire building that contained satellite phones. She wasn't relishing crawling around in the ducts again but headed back to the janitor's closet. She was almost here when a man stepped around the corner. Ms. Wilson put a bullet between his eyes before he could register her. Unfortunately, someone came running in her direction. Instead of waiting, she slipped into the janitor's closet, barricaded the door and slipped back into the ductwork. She finished securing the grate when a man kicked the door in. He looked around the room.

"Fucking decoy!" the younger guy said before pulling a walkie-talkie from his belt and speaking into the device, "Henderson is down."

"For fuck's sake!" a woman's voice came back. Ms. Wilson recognized the voice but couldn't place it. "Find this person and put them down. It shouldn't be that complicated."

"Sure thing, Mrs. Jackson."

"How many times do I have to tell you not to use real names? What have they been training you at redneck gun camp?" The woman on the walkie-talkie let out a stream of obscenities that would make a hardened sailor blush.

Ms. Wilson thought about putting the young men out of their misery but decided she needed answers first. After the woman's tirade ended, the man promised to check back in in ten minutes. Ms. Wilson quietly slipped the grate into the duct before she fell out of the ceiling, lacing her legs around the man's neck. He tried to reach for the walkie-talkie, but it fell to the ground. She squeezed harder. She focused pressure on the carotid arteries and counted backward from twelve. At ten, the man slumped to the ground and Ms. Wilson landed quietly on her feet. She took the walkie-talkie and clipped it to her belt. It was big and bulky, but it should fit with her in the ducts.

She searched for something to restrain the man. There was a roll of duct tape on a shelf. She spread the man's arms behind his back and duct-taped them to opposite ends of a broom, before winding his feet together. She then fastened the broom to a shelving unit with his arms stretched back behind him, enough to make it very difficult for him to be of any danger to her. In fact, in the position she'd strung him up in, he wouldn't be a danger to anyone for quite some time.

When ready, she patted him on the cheek until he woke. "Wakey, wakey," she said in a sing-song voice before she slapped him once hard across the face.

The man tried to yell, but the rag in his mouth, fastened by the duct tape, prevented him from making too much noise. The man tried to squirm, but quickly realized his predicament and stared at the woman.

"Okay, now that I have your attention," Ms. Wilson said, "we'll have a conversation. And if you get out of hand, I will slice off one of your testicles and feed it to you. And guess what? You have two of them. Do you understand?"

The fear in the man's eyes was obvious. He shook his head vigorously in agreement. She unwrapped the duct tape and pulled the cloth out of the man's mouth.

"What kind of munchkin demon are you?" he asked around the cloth.

She tilted her head sideways before reaching out and slicing off the bottom part of the man's earlobe. He screamed, but she shoved the rag back in and smacked him once across the face until he quieted.

"Now that I think we understand each other, we can proceed. I will not tolerate any disrespect."

The man nodded once.

"Who do you work for?"

"An oil company," the man said.

Again, Ms. Wilson brandished the blade. "You know that's not what I'm asking." She moved to the man's other ear as if she would take off another chunk.

"Okay, okay. I'm a member of the Constitutional Liberation Army. My rank and serial number a—"

Ms. Wilson shoved the rest of the rag back into his mouth. He writhed again as she taped his mouth shut.

"Most people don't realize how potent the chemicals are in their cleaning supplies. Did you know that bleach, when mixed with certain glass cleaners, makes a sort of do-it-yourself chloroform?" She nodded at a rag that was soaked, sitting on a shelf. She picked up a pair of gloves and snapped them onto her hands. "I hope I got the recipe right," she said before she shoved the wet towel in the man's face. She waited until he calmed down and passed out. She stripped off the gloves and checked for a pulse. "Look at that. I didn't kill you after all." With that, she crawled back into the ductwork. She had one thought on her mind. She needed to call Hennigan.

Chapter Twelve

Dr. Hennigan

Hennigan listened attentively to Ms. Wilson's tale of the past twenty-four hours. "Have you slept?" Hennigan asked after Ms. Wilson finished explaining, grabbing the satellite phone and returning to their offices to make a call.

"Who needs sleep?" Ms. Wilson joked. "I'm having too much fun. It's been ages since I last got to kill anyone. I forgot how much I missed it."

Hennigan glanced at the three civilians in the room and almost chuckled at the horror washing over their faces. They had never encountered someone like Ms. Wilson before, and they likely never would.

"How did you find me?" Hennigan asked, sensing Ms. Wilson's story had come to an end.

"I knew your cell phone would be trashed, as would Denzili's and Richardson's. So, I thought about what I would do if I were you. Where is the last place someone would expect you to go? Then I remembered your new pets — and voilà, there you are."

"Pets?" Ethan said.

"Shh," Denzili said, "the grownups are talking."

Ms. Hennigan could tell that Ethan wanted to say something else, but Blayne reached out his hand and grabbed Ethan's. With one simple squeeze, Ethan stood down.

"Is that Denzili?" Ms. Wilson asked.

"Yes, she's here with me, as well. I haven't heard from Richardson." Then, almost as an afterthought, Hennigan asked, "Have you?"

"Not yet. I tried finding you first. After you, I'm going to call in the reinforcements."

"Who are you going to call? Someone has betrayed us. I don't know who to trust."

"I know someone who wouldn't betray us." The words came from the phone, but Dr. Hennigan sensed the strain behind them.

"What are you thinking, Ms. Wilson?"

"My ex."

Denzili let out a low whistle as her eyes widened.

"Is that best?" Hennigan asked.

"She's the only person I trust besides the inner circle." Hennigan knew she was referring to herself, her mother and her grandmother. Wilson didn't even trust Denzili and Richardson. She tolerated them and had promised Hennigan not to kill them unless they deserved it.

"Have at it," Hennigan said. "Keep me updated."

"How long will you play house with your pets?" Ms. Wilson asked.

"Not too much longer. We're going to go to ground. We need a secure place to hold until we know what's happening."

"I think I can do that. Now that I have the satphone, I can connect to the internet. I purchased three off-the-books locations after last month through a couple of shell corporations I play with. I'll double-check their security. Give me thirty minutes." And with that, Ms. Wilson hung up the phone.

"Who is she?" Kira asked.

"She's the last person on earth you want to fuck with," Denzili said with a broad smile. "You think I'm scary? This is the woman who gives me nightmares."

"It's a good thing she's on our side," Hennigan said. "Technically, she's my research assistant. But as you just heard, she's so much more than that. The only people who truly know her value outside my team are my mother and grandmother."

"Tell them about your mother and grandmother," Denzili said. "They're also scary women you don't want to fuck with."

"I'm seeing a pattern here," Blayne said flatly. "But is it just bolstered bravado?"

"Maybe," Hennigan said, not giving anything away. "I guess this is as good a time to tell our story. As you've figured out, I work for an off-governmental organization called The Foundation. My ancestor, Deborah Sampson, established us after the Revolutionary War. Ever heard of her?" She looked at Blayne, Ethan and Kira's blank faces. "I'm not too surprised. She's not discussed in American history textbooks, which is a sad oversight. She was born on December 17, 1760, in Plympton, Massachusetts, about ten miles east of Plymouth. When she was five, her father was lost at sea, assumed shipwrecked. In reality, he'd left his wife and seven children to start a new life in Fayette, Maine. To say that being a single mother in the 1700s was difficult is an understatement. Her mother, also named Deborah, placed her children with other families when she could not afford them. At age ten, young Deborah was indentured to Deacon Benjamin Thomas, a farmer in Middleborough."

"Wait! She was an indentured servant at ten?" Ethan asked, his eyebrows shooting up toward his hairline as his eyelids retracted slightly.

"It's how things were done then. If you couldn't care for your kids financially, you found someone who could. Anyway, at eighteen, she finished her indenture and went to work as a teacher. She was self-educated. Don't think the family she worked for provided her with an education. It wasn't part of the servitude. It's important to remember that the Revolutionary War had been raging for three years before Deborah turned eighteen. After teaching for two years, she decided she wanted to join the war effort. She disguised herself as a man to join the Fourth Massachusetts Regiment, renaming herself Robert Shurtleff. 'Robert' quickly rose through the ranks and ended up at West Point, leading scouting and raiding parties. She escaped detection for two years. There were a couple of close calls, sure. Once, she had a gash on her forehead from a sword, and another time, she dug a ball bearing from her body to avoid a surgeon finding out her sex. She was ultimately discovered when she became seriously ill because of a raging epidemic in Philadelphia."

"That's so fucked up," Kira mumbled. "I'm sorry, but it just is."

"Trust me, I agree with your sentiment completely," Hennigan said. "She was honorably discharged from the army and retired to Massachusetts, where she settled down with Benjamin Gannet in Sharon."

"Deborah was the only woman in the Revolutionary War to receive a full pension for her service," Denzili said. Hennigan looked at Denzili, who sat like a school child hearing her favorite story.

Hennigan nodded her agreement. "After the war, Deborah was restless. Although she loved her husband and the life she was creating, she wanted more. She missed the days of scouting and raiding, but she found it hard to take part in that world as a woman. She attended underground meetings and occasionally donned her Robert Shurtleff personality."

"Do you think she was a transgender man?" Blayne asked.

"Not by our modern sensibilities. From her diaries, Robert Shurtleff was less who she desired to be than who she had to be. She knew that to live in a world where men dominated all aspects of public life, she had to become a man. She didn't want to *be* a man." Blayne nodded, clearly accepting the explanation. "Anyway, in her early forties, she started lecturing around the country, telling her story. She met many women who were similarly disgruntled with their station in life. She put together a network of women with similar sensibilities. By the time the US entered the war of 1812, The Foundation was firmly established in all eighteen states and five territories. Admittedly, the extent to which she was in the territories is fuzzy. By the time she died in 1827, The Foundation had its fingers in every aspect of American politics behind the scenes. When her mother passed, Deborah's eldest daughter Mary took over the day-to-day running of The Foundation. And every generation since, Deborah's descendants' eldest daughter has been entrusted to run the organization. When my grandmother passes, my mother will take over. When my mother passes, the torch will be passed to me. And that's our story."

"That's quite a—" Blayne started, but his phone vibrated. He didn't recognize the number, so he handed it to Dr. Hennigan.

"Hennigan," she answered, putting the phone on speaker mode.

"All three of the new properties are still operational. The closest to your current location is maybe fifteen miles from where you are in an old industrial park." Hennigan hit the speaker button and held the phone to her ear as Ms. Wilson provided more information. She 'trusted' the people in this room but wasn't willing to take chances with her safety and security.

"Inside the facility, you'll find a Faraday cage, four bunks, a small kitchen, a training room and all the other accoutrements you would need to invade a small country," Ms. Willson explained.

"You thought of everything."

"Not quite. You'll need to get food before you go."

"I think I can manage that." Hennigan paused before asking, "What will you be up to?"

"I'm going to find Richardson, contact the senior leadership, call Ms. Brighton and see if I can be a general nuisance around here."

"How will you contact me?"

"There are five satphones in the safe house. I'll call you on the one marked 'A'."

"How did you set this up without stepping out of The Complex?"

"I work in mysterious ways." Her voice held a hint of mirth.

That was the only answer Hennigan was going to get. Before she could ask another question, there was the sound of a scuffle on the other end of the line.

"Sorry about that. I'm not in the most secure location. These damn satphones are persnickety little devices. Anyway, there are at least two fewer CLA roaches running around these halls. I swear, every time I take one down, three seem to replace it."

"When you get a chance, can you send me everything about the CLA? It's clear that we underestimated them."

"That we did. Someone is pulling their strings. This is not the same ragtag group we previously profiled internally. So far, the ones I've interrogated don't seem to have much information." There was a burst of gunfire. "Roaches, I tell you." With that, the line disconnected.

* * * *

Agent Murphy

By six p.m., Murphy was ready to go home. Unfortunately, she had another meeting with the President's Chief of Staff, Sepi Amin, who, this time, wanted an up-to-date briefing.

She rolled her neck, trying to get the kinks out, when there was a soft knock on her door. "Enter." She finished typing the email before turning to find her partner sitting in one of the guest chairs.

"How are things?" Ben asked.

"As you can imagine." Murphy took in a deep breath. "God, I need more coffee. Walk with me?" She glanced at her watch. "I have thirty minutes before my next meeting with the White House."

"Oooh, look at you, taking meetings with the White House," he said, trying to add some levity to the room, but Sarah could only manage a weak smile. Ben looked at his partner. "That bad, huh?"

"You have no idea."

"Then the coffee's on me."

"Perfect!"

They walked down the hall to a small breakroom where a pot of coffee was always brewing. Sarah hadn't figured out who kept the pot full, but she was grateful that someone did.

Ben grabbed a mug that read, '*I'm an FBI agent, what's your superpower?*' He filled it and handed it to Murphy. He then grabbed a mug with an image of Jesus in a cowboy hat petting a dinosaur that read, '*Jesus was an American.*'

"Who buys these things?" Sarah wondered aloud.

"I don't know, but they at least make me laugh," Ben replied.

"There was a '*Female Body Inspector*' mug that may have accidentally met its end on my first day here," Sarah said with a sly grin. "Funny, I don't mind. Sexist? Not on my watch."

They stood in the breakroom, sipping their coffee.

"How's Kira?"

"Strong. She didn't seem shaken by last night at all. She's tough as nails. What about you? Any movement on the dating front?"

"Nah. I'll stick to dogs. They're more loyal." He quickly added, "No offense."

"None taken." Sarah took a sip of her coffee. She'd had a lot of FBI office coffee in her career. The brew at the Emerald City was one of the best. She'd asked a few people where it came from, but no one seemed to know. It was like there was some coffee fairy who showed up every night and just put fresh grounds around the building.

"What have you learned about this CLA group today?" Ben asked.

"So far, we don't have much. They were on everyone's radar, but no one worried about them. They seemed all rhetoric and no bite. We still do not know why they met with a far-right German nationalist group. Plus, we're not completely sure who shot whom first. From the surveillance we've pulled, it looks like the CLA ambushed the Germans, but we don't know why. It's all bizarre." She glanced down at her watch. "On that note, time to face the music. I'll see you tomorrow."

"Sure thing, boss."

She rolled her eyes. "If you ever call me that again, I will transfer you to Fairbanks."

"That's just mean. You know I can't handle the cold. This bayou boy thinks Houston is in the north."

"How did you survive Quantico?"

"I don't know. I've put that horror show out of my mind. There was this white shit that was everywhere. I thought I was a popsicle from when I got there to when I landed back in NOLA."

Sarah couldn't help but let out a slight chuckle. "Anyway, time to play politics." Murphy raised her mug at Ben as she left the breakroom and headed to the elevator. The doors opened, and the car was empty. The elevator ride to the basement provided a brief respite from the chaos. She navigated through the maze of corridors until she reached the SCIF, using both a palm print and a retina scan to access the room.

Inside, she entered the conference ID information and waited. A message on the screen said, "*The Host Will Be with You Shortly.*" Sarah sat down in the lone chair in the room and waited. Ten minutes after the designated time for the meeting, a professional woman with black hair in an updo appeared on the screen.

"Agent Murphy," Sepi Amin greeted.

"Good evening."

Amin didn't respond kindly. "Status report."

Murphy provided a brief report of all the information the FBI had gathered that day. Amin took copious notes during the entire conversation. Amin periodically asked for clarification, but the woman mostly let Murphy provide what they'd learned.

"You're telling me, we still don't know what the meeting was about?"

"Unfortunately, no. Various intelligence agencies had not given the CLA a serious enough threat level to attempt infiltration, so we're still trying to find an asset willing to talk."

"Any idea why we're so far behind?"

"I wish I had an answer. I have a few theories—"

"Do tell." For the first time in minutes, Amin looked directly into the camera.

"Again, these are just theories."

"I understand."

"First, it's possible that the CLA simply flew under the radar. The group operated within legal loopholes or blind spots. Simply put, they've exploited the limitations of existing intelligence practices. If this is the case, they know a lot about how HVEs are assessed and how to avoid raising their profile until they were ready to strike. Another theory is that the CLA has infiltrated key intelligence agencies, which could allow them to manipulate or disable surveillance systems, forge documents or tamper with intelligence reports."

"How easy would that be?" Amin asked.

"I would like to tell you it's impossible, but we both know nothing is impossible."

"True. Do you have any other theories?"

"New leadership," Murphy said. "It's possible the group has new leadership that has urged them to a more militant and militaristic stance."

"Or maybe the existing leadership became frustrated with their lack of progress and decided that violence was the only way to achieve their goals," Amin added.

"Possible. Again, we just don't have enough information."

"What do you need from our end?"

"I'm waiting for a warrant to search Benjamin Jackson's property. He's the last-known leader of the group. We're hoping to obtain it in the morning and conduct a raid on the ranch where he resides in West Texas."

"And you're coordinating with the Dallas and Oklahoma field offices?" The question came off less as a question and more as a statement.

"Yes, ma'am."

"Good. Do you know who the judge is assigned to the warrant?"

Sarah rattled off the name. Amin turned her head to the side, clearly putting pieces together. "I believe Cleo Barnes went to school with his wife. I'll have her reach out through back channels. You'll have that warrant in hand by nine a.m. Anything else?"

"Not that I can think of right now."

"If you come up with anything else, please let us know. We want this taken care of quickly. So, let's bypass the bureaucratic red tape." Sarah thought the conversation was over, but Amin had one last thing to say, "Oh, and, Agent Murphy, please keep this conversation between us. There's no need to tell Director Steele."

"Understood, ma'am."

"Good." With that, the camera on the other end went dead.

Sarah felt a headache coming on. She hated politics.

* * * *

Blayne

Blayne walked Denzili and Hennigan to the door. When Dr. Hennigan walked out, she said, "We'll be in touch." Blayne wasn't sure if that was a good thing or a threat. He shut the door behind them, locked it and leaned against it as he let out a long breath. The conversation he was about to have with Kira wouldn't be fun.

He pushed himself off the door and walked back into the living room. Kira had moved to the couch, crossing her legs at the knees with her arms folded in front of her. All she asked was, 'What the actual fuck?' Kira turned her head between Blayne and Ethan, waiting for a response.

"Don't look at me," Ethan said. "I wanted to let her bleed out on the couch."

"Why didn't you call me?" Kira asked. "You realize you were harboring one of the most wanted women in America. And if half of what she's told us tonight is true, she may be single-handedly one of the deadliest people on this planet. Again, what the *actual* fuck!"

Blayne tried to form words to explain why he'd allowed all this to happen, but he didn't understand his decision. "I thought it was the right decision."

"That goon of hers shot you!"

"Trust me, you don't think I know that? When she showed up here last night, of all places, I knew we had to help her."

"You aided a terrorist," Kira responded. "Do you know the legal jeopardy you put yourself in? The legal jeopardy you've put Ethan, Dr. Giest-Mueler, and…me in?"

What she said was true, but Blayne still believed in his guts he was making the right decision. He finally sat down. He rested his elbows on his knees as he leaned forward and looked Kira directly in the eyes.

"I do," he finally said. "God knows, I do. You don't think I've been practically shitting myself for the past twenty-four hours? None of this makes sense to me. All I know is that Dr. Hennigan —"

"Assuming that's her real name."

"It is," Ethan said. Kira spun her head in his direction. "She went to the bathroom, so I searched for her online. Her full name is Dr. Phillipa Hennigan, and she's a board-certified psychiatrist."

"You had the means of calling for help all day?" Kira rolled her head in frustration. "I at least thought you had a gun to you the whole time and couldn't be stupid enough to be party to this mess."

Ethan's mouth dropped open as he searched for something to say.

"That's not fair," Blayne responded. "You weren't there. She needed our help and promised to tell us about last month. I wanted answers."

"If she'd been arrested, you would have gotten answers," Kira said.

"Yeah, she told us she wouldn't live long enough to answer questions if she was taken in," Ethan said. Kira started to respond, but Ethan held his hand and plowed forward. "Trust me. I didn't think the argument was very strong either. But, the more I've considered it, the more I think she was right. We've seen what they would do to destroy a fucking cell phone. You think they'd let one of their own end up in police custody?"

Kira sat there for a moment, seething. After a beat, resignation washed over her face. Blayne noticed her foot bopping up and down rapidly.

"Now what?" she asked.

"Now, we're stuck between a rock and a hard place," Blayne admitted. "We can't tell anyone without incriminating ourselves. We have nothing actionable. All we can do is wait."

"Do you think those two will show back up?" Kira asked.

"I wish I could say 'no,' but we'll see tomorrow. Something is going down, and Dr. Hennigan believes it involves Pennington University."

"She could have been feeding you a line of bullshit."

"Maybe, but I doubt it. She could have left any time she wanted to today," Blayne said. He looked at Ethan. "Did she even try?"

"Nope. She even insisted on waiting for you to get here before she'd tell me everything. She had no plans to leave here until she talked to you."

Kira took a breath through her nose and let it out. "Legally, you have no grounds. If caught, tried and found guilty, you will go to jail. As your lawyer, I can say we could argue Stockholm Syndrome. After what happened last month, clearly, neither of you are in your right minds."

"That's not—"

Kira lifted one finger to cut Blayne off mid-sentence. "The legal ground is shaky. But, if the larger, looming threat proves true, then your actions can be justified. There's a legal theory that works in some states called 'competing harms'."

"Oh great, she's going lawyer-speak on us," Ethan tried to joke.

Kira shot him a side-eye and continued. "Say you're in a situation where you think you or someone else is about to get hurt badly—physically, I mean. At that moment, you think the best thing to do, the only thing to do, is something that technically breaks the law. Now, the law says it's okay if the average person, using common sense, would say, 'Yeah, that makes sense. The risk of getting hurt was too high compared to the harm of breaking the law.'"

"What if you just think the law is bad?" Blayne asked.

"Here's the kicker. Your decision to break the law can't be based on whether you think the law is moral or right. The law's the law, regardless of personal opinions. And that, my friends, is Criminal Law one-o-one for the night." She uncrossed her legs, placing both feet on the ground before standing. Blayne followed suit.

"You know I'm sorry about all this," Blayne said.

"I do," Kira replied. "I don't like it."

"Makes two of us," Ethan chimed in.

"Bu-ut," Kira said, drawing out the word, "I understand why you're doing what you're doing. I just hope this doesn't come back to bite all of us in the ass. Orange isn't a color that would look good on any of us. The one thing we have going for us is that your new friend appears very connected. I just hope her connections save us in the end. And I hope we're making the right decision."

"Time will tell," Blayne said. He reached out and pulled Kira into a hug. At first, she didn't hug him back, but she eventually threw her arms around him in response.

"Ahh," Ethan said. "Group hug." He came and joined them.

Kira pushed away and looked at them. "When this is all over, we will discuss life choices. But you little shits, if this blows up in our faces, I will ensure your lives are so unpleasant that you'll wish you were detained in Guantanamo." She looked between Blayne and Ethan before saying, "I still love you both." An exasperated breath escaped her. "What the actual fuck?"

Ethan

Ethan didn't want to be all '*I told you so*' when Kira left, but stared at Blayne knowingly when he came back into the room after he'd armed their security system.

"I know, I know. I've royally screwed the pooch here."

"We've messed up big time," Ethan admitted. "And while I will tell you at every turn that I think this is a horrible, horrible idea, I don't think there was a better option."

"Really?" Blayne said. He picked up one of the kitchen chairs and carried it back to the kitchen table.

"Yeah. I had a long time to talk to Dr. Hennigan today. She's probably the scariest person alive. I'd rather be stuck in a room with one hundred Kiras than face off with one Hennigan. She's that kind of scary. But, as scary as she is, I don't doubt her sincerity."

"True, but you can be sincerely wrong," Blayne said. He walked back, grabbed another chair and put it back where it belonged.

"Oh yeah. She's crazier than a soup sandwich," Ethan said. Blayne let out a sharp laugh. "But she's sincere."

"In the immortal words of Oscar Wilde, '*A little sincerity is a dangerous thing, and a great deal of it is absolutely fatal.*'"

Ethan shook his head in agreement. "We're in deep trouble if this backfires."

"Yep."

"Speaking of fucked…"

"Wow," Blayne drew out with a laugh. "Now, that's what I call a transition."

"Hey, I've been stuck at home all day. You got to go out, see people and do things." Ethan pushed himself off the couch.

"Yeah, like get accosted by a tiny scary woman with a gun."

"Is that a gun in your pocket, or are you just happy to see me?" Ethan joked.

Blayne smiled. "I'm always happy to see you."

Ethan walked over to Blayne and pulled him in for a big embrace. "What fresh hell have we gotten ourselves into?" he said as he pulled back and looked up into Blayne's face.

"I don't think we've gotten ourselves into anything new. It's just a continuation of the shit from last month. Now we just know more about what's going on."

"I hope so," Ethan said, reaching his hand up to trace the line of Blayne's jaw with his thumb. "I hope so."

Blayne lowered his lips to Ethan's.

Blayne lifted Ethan from the ground, and Ethan wrapped his legs around Blayne's waist. They kept kissing as Blayne walked down the hallway to his bedroom. Ethan reached out behind him, grabbed the doorknob and turned it. Blayne kicked the door open and walked over to the bed before tossing Ethan on the mattress. He bounced slightly as he landed. Ethan quickly perched on his elbows, his legs hanging off the side of the bed, as he stared up at Blayne. The room was illuminated by a lone lamp. Ethan unbuckled his belt.

"Stop," Blayne commanded. "Let me."

Blayne lowered himself between Ethan's legs. He reached out, grabbed the leather strap and pulled it free from the buckle holding it in place. Ethan let his head drop back as he moaned slightly at Blayne's fingertips caressing his abs before he popped the button on his jeans. Blayne lowered his mouth and grabbed the zipper in his teeth before gently pulling it down. Blayne raked his chin across Ethan's cock, causing Ethan to let out another whimper of anticipation.

"I've always wanted to try that. It looks sexy in porn, but I wasn't sure it would work."

"It worked," Ethan responded breathlessly. He sat up and pulled Blayne toward him and brought their mouths together again. Ethan reached down and started unbuttoning Blayne's shirt. Then, as he undid the last button, he pulled the shirt out of Blayne's pants. Blayne finished the job for him and pulled off his T-shirt. Ethan took off his T-shirt, too.

Blayne reached forward and grabbed Ethan's head as they brought their mouths together for another kiss. Ethan plunged his tongue into Blayne's mouth, and they explored each other. Blayne then sucked gently on Ethan's, encouraging it to probe deeper into his mouth.

Ethan started rocking his hips. He was hard as a rock now.

"Are we good?" Ethan's voice, barely above a whisper, held a weight that seemed almost absurd in its seriousness.

Blayne's fingers found Ethan's waistband, his smile answering the unasked question in the air. "Now we are," he replied. He glided his hands under Ethan's ass before helping Ethan slide his jeans from his hips. Blayne took his time taking off Ethan's pants. Ethan looked down at the wet stain forming on his boxer briefs. The metallic lettering of the Italian designer's name on the waistband shimmered in the lamplight.

Blayne used his shoulders to push Ethan's legs wider as he lowered his face. He kissed Ethan's treasure trail until Blayne put his hands on either side of Ethan's hips. Blayne rested his chin on Ethan's lower abdominal muscle and looked up, locking eyes with Ethan. Ethan's cock pressed into the underside of

Blayne's throat from beneath the cotton separating their skin.

Blayne smiled before he turned his head and rubbed his cheek against Ethan's erection, causing Ethan to squirm. He traced the erection through the boxers with his tongue, causing Ethan to whine in response. Blayne lifted Ethan's hips slightly, and his boyfriend rocked upward to help Blayne get his hands under the waistband of his boxer briefs before Blayne slid them entirely off.

Ethan stared down, his dick fully erect, lying flat on his stomach. Pre-cum oozed out of the tip. Blayne grabbed the base of Ethan's cock and lifted it gently away from his torso. He looked up at Ethan as he let his tongue slip around the underside of the cockhead, teasing it. Blayne then swirled his tongue until he was gently circling the head. Ethan lay back on the bed, rolling his eyes into the back of his head as Blayne swallowed all seven and a half inches of him down to the base. Ethan inhaled suddenly at the movement. He lay there for several minutes as Blayne expertly worked his balls, shaft and head. There was a slight slapping sensation as Blayne let go, and Ethan's dick struck his abs.

"Whoa," was all Ethan muttered. Blayne got off the ground and stood. Ethan reached out and pulled Blayne to him. Ethan kissed Blayne's runner's body. He quickly worked on Blayne's pants and boxers before staring at the monster before him. Ethan wasn't nearly as adept at cock sucking as Blayne was, but he gave it his all. He pointed Blayne's dick toward his lips and did his best to deepthroat it before he gagged. Blayne gently withdrew his dick before slowly pushing it back into Ethan's mouth. With each stroke down his throat,

Ethan could take more and more of Blayne without gagging. Before long, Ethan was taking three-fourths of Blayne's cock and stroking the last part with his hands as he serviced his boyfriend. Ethan was getting into a rhythm when Blayne pulled out.

Ethan looked into Blayne's eyes. "What'd you do that for?"

"I was about to come," Blayne said with a smile. "I wasn't ready for that yet."

"Me neither," Ethan said. He reached out a hand to grab Blayne's and gently pulled him onto the bed on top of him. They lay on the bed kissing each other, feeling each other's naked bodies.

"I want you in me," Ethan whispered into Blayne's ear.

Blayne looked up at Ethan with a surprised look on his face. "Are you sure? I'm not exactly the easiest dick to take."

"I know, but I call myself verse. Time to prove it," Ethan said with a cheeky grin.

Blayne extended his arm toward his side of the bed, effortlessly retrieving the bottle of lube from its place atop the dresser and popping the lid open.

"How do you want to fuck me?" Ethan asked.

"Should probably have you sit on it. That way, you can control how much you take and when."

"Okay. Not the sexiest discussion, is it?"

"Sex never is," Blayne joked as he squeezed a healthy amount of lube onto his dick and let it dribble down the sides. "Are you sure you want to bareback?"

"You've been tested, and I've been tested. And I trust you haven't been fucking around on me. Why would you go elsewhere when you have all this?" Ethan joked as he gestured to his naked body.

"And you're not fucking around on me, because when have you had time? The only person who gets one-on-one time with you is your twinky personal assistant."

"And don't worry. That would never happen. One, he's too…Lucas." Ethan scrunched up his face.

"You mean he doesn't need to get fucked because of that stick shoved up there?"

"Exactly." They both broke out into laughter. "And speaking of shoving things in somewhere, let's do this."

"So bossy tonight… I like it."

"That's me, the resident bossy bottom."

Ethan got up and straddled Blayne's hips. He reached for the bottle of lube. He put a healthy amount on before he slipped one finger inside himself.

"I can do that," Blayne offered.

"You have gigantic hands."

Blayne's eyebrows furrowed in confusion, his eyes widened slightly and he parted his lips in a mixture of surprise and disbelief.

"That made no sense," Ethan realized.

"None whatsoever—especially given the much, much bigger thing that's going to be in there in a minute."

"Just trust me. I've done this before, just not with something," Ethan said, gesturing to Blayne's still erect dick, "that big."

"I bet you tell that to all the guys."

Ethan acquiesced. He angled his bottom toward Blayne, who applied more lube before slipping in one finger. Ethan's breath caught in his throat as it slid in.

"Breathe," Blayne coached.

Ethan took in a breath as Blayne started fingering him. "I can guarantee you I never had this problem with…" There was a hesitation in his voice.

"With…Danny. It's okay to say his name around me. We both have a sexual history. Hell, we had one of my hookups here last night performing surgery on my kitchen table. If you can put up with that, I can put up with the fact that my glorious manhood is like an Eiffel Tower compared to his Washington Monument."

Ethan groaned. This time, it wasn't from ecstasy. He swiveled his head to look at Blayne. "That…that was just bad."

"True, but you didn't even notice when I put my third finger inside you."

Sure enough. Blayne slowly punched Ethan's hole — not in a 'fist fucking' kind of way, but in a 'loosening him up for the main event' kind of way. Ethan had never been fisted. He had no desire to be fisted, but he also knew that taking Blayne would need all the relaxation he could muster.

After a few more minutes of having his ass played with, Ethan said, "I think I'm ready."

"Straddle me," Blayne said. Blayne held the base of his cock. Ethan hovered over Blayne, grabbing the top part of his dick and hovering it next to his hole. Blayne's cockhead rubbed against him. The sensation of Blayne ready to enter his ass excited him. He lowered himself on top of it. The sharp knifing sensation as Blayne's cock passed his sphincter caused his toes to curl. "Just breathe," Blayne encouraged. "Take all the time you need."

Ethan hovered for a second, letting himself get used to the girth. The first step was the girth, and the second was handling the length. Ethan allowed himself to slowly slide up and down without taking Blayne's dick out of his ass. With each little slide, he went down farther until Ethan breathed in and sat down until his ass hit Blayne's pelvic bone. He opened his eyes and found Blayne staring at him. There was so much warmth in those eyes. Blayne reached up and ran his finger over his cheek.

Ethan slid all the way until he could feel the mushroom head inside his ass on the verge of slipping out, and he slid all the way down again. Blayne let out a quick gasp. Ethan felt a sensation he'd never known before. He sat there for a moment. "I think something just broke," he said.

Blayne got a worried look on his face. "What are you feeling?"

"I feel like you just entered me again."

"That's me hitting past the second sphincter. It's normal. Just wait a second. You should feel a sudden release as your body adjusts and becomes okay with it."

"I've never felt like this before," Ethan said.

"Probably because you've never tried to impale yourself on a baseball bat before," Blayne joked. Ethan tried not to laugh because that caused the sharp sensation to pulse.

Ethan took a few deep breaths. Sure enough, he sensed the new sensation as his body opened. He lifted himself up then down again. When Blayne passed the second sphincter this time, he didn't recoil.

Soon, Ethan's whole body shuddered every time Blayne pushed past the internal barrier, bringing a new layer of pleasure Ethan had never experienced. When Ethan got into a rhythm, Blayne reached out his hand and started stroking him with his giant hands. Blayne's hands felt like magic as they traced over every vein in his cock.

"I'm getting close," Blayne said.

"Me too."

That just caused Ethan to speed up, and Blayne did likewise. When Blayne came, Ethan saw white lights as the giant cock inside him throbbed and pulsed. He looked down to see Blayne's stomach muscles contract as Ethan kept moving. Before Blayne had finished coating his insides with cum, Ethan painted Blayne's stomach and chest. He collapsed onto Blayne and just lay there panting. Ethan could feel Blayne's own calming breath beneath him. He closed his eyes and finally felt the last popping sensation as Blayne's dick slid out of his ass.

"Whoa," Blayne said between breaths. "That was the most amazing fucking sex I've ever had."

"Once I got comfortable with you inside me, it blew my mind, too. I don't think my body could handle that daily, but I'm game to do it again…soon."

"Don't worry. I call myself a verse bottom for a reason. I love to get fucked, but I've also never tried taking something as large as me other than a dildo, which isn't the same."

Ethan looked up and stared into blue eyes. He could lie like that forever, covered in sweat and cum.

"Shower?" Blayne asked.

"Just a few more minutes, then I'll let you clean me up."

"For you, anything, babe." Blayne reached down and laid his arm across Ethan's back. Ethan's ear was pressed to Blayne's chest, and he could hear the thumping sound of Blayne's heart. A heart he knew he'd won.

Chapter Thirteen

Blayne

The morning sun filtered through the slits of the blinds, casting rays of light across Blayne's bed. Blayne rolled over to get the sun out of his eyes and snuggled up to Ethan's back. Their freshly scrubbed bodies, clean sheets and clothes smelled like a little slice of heaven. Aromatic tendrils of freshly brewed coffee wafted through the air, filling the room with a delightful aroma that awakened the senses. It was a moment of tranquil bliss, as the smell of clean linens and coffee seamlessly intertwined.

Blayne shot up, exclaiming, "What the fuck?"

"What?" Ethan replied, still clearly in a foggy state.

Blayne nudged the sleeping man. "Ethan, you need to get up now. We have… We have a visitor."

Ethan turned his head and stared at the woman sitting at Blayne's desk, holding a cup of coffee and pointing a gun at both of them.

"Where is she?" the woman asked.

"You've gotta be fucking kidding me," Blayne muttered.

This was clearly not the reaction the woman had expected. Blayne observed the features of the ethnically ambiguous woman with long black hair pulled back into a ponytail that cascaded over her shoulder. She was dressed in a black pantsuit.

"Do all of you shop at Assassins 'R' Us?" Blayne asked. "I mean, I'm not exactly known for being a fashion queen—just ask this one"—Blayne gestured toward Ethan—"but I swear you all buy off the rack."

A flash of indignation ignited within her eyes. She furrowed her eyebrows sharply, and her jaw clenched, her muscles visibly tensing as a wave of disbelief washed over her face. *Maybe 'off the rack' was a step too far?* And she started laughing.

"I'll have you know…I have impeccable taste and a unique fashion sense. And before you test me, know that my two-thousand-dollar pair of heels could kill you just as fast as my gun can."

"Maybe it's best not to anger a woman with both heels and a gun," Ethan whispered to Blayne.

"I haven't had my coffee," Blayne said flatly.

"So," she let the word hang in the air for a moment, "where is she?"

"I don't know," Blayne replied through clenched teeth. "Now, if you don't mind, I'm going to drag my obnoxiously hot boyfriend into the bathroom for a quick shower. Once we've freshened up, we'll join you."

Blayne threw the covers off him, swung his legs over the side and stood. He looked back at Ethan and extended his hand. "Honey?"

Ethan glared at the woman and Blayne, then stretched his arm toward Blayne, who helped him out of bed. Blayne positioned himself between Ethan and the woman and guided Ethan toward the bathroom. When they reached the door, he turned and addressed the woman.

"Why don't you be useful and make breakfast?"

Blayne shut the door behind him.

Ethan

The door clicked behind Blayne, and Ethan whirled on his boyfriend. "What the fuck are you doing?" he screeched out in a high-pitched voice.

"I'm over it. These people just keep invading our lives. I'm just over it."

"They're trained fucking assassins!" Ethan's voice seemed to get higher with each word.

Blayne put his hands on Ethan's shoulders, looked him in the eyes and said, "Calm down."

That was it. Ethan exploded. "I will *not* calm down. You need to…what's the opposite of 'calm down'?'"

"Get fired up? Work myself into a frenzy?"

Ethan made a screeching noise as panic surged through his veins like an electric shock. His breaths came in rapid, shallow gasps, his chest heaving as he desperately tried to catch his breath.

"Oh fuck," Blayne said. "You're having a panic attack." Blayne shut the lid on the toilet before helping Ethan down. Ethan had a history of panic attacks, and he had told Blayne about his early days as a singer when they happened regularly. Ethan put his head between his legs as he tried to breathe, while Blayne leaned against the sink, rubbing his back. "You're going to be okay. I'm here. I won't let anyone hurt you."

After a couple of minutes, Ethan's breathing normalized, and he finally looked up at Blayne and asked, "Have you lost your ever-fucking-mind?"

"What do you mean?"

"You just told an assassin to go cook breakfast."

"I did, didn't I?"

Ethan stared into Blayne's face. "She could have killed you. She could have killed me." Ethan heard his voice rising again, so he forced himself to take deep, calming breaths. "What possessed you —?"

"I don't know," Blayne cut him off. "Now's probably not the time to tell you I had a similar reaction yesterday when Denzili came up behind me with a gun and shoved it in my back."

"You told her to cook you breakfast?" Ethan's mind struggled to comprehend the absurdity of the situation.

"No. I invited her to coffee."

"You did *what*?" Ethan's emotions unraveled like threads in a fraying tapestry. He slipped from the toilet to the cold tile of the bathroom floor. Tears stung the corner of his eyes as he wiped them away.

Blayne slumped down to the floor and enveloped Ethan in his arms. "I'm so sorry. I wasn't thinking. My mouth ran before I thought about the consequences of what was coming out of it. I didn't mean to sound glib."

Blayne used his thumb to wipe a tear from the corner of his eye.

"Just stop..." Ethan looked up into Blayne's face. "Just stop poking the bears. As Ms. Wilson said, they see us as pets, as playthings. Right now, they find us charming. Tomorrow, they may very well put a bullet in you. I can't live with that. I can't live without you."

Ethan grappled with the paralyzing grip of panic that wanted to overtake him and the suffocating weight of his own vulnerability…of *their* vulnerability.

"I promise to stop poking the bears. You're the one I want to poke." Blayne gently jabbed Ethan in the rib cage affectionately and said, "Poke." He waited a few seconds, and when Blayne didn't get a response, he did it again. "Poke."

This time, Ethan chuckled and shook his head. Tears were dying to escape, but he closed his eyes and willed them back. *The only way through is forward.*

"I think you're crazy, Mr. Blayne Dickenson. But for some reason, I love crazy." Ethan let Blayne pull him in for another hug and laid his head against his chest. Ethan closed his eyes, took a deep breath and smelled the comfort of Blayne's scent around him. He let out a whistle, pushed away from Blayne and shook his head, like he was shaking out the morning fog. "Now what?"

"We get ready and go see what Ms. Ponytail wants?"

"Her name is Richardson." Ethan stopped for a second. "At least, I assumed that's Richardson. God, what if that's not even Richardson?"

"I'm pretty sure that's Richardson. If it wasn't, I don't think my brief outburst wouldn't have gone over as well as it did."

"How so?" Ethan asked.

"I tested a theory I had yesterday when I met Denzili. Something Dr. Hennigan said made me realize their group has a code. They don't kill indiscriminately—"

"I know about a plane full of people who would disagree with that."

"I mean, they don't just kill for the sake of killing. In fact, killing is the last step for them. They won't shy away from it but must have a reason to do it. Not only that, but there also seems to be a clear hierarchy related to who gets to decide who lives and dies. And those people down at Denzili and Richardson's level don't make those decisions. They're the pawns."

"A chess metaphor? Really?"

"Think about it. Denzili and Richardson are pawns. Her grandmother's the queen. Her mother's clearly the king."

"What does that make Hennigan, a bishop?"

"Nah, a knight. Bishops are great and can do a lot of damage when they're on their own. Knights rely on their pawns to get in the bishop's way and form points of support for the knight."

"You realize I've never played chess, right?"

"Uh, now I do. We'll have to rectify that at some point. It's all about strategy. And right now, we've found ourselves in a chess game played by some scary talented players."

"Are we sure they're even playing chess? I feel like I'm playing Chutes and Ladders."

Blayne chuckled. "Oh, they're playing chess."

"So, are we pawns or just cannon fodder in this little analogy of yours?"

Blayne's brow furrowed, and his gaze went distant for a couple of seconds before he slowly said, "We're new players on the board. We're neither the black nor the white side. We're a complication. The question becomes, whose life are we complicating? We complicate things for this domestic terrorist group, the CLA. I've never been a big fan of right-wing extremists, so they seem like the worse of two evils."

Ethan shook his head. He wasn't sure if he ultimately agreed with Blayne, but he couldn't find fault in the man's logic. "What now?"

"Let's pull ourselves together, get dressed and make nice with our new favorite assassin."

Blayne stood up and pulled Ethan up with him. They brushed their teeth, completed a quick shit, shower and shave before getting dressed and heading into the living room.

Ethan's nose was met with a fantastic fragrance. "Whoa!" he said absently as he walked toward the kitchen.

"I made a big breakfast," the woman said. "Your room still had their air of sex in it, so I figured you two needed to replenish your energy." The woman gestured to the kitchen table, which had been set. "Please take a seat. Coffee?"

"Yes," Ethan said before quickly adding, "please."

The woman smiled at him. "So polite. That's one thing I love about you Southerners, your politeness. Faced with almost anything, you're going to be polite."

Ethan noticed the hint of an edge in the statement that worried him, but he smiled and said, "Thank you."

She poured them coffee and set down plates with omelets, toast and jam.

"Bon appétit," she said, sitting at the table and taking a swig of her coffee. Ethan and Blayne hesitated for a second. "Don't worry. They're not poisoned."

Blayne cut into his omelet and forked a piece into his mouth. A sound came out of Blayne, one Ethan had only heard when they were in bed.

"This is amazing. What's in this?" Blayne asked.

"A little of this, a little of that."

"I didn't have that much here. How did you throw this together?" Blayne asked as he forked another mouthful in.

Ethan followed suit. The flavor combination in the omelet was unlike any he'd tasted before.

"You'd be amazed at how a well-trained chef can make a five-star meal with the barest ingredients."

"You're a chef?" Ethan asked.

"In another life."

"I take it you're Richardson," Blayne asked as he took a bite of toast.

"So, you have heard of me?"

"We've met your friends," Blayne said noncommittally. "How do we know you are who you say you are?"

"You don't, but since you didn't call anyone or even try to call someone, you've already made that determination."

"True," Blayne said.

"This is pretty remarkable," Ethan commented. "Tell us about yourself." He didn't mean to say that, but he felt like he was having a pleasant breakfast, which was the most natural thing to say.

"For obvious reasons, I won't tell you much, but I've worked for The Foundation for several years. I was recruited while I was in culinary school studying to be a chef. After…training, my first assignment was to liquidate one of my professors."

"Liquidate?" Ethan asked.

"Liquidation, in simple terms, involves closing a company and selling off assets to generate cash, typically to settle outstanding debts. In my world, it's not a company we're closing, it's someone's existence on this planet. Someone has either committed great atrocities or been found guilty of a heinous crime against the United States. When that person is untouchable by the US government for whatever reason, we step in and ensure the debts are settled."

"How does that philosophy mesh with you taking out an airliner to destroy Ethan's phone?"

"Hennigan told you about that?" The woman raised one of her perfectly shaped eyebrows thoughtfully. "She trusts you more than I expected. You don't know how special that makes you two." Neither man said anything, so Richardson continued. "I don't give the liquidation orders. I execute them. I'm very good at what I do. Take the professor I was talking about. He was a contract Russian assassin. Because of his culinary skills and association with my college, he could travel the world. He was a renowned chef, so he easily slipped in and out of countries executing people on behalf of the Russian government. Then he made the mistake of killing a member of the British parliament who was the deciding vote on a matter that involved both the United States and the Russians. The member of parliament who was executed was more favorable to US interests. It was determined that he needed to die—and I, his student, would be the tool of his execution."

"Was it hard to kill someone you knew like that?"

"He was like a father to me. But no, after I read his record, I became aware the world was safer without him. I had no qualms about killing him. I used NeuroCelerin, a swift-acting neurotoxin. He would taste our work, so getting him to taste my food was never a problem." Ethan shot Blayne a quick look. "Don't worry. It's a fast-working toxin. If I had poisoned you two, you'd already be dead. Anyway, the night before, we had a party on campus and all my peers were there, so I ensured they all ingested the antidote. That way, anyone who tasted my food would already have the antidote running in their systems. My professor died just as planned. The medical examiner wrote it up as a heart attack because NeuroCelerin can only be detected if you're looking for it. The chemical agent doesn't appear on a standard tox screen if you're not specifically seeking it. It's one reason it's so popular in my line of work." She glanced between Blayne and Ethan. "Where are they?"

Chapter Fourteen

Agent Murphy

Dear God, I've entered the third rung of hell, Murphy thought as her plane touched ground at the Ann Lee Doran Memorial Airport. They hadn't flown into the town's larger Rick Husband Amarillo International Airport because they wanted to get in and out of the area quickly with little fuss and even fewer eyes on the operation. The plane taxied around the runway before stopping in what looked like the middle of a field. Security at this little airport was nonexistent.

The air was clean and empty. That's one thing she could say for West Texas. They didn't have the haze of a larger city. Blue sky stretched in every direction, not a cloud in the sky. Around them was nothing but a sea of concrete or dirt. Why anyone in their right mind believed this was a great area to settle was beyond her.

"Welcome, Agent Murphy." A man stepped out of a building, looking every bit the stereotype of a West Texas lawman. He wore the standard FBI black suit but had a silver bolo tie that glinted in the mid-morning light. He also had a white cowboy hat sitting on his head.

"Agent Mitchell, I presume."

"Please, call me Big D. Everybody does." He extended his hand, and she shook it once firmly. Agent Michael Davis was the Special Agent in Charge of the Dallas Field Office, which covered Dallas and most of northern and West Texas. "Let's get to the staging area. It's about a twenty-minute whirlybird ride as the crow flies."

Murphy just looked at him, understanding about fifty percent of what he said. When he started leading her toward a helicopter, she got the gist. "Who's coordinating efforts on the ground?" she asked.

"One of my agents from the Amarillo office is coordinating efforts on this side. There are two different complexes we're raiding. There's one just outside Texline and another in the middle of nowhere on the New Mexico side. Ben and Laura Lee Jackson own the one on the Texas side. The other is owned by William Johnson. That operation is being coordinated by agents from the Albuquerque Field Office." He stopped and turned to look at Murphy. "Have you met Euphrasia Via?"

"I can't say that I have."

He turned and continued leading her toward the helicopter in the distance. "Agent Via oversees the Albuquerque office. She'll be at the staging area. Interesting woman. She's one of those New Mexico Indians—"

"You mean she belongs to one of the indigenous tribes?"

"Ahh, you're one of those new politically correct types. Nothing wrong with that. Anyway, yep, she's a native."

Sarah was glad the man was in front of her as the look of disbelief washed over her. *Is he for real? Who talks like this anymore?* She realized she'd stopped dead in her tracks and hurried to catch up. "Any idea which tribe she belongs to?" Sarah asked.

"The New Mexico one," Agent Davis said.

"You realize there are twenty-three recognized tribes in New Mexico?" Murphy had researched all the key players in the tri-state area when she'd agreed to take over the Houston Office. Unlike 'Big D,' which Murphy was beginning to think stood for 'Big Dumbass', Murphy knew that Agent Via was a member of the Mescalero Apache Tribe, which had their reservation just south of Ruidoso.

Agent Davis kept talking, but Murphy just tuned him out. He was clearly a man who liked to hear himself speak. Thankfully, the pilot had seen them coming and had already started prepping the copter for takeoff. In minutes, they were in the air and flying over the West Texas landscape to the small town of Perico, Texas. Agent Davis explained that Perico was an actual ghost town.

"Perico was once known as Farwell. The town was built in 1888 as a Fort Worth and Denver City Railway shipping point. It grew as a center for supplies and education by the turn of the century. Bu-ut" — he drew out the word with his Texas drawl — "with time and highway improvements, the railway stopped coming this way. By the mid-1980s, Perico had dwindled to two residents and one operating business, a grain elevator.

Now, it's just a husk. Kind of perfect staging point for us, though."

The helicopter descended a couple hundred yards from other vehicles to avoid creating a dirt storm around the agents on the ground. Before they were out of the helicopter, a woman in her early fifties approached and extended her hand, yelling, "Agent Sarah Murphy, I presume. I'm Agent Euphrasia Via."

Sarah shook the woman's hand enthusiastically. Murphy noticed how Via didn't bother saying anything to Agent Davis. Agent Via led Sarah to an FBI mobile command center. The FBI mobile command center was an impressive sight—a technologically advanced and fully equipped operational hub on wheels, the FBI's seal blazoned the side of the large truck. There was no questioning what its purpose was. Sarah followed Agent Via into the command center. Inside, three different agents sat at laptop terminals. Small and large monitors were on the truck wall before the agents. A giant digital clock sat above it all with the current time. The truck had a slide-out, which created a little alcove where two more agents were pouring over real-time satellite images.

"Damn," Sarah said. "I'm going to have to get me one of these."

"I was lucky enough to get one of the first of this newer model," Via explained. "It's state-of-the-art. It features secure communication systems, three built-in computer workstations that can expand to five and it's equipped with onboard Wi-Fi and satellite communications technologies. There are even a couple of fold-out cots in one of the undercarriage storage compartments. They thought of everything."

Sarah let out a low whistle as she took it all in. "So, where are we with the infiltration?"

"Honestly, we were just waiting for you to get here. We can infiltrate both ranches in under ten minutes."

"Movement at the ranches?"

"Nothing. It's been silent at both places."

That worried Sarah. If there was no movement at either ranch, that possibly meant the owners had already vacated the premises, so who knew what type of intelligence would still be there?

"Let's get this show on the road," Sarah said.

Via immediately started barking orders. Sarah heard vehicles leaving their location, the sound of their wheels spinning on the dirt and gravel as they drove away. Then drone footage overhead followed the convoys in both states as they sped toward their targets in single file.

The infiltration was textbook. The vehicles spread around the complex, and teams of agents slowly picked their way from the outer rims of the properties inward toward the major structures. Periodically, you'd hear a mobile unit say, "Barn is clear." Everything was perfectly smooth.

The New Mexico ranch was smaller, so the infiltration team reached the main house faster. The largest monitor picked up the feed from that team leader. Over the intercom system, Sarah heard the team leader yell, "FBI! Search Warrant! Open up!" Nothing happened. The team leader motioned to one of his team members, who held a tactical breaching kit, and the agent smashed the battle ram into the door. The monitor cut out.

"What just happened?" Via asked.

"Switching to drone footage." The screen filled with a different viewpoint, and nothing happened. The monitor was black. "I'm maneuvering the drone to a higher altitude." As the drone rose, the image of tendrils of black smoke filled the screen. The ranch house was a blazing inferno.

Via didn't wait. She grabbed the team. "Alpha team, stand down. Repeat, stand down. Bravo team's target was armed. Repeat, Bravo team's target was armed."

"This is Alpha Team Leader. Please repeat orders."

"Alpha Team Leader, this is the nest. Do *not* enter the main house. I repeat, do *not* enter the house. We're sending in the bomb squad."

* * * *

The next couple of hours were a lot of standing around and taking phone calls explaining to everyone from the White House Chief of Staff to the Director of the FBI what had happened in New Mexico. Thankfully, the bomb inside the house imploded rather than exploded. Essentially, everything inside the home was turned to ash. The agents only suffered cuts and bruises from the fragments of shattered glass, wood and concrete being forcefully propelled in all directions. The paramedics were on the scene, and a couple of agents were carted off in ambulances to receive stitches for more severe lacerations.

"This could have been a lot worse," Sarah muttered.

"What was that?" Agent Via asked.

"I said, '*This could have been a lot worse*.'"

"We got lucky," Via admitted. "So far, we've underestimated this group at every turn. The fact that this was an implosion and not an explosion tells us that the bombmaker knew what they were doing."

"Agent Via," a technician said, "we're ready to roll."

"Let's go," Via replied.

The hydraulics on the slide-out whirred as the alcove disappeared. Via pointed to a handful of seats built into the wall, and Murphy walked over and buckled in. The leveling hydraulics settled as the truck's engines came to life. The truck pulled out of their staging location and headed to the Texas ranch.

In thirty minutes, the mobile unit was fully operational again. Murphy, Davis and Via, entered Benjamin and Laura Lee Jackson's house. A team of FBI agents were already photographing and tagging anything that could be potential evidence. As a home, everything was very West Texas Americana—lots of imagery of the west decorated the place, along with patriotic red, white and blue motifs. A giant family Bible sat prominently on the coffee table before the couch. A very thin layer of dust had covered things.

"They haven't been here in at least a week," Murphy guessed.

"How do ya figure?" Davis asked.

"The dust. Look at this place. It's immaculate. The only thing out of place is the dust."

"Good observation," Davis admitted, "but this is West Texas. Dust happens faster out here. All it takes is one of those haboobs coming from New Mexico, and everything can be dusty tomorrow."

"A what?" Murphy asked.

"A haboob," Davis repeated. "It's a powerful dust storm that can descend upon West Texas with tremendous force. Basically, air comes rushing over the Rockies, picking up speed and dust along the Western

Plains of New Mexico until it hits Texas. You'll look out on the horizon and see this massive wall of swirling dust barreling down on you. When a haboob rolls in, all you can do is take cover. And if you must be out in it, don't open your mouth. New Mexico doesn't taste that great."

"I'll take that under advisement."

"Agents?" a young agent said, entering the room. "You need to come see this."

The three senior agents walked through the house and into the kitchen. "We almost missed it," the agent said. He pointed to a rustic china cabinet with various dishes and serving platters of different sizes and shapes. "We were going to inventory the china when we accidentally pulled on the door harder than needed and the entire cabinet moved." He reached out and slid the cabinet outward, revealing the entrance to a basement.

"Has anyone been down yet?"

"No."

"Let's clear it first. Go get someone from the bomb squad in here."

Twenty minutes later, the three supervisory agents were assured the basement was safe, so they ventured into the room to find the epicenter of the CLA.

"Holy shit," Davis said. "We just hit the mother lode."

"We'll be dissecting this mess for weeks," Via agreed.

The three took out their phones and started documenting the room's content. They'd get other agents down there to go through the material thoroughly. But for now, they took videos and pictures on their cell phones of anything that looked immediately important.

"Agent Murphy," Via said, "come look at this." Murphy wandered toward Via and looked at a corkboard on the wall. "Pennington University... Isn't that in Houston?"

"Yes." Murphy's eyes grew as she started snapping pictures of everything on the corkboard. Murphy could see the corner of something sticking out from one sheet of paper on the wall. Using her gloved hand, she moved the sheet of paper aside and found the picture of a woman with a bullseye marked over her in red marker. "Now, who are you?" Murphy took a picture of the photo.

* * * *

Blayne

Blayne and Ethan proceeded to clean up the dishes after their breakfast with Richardson. She sat down at a table with a cup of coffee. Fortunately, she had put away her gun, which was a step in the right direction. As Richardson relaxed, Blayne wasn't concerned that she would become trigger-happy. Richardson seemed resigned to hanging out in their apartment all day, but Blayne had class. He glanced down at his watch. He still had plenty of time.

Just as Blayne finished putting the last of the dishes in the dishwasher and starting it, his phone buzzed in his pocket. He dried his hands on a dishtowel. He glanced down and saw the nine-one-five area code on his phone.

"I should answer this. I think it's Ms. Wilson."

"Put it on speaker," Richardson replied.

"Good morning," Blayne greeted as he did so. "You're on speaker. Ethan is here with me, and we've been joined by Richardson."

"Richardson? Are you there?"

"It's me, Ms. Wilson."

"We've been trying to find you."

"I figured as much," Richardson replied before sipping her coffee. "I went to ground. The boys have been catching me up on everything. What's the status of The Complex?"

"It's still under siege. Don't worry. I'm coordinating efforts to put an end to that. It's a game of Whac-A-Mole around here. I kill one CLA agent, and two pop up in his place."

"What's your body count so far?" Richardson asked, as if this was the most ordinary conversation.

"I lost count after the first dozen. I've had other things on my mind. There is also a trio of recruits doing a pretty good job of racking up their own body counts. I almost feel like a proud mother."

Richardson let out a short laugh. "Can you direct me to the new safe house?"

"No," Ms. Wilson replied. "Until Dr. Hennigan lays eyes on you herself, she'll want to maintain distance. You know, standard protocol in these situations."

"You think there's a mole?"

"Most assuredly. Someone coached these CLA thugs on how to bypass our security systems. That requires intimate knowledge of how The Complex works."

"How did they find Mesa —?"

"As much as Dr. Hennigan trusts the men with you," Ms. Wilson said, cutting Richardson off, "she has not revealed where The Complex is located or its full name. I say we keep it that way."

"Fine with me," Ethan said. "The less I know, the better."

"Besides catching up with Ms. Richardson, why did you call?" Blayne asked.

"Oh yes," Ms. Wilson said. "Just a second." There was the sound of three rapid gunshots. "Look at that. I have at least a baker's dozen now. Anyway, Dr. Hennigan wanted you to know that she'll be at Mr. Dickenson's apartment tomorrow morning at nine a.m. for a meeting. Ms. Richardson, I would plan on being there then."

"I have a burner," Richardson stated before quickly providing the number, "just in case Dr. Hennigan wants to contact me before tomorrow morning."

"Perfect." They could hear the echoing sound of boots on a marble floor over the phone, followed by another burst of gunfire. "They make this too easy. Anyway, I will text the burner phone the address for a secondary safe house that has already been vetted. You'll have access to everything you need there." There was a sound of running. "Sorry. I really must go."

With that, the phone went dead.

"Is she okay?" Ethan asked.

"Trust me," Richardson said with a broad grin. "That woman will outlive us all." Richardson stood and nodded her head toward Blayne and Ethan. "It's been fun. Thanks for giving me free rein in your kitchen this morning. It's always fun to flex those muscles for a change. I'll be seeing you soon."

Richardson picked up her coat and left the apartment.

"I don't know if I can handle too much more of this," Ethan admitted, shaking his head. "Wow, just wow."

"Well, it looks like today will be a normal day."

"Normal! Has any day in your life been remotely normal since you met me?" Ethan groused.

"Nope," Blayne said as he kissed Ethan. "And I wouldn't have it any other way. Now that she's gone, I should head to school."

"You're not wearing that, are you?"

"I was planning on it."

"Blayne, I swear you're a hopeless case regarding your fashion. Let's pick something out for you to wear. I don't want you looking like a slob in front of your class."

"I'm hardly a slob. I'm not even the worst-dressed faculty member on campus. There's one older professor who wears a torn-up T-shirt and shorts with holes to office hours, and another one who regularly shows up in yoga pants after her yoga sessions. I figure, if I'm dressed better than them, I'm in great shape."

Ethan groaned, grabbed Blayne by the hand and led him back to the bedroom for an impromptu clothing makeover.

* * * *

Thirty minutes later, Blayne left the apartment and went to campus. The afternoon flew by. He had two back-to-back sections of composition. As usual, his students weren't ready for their peer workshops. As he walked around the room, he saw at least one apparent case of a student who had used generative artificial intelligence to write the paper.

"Mr. Bixby, I would rewrite that paper before you hand it in next week. I can tell you didn't write it. I've seen enough papers written by large language models to spot them from a mile away."

"I didn't use—"

"Don't. Please don't," Blayne said, cutting the student off. "We both know you didn't write that. I've seen your writing. That's not it."

As Blayne walked away, he heard the student grumble, "I swear the guy I bought the paper from promised it was written by an actual human."

Blayne thought about spinning around and saying something but decided it wasn't a battle he wanted to engage in that afternoon. He'd learned long ago that some confrontations weren't worth having when it comes to teaching. You never lower your standards, but always consider the possible costs before engaging. If you nitpicked at everything and took on every fight, your teaching evaluations tanked, and you wouldn't create a classroom environment that fostered learning.

Thankfully, Blayne kept himself busy reading over students' shoulders and answering questions. By the time the class ended, he was ready to go home.

Blayne packed up his bag and joined the stream of students as he left the classroom. He turned the corner in the Akokisas Lecture Center and found security guards outside a classroom. "What's that about?" Blayne asked himself.

"That's Dr. Martinez's political science class," Emma Davis said, coming up on Blayne's right.

"Oh…hey, Emma. I didn't see you there."

"Then who were you talking to?" Emma inquired.

"I was talking to myself."

"That's either a sign of genius or insanity," Emma replied.

"Hopefully, it's the former not the latter," Blayne joked. "But why the security?

"Oh, apparently, she's been on TV talking about the attacks at the arena. My roommate has her for Intro to Poly Sci. She says all Dr. Martinez talks about are White-people terrorists, probably because she's Hispanic."

"Wow." Blayne looked at his student. "You just said the unspoken part out loud, didn't you?"

"Huh?" Emma replied. "I don't understand. Of course, I was talking out loud. I'm not psychic like my aunt."

"And with that" — Blayne did everything to control his facial expression — "I'm going to go sit in on her lecture."

He made his way to the door. A security guard checked college ID cards against a class roster, so Blayne couldn't just attend the lecture. He looked at the guard, "Any chance I can sit in on her lecture?"

"No. Per the campus higher-ups, only registered students are allowed in this room."

"Oh well, thanks," Blayne said politely. "Well, it was worth a try."

He walked away. The lecture center was designed with a curved wall then a staircase down to the next level. He had just hit the stairs when he heard someone yell, "Mr. Dickenson." He turned and found his favorite barista, not exactly his best student, Todd Rice, poking his head out the door. "Over here." Blayne scrunched up his face in confusion. "It's Martinez's class."

This was probably a bad idea, but he hustled over, and Todd let him through the side door into the lecture classroom. The place wasn't packed, so there was room for an extra student or two. He followed Todd to the back of the room, where his student had his stuff.

"I noticed you were trying to get in. They're such hardasses about this," Todd said.

"You probably shouldn't have let me in, Todd," Blayne said, looking around the room to see if anyone would throw him out of the classroom.

"I know you're not here to kill Professor Martinez, so I didn't think letting you in was a big deal. Besides, it's not like the room is full."

A side door opened at the base of the lecture hall, and a guard held the door as Professor Martinez entered the room. She had a refillable bottle of water that she sat on at the front desk before she started up the classroom technology. One student approached her. The guard at the bottom of the room eyed the student but didn't move to intercept her. The student and professor had a brief conversation as Dr. Martinez continued preparing for class. The overhead projector screen rolled down in the room's front as the light in the box bolted into the ceiling turned on, showing the university logo as the professor logged into her account. Dr. Martinez had her slide deck up and running in a few minutes.

Professor Olivia Martinez stood at the front of the lecture hall with a presentation clicker as she scanned the rows of seats. For a second, Blayne thought the professor's gaze lingered on him too long, but she said nothing. "Good afternoon, everyone," she began a little louder than necessary. Her voice resonated off the walls, causing the students to stop talking or playing on their smartphones. "As promised, today, we delve into a relevant and alarming topic — the rise of right-wing authoritarianism. Let's start with a simple question."

Dr. Martinez clicked her remote, and the slide switched to one with the words "What is right-wing?"

"Republicans!" a guy in the front row called out.

"Not exactly," Martinez started. "Your assumption is one I'm commonly met with when I ask this question. But it's important to note that the philosophical underpinnings of 'right-wing' and 'left-wing' are much older than the United States. The labels 'right-wing' and 'left-wing' originated from the French Revolution and were initially tied to one's seating position in the French parliament. The left-wing was the party of movement, and the right-wing was the party of order. These terms have been broadened today to encompass more complex philosophical ideas."

Dr. Martinez clicked to the next slide that provided generic definitions of the terms. Instead of reading the slide, she explained, "The term 'right-wing' broadly encompasses ideologies prioritizing tradition, limited government, free-market capitalism and individualism. The Republican Party encompasses an array of ideological stances that align with conservative principles. However, the party contains a multitude of different factions, including libertarians,, economic conservatives and social conservatives, among others, who would not align with right-wing ideology. Some members of today's Republican political party consider themselves centrist or even left-leaning on specific issues."

She gazed around the room before continuing. This time when she clicked, the words 'Right-Wing Authoritarianism' shone on the screen. "The problem we face is less about political philosophy here and more about *authoritarianism*. To understand this, we need to turn to one of my mentors, Bob Altemeyer, a psychologist at the University of Manitoba. He sketches the right-wing authoritarian personality in a rather specific light. Right-wing authoritarians are" — she clicked the button and the first bullet point appeared — "individuals who inherently agree to the will of authority figures they view as legitimate." She clicked again, "Two, these individuals are prone to exhibit aggression — not aimlessly, but in the name of those authority figures they hold in high regard. These could be political figures or religious figures. And finally, these individuals adhere to conventional thought and behavior, a sort of comforting conformity, akin to a river flowing along its well-worn path. Unfortunately, right-wing authoritarianism often coincides with ethnocentrism, nationalism, xenophobia, religious fundamentalism and protecting 'traditional' values norms."

A hand shot up in the second row, and Martinez nodded in the student's direction. "Are you trying to say people shouldn't believe these things?"

"It's not the political philosophy that is problematic here. It's the authoritarianism. Authoritarianism is a structure. There's limited political pluralism, where individual freedoms are restrained and dissent is typically not tolerated. Adherence to the party line is maintained by force, and compliance is rewarded while resistance, I'm afraid, faces harsh retribution."

"Well, what about the left-wing?" someone called out. Blayne looked in the direction he heard the voice but couldn't figure out who had spoken.

"Are there left-wing authoritarians? Definitely. Now, I will say that Bob Altemeyer strongly disagrees with this point, and in fact, argued that left-wing authoritarians were mythical creatures like Nessie and Bigfoot created by the right to play a game of 'but what about them?' which political conservatives love to play when taking attention off themselves. Unfortunately, we've seen over the last several years that there can be people who are just as authoritarian on the left. However, we still do not see the intensity or the numbers of people who are authoritarians on the left as we do on the right. Now, I want to make this clear. As a political scientist, I stand against authoritarianism… period. I don't care what side that authoritarianism comes from. I stand against it."

A hand shot up in the third row. "Professor Martinez," a student began, "how does this connect with the ideology of the group who attacked the concert the other night?"

"Great question," Martinez responded, pointing at the PowerPoint slide projecting behind her. "First, I've talked to my friends in the FBI, and they cannot definitively say that the events that happened the other night specifically targeted the concert. In fact, it looks like the CLA was meeting with a different right-wing authoritarian group from Germany, which is a whole other can of worms. For now, let's say that the CLA believes that the United States government has overstepped its bounds, infringing on the rights of citizens and straying from the original intent of the Constitution. They see themselves as defenders of American values and the Constitution, viewing their cause as a moral, even sacred duty."

She switched to the next slide. "The CLA has identified the 'liberal ideology' as the culprit behind the nation's decline, arguing that radical action, even violent resistance, may be necessary to restore the country. The group rejects the federal government's authority, advocating for a region or nation governed strictly by the Constitution's original intent. They've even supported secessionist movements."

Another hand rose, and Martinez gestured to the student. "But, Professor, isn't their claim legitimate? I mean, the government has grown significantly over the years."

"Indeed," Martinez nodded, "and that's a concern many share. But the debate is whether the perceived problems warrant the CLA's radical and violent solutions. We should remember that authoritarian solutions undermine democratic values and individual freedoms. The government's growth is not inherently bad. It's about whether the growth is controlled, responsible and for the benefit of the people. To believe that the legal system and Constitution originally designed to govern thirteen colonies should be the same to govern fifty states and five major US territories isn't realistic. Our nation has grown, and so has the necessity of changing governmental structures with it."

The following slide featured photos of John Black, Rebecca Watson and David Collins. "Let's look at the CLA's original leaders. John Black, the founder, is a former Marine and constitutional scholar. Rebecca Watson, a charismatic figure, brought the group into the mainstream. David Collins, a hardliner, advocates for forceful means to achieve the CLA's objectives. Again, these three people created the CLA. But none of them are currently associated with the group, according to my research and that of the US government."

A student in the back row interjected. "If they were just about discussions and nonviolent protests, wouldn't that be acceptable?"

"Certainly," replied Martinez. "Freedom of speech and assembly are fundamental rights. The problem arises when speech incites violence, or peaceful protests become violent. The CLA's recent shift toward violence is alarming and seriously threatens public safety and social order. Someone new is the voice of this group, and we aren't completely sure who that is or what their ideology is. Many of our assumptions about this group are based on the founders' writings. If those people are truly out, we aren't sure what ideology drives them now."

The professor paused again, making sure she had everyone's attention. "Understanding the CLA and its ideologies is crucial to combating homegrown extremism. By studying their beliefs, rhetoric and actions, we can develop strategies to address the root causes of such extremism and maintain our societal harmony while preserving the democratic values we hold dear."

"Professor Martinez," a male voice from the back of the room asked, "why do some people feel drawn to groups like the CLA? Is it solely political?"

Martinez nodded, leaning against the edge of the computer station that filled the front part of the auditorium. "That's a very insightful question. The reasons are multifaceted. First, people who feel alienated or disenfranchised often look for a solution, and these groups offer one. Not only that, but they also often offer a specific scapegoat. I'm always amazed at how many people complain about their economic health then vote for political parties that put policies in place to prevent economic equality. These groups offer a place for individuals who feel their voices are being ignored or perceive themselves as victims of societal changes. Progress has happened, and it scares people, or all the good jobs are going to immigrants, even though most of the jobs taken by immigrants are not the ones they are clamoring to get. The CLA and similar organizations play on these sentiments, offering a sense of purpose, camaraderie and a clear enemy — in this case, the 'liberal elites' and the federal government."

Another student raised a hand. "These groups can become dangerous quickly, right? Especially when they have members with military backgrounds, like David Collins?"

"Yes, you're correct," Martinez responded. "When such groups contain individuals with military training, the potential for violence escalates dramatically. That's one reason why the recent actions of the CLA are particularly concerning. It appears they're shifting from ideological advocacy to operational militancy."

The room fell silent for a moment before another student chimed in. "So, what can be done about groups like the CLA? How can we combat this kind of extremism?"

Martinez sighed lightly, a somber look on her face. "It's a complex problem with no simple solutions, but it begins with education and understanding. We must understand the causes behind such movements, address feelings of disenfranchisement and promote inclusive dialogue. There's a reason I've dedicated my life to understanding and speaking out about these groups. Everyone here today sees the real threat these people pose. The security guards," Dr. Martinez gestures to the man sitting in the front and lecture hall's doors, "are here to protect you as much as they are to protect me."

"Remember." She paused, clearly trying to parcel out what she would say. "The goal isn't to suppress voices or ideologies. I firmly believe in free speech, even when that speech is mean and hateful. I may not like what's coming out of someone's mouth, but I will fight for their right to say it. Instead, our society must strive to de-escalate conflict, promote understanding, and work toward solutions that uphold our democratic values. Governments and communities must work together to address economic disparity, social inequality and other root causes that fuel these extremist movements."

She took a sip of water, then smiled at the room. "This brings us to the end of our lecture." The sound of closing notebooks and the zippers of bags opening filled the room. Dr. Martinez raised her voice to be heard over her students. "Continue pondering these issues. We'll pick it up from here next time. Oh, and one more thing... Don't forget about the rally against extremism tomorrow. I hope to see you all there."

"She's good, isn't she, Mr. Dickenson?" Todd asked next to him.

"She is. She most definitely is. I can understand why the CLA might target her. She has a pulpit. These groups like to work in the shadows. I'm sure her calling them out and making them national news isn't winning her many friends."

"Well, they did attack Houston," Todd said.

Blayne turned and looked at him. *Did he totally miss that part of the lecture?* "Well, I better get out of here," Blayne said noncommittally. "I'll see you next week in class." Blayne stood, grabbed his attaché case, slipped out of the auditorium with the stream of students and walked right by the security officer who hadn't let him in earlier. There was not a hint of recognition on the officer's face. *So much for our crack team of security guards.*

* * * *

Ms. Wilson

Ms. Wilson hadn't had this much fun in decades. She may have appeared like a cross between a judge and a librarian, but she still had skills at sixty years old. Now she was just being inventive because she was waiting. She could only do so much business on a satphone. What she needed was to get her full communications array back up and working. She felt like an appendage had been ripped from her body, so she took great joy in returning that feeling to their unwanted guests.

Ms. Wilson turned the corner and gasped loudly, catching the attention of three hulking brutes. She wanted to scream, "Come and get me boys," but she held back. "Oh no," she said in her best little old lady voice. The three men took off after her. *Perfect*. She ran down a hallway and turned around just in time to see the last one run over a grate in the floor. She hit the wall light switch, sending a metal spike from the ceiling. It connected with the man, completing the electrical connection. Immediately, the sound of sizzling permeated the walls.

The men stopped and looked at their friend as his body convulsed. One guy tried to help his friend, but Ms. Wilson's *tsk*ing sound stopped him. "Sizzles like bacon. That smell is going to take forever to get out of here."

The man growled at her. "I'm going to kill you."

"Good luck with that," she said with an eyebrow flash and a cheeky grin. "Come and get me, sweet cheeks." Then she blew them a kiss. She wasn't sure if it was the grin, kiss or calling them 'sweet cheeks', but the men came after her like two linebackers at the Super Bowl. She darted down the hallway and threw herself inside an open door, locking it behind her. Ms. Wilson crossed through the room and opened the next door, which she closed but left slightly ajar.

She heard the crashing sound of the wooden door as the men tried to punch and kick their way through it. "Use the ax in the fire case, you two apes," she mumbled. Sure enough, seconds later, there was the splintering sound of wood cracking against the force of the ax.

She pulled up a small monitor on her phone to time this one just right. The men crashed through the open door and into the room framed by three glass walls. The first man crossed the room to the only other door and found it was locked. He turned to look for a second door. The second guy was just seconds behind him, but that's all she needed. She triggered the containment cage. A glass wall slid up the middle of the room, separating the men. The second man turned to exit the way he came, but his path out was now blocked.

She flipped on the intercom and said, "Breathe deeply. It will go faster." A chemical fog seeped in from the ceiling. Immediately, the man in the glassed-off room started coughing then choking, falling to his knees. He reached out toward his friend, but his body went limp. She glanced down at her watch. *Tick-tock.* The last man standing pounded on the glass walls. She turned on the intercom again. "Don't bother. That's a chemically enhanced borosilicate glass. It's stronger than your average bulletproof glass. Your little meatpaws won't break through it."

"Where are you, you fucking — ?"

"Language!" Ms. Wilson spat like a schoolteacher from the fifties. She walked around the glass, running her fingers over the transparent wall that separated them. The man turned and eyed her as she left fingerprints on the outer glass wall. "Don't make me punish you." She paused, as if reconsidering. "On second thought, please... Please, let me punish you." She gave the man a Cheshire-cat grin through the window. She kissed the glass, leaving a bright red lipstick smudge for him. Then she purred like Eartha Kitt, and said, "Come and get me." She hit a button on her watch, and the gas from the first room was sucked out via an HVAC system. When the toxic fumes were gone, the glass walls rescinded. There was an audible click as the glass door unlocked.

Ms. Wilson let out a cackle as she ran away. She was barely around the corner when she heard the glass door crash open, and the man tore off down the hall after her. Ms. Wilson turned, standing at the end of the next hall. The man came to an abrupt stop.

"Out of tricks, old woman?" the man asked.

"Gained any IQ points?" Ms. Wilson responded. "I believe a rodeo has lost its clown."

The man seethed. The veins on either side of his neck pulsed in rage as his face turned a scarlet red, and the man barreled down on her like a raging bull. Of course, that's exactly what Ms. Wilson wanted. He was the animal bearing down on the human, and she was the skilled matador. Sure, the bull occasionally caught someone with their horns, but in a bullfight, at least the matador knew what game was being played. The man lunged as she whipped out a can of bear spray and leveled it at his face. A scream pierced the hallway as the toxic chemicals clouded his vision, stinging his eyes. He grabbed at the air where Ms. Wilson had been a fraction of a second earlier, but she'd slipped to the side and used the man's momentum to throw him off balance as she gutted the man with her knife. He landed on the ground, and she struck one more time with her knife into the center of the man's lower back.

She crouched and wiped the blood from her hands onto the back of the man's pants. "Clean up on aisle three."

The man lay prone. If he didn't die from blood loss or sepsis, he wouldn't be walking again soon. The man grumbled something on the ground.

"Excuse me. You'll have to speak up. I couldn't hear you," Ms. Wilson said to the man dying in the pool of blood at her feet.

"I'm going to kill you, bitch," the man stammered between haggard breaths.

"I seriously doubt that." She pulled out her gun and put two bullets in the back of his head.

Slow clapping from the other end of the hall caused Ms. Wilson to spin her head.

A woman with bright red hair in an American flag shirt, jeans and cowboy boots stood clapping as she leaned against the wall. "I never did like Frank," she said.

Ms. Wilson cocked her head. There was something familiar about this person, but she wasn't sure what it was. Ms. Wilson leveled her gun at the woman.

"Oh please, Ms. Wilson, put that little toy away. If I wanted to shoot you in the back, I would have."

"What are you? Raggedy Ann's evil stepmother?"

"Only thing sharper than your mind was that tongue of yours," the woman said.

"I'm sorry. Clearly, you were forgettable the first time we met. Care to reintroduce yourself so I can forget you again?" Ms. Wilson asked with a smile that went nowhere near her eyes. She kept her ears open. Ms. Wilson heard people trying to be quiet moving around her. She took stock of her options. *Keep her talking.* "Did we go to high school together?"

"I'm not that old," the woman responded. The bottle redhead tried to hold the disgust of that idea from her tone, but it didn't work very well.

"Well, you look like you've had a little work done. It's so hard to gauge people's ages these days."

"If you must know, I'm Laura Lee Jackson — and I'm the last person you'll ever see alive."

"Not if I kill you first," Ms. Wilson said.

She fired two shots in Laura Lee's direction, who was already moving before Ms. Wilson fired the first round. The other woman drew two guns and fired back. Ms. Wilson expected this move and dove toward the hall where men had been trying to box her in. She tore through three men in seconds and was running. She heard the clattering of cowboy boots behind her, and Laura Lee Jackson screaming behind her, "Don't kill her. Bring her to me."

"Bloody unlikely," Ms. Wilson said as she slipped into a room and locked the door behind her. She turned and found a guy strung up to a shelving unit. "They haven't found you yet? I guess I've been keeping them preoccupied." Ms. Wilson looked around the room to find something to knock the man out. She couldn't find anything, so she looked at the man and said, "Sorry, but this is going to hurt." The man screamed something through the duct tape and rag over his mouth as she flipped her gun over and pistol-whipped him against the side of his head. There was a crunching sound, and the man's head went slack.

Ms. Wilson scrambled back up into the air duct system. She'd gotten faster and faster at traversing this path and made it back in fifteen minutes. She went to her computer and flipped through all the cameras she'd installed while out. Finally, the image of the woman with fire-engine-red hair appeared on the screen. Ms. Wilson turned on the audio, but the man she was talking to had his back to the camera, so she could barely hear him.

"*Don't worry…she'll pay… I know, Lizzy…dead…all of them.*"

The redhead, who called herself Laura Lee, wasn't audible because she was anger-whispering. Ms. Wilson enhanced the image for a few seconds until she could see the woman's face more clearly. She studied it for a moment. Something just wasn't clicking. She made out the words "Pennington University" and "rally."

Then it hit her like a ton of breaks. "Did the man call her 'Lizzy?'" Ms. Wilson rewound the audio and enhanced it as best as she could, and she was pretty sure the man called the woman Lizzy, not Laura Lee.

Ms. Wilson searched her system for the name "Elizabeth." She searched personnel files and finally saw an image she hadn't thought about in twenty years. "Well, *fuck*!"

Chapter Fifteen

Ethan

Ethan was bored enough to watch RTN but tired of hearing about the Houston arena, so he popped in one of Blayne's *I Love Lucy* DVDs.

"Kicking it old school," he said to himself, putting his feet up on the coffee table and folding his arms behind his head. He was asleep halfway through the first show.

A knocking jarred him from his sleep an hour later. He got up, rubbed the sleep from his eyes and yelled, "Give me a second," through a yawn. He wondered if he should have cried anything.

"Open up already," he heard Ric's voice call.

"Dude, give him a minute," Orr said over his bandmate.

"What if he's *schtupping* Blayne in there? Do we really want him answering the door?"

Blayne opened the door. "There's no *schtupping* going on here. I was sleeping. What are you three doing here?"

"We haven't seen you in days," Orr said.

"You weren't answering your phone," Ric added.

"I'm just here for the pizza," Zach said.

"Pizza? I didn't order —"

"We come bearing," Ric said as Lucas came around the corner with a stack of pizzas, a box of beer and a couple two-liter bottles of soda.

"You're using my assistant as a pack mule?"

"He was bored," Orr said as he patted Lucas on the back. The slap almost made Lucas stumble.

"Get in here," Ethan said, grabbing the pizzas from Lucas' arms.

In minutes, the guys were lounging around the kitchen or on the sofa, eating pizza and tossing back beers.

"So, what's going on?" Ric said. "This is an intervention."

"Yeah, I see that nasty bruise on your arm," Orr said. "Did Blayne hurt you?"

"God, no!" Ethan let out.

"Then what?" Ric asked. "Something's going on. You're pulling back again. The last time you pulled back like this..." His voice trailed off.

"Was last month," Ethan said. "I'm very aware of what happened last month. And I promise, no one is trying to get my cell phone or kill me." Ethan paused momentarily and tried to shoot his bandmates a reassuring smile.

"Dude," Orr said. "What the fuck was that?" He turned to Ric, "Did you just see that?"

"The fake-ass smile after he said, '*No one is trying to kill me*?'" Ric replied in a higher-than-normal pitched voice that mimicked Ethan's. "Yeah, I saw that."

"I do *not* sound like that," Ethan said.

"And now he's being evasive," Zach added.

"I'm not being evasive," Ethan said faster and higher than he intended. He took a deep breath, centered himself and said, "I'm perfectly fine."

"No one's buying it," Lucas said.

"Tell us, or I'm calling Mr. J.," Ric said, pulling out his phone for emphasis. "You know he'll get to the bottom of it."

"You wouldn't dare," Ethan said. The group had always used calling Mr. J. as the ultimate threat when one of their members wouldn't get in line. They weren't exactly scared of their bodyguard, but they knew him well enough to know he could be terrifying.

Zach turned on the screen, shuffled for a few seconds and showed Ethan an image of Mr. J.'s bald white head over a green button that said 'call'.

Ethan deflated in front of the group.

"Just tell us," Zach said. "There's nothing you can't tell us."

And it all came flooding out of Ethan's mouth, every last thing that had happened over the past few days — from coming home and finding Ms. Hennigan in the house, to giving her blood, to spending the day with an assassin, making friends with another assassin and waking up to find a third assassin sitting in their bedroom.

"That security system I had installed is patently useless against these people. I might as well have installed a turnstile!" Ethan frantically looked at the guys as he took quick breaths. He looked at Ric and added, "And no, I'm not having a panic attack!"

"Well, who had international conspiracy and assassin in the betting pool?" Orr joked.

"My bet was that Blayne had turned Ethan into his personal gimp," Zach said.

"I had you two running off to Paris to get married," Orr said. "I was on team Blay-than… Eth-lane just didn't work for me."

"I had they were having a massive orgy," Ric joked. "I guess that's kind of what happened," he said with a shrug.

"What about you, Lucas?" Blayne asked his assistant. "What did you think we were doing here?"

"I had no idea and didn't think it was my place to guess."

"Trust me," Orr said. "We tried to get the little guy to talk, but he wouldn't."

Ethan shook his head. "So now what?"

There was silence for a few minutes. Finally, Ric broke the silence. "I guess that depends. What do you need from us?"

"I… I…uhh…" He tried to form the idea of what he wanted to say. He finally came up with, "I don't know."

"Do you want us to take you away from here? Get you unentangled from all this?" Orr asked seriously.

"No," Ethan said, looking up. "I don't. How fucked up does that make me? I won't leave Blayne to handle all this alone."

"Wow," Zach said, "you really love him, don't you?"

"Yes," Ethan whispered. "I do. I love him. And yes, all this is completely fucked up. And yes, I didn't want to get suckered into this mess, but I am, and I'm not about to leave Blayne on his own. I brought this to him."

"No, you didn't," Ric said.

"Of course, I did. Blayne would never have been dragged into any of this if he had never met me. He would never know that any of this…whatever existed."

"The dude doesn't blame you for getting shot, does he?" Orr asked.

"Not at all. Blayne's glad he got shot and not me." Ethan looked around at his friends. In that moment, he knew this group of guys would always be there for him. They were brothers.

"Lucas, if you want to leave, now would be the time. As it is, you already know more and could have a target on your back. You have the option to walk away from all this. In fact, if anyone wishes to step back from this, feel free to do so. ZERO can always replace me—"

"Don't even think about that," Ric said. "I never want to hear those words from your mouth again. Is that understood?"

"I knew you had discussions about it last month when I disappeared," Ethan said flatly. "Stephanie told me."

"We," Orr said, pointing around the group, "didn't have discussions. Were there discussions? Yes. We"—he pointed at the bandmates again—"would rather have disbanded forever than replace you."

Ethan hadn't realized how much he needed to hear the group say this after the trouble he'd caused them the past month. He wiped a tear away from his eye.

"Okay, enough sappy shit," Ric said. "Pile on." He dove on top of Ethan, and the other guys followed suit. They'd done it with each other since they were in college. When someone needed to be reminded that they were brothers, they all dog piled on top.

"Clearly, I missed something," Blayne's voice cut through the laughter. "What's going on here?"

"I'm here," Ethan said from the bottom of the dog pile.

"Are you okay?" Blayne asked. From the tone of his voice, Ethan could tell Blayne wasn't worried, so he shoved his arm between the guys on top of him and gave his boyfriend a thumbs-up."

"Pizza?" Lucas asked. "And you'll probably want a beer."

The guys started rolling off Ethan. When Ric was finally off, he sat up and looked at Blayne, who had opened the pizza boxes and was investigating what the guys had brought.

Blayne sat down at the table next to Lucas, held the pizza up to his mouth and asked, "What did I miss?" before chomping down.

Lucas looked at Blayne and asked, "Did an assassin make you breakfast?"

Whatever Blayne had been expecting to hear, that clearly wasn't it, as he immediately choked on his food. Ethan jumped up, ran to his boyfriend, and got to him just in time to see Blayne take a massive swig of the beer Lucas had handed him.

"I told you you'd need a beer," Lucas said.

"You told them?" Blayne asked, looking at Ethan.

"It kind of came pouring out of me. At first, they thought you were beating me up or using me as your sex slave, so telling them what was happening seemed like a lesser evil."

There was a knock at the front door.

"Are we being too loud?" Orr asked. "We've had hotel security called on us a few times for that. Once someone swore we were having some wild orgy, we were just gaming and got a little louder than we should have."

"I'll get it," Zach said.

He popped off the couch and was already heading to the door when Ethan and Blayne yelled "No!" in unison.

They jumped out of their seats when they heard the front door open, and Kira's voice said, "Oh! Not who I expected."

Ethan rounded the entryway just as Blayne did. "Oh, thank God," Blayne muttered. "It's just you."

"What kind of fucked up welcome is that?"

"He was probably afraid it was one of your new assassin friends," Zach said as he closed the door behind Kira.

Kira shot them a look.

"They know," Ethan said.

Kira looked at them and said, "I need a beer for this." She thought about it for a second. "I need something stronger. What do you have?" She turned to look at Blayne.

"I have vodka in the freezer."

"Perfect. Just bring me a glass and the bottle."

Once Kira was settled and started drinking, the group took turns catching her up on the day's events.

"Heard anything from Murphy?" Blayne asked.

"I've been avoiding my girlfriend. You know I can't lie to her. She'll see me and immediately know I'm hiding things from her."

Blayne looked at the band and said, "She's an amazing liar. Don't let her fool you."

"I'm a bluffer," Kira said. "I can bluff in the courtroom, I can bluff at a poker table in Vegas. With my girlfriend who works for the FB fucking I, I can't bluff." Kira took another swig of vodka.

"So, why are you here?" Ethan finally asked.

"I received a text message about a meeting here. I figured you had one of your friends send it." She gestured with the bottle of vodka at the band.

"No. No one sent a message," Ethan said.

"That's because I sent it."

Dr. Hennigan

All the heads in the room spun to face Dr. Hennigan as she spoke. Denzili and Richardson had entered behind her and immediately fanned out, drawing their weapons and pointing them at the people who sat around the living room.

"You're them? Aren't you?" Lucas squeaked out.

"Them who?" Dr. Hennigan asked.

"The psychopathic killers?" Lucas said before he closed his eyes.

Dr. Hennigan wondered if the poor young man was about to shit himself. She looked at Ethan. "Is that how you described us?"

Ethan looked at her and rolled his eyes. "No. I'm sure my language was much more colorful and dramatic than that." Ethan turned and looked at Richardson. "But I raved about your breakfast. Gave you a five-star review."

"She made you breakfast?" Kira asked, seeming to get her wits back.

"We woke up, and she was sitting in our room," Blayne started.

"Don't worry. We were fully dressed," Ethan added. "And Blayne was like, I need to help pull my boyfriend together before his meltdown. Please cook us breakfast — and so she did."

"Babe, are you okay?" Blayne asked, turning to Ethan.

Ethan briefly thought about it. "I'm actually okay."

"You must be the rest of ZERO." She turned and looked at each member. "Zach, Ric and Orr." She looked around the room and caught Lucas, the young man who looked like he would have problems with his bodily functions. "And who are you?"

"Lucas Andrade," the young man squeaked out.

"Speak up. I couldn't hear you."

"Lucas Andrade," the young man yelled this time.

"Ah yes, Ethan's new PA." Dr. Hennigan smiled one of her frighteningly charming smiles. "I am Dr. Hennigan, but I'm assuming all of you already know that from the looks on your faces. These are my associates Denzili and Richardson." She gestured to the woman and said, "You can put your guns away. Now that we're all acquainted, there's no need to flash them around."

Denzili put her gun behind her back, tucking it into her pants while Richardson placed hers inside a shoulder holster.

Denzili turned and looked at Hennigan. "Mind if I get a beer and a slice?"

"Don't ask me. It's their party we're crashing."

Denzili looked at the group and gave them a gesture that clearly meant, '*Do you mind?*'

Everyone quickly mumbled their assent for her to drink up.

"Would you like anything?" Blayne asked.

Hennigan looked around the room and said, "Do you have any wine?"

"Sure." Blayne stood up and went into the kitchen. He pulled out two bottles and read the labels. "I have a Shiraz and a Malbec. I may have a white —"

"The Malbec will do. I love a good Argentinian Malbec. It is from Argentina, isn't it?"

"I may not be a sommelier, but I promise my Malbecs come from Argentina, and my Shiraz is from Australia."

"I would love to take you to this amazing Argentinian vineyard. They have the most amazing futures there. I don't know who runs it now. I had to kill the last owner." She looked around the room dramatically. "Not because of the wine. The wine is amazing. He was a Nazi that needed to be put down— and I mean, a real one. One of those fuckers from the Third Reich. He was in his nineties. He'd never make it to trial at his age, so I ensured he met divine judgment a little sooner than he had expected."

There was a popping sound as the cork came out of the bottle. The men in the room jumped at that, exactly where she wanted them, disarmed by her charm and scared. She'd learned long ago from her mother, grandmother and Ms. Wilson that the nicer you were, the scarier you'd seem to people. It was that juxtaposition of the fear of death combined with a pleasant smile that put people on edge. And if you used it to your advantage, you could quickly work a room.

Blayne handed her a glass of wine. She sniffed it, swirled it in the glass. The wine had decent legs. She then tasted just enough to get a good sense of the vintage. "The bouquet is full and complex—floral hints of ripe black fruit are at the forefront, with black cherries, plums and blackberries underneath. Then you're hit by the secondary notes of vanilla and chocolate. These are probably the byproduct of oak-barrel aging. Even a subtle touch of tobacco and leather gives it an earthy undertone. Excellent choice, Mr. Dickenson."

Hennigan looked over at the couch, and immediately, one of the band members moved to the floor so Hennigan could sit. She strolled over and made herself comfortable before taking another sip, aware that everyone was watching her.

Blayne's phone rang.

"Right on time," Dr. Hennigan said to the group. "Please answer the phone. That would be Ms. Wilson calling with an update."

Blayne pulled out his phone and said, "You're on speakerphone."

"Dr. Hennigan?" Ms. Wilson started. "Are you there?"

"I'm here, Ms. Wilson. As Mr. Dickenson told you, you're heard by everyone. Everyone from Munchkin Land has joined us today."

There was a pause on the other end of the line. "Shall I continue?"

"Of course. Everyone here has gone over the rainbow."

"What the fuck is she talking about?" Orr asked Ric, who was sitting next to him. Ric just shushed him.

"What information do you have for us, Ms. Wilson?"

"Well, I found out that our little roach problem here is led by a queen roach you know." There was a pause before Ms. Wilson said, "Lizzy Cleburne."

Hennigan took a subtle breath and forced her face to remain impassive. "Interesting," was all she said before she sipped the Malbec. "I thought that specific roach was terminated twenty years ago."

"That makes two of us," Ms. Wilson agreed. "But you know how some roaches are. They just don't stay dead, no matter how many times you step on them."

"Anything else?" Dr. Hennigan asked.

"Yes, our intelligence about Pennington was confirmed this evening. I couldn't make out the entire conversation, but I believe the target will be at a rally."

"Like a pep rally?" Hennigan. She turned and looked at Blayne. "Does your school even have pep rallies?"

"We have bonfires occasionally, but not one this weekend."

She stared at Blayne and saw a look of recognition crossed his face. "What?" she asked. "You just had an idea."

Jason Wrench

"I snuck into a lecture today about ring-wing terror groups. There was a professor I'd seen on TV who works at Pennington. She mentioned something about a rally against extremists."

"Ms. Wilson?" Hennigan said.

"Pulling it up now." Everyone hitched their breaths. "Yes, there is a rally against right-wing extremists on the Pennington University Quad tomorrow afternoon. It's been organized by Dr. Olivia Martinez. Dr. Martinez is a political scientist who specializes in homegrown violent extremists. She's literally written the book about the Constitutional Liberation Army. I'm sending the book information to Mr. Dickenson's phone." There was another pause on the line before Ms. Wilson started speaking again. "Dr. Martinez would make an excellent target. She's actively gone after the CLA and was one of the first to publicly label the CLA as a terrorist organization. They've been on her radar longer than they've been on ours. She had a cousin who got involved in them, so she became interested in the group as a scholar. Dr. Martinez has made it her life's work to bring these people kicking and screaming into the light."

"Well, you've given us much to consider, Ms. Wilson. Any news on fumigating our home to rid us of our roach infestation?"

"Yes, the friendly exterminator from out west is coming tomorrow."

"Great, then we can tidy up this little mess here tomorrow and return home. Sounds like a perfectly delightful way to spend our day," Dr. Hennigan said. "Call back with any additional details as they emerge."

"Will do. For now, I'm going to go kill a few cockroaches."

"What is your count up to?" Denzili asked.

"Oh, I think I really lost count after thirty. I'm having to become more and more *inventive* with how I exterminate them to prevent myself from getting bored."

"I'm sure you'll kill those roaches in the most delightful ways."

There was a bark of laughter from Ms. Wilson's end of the line before she hung up.

"I don't think she was referring to cockroaches," Zach said.

Hennigan turned and smiled at him. "Gold star for you." She turned back to Kira. "We need reinforcements. And the person we need to contact is not someone I can contact directly. I need you, Ms. Strickland, to make a call for me."

"Who are you going to have me call?" Kira asked. Clearly, the lawyer didn't trust Dr. Hennigan, nor should she. Of the people in the room, Kira Strickland was most likely to be recruited by The Foundation. She was much stronger than she even realized.

"I need you to call Cleo Barnes."

"That's funny. You want me to call the First Lady? Sure, why not? I'll get right on that." Kira looks at her and mimics holding a phone. "Hey White House, it's me, Kira. Put the pres's wife on the phone."

Dr. Hennigan rolled her eyes. "Well, I would hope you'd adopt a more professional tone. But I need you to call Cleo Barnes. I don't have her personal cell phone number, but I have the White House operator's number and the private residence's extension number, along with the relevant passwords."

There was silence in the room.

"You're not joking, are you?"

Dr. Hennigan let out a slight sigh before smiling her most condescending smile. "You should know by now, you should *all* know by now" — she took a moment to look around the room — "when it comes to the security of this nation, I never joke."

Ethan

Everyone took Dr. Hennigan's veiled threat seriously. Even the usual jovial Orr seemed to take pause. Poor Lucas looked like he was about to take Ethan's place as most likely to have a meltdown.

"Dude," Zach finally said, "she's like scarier than my stepmother."

"Unless your stepmother can kill you with her bare hands without scratching her manicure, she's scarier," Orr said. "Not as scary as Ji Chu-young when she gets pissed off, though."

"Who is that? She sounds like my type of woman," Hennigan joked.

"That's our concert director," Ethan said. "She's a bit of a taskmaster."

"Well, there's no need for anyone here to worry. I never get pissed off," Hennigan said.

"Why don't I believe you?" Lucas asked.

"She really doesn't," Denzili responded before taking a sip of her beer. "Trust me. I've known her for years and never seen her pissed. Peeved? Occasionally. Annoyed? Hourly."

As if to emphasize Denzili's point, Hennigan rolled her eyes and cleared her throat. "My mother taught me long ago that extreme emotions prevent someone from being centered and aware of what's happening around them. When we experience extreme emotions — intense joy, crippling sadness, debilitating fear — we narrow our focus."

"Like tunnel vision?" Lucas asked.

"Precisely, my dear Lucas," Hennigan said. She tilted her head to the side before adding, "You don't mind if I refer to you as 'dear'? I was recently informed that not everyone appreciates it." She shot Ethan a meaningful look but didn't call him out.

"I...uh...don't mind," Lucas said.

"Perfect," Hennigan practically purred. "Think of it like being in a brightly lit room, but your focus is solely on the tiny, flickering candle in the corner. You become engrossed, whether it's a flame of joyous excitement or a wick wavering in fear. Everything else fades into shadow, forgotten and unnoticed."

"But why?" Lucas continued.

"I take it you've been plagued by extreme emotions most of your life," Hennigan said it as a statement and not a question. Lucas nodded. She took a deep breath, and a look of tenderness crossed Hennigan's face that Ethan found almost endearing. "Survival, mostly. Negative emotions trigger our fight-or-flight response. Our brain wants to protect us by concentrating on the 'threat' or the source of our emotions. Unfortunately, some people get into this cycle and can't escape. Whether severe anxiety, depression or terror, they focus on extreme emotions. As for intense joy or excitement, it's more about cognitive resources. We're so caught up in the moment that the brain doesn't process peripheral information as effectively."

"Are you a psychologist?" Lucas asked.

"Same general ballpark. I'm a board-certified psychiatrist, as Ethan can attest. I also hold a master's in public health and a PhD in bioengineering."

"How'd you know I searched —?" Ethan said.

"I'm alerted anytime anyone searches for me. In my line of work, it's always good to know when someone is looking for you online."

"So, you're saying we see less when we feel too much?" Lucas asked.

"Precisely. In my profession, seeing less will get me and others killed." She turned to Kira and said, "So, let's make that phone call."

Dr. Hennigan

Dr. Hennigan wrote the instructions on a pad of paper and explained that the steps had to be followed precisely for her to be put through to the First Lady. Dr. Hennigan could tell Kira was skeptical, but Kira followed her instructions to the letter.

"Hello?" a woman's voice said on the other end of the line.

"Yucca glauca," Kira said, looking to Dr. Hennigan to ensure she said the name correctly.

"This is Cleo Barnes. May I ask who's calling?"

"My name is Kira Strickland. We have a mutual acquaintance—"

"Is our friend with you now?" Cleo asked.

"Yes."

"Honey, I need to take this call in the other room. I'll be back in a few minutes."

"Hurry back. I wanted to go over the protocols of the State Dinner with you," President Jeffery Barnes was heard saying in the background.

There was a rustling of a fabric followed by the opening and closing sound of a door. "This line is secure," Cleo said before lowering her voice and asking, "What the hell is going on?"

"Cleo, it's Phillipa. You're on speakerphone."

"Is Kira a recruit?" Cleo asked.

"She's…not one of us."

"Wait a second," Cleo said. "She was the best friend of the guy you shot last month. What is going on out there?"

"It's been an interesting few days, dear. The Complex has been temporarily hijacked. Don't worry, the Chair and Vice Chair are secure, and Ms. Wilson is causing as much mayhem as possible. We're working to re-secure The Complex as soon as possible. I'm calling tonight because of the problem we started at the concert the other night."

"This is hardly the normal channels we connect through. How do I even know this is the real Phillipa Hennigan?"

"I have two words for you, 'Lizzy Cleburne'. She's resurfaced."

There was a gasp on the other end of the phone. "We left her for dead in Appalachia. Why and how the hell did she claw her way back?"

"Some people just don't take a hint and stay dead," Hennigan replied.

"Let me guess. She's the one who infiltrated The Complex?"

"Her and someone else on the inside. We'll scurry out that mole in due time. For now, there are more pressing concerns. How familiar are you with the Constitutional Liberation Army?"

"Until two days ago, I don't think anyone in the White House had heard of them. Now, they're all anyone is talking about."

"Have you heard of one of their leaders, Laura Lee Jackson?"

"I'm sure I have."

"Well, that's our old friend Lizzy."

There was a stream of obscenities that flew out of the speakerphone.

"We have a more urgent matter. Our intel suggests there will be an attack on a university campus in the Houston area. We need your assistance in coordinating with other key individuals."

"Whoa," Cleo replied. "You realize the risk we're taking? You could expose my cover."

"That cover we both have worked hard to create. Trust me, I wouldn't have you betray your cover unless it was dire. Give me a couple of hours. Who should they contact as the point person on the ground? Just have them call this number."

"Fine. Jeffrey won't enjoy having his plans interrupted. Tonight was supposed to be date night."

"Give my regards to Jeffrey."

With that, the phone call ended.

Hennigan looked around the kitchen and living room.

"That was really her," Blayne said. "Wow. You had the First Lady of the United States of America on the phone in the blink of an eye without anyone even bothering to notice at the White House."

"Yes," Hennigan replied. "And trust me, I can count the number of people who know about my relationship with Cleo Barnes on one hand." She looked around the room. "I hope you all recognize the seriousness with which I'm treating this threat."

"Any chance she can get us a tour of the White House when we're there on tour?" Orr asked. Zach, sitting next to him, elbowed him in the rib cage. "Ow! What was that for?" Zach just shook his head in frustration.

"I'm sure we can arrange something when all this unpleasantness is behind us," Hennigan said. "For now, we wait. I recommend calling it a night."

Initially, the group seemed reluctant, but everyone agreed that not much else could be done until they had better intelligence and help from local contacts. Lucas called up Mr. J. and requested transportation back to the band's hotel. Hennigan watched the room, taking in the various dynamics.

Blayne

For the first time since he'd gotten home, Blayne pulled Ethan away from the rest of the group and enveloped him in his arms.

"I missed you today," Blayne confessed.

"I think…I'm going back to the hotel tonight," Ethan said.

"Why?" Blayne asked, concern in his voice.

"All this," Ethan said. "It's been a long day. I need clean clothes. And I know the guys will have more questions once we're away from…them," Ethan said, glancing at Denzili and Richardson, who were whispering in the living room. "I just need a break." There was a sudden slump in Blayne's posture, so Ethan quickly added, "Not from you. I still love you, and I love you more than ever. But I just need to get away and have a break, return to my normal life for this evening, even if it's not a true escape."

"I could come with you," Blayne said, trying to put a puppy-dog look in his eyes.

"You and I both know you're needed here. Kira needs you, and the guys need me. It's just for one night."

"As long as it's only for one night," Blayne said, pulling Ethan into a hug and planting a kiss on the top of his head.

Ethan looked at Blayne's face and said, "Just for tonight." He put his arms around Blayne's neck and kissed him.

There was a knock at the door to the apartment.

"I believe that's our ride," Lucas said, pointing to the door.

Blayne turned to go answer the door. Much to the evident surprise of everyone in the room, Hennigan opened the front door.

"Phillipa?" The man's voice held shock, causing everyone in the room to fall silent.

Blayne and Ethan reached the entrance hall just in time to see a bewildered Mr. J. standing at the front door.

"James." She reached out and kissed the man on his cheek. "It's so good to see you. It's been ages."

"Since I worked on the security detail for Barnes' senatorial campaign. That was ages ago now. Do you keep in touch with Cleo?"

"As a matter of fact, I spoke with her tonight."

Hennigan talked with Mr. J. as if he were a long-lost friend or former lover. *No? Could they?*

"Are you thinking what I'm thinking?" Ethan asked.

"Probably," Blayne replied. "I swear. Whenever I think I know what's happening, there's another twist."

"What are you doing here?" Mr. J. asked Hennigan. "Hanging out in a college apartment isn't your usual scene."

"I'm an old family friend of Levi and Grace Dickenson, Blayne's parents," Hennigan explained. "They informed him that I was in town for business, so he invited me over." Hennigan flirtatiously placed her hand on Mr. J.'s chest. "I don't think Blayne realized there would be a party here. But we shared a glass of wine and caught up on old times."

Blayne couldn't help but be amazed at Hennigan's effortless ability to fabricate a believable lie. There was no stumbling or mumbling—just a smooth flow of outright bullshit from her lips.

"Well, if you're in town for a few days, I'd love to catch up and have dinner," Mr. J. said.

"I would love that," Hennigan responded, patting him once on the chest before withdrawing her hand. "Do you still have the same cell phone number?"

"I've had it for twenty years, not getting rid of it now," Mr. J. joked.

"Perfect. I'll call you." Hennigan stepped back before saying, "It really is good seeing you, Jameson."

"Likewise, Phillipa. I'd love to chat more, but I need to take the band back to the hotel."

"Of course. I remember all too well what your life is like in personal protection. These boys are fortunate to be in such capable care."

Ms. Hennigan stepped aside, and Mr. J. said, "Let's go."

The members of ZERO piled out of the apartment. Each one was a little dumbstruck as they passed Mr. J.

"I'll talk to you soon, Jameson," Phillipa yelled after them as Blayne shut the door.

As soon as the door shut, Blayne turned and looked at Hennigan. "You and Mr. J.?"

"We've known each other for years, and occasionally our paths cross."

"Oh, come on," Blayne said. "You know that's not what I meant."

"Mr. Dickenson," Hennigan said, raising an eyebrow and narrowing her gaze. "I, for one, am not one to kiss and tell."

Chapter Sixteen

Agent Murphy

The remainder of the afternoon was spent reviewing evidence that had been scanned by the local field office. There was enough proof to place the CLA at the arena. They had plans for the Houston arena and contact information for leadership in the National Democratic Party of Germany. What they didn't find was an apparent motive.

Murphy disembarked from the plane in Houston around ten p.m. at a small airstrip approximately twenty miles from the Emerald City. She exited the small jet and found her driver on the tarmac. The junior agent who'd gotten her driving detail was always very polite.

"Good evening, ma'am. Where would you like to go?" he asked, opening the side door for her.

"Take me to Ms. Strick... No, actually, I need to head back to the office. Take me to the Houston Field Office." Even though everyone called it the Emerald City when they weren't at work, agents knew that internally the higher-ups didn't appreciate the colloquial nickname. So, at least when they were on duty, the formal name was used.

She settled comfortably in the backseat of the SUV. Thankfully, she'd charged her phone on the plane, so she pulled out her cell phone and started flipping through messages. Sure, she could have taken her phone out of airplane mode the entire hour and twenty-minute trip, but after her day, she'd just wanted to kick back and close her eyes for a while.

She'd received a text message from Director Steele's secretary, urging her to call him immediately. She hit the number and listened to it ring. Finally, there was a click as the Director picked up. "Director Steele," the voice said. Murphy heard partygoers in the background.

"Sorry, Director. This is Agent Sarah Murphy. I just landed in Houston and read the message from your secretary. I didn't mean to take you away from a social gathering."

"That's fine, Agent. Just a moment," Director Steele responded. There was then mumbling, and the sounds of the social gathering started fading into the background. "Apologies for the interruption. I'm currently at a dinner party that has dragged on for far too long. Any updates?"

"I'm on my way back to the office to file my report now. I expect to have it to you within the hour."

"Hold off on that. We've just received a new batch of intelligence from the White House. There's an urgent threat assessment regarding a university in the Houston area. Are you familiar with Pennington University?"

"Yes, sir. Quite familiar with it, actually."

"Excellent. I'll send you the contact number of someone on the ground. They will serve as your liaison to…well, I'm not entirely sure how to categorize them. This group is a team of highly trained specialists the White House works with. They'll update your intelligence in real time. This takes priority. Your report can wait until the morning."

"Understood, sir. I'll speak with you in the morning."

The Director hung up, and a few seconds later, a text pinged on her phone from an unknown number. The message said, "*Call them now*," followed by a phone number. Murphy hit the number without even paying attention to it.

"Hello?"

"This is Special Agent Sarah Murphy. I'm the acting Special Agent in Charge of the Houston Field Office."

"Sarah? It's Kira. Did you hit the wrong number?"

"Oh, hey. I must have done something wrong. Let me figure this out. I'll call you back in a few minutes."

"Sure thing," Kira said.

Sarah looked back at the text. This time, she recognized the number as Kira's. She texted the unknown number back.

This is Special Agent Sarah Murphy. Please confirm who this is and the number sent.

About thirty seconds went by, she received another text.

It's Director Steele. The number of the local contact is and he sent Kira's cell phone number again.

Thank you for the confirmation.

She hit Kira's cell phone number.

"Hey there, get the wrong number straightened out?" Kira asked when she answered.

"Apparently not. This is the number Director Steele gave me for my *local* contact here in Houston." Kira cursed on the other end of the line. "What's going on?"

"I'm at Blayne's. You might as well get over here. This is a face-to-face type of conversation."

"What's wrong?" Sarah asked.

"Just come over here. We'll provide you with all the details."

Kira disconnected the call. Sarah caught the driver's eye in the rearview mirror. "Change of plans. We're heading to the suburbs."

* * * *

Blayne

Blayne searched Kira's face as she hung up the phone. He couldn't figure out what was going on inside her head.

"That was the local contact Cleo Barnes promised to get us."

"Wait a second. I thought you were talking to Sarah," Blayne said.

"I was," Kira replied.

It took a second to realize what Kira said to hit Blayne. "Oh, fuck."

"The shit's about to hit the proverbial fan," Kira agreed.

"Well, this is an interesting turn of events," Hennigan said. "I don't think a big gathering is necessary. Denzili, Richardson, I want you to conduct a brief reconnaissance mission on campus. We know the rally is to be held in the quad area. Please go scope it out. Look for choke points and areas where a sniper could set up shop. War-game every scenario you can come up with."

"Understood," Denzili said. Without hesitating, Denzili and Richardson left the apartment.

"And then there were three," Blayne said as the front door closed. Blayne walked into the kitchen and sat with the other two women at the table. "On a scale of zero to one hundred, how pissed off will Sarah be?"

"Oh, pissed off will not come close to what Sarah will be when she finds out what's happening."

"How will you explain everything?" Hennigan said. "Remember… If you tell her everything, she can't unlearn it. She should have the right to walk away before being drawn into this."

"We both know that will not happen. Sarah will be pissed that I didn't tell her yesterday when I found out about you."

"Blame me," Hennigan said. "Tell Agent Murphy I threatened to kill her if you told her anything." She downed the last sip of Malbec in her glass. "I'm used to playing the villain. I've gotten quite good at it over the years."

"But you're not, are you?" Blayne asked. "A villain, I mean," he clarified.

"I am many things to many people. Some see me as the boogey-woman who goes bump in the night, the one they warn their kids about. For others, I'm a superhero who swooped in at the last second to save their lives. You want there to be a world of black and white, Mr. Dickenson. I live in a world of grays, more grays and nothing but grays."

"Would you like a refill?" Blayne asked, gesturing toward the empty wine glass.

"No, I should keep my wits about me. I'll use the ladies' room before Agent Murphy arrives. Don't worry. I remember where it's located." Hennigan pushed herself up from the table and crossed through the living room toward the guest bedroom.

Blayne needed something to do, so he set about straightening the apartment. He started a stack of empty pizza boxes.

"Apparently, the band thought they would feed an army. Little did they know," Blayne said. He opened a drawer next to the fridge and pulled out a box of generic resealable bags. He took the remaining pizza and shoved the leftovers into the plastic bags. When he was done, half the bags he put in the fridge and the other half in the freezer.

He then filled the dishwasher with empty glasses and mugs.

"I'm going to take the empty boxes out to the trash. I'll be right back," he told Kira, who had barely paid him any attention while Blayne had been straightening the apartment. Kira was clearly lost in her own world. Blayne sat the stack of boxes on the table before reaching down and patting her shoulder. "It's going to be okay." Kira reached up and grabbed his hand before looking at him.

Tears were trying not to escape from the corners of her eyes. "Thanks. You don't know that, but thanks."

Grabbing the stack of pizza boxes, he walked toward the door. He turned the boxes sideways and squished them against his side as he fumbled with the knob.

Blayne turned the door handle then snaked around the door with the boxes into the night air. The night sky was clear. He could see a few pinpoints of light in the sky, but none like he'd seen growing up in West Texas, where light pollution didn't block the majesty of the stars in the heavens. He walked over to the dumpster. The last user had forgotten to close the lid, so he quickly threw the stack of used boxes into the bin. He closed the cover then leaned against it. He lightly bit his lower lip as he took a second to take stock of the insanity that had been his life.

"Dear God, help me out here," he said, gazing up at the sky. "I don't know what I'm doing. I know I don't pray that much anymore, but for fuck's sake, how much can one man take before he breaks? Sorry about the cursing." He paused briefly before asking, "Do you even care about cursing? I mean, you created humans, and we sure like to cuss up a shit storm. Hell, maybe you invented cussing. I don't know. I don't know how you could sit in heaven and not look at us humans and say, '*what the fuck?*' at least a million times a day." Blayne let out a huff, and for the first time that season, tendrils of his breath were visible in the cold air. A rumbling sound caught Blayne's attention, causing him to turn his head. A black SUV entered the parking lot. "If you could do me one quick favor," Blayne said, praying into the night, "just keep Sarah chill enough so she doesn't hurt Kira tonight." He waited for the SUV to pull into a parking space before he added, "Amen."

The back door opened, and Sarah stepped out of the vehicle.

"Well, fancy meeting you here," Blayne said, feigning enthusiasm.

"Do you need me to stay, Agent Murphy?" a young guy in a dark suit said.

"I can handle it from here. I'll see you in the morning."

Sarah turned and looked at Blayne. They stood in silence until they heard the door to the SUV shut.

"It's not... Actually, it's probably worse than you think," Blayne admitted.

"Let me stop you right there," Sarah interrupted, raising a finger to stop him. "Wait for him to go."

They stepped out of the way as the agent pulled the SUV into reverse and started leaving the parking lot.

"Remember, it's the FBI. Always assume there are eyes and ears everywhere." She then spun and looked up at Blayne. "What did you get yourself into?"

"A Texas-sized shit show. And before we go in there, don't blame Kira. It's...it's complicated."

"All right, I'm ready to hear just how complicated you're about to make my life," Sarah said, seemingly bracing herself.

* * * *

Dr. Hennigan

Hennigan washed her hands and splashed water on her face to freshen up. She'd been running at full pistons ahead and hadn't really breathed for a few days. She lifted her shirt to inspect the sutures on her side. Thankfully, they didn't look infected, which was her primary concern. As much as she acted calm, cool and collected, the pain in her side was constant. If she took one hit to the injury, she'd blackout from pain. But in her line of work, you often must suck up the pain until you could step back and deal with it directly.

She left the backroom and headed into the living room. Kira's back was to her in an otherwise-empty apartment.

"Where's Mr. Dickenson?" Hennigan asked. Kira's shoulders jumped. "Sorry. I didn't mean to startle you."

"I was lost in my head. Blayne took the empty pizza boxes out to the garbage. He'll be back in a second."

"How are you holding up?" Hennigan asked.

"I don't know what to think about any of this," Kira admitted. "One day, I thought you were the devil incarnate, and the next, I'm having a phone conversation with your bestie, Cleo Barnes. Cleo Barnes, who is, of course, married to Jeffrey Barnes, the most powerful person in the world."

"Yes, I can see how this could be overwhelming."

Kira took a deep breath, trying to gather her ideas amid the whirlwind of information and revelations. Hennigan walked around the table and stared at Kira.

"I can't even begin to imagine what you're going through," Hennigan empathized. "This is the world I grew up in. It's my normal. It's a lot to process, Kira. The sudden unveiling of this hidden world and the interconnectedness of those running it can be overwhelming. The truth is far stranger than anything can imagine."

Kira let out a hollow laugh. "I know there are little 't' truths and big 'T' universal truths in this world. But your world takes the idea of truth, spins it around, molds it, reshapes it and spits it out as something that I don't even recognize."

Hennigan was about to stretch out her hand and touch Kira reassuringly when the front door to Blayne's apartment opened. Hennigan slipped her hand into her pocket, rested it on the gun that sat there and put on her most comforting smile.

"Look who I picked up next to the dumpster," Blayne tried to joke. The joke fell flat in the room. "Okay, uhh...I guess introductions are in order."

"Agent Sarah Murphy," Hennigan said. "It's so good to see you again, especially since I'm not shooting at you. Your dad was a professor at Tulane until he retired four years ago, and your mother was an FBI agent who died of cancer...almost a decade ago now, I believe."

Agent Murphy's gun was leveled at Dr. Hennigan before Hennigan even realized she was going for it. *She's fast.*

"Put that thing away, Agent," Hennigan ordered, her tone firm. "I currently have my weapon leveled at Kira under the table. You shoot me, I shoot her and Blayne must clean up the blood in his kitchen...for the second time this week."

"Who are you?" Murphy demanded, keeping her weapon raised.

"Do you really want to know?" Hennigan asked. "Everyone else in this room knows. This is your only chance to walk away from all this. Out of courtesy to Ms. Strickland, I'm allowing you to walk away."

"Yeah, that's not really an option," Murphy said. "So, let me repeat my question in case you missed it the first time. '*Who are you?*'"

"That's a complicated answer, and we don't have time to go into it now. Instead, we will focus on why I had Kira call the First Lady, who called your director, who called you."

"Okay, so you're connected. That doesn't make you above the law," Sarah said flatly.

"Of course not. I'm just not subject to the same laws you are. You may find this hard to believe, but we are on the same side...at least right now. Now please" — Hennigan gestured to the chair next to Kira — "sit down and let's have a civilized conversation about how we're going to save Pennington University tomorrow before there are a lot of victims."

Hennigan then laid out the intelligence they had about the CLA and their meeting in Houston and the subsequent fallout.

"You think the meeting was a sham? They came to Houston to kill the Germans?" Sarah asked.

"That seems to be the most logical conclusion," Hennigan said. "Everything about it from my vantage point was a setup. Part of me wonders if the whole thing was to get my team in the arena, while they conducted a separate operation."

"What 'separate' operation?" Sarah asked.

Hennigan had hoped to keep this part out of their conversation, but decided the truth was the best path forward with Sarah. "The Foundation operates a facility we call The Complex. While we were incapacitated here, they infiltrated the facility. The woman who seems to call the shots, Laura Lee Jackson, is one of our former operatives."

"Why is one of your former operatives associated with the CLA?"

"We don't know. In fact, until earlier this evening, she was presumed dead — and I mean a long-time dead.

No one has seen or heard from her for over twenty years."

"Do you frequently lose your operatives?" Sarah asked.

"No. Operatives don't retire." Dr. Hennigan stared into the other woman's eyes and knew she didn't need further explanation.

"Okay, so we have a former secret governmental spy agency operative who hooked up with some homegrown extremists. To do what? What's her end game?"

"That, no one knows. All we know right now is that she's here. Well, she was at our facility earlier today, but I doubt she'll miss the opportunity to take part in this offensive action of theirs tomorrow."

"And the only intelligence you have is that they're targeting Pennington and a rally. And because Blayne heard about a rally in a class he snuck into today, you're assuming that tomorrow's rally is the target?"

"Yes." Murphy sat back in her chair and crossed her arms. "You do realize this intelligence is quite thin, don't you?"

"Most intelligence is," Hennigan admitted. "We act based on the most up-to-date information. Those facts are constantly evolving. So, today, we raided two CLA facilities—one in West Texas, the other in Eastern New Mexico."

"Interesting," Hennigan replied, steepling her hands under her chin, then signaling for Murphy to continue with a gesture.

"Both homes were rigged to implode. We triggered one during the raid and received no actionable information. On the other, we let the bomb squad do its thing before we entered. We found an underground bunker that had a lot of intelligence."

Hennigan made a mental note to have Ms. Wilson hack into the FBI's computer networks and retrieve any of the digital files from the operation.

"And?"

"We found detailed blueprints of Pennington University. We're talking blueprints that go back to when the original campus was built. Underneath the blueprints, I found one picture." Sarah picked up her cell phone, which had been placed on the table in front of her, unlocked the phone and scrolled through the information on her phone. She turned her phone around when she found the file she was looking for. "Do you know who this is?"

The woman in the picture appeared to be a young Latinx woman, possibly in her late twenties or early thirties. Someone had drawn a red bullseye around the woman. "I don't know who that is."

"Damn," Agent Murphy said before putting the phone on the table.

"Wait! Show me that photo," Blayne said. The three women turned to look at him, but Agent Murphy didn't hesitate to do as requested. "Wow, that's her. That's Dr. Olivia Martinez. She's the political science professor who is organizing the rally tomorrow."

Chapter Seventeen

Agent Murphy

After the tête-à-tête the previous evening, Kira had driven Murphy back to her place. They had talked into the early morning hours. Murphy was not happy with this situation, but she understood it from Kira's point-of-view. However, she still thought Kira should have confided in her. *To what end?* Murphy pondered as she was chauffeured to the Houston Field Office. If this continued, she would need to purchase a new car. She hadn't needed one in New Orleans, but Houston was more spread out and didn't have NOLA's tight public transportation system.

"Ma'am? Do you need me to get the door for you?" The agent in the front seat turned around, looking at her.

How does he drive like that? Then she realized they weren't moving anymore. "Sorry about that," she said. "I got lost in my thoughts."

"Happens to us all, ma'am."

She would have to put a stop to this younger agent constantly addressing her with "ma'am." He meant well and was trying to be respectful, but she was an agent just like him.

"I'll see you at the operations meeting later this morning," Murphy said as she exited the vehicle. She didn't wait to see if the younger agent followed her into the building. She walked up the path and in through the glass doors of the Emerald City. She sailed through the new automated security measures at the building after the impromptu protest the month before. That had been one of her first jobs when she took over the post. The only sound in the building at this early hour was her heels clicking across the marble atrium as she headed to the elevator bank. She waited for a second and heard the ding of the elevator car arrive.

"Hold the door," a man's voice called out. Murphy stuck her arm through the closing doors.

"Morning, Murphy," Agent Benjamin Harper said as he entered the elevator.

"Morning, Harper."

"I got a text that we had an all-hands-on-deck meeting at nine. Any idea what this is about?" Harper asked.

"I should know, considering I'm the one who called for it," Murphy replied.

Harper took a swig of coffee from his travel mug. "Well, don't keep me waiting."

"I don't know what I can tell you yet. I have a meeting with the White House and Director Steele at seven-thirty."

"That doesn't sound good," Harper responded. "I hope they're not planning to send us back to New Orleans. I just finished unpacking."

"How much crap did you bring? You know this is temporary for both of us," Murphy said.

"Well, I had to bring my computer, television, clothes, golf clubs and other essentials. Why? What did you bring?"

"My to-go bag. I just keep recycling through my suits. I have three at the dry cleaners, two hanging in Kira's closet and the one on my back."

"Damn, you pack light," Harper said. "I need at least two full suitcases if I go to an all-expense paid clothing-optional resort."

"Eww," Murphy said. "I didn't need that mental picture before I've had coffee."

"You and Kira have a late night?"

"Not the kind you're thinking of." She reached out and pushed the emergency stop button on the elevator. She'd learned this was one of the few places to hold a conversation, but you could only do it for twenty seconds or the fire alarm would go off. "Here's the deal. The people from last month are back. They're apparently working for or with DC, and somehow Kira got herself wrapped up in this mess. It's a clusterfuck." With that, she pushed the button and the elevator continued.

Ding! The door to the elevators opened, and she exited, leaving Harper in stunned silence behind her. She heard him scramble to exit the elevators before the doors closed.

"You can't drop a bomb on me like that then walk away."

"I don't know what you're talking about," Kira denied. "I said nothing. And more importantly, you know nothing." She got to her door, pulled out her keycard, opened the room and said, "I'll see you at nine. And clear the rest of your day quietly. It's going to be busy."

She shouldn't have said anything to Harper, but they'd been partners for years, so she believed she owed him. He'd been dragged along to Houston as her partner, but she was put into this leadership position, making her his boss. The whole thing was messed up, and neither of them enjoyed playing politics.

After logging into her computer and responding to several emails, she proceeded to the SCIF in the basement. By seven-thirty, she logged in and stared at a screen with Director Steele, President Barnes and Sepi Amin.

"Good morning, Agent Murphy. I just read the report you submitted last night," President Barnes said. "For obvious reasons, this report has been labeled Top Secret. Not even my Chief of Staff, he nodded his head toward Amin, could read this document. As you can well imagine, there is information that you included in your report that is beyond dangerous to our national security. After today, I recommend destroying any notes you have on this subject. There will be only a single copy of this report, and it will be held here in the White House in our secured digital archival vault."

"Yes, sir," Murphy responded.

"And, Murphy," Steele said, "this is covered under the Counterintelligence and Security Enhancements Act of 1994. As of eight p.m. last night, you were officially made a National Counterintelligence Policy Board member in absentia. This is covered under

Section "E", Coordination of Counterintelligence Matters with Federal Bureau of Investigation. To learn more about these provisions and the corresponding laws, read the *Intelligence Community Legal Reference Book* by the Office of the Director of National Intelligence and the Office of General Counsel."

Murphy could tell that Steele was reading from a script. The FBI's lawyers probably gave him the exact verbiage to say that morning. *What kind of fucking shit show did I step into?*

"Now I'm going to ask Ms. Amin to leave, as she doesn't have clearance for the upcoming conversation," Director Steele stated.

The President nodded his head as Amin stood and left the White House situation room.

"Now that it's just the three of us, feel free to speak openly," the President encouraged.

"Is there any new intelligence beyond what I submitted last night?" Murphy asked.

"No. We still do not know why Dr. Martinez is being targeted," Director Steele said. "Sure, Dr. Martinez has been a pain for the CLA, but our analysts and their foreign counterparts can find no direct link between the women that would level this type of attack."

"What about between Dr. Martinez and Benjamin Jackson, the husband?" President Barnes asked.

"Believe it or not, that's even murkier," Steele admitted.

"Is Martinez part of this Foundation group?" Murphy asked.

"That would be something you'd have to ask your contact on the ground," Steele said. The look on his face showed that this was a line of questioning he wasn't comfortable with, even on a secure line.

"To what extent should I trust The Foundation?" Murphy asked as her follow-up.

"Murphy, for the record," President Barnes said, "The Foundation does not exist. We" — and he looked directly into the camera — "and I mean all three of us, have never heard of them, nor have any of my predecessors."

"That's correct, Agent Murphy. Sometimes concerned citizens, independent of governmental agencies, bring their concerns to the US government, and we fully investigate those matters," President Barnes clarified. "It's like a knitting club that calls the police when they see someone's house being broken into."

Well, I was just put in my place. The message was clear, *'toe the fucking line'.*

"Yes, sirs. I completely understand you, sirs."

The rest of their meeting flowed in this same vein. Murphy would try to ask a question and be immediately informed that the information either didn't exist, the players involved didn't exist or no one had any idea what she was talking about. She also got the sneaking suspicion that every question she asked also told the men something. They all spoke in code about something that didn't exist. It was a game of Schrödinger's intelligence.

By the time she got into their large conference room with her agents, she was still trying to figure out how to spin everything.

"Good morning," Murphy began as she walked to the front of the room. "Concerned citizens have provided actionable intelligence about an imminent attack against the life of Dr. Olivia Martinez, a professor of political science at Pennington University."

She looked around the room as everyone started taking notes. "We've been in touch with the head of security at Pennington University, and they've decided not to cancel the anti-extremism rally scheduled on campus," Murphy informed. "If they won't cancel it, then we need to secure it. I need ideas on my desk by eleven. We'll have a full meeting at noon before heading to the campus. Put everything else aside. Protection of this event has been made our top priority," a few people in the room grumbled. "This came from the President of the United States himself. I had a meeting with the President and Director Steele today. *They*, and as a result, *we*, are taking this seriously. Is that understood?" She scanned the room to see if anyone would openly object. When no one did, she said, "Questions?"

* * * *

Ethan

Ethan tossed and turned all night long. He needed to talk to Blayne, so he woke up early and had Ms. Z. drive him to Blayne's apartment but not before stopping by the Dream Bean for coffee and breakfast sandwiches. Ethan promised to call Ms. Z. and report in if he left the apartment. He also texted Lucas and said he was at Blayne's and to call him on his cell if he needed him.

Ethan walked up to the door and pulled out his key but wasn't sure if he should use it. He knocked. He waited. Blayne didn't answer the door, so he knocked again.

Finally, he pulled out his cell and texted Blayne.

Are you awake? Why aren't you answering your door?

A few seconds later there was a click, and Blayne stood with ruffled hair, wearing only a pair of pajama bottoms.

"Morning, sunshine," Ethan said.

Blayne grumbled acknowledgment before holding the door open for Ethan to enter. Ethan walked into the kitchen and did a quick look at the place.

"Anyone else here?"

"Just us," Ethan confirmed, handing Blayne the cup of coffee. "Drink up. It'll help you feel better."

Blayne nodded and took a sip of coffee before sitting down at the table.

"Late night?" Ethan asked.

"Yeah. Murphy got here. Wow, was she fucking pissed off."

"I'm glad I left before all that went down."

"I wish I could have gone with you," Blayne said. "How are the guys?"

"Confused. Concerned. They asked a lot of questions. Some I had answers to, and the rest I couldn't explain without telling them other things that I don't think they would be ready to handle yet. I'm not cut out to be a spy."

"You and me both," Blayne said. "I honestly don't know how Dr. Hennigan keeps track of all the lies and her real life. The number of balls she has in the air is beyond me. We're both busy guys, but I don't think we come close to her level of busy. I can barely handle graduate school, teaching and dating you. She did that and worked as an international assassin on the side."

"Eat your sandwich," Ethan said. "You're going to need your energy today, dear."

Blayne picked up the croissant layered with scrambled eggs, sausage and cheddar and took a bite.

Ethan let a breath out through his nose. "Is there any chance I can convince you not to go to campus today?"

Blayne shook his head as he chewed.

"I didn't think I could, but I had to ask," Ethan replied. "So, it looks like you're stuck with me. Everywhere you go, I go. Unless I'm at your side, I won't have you running headfirst into danger. Is that understood? Oh, and if we go out in public, we might be accompanied by at least one of my guards."

"Don't you think Mr. J. would attract attention in a crowd? He's not exactly inconspicuous," Blayne asked, taking a sip of his coffee.

"Oh, I don't want him to be inconspicuous. I want him to be a big-ass deterrent."

Blayne chuckled. "Fair enough. What did you tell him?"

"As little as humanly possible. I deflected more than anything. Thankfully, the guys helped me with 'operation deflection'. I think he's suspicious—but doesn't know what he's suspicious about."

"Well, fingers crossed, this is all over in eight hours," Blayne said.

"From your mouth to God's ears."

* * * *

Ms. Z. showed up in an SUV to drive Blayne and Ethan to a drop-off point right at the opening of the quad. Inside the spacious SUV, Blayne and Ethan sat beside each other, their fingers gently intertwined as they stared out of the windows. Ms. Z. skillfully maneuvered the vehicle through the labyrinth of cars and pedestrians.

"Geez, this is turning out to be quite the circus," Blayne commented.

"We're going to have to get creative," Ms. Z. said, her voice laced with determination. "Everyone's headed to the quad. I will do my best to get as close as possible — but not sure how close that will be."

Blayne could see the Unity Tower in the middle of the quad through the front window. News vans were scattered along the street, impeding traffic. The campus police were supplemented by the Houston Police Department. Still, they seemed a little overwhelmed by the sheer number of people. Honestly, it reminded Ethan of the first time the band had shown up at a television studio, and they were greeted by throngs of fans hoping to get seats inside. The television studio, just like the campus, was clearly overwhelmed by the turnout.

Blayne leaned forward slightly, surveying the chaos unfolding before them. "Yeah, you can drop us off anywhere. I think you'll have a better chance of finding an actual parking space in the western lot, on the other side of the medical center."

"Are you sure?" Ms. Z. questioned. "I'm supposed to stay with you."

"The guys are already here. I'm sure they'll have the rest of the crew with them."

"Fine, but I'll double-check before making any decisions," Ms. Z. confirmed.

Ms. Z. pulled out her cell phone and quickly called Mr. J., who gave her the okay and told them they'd meet at the entrance to the Harmony Gardens.

"What's the deal with this place?" Ethan asked.

Blayne, in his best tour guide voice, replied, "The Unity Quad is a major feature in the southern part of the campus. In the heart of the quad stands the magnificent Unity Bridge and Tower, a majestic structure that gracefully bisects the west and east sections of the quad. The tower is a powerful symbol of connection and convergence, drawing people from all walks of life toward a shared destination."

"Uh...you sound like you've said that a few too many times," Ethan joked.

"I spent my first summer working as a campus tour guide. Not the most glamorous job, but it kept me fed."

Blayne explained that unity is broken into four distinct concepts—harmony, synergy, collaboration and purpose. "The Harmony Gardens is in the Southeast part of the quad. I can't imagine how much water they use in that part to keep all the flowers from dying in the Texas heat. From there, we have the southeast section, Synergy, where '*students and faculty come together, fueled by a collective spirit of cooperation and innovation.*' I don't think I've ever seen faculty and students there, but there is a small playground and a bunch of picnic tables. There are also more trees in that part of the quad than in the other three. From there, we have the Northwest part, which is Collaboration, and is '*a haven for interdisciplinary projects and joint ventures.*' Yeah, I think they have an outdoor art show once a year. They hold honors graduation there as long as it's not over ninety degrees outside. Last, but certainly not least, is Purpose. This is where the main rally will be held. The western edge has the Purpose Pavilion, allegedly '*a beacon of inspiration and a gathering point for those driven by a common cause.*' It's also the location of our free speech zone on campus, which is why all kinds of rallies happen here."

"Well, it's nice to know I'm with someone so ready to be my tour guide. I'll be sure to tip him when we're done."

"Here we go," Ms. Z. cut into the conversation as she pulled up to a spot near the entrance. "I'm going to go park, then I'll find you. Go straight to this—"

"Harmony Gardens," Blayne helped.

"That's it. Don't make Mr. J. have to look for you."

"Aye, aye, captain," Ethan joked as he opened the door to the SUV. Blayne slid across and followed Ethan out. Blayne stood for a second on the sidewalk, and Ethan closed the door. "Where to, Mr. Tour Guide?"

Blayne turned in time for Ethan to see the over-exaggerated roll of his eyes. "Why do I feel like I will regret letting you come with me?"

"Oh, you didn't *let* me do anything."

"Isn't that the truth," Blayne said with a smile. "Stay close. I don't want to lose you." Sure enough, they were almost immediately swept away by the crowd. Thankfully, they got to the entrance of the Harmony Gardens without losing each other.

Ethan was surprised that Harmony Gardens lived up to its name. It was like being transported into a lush green space more reminiscent of the East Coast than Texas.

"Wow, the gardeners here do an amazing job," Ethan remarked.

"Yeah, I've always been impressed myself. They have huge retractable shade devices for some parts of the garden to prevent some plants from overheating during the summer. I swear, the campus takes better care of this little part than the students who live in the dorms. One dorm finally got AC like two years ago.

Can you imagine living in the Houston heat and humidity and not having central air?"

"Hey!" Ric's voice cut through the crowd. "About time you two showed up. I was beginning to think you weren't going to make it."

"What the hell are you three wearing?" Blayne asked.

Ric wore holey jeans topped off with a purple and yellow Aloha shirt. He had a giant pair of reflective sunglasses that covered half his face. Then there was Orr, who had opted for a mismatched yet oddly coordinated outfit. He sported a pair of baggy patchwork jeans featuring various fabrics and patterns, each panel telling its own story. The jeans looked like they came from the stage closet of a musical from the seventies. He topped it off with a vintage band T-shirt, layered with an oversized red blazer. He wore a pair of blue sunglasses. Then there was Zach, who donned a pair of high-waisted, wide-legged trousers in a vibrant shade of teal, paired with a form-fitting, vintage-style graphic T-shirt. And by form-fitting, you could see every one of his ab muscles through the T-shirt. He wore stylish shades and topped the ensemble with a Pennington University baseball cap that had clearly been purchased recently.

"You guys look like three rejects from clown college," Ethan remarked, holding back a laugh.

"Wow, just...wow," was all Blayne got out of his mouth.

Blayne

His phone buzzed in his pocket, and he quickly retrieved it to read a text message.

Check your other pocket. Give the second one to Ethan.

He reached into his pocket to find two objects the sizes of pencil erasers. Blayne turned his back to the group.

They go in your ear, a follow-up text message.

He was about to ask how they got in his pocket when he remembered bumping into a goth girl in the crowd. She'd done the usual angsty teen, "Watch it," and shot him a glower, but he'd really paid attention to her. In retrospect, how he hadn't realized it had been Denzili in the black lipstick and thick mascara was mindboggling.

He took one device and put it into his ear.

"And good afternoon." Dr. Hennigan's voice came through the earpiece. "Don't respond. I know this can be a little disconcerting. You need to pull Ethan aside for thirty seconds and give him the other earpiece."

Blayne turned around. The guys were still talking as Ethan further mocked their clothing choices.

"Hey, Ethan," Blayne interrupted, "can I borrow you for a minute? I want to show you something in the garden. We'll be right back."

Without waiting for an answer, Blayne reached out and grabbed Ethan's hand and pulled him behind him. After a couple of turns in the garden around a few six-foot tall hedges, Blayne stopped and looked around to ensure they hadn't been followed.

"What's up?" Ethan asked.

"Here," Blayne said, holding out the earpiece.

"Is that?" Ethan said as he took the device. "Damn, it's small." He placed it in his ear and said, "Hello?"

Blayne heard Ethan's "Hello" in his ear.

"Good afternoon, boys," Dr. Hennigan's voice came through the earpiece. "I've set these to a personal channel. You'll hear crosstalk between different police agencies, but we'll only hear each other when you speak. Your job is to stay alert. If you see anything, say something, and one of us will investigate. Is that clear?"

"Crystal," Blayne said.

"Where are you?" Ethan asked.

"We're around."

Almost immediately, they started hearing police chatter in their ears.

"Wow, this is going to take some getting used to," Blayne said.

"If it gets too much, just tap your ear twice. That will cut the local channel chatter," Denzili's voice said in Blayne's head. "It takes some getting used to."

"Thanks," Ethan said.

"Yeah, this is freaky," Blayne said, turning his head toward Ethan's voice but realizing that it was the earpiece he turned toward, not the actual person.

"It's called localization," Ethan explained. "We had to get used to earpieces at concerts. Trust your eyes and not necessarily your ears."

"Okay," Blayne said, not really convinced. "We better get back to the guys."

Ethan took hold of Blayne's hand and looked into his eyes. "We've got this."

* * * *

Dr. Hennigan

Dr. Hennigan had spent the morning poring over the layout of the Pennington University Quad. There were too many places where someone could hole in a sniper's nest. They'd checked the roofs of Jordan Hall to the east of the Pavilion, the K. G. Johnson building to the northeast and the Ann Richards Arts and Sciences Building to the immediate north. Mostly, they found the FBI on those rooftops, so they at least had those vantage points covered. Admittedly, there were many windows in each of those buildings, but the FBI was already doing a floor-by-floor check.

"Richardson," she said, confident that the other woman would hear her. "When was the last check done on the tower?"

"Ten minutes ago. The museum is still locked up tight."

In the debriefing after their surveillance the night before, Denzili and Richardson had informed her that the tower was securely locked. The tower's base was a square building that served as a small museum. Access to the tower was only through the museum. You could access the tower's entrance, but it was padlocked shut. The bridge was a bridge to nowhere. It rose over the museum and went around the tower, but there were no entrances from the bridge. The architectural design of this place made no sense. Why build a tower, encase it in a museum structure, then construct a bridge that served no purpose other than to pass over the museum? Someone was either high when they drew up these plans or was too rich for their own good and was like, "*Build me a bridge!*"

"Agent Murphy," Hennigan said through her earpiece. "I see you're monitoring the buildings. Have you observed anything?"

"Who is this? This channel is reserved for official FBI personnel only," Sarah replied.

"You'll notice that no one around you can hear us," Hennigan mentioned. She walked through the crowd, holding her cell phone discreetly in her hand to avoid drawing attention.

"Who is this?"

"It's your new friend. How quickly you forget."

"Hennigan?"

"Who else would it be?"

"Leave me alone," Murphy responded firmly. "I have enough to handle without you talking in my head."

"I'll only contact you from this point forward if I need something or have intelligence. Overall, your surveillance approach is the same as I would have taken."

"We know what we're doing," Murphy replied.

"Take the compliment."

Hennigan switched channels and let Denzili and Richardson know they were ready. They had plenty of eyes everywhere for whatever was going to happen over the next hour.

"Remain vigilant," Hennigan instructed the team. "They're here. I can feel them."

* * * *

Agent Murphy

Murphy was set up in a small command vehicle on the southwest corner of Purpose Park. It wasn't nearly as nice as the semi-truck she'd been in the day before. This one was more like a seventies food vendor reject. She kept waiting for someone to come up and try to order ice cream. The mobile command had two computers and four monitors built into it. On a good day, you could squeeze four agents into the back. With her and Harper, they had five—and it wasn't air-conditioned. Thankfully, the fall air wasn't too hot, just in the low seventies, but the inside of the tin can was pushing ninety with the body heat.

"I need to step outside for some air," Murphy said.

"I'll join you," Harper replied.

She turned to her team. "Please make sure you stay hydrated. If you're not careful, this tin box could cook you and the equipment."

Note to self, upgrade the mobile command unit. She stepped out the back and took in her first breath of actual air. She leaned back against the truck and watched as students and people from the public entered Purpose Park.

"So, will you ever tell me what happened this morning?" Harper asked.

"I wish I could. You learned more during my little elevator breakdown than you should have. I just needed to tell someone. Saying nothing, I was told in no uncertain terms that what I told you never happened, could never happen, and if it did happen, the level of security surrounding it was so high only about eight people in our country have that level of clearance."

"Fuck," Harper drew out in his thick bayou accent that rose its head occasionally.

"Fuck is right."

"Oh, and while we were in there"—she motioned to the truck—"my new little nightmare hacked into our signal to say hello."

"That shouldn't even be possible," Harper said once he'd regained his composure.

"Tell me about it," Murphy said.

"Agent Murphy," a voice in her ear said.

"Yes?" she responded.

"It looks like the rally is about to start."

"Thanks," she replied. She took one more breath of fresh air. "Ready to go back into the oven?"

"This tin can isn't that bad. You should try the heat and humidity in the bayou in August. You'd be clamoring for a nice cool box like this one," Harper said as he patted the side of the truck. He opened the door, and Murphy climbed in. She had three drones in the sky that were being monitored. Plus, they had one stationary camera to see the pavilion itself.

"It's showtime, people," Murphy said. "Check in."

The different teams that were in place quickly checked in as the first person took the stage.

* * * *

Dr. Hennigan

The first woman to walk up to the microphone was the type of college revolutionary she'd seen on college campuses forever—young, idealistic, thinking they were the first to tackle the evils of society.

"Ladies and gentlemen, today I stand before you to address a menacing force that threatens the very fabric of our society—the venomous serpent of extremism!" A cheer erupted from the crowd. Hennigan refrained from rolling her eyes—not that anyone could see her eyes behind her designer sunglasses. But she didn't want to stand out, so she politely golf clapped. "It slithers through the shadows, poisoning minds, sowing division, and igniting the fires of hatred. But fear not, for we shall face this abomination head-on and vanquish it with the blazing power of truth and *unity*!" The crowd erupted at the last word.

"Check in," Hennigan said.

"Nothing here," Denzili said. "I'm north of the lawn, walking on the sidewalk."

"South here, next to the gardens. Going to recheck the bridge," Richardson replied.

"Wow, look at that," Ethan said. "I'm… Where the hell am I?"

"You're southwest of the actual pavilion," Blayne said. "We're about one hundred yards back."

"Hey, what's the deal with the drones?" Ethan asked. In the background, Hennigan overheard one of his bandmates explaining it to him.

"Just nod your head and pretend you're listening," Hennigan advised. "There are about five drones in the vicinity. Three are operated by the FBI, and two are remotely controlled by Ms. Wilson."

"How the hell?" Blayne spat out.

"She's using the satphone," Hennigan said. "Don't ask me how she does what she does."

"I can also hear every word," Ms. Wilson's voice cut through the chatter. "Hennigan, switch to operation two lines."

Hennigan immediately switched. "Status update?"

"There was a drawdown of personnel last night. There are still about twenty or so cockroaches scurrying about. Ms. Brighton will execute operation 'Take Back' in twenty-eight minutes and counting."

"Just keep your head down," Hennigan said. "How defensible is your current position?"

"I'm perfectly safe. I'm fine if the yokels don't know how to track satphone signals. And so far, I've seen no sign that these imbecilic clodhoppers even know they exist."

"Just don't take any chances."

"May our fervent call for unity and understanding resonate through the ages, inspiring future generations. Let it be known at this very moment that we proclaim with unwavering conviction that extremism shall be banished into the depths, eternally conquered by the unwavering spirit of humanity united!"

Dear God, she sounds more like a Southern Baptist preacher than a revolutionary.

I now want to bring to the stage our next speaker, Dr. Olivia Martinez!"

The crowd erupted.

"Keep your eyes open, people. The main event is starting."

Chapter Eighteen

Ethan

The crowd extended in all directions, a diverse mix of people of all ages, genders and ethnicities. Some held signs and banners, while others seemed to be there just to see what was going on. Among the attendees were the usual students, as well as individuals dressed in business attire. Of course, Ethan wasn't sure if the people in suits were professionals who had come to campus or were FBI agents milling about the crowd. The rally had transformed into a focal point of unity, where individuals fostered an atmosphere of awareness, acknowledging the urgency of the issues and the necessity for collective action.

"Ladies and gentlemen, distinguished guests," Dr. Martinez said. Ethan only knew what the woman looked like because he'd run an internet search on her this morning after Blayne had explained what they'd learned the previous night. "Today I stand before you to address a growing concern that threatens the fundamental principles of democracy and individual liberties — homegrown extremism. Our politicians want to point at people from other countries and scare you into believing that the biggest threat to democracy is immigrants and foreign nationals. Yet, homegrown extremists are repeatedly allowed to prosper and thrive because certain politicians know that denouncing extremists and their actions is denouncing a portion of their voter base. These politicians would prefer the streets of the US run red with the blood of its citizens rather than admit the hard truths of our reality. As a society built upon the pillars of reason, justice and freedom, it is our responsibility to shed light on this pressing issue and engage in a thoughtful discourse that transcends mere rhetoric."

Ethan found himself genuinely impressed with Dr. Martinez's eloquence. "Was she always this captivating during her lectures?" he asked Blayne.

"She's a bit larger here, but yeah, she's just that good."

Dr. Martinez continued, "We must underscore the significance of cultivating democratic values and promoting civic engagement. It is imperative to encourage active participation in democratic processes, empowering all citizens to voice their concerns, hold institutions accountable and advocate for policies that safeguard democracy and condemn extremist conduct."

Ethan had been oblivious to the sign language interpreter, but he witnessed her collapsing to the ground just moments before the deafening sound of the gunshot that claimed her life reached his ears.

The rally, once filled with hope and unity, erupted into chaos. Panic seized the crowd like a vise, spreading rapidly through their ranks. Fear surged through the air, triggering a cascade of reactions among the attendees. People scattered in every direction, their movements frenzied. People pushed and shoved, desperately trying to find an escape route. Others tripped and stumbled, their attempts to flee impeded by the sea of bodies around them. The air filled with cries for help, desperate pleas for safety.

More shots pierced the air, and Ethan witnessed a young woman, just ten feet ahead, collapsing lifelessly onto the ground before even touching the grass.

"Down!" Mr. J. yelled. Immediately, the ZERO security team surrounded their group.

"Mr. Bond, there's an active shooter at nine o'clock."

"Shooter, nine o'clock," Ethan hollered. He watched as the shooter crumpled to the ground but wasn't sure which guard took the shooter down.

Of course, that brought the snipers' attention to their group. Ethan looked chaotically around them for an escape route. A young man behind them went down.

"There's a sniper in a nest on the top floor of the door west of your position," Ms. Wilson's voice cut through the chaos.

Blayne turned his head in that direction. "Eberly," he yelled. "That's Eberly Hall."

"Relaying information to the FBI," Ms. Wilson said.

"Run!" Mr. J. called.

Acting on instinct, Ethan seized Blayne's hand and sprinted alongside him.

* * * *

Agent Murphy

Murphy watched in horror as panic erupted among the crowd, seeing people scattering in every direction, seeking safety.

"Where are the shooters?" she yelled, keeping her eyes fixed on the monitors.

"It looks like someone in private security just took someone down," an agent said, glancing up at Murphy for a moment.

"Did you know there was private security on the ground?" Barnes asked.

"Can you get me a better angle?" Murphy asked. A second later, one drone zoomed in on that area. "What the fuck are they doing here?"

"Is that...?" Barnes trailed off, pointing at the screen.

"Yes, it's our beloved boy band," Murphy confirmed, rolling her eyes.

"What the hell are they wearing?"

"Agent Murphy," a voice interjected in her earpiece, "there's a sniper's nest on the top floor of Eberly Hall. Your agents positioned on the roof of Jordan Hall have the best chance of eliminating the sniper."

Without even responding, she relayed the information. She turned to the drone pilot. "Get me a visual on Eberly."

The drone captured the sight of FBI agents rushing across the rooftop. Murphy anxiously scanned the footage, searching for the threat. And there it was — the flash of a muzzle.

"Third window down from the...north," she said.

One of her men set up the shot. Seconds later, the sniper tried to take another shot and was immediately taken down by one of her team.

She turned back to the drone pilot and asked, "Can you zoom in on that room?"

There was a dizzying motion on the computer monitor, but the drone hovered just outside the room. The dead body of the sniper was clearly visible.

"Ground team, you are cleared to sweep Eberly Hall," she said.

The video monitor went dark. Then another one went dark.

"Fuck," the pilot said. "Someone's taking down the drones. It looks like we have a second sniper on our hands."

The screen then caught what looked to be an audience member pulling their concealed weapon and shooting. *At whom?* Murphy had no idea.

"Or someone in the crowd thinks the drones are part of the attack," Murphy said. "Where the hell is crowd control?" Murphy watched the screen, where no one seemed to direct the people on the ground. "The people in the crowd will be responsible for more deaths than the shooters."

"Agent Murphy," the agent said. "We have a confirmed second sniper."

* * * *

Blayne

Blayne was a runner, but he was also a tall moving target. At some point, he lost Ethan's hand, but kept running.

"Don't run in a straight line," Ms. Wilson said.

Immediately, he swerved in a new direction, hoping the sudden change would throw off whoever was shooting at them.

"Blayne," it was Ethan. "I'm right behind you. Keep running."

"The safest place is under the overhang next to the bridge. Get there and press your body against the wall," Ms. Wilson said.

Blayne didn't need to be told twice. He altered his course to head toward the bridge. Blayne heard a bullet hit concrete somewhere nearby when he left the grassy area but didn't slow down. He practically slammed into the wall and waited for Ethan to hurry up behind him.

Ethan was hunkered down behind a short concrete wall separating Purpose Park from the pedestrian sidewalk.

"What are you doing?" Blayne asked. As if to answer him, a chunk of concrete from the top of the wall splintered as a bullet hit it. "Fuck!"

"It's coming from the bridge," Ethan said.

Blayne leaned away from the wall and looked up. He had just enough time to see a rifle at the bell tower's top.

"How the hell?" Blayne started. "The sniper's in the bell tower. He has Ethan pinned down."

"Stay where you are," Hennigan said. "Ms. Wilson, can you verify the location?"

Blayne heard a buzzing motion overhead followed by a shot. A drone crashed on the sidewalk, maybe fifty feet in front of Blayne.

"Was that enough confirmation?" Blayne asked.

"We're on our way," Hennigan said. "Stay where you are."

Blayne carefully crept his way down the side of the wall next to the museum. *If I can just get to the door.*

"Mr. Dickenson, I told you to stay put," Hennigan's voice said.

Blayne looked back to see another chunk of the wall where Ethan hid crumble away as another bullet struck it. "Sorry," Blayne said. He removed the earpiece from his ear, flung it on the ground and crushed it under his foot. He was tired of being bombarded with so many voices in his head.

The glass door of the museum lay shattered. All Blayne needed to do was cross the threshold into the museum. The padlock locking the old metal door on the tower was broken off. Blayne put his hand on the door and pulled lightly. He expected it to groan under the weight of the metal grating against metal. Someone had done a great job of keeping the metal door lubricated, because it barely made a sound.

Blayne entered the tower and found a round stone staircase leading up to the belfry. *I'm fucking nuts*, he thought as he put his foot on the first step. He kept his back to the wall and focused on what was happening above. He'd heard the brief pause before the sniper shot another round. Blayne didn't know much about guns, but he knew this one had to be semi-automatic, because he didn't hear the gun loaded and cocked between shots. Blayne had only fired guns once in his life. He'd gone hunting on a West Texas ranch with his best friend. He still remembered the pain from the shotgun as it recoiled against his teenage shoulder. What he heard above him sounded nothing like that.

Blayne took one stair at a time. Slowly he climbed, the sounds of the shots getting louder and louder with each step.

"Base to Platoon Leader," a voice cracked over a walkie-talkie above him.

"Give me a second. Got ear protection in." There was a scuffle above him. "What was that?"

"Platoon Leader, this is base. Sniper Two is down. Our three men in the crowd were killed. Meet at the exfiltration point in five minutes."

"Roger that," the sniper above him said. "Time for a few more shots."

Blayne covered his ears, waiting for the next shot. The higher he got, the more stairs he tried to climb each time the sniper took a shot. He figured with the gun reverberating off the bells above him, the sniper wouldn't be able to hear him on the stairs if there wasn't some kind of trap along the way.

After the next shot, Blayne was just below the wooden planks of the belfry. He could see the sniper on the other end of the landing from the staircase. He'd only get one chance to do anything.

"Come on, little boy-band fucker, poke that head up from behind that wall. Let's play peek-a-boo. I know you want to," the sniper mumbled before taking another shot.

Blayne made it to the belfry and crouched. The sniper stood before him, perched in one of the giant window areas next to one of the two bells.

"There you are," the sniper said.

Fueled by a surge of adrenaline, Blayne charged the sniper as a raw and guttural roar escaped his mouth. The sniper turned and tried to level his gun at Blayne, but it took him a second too long. Blayne shoved the man toward the window. The sniper rifle crashed to the wooden floor. Blayne grabbed the side of the bell and crashed it into the guy's head as he tried to regain his balance and went stumbling right out of the window. Blayne heard the sniper's cry echo off the outside wall before the sound of his body hitting the ground with a solid thud.

"Platoon Leader, do you copy?" the walkie-talkie squawked. "Ben, are you there?" the woman's voice yelled.

Without thinking, Blayne picked up the walkie-talkie and said, "Sorry. Ben isn't here to take your call," then hurled the device out of the window.

Blayne found himself alone in the bell tower. A faint ring resonated from the brass bell as his adrenaline-fueled bravado gave way to a flood of conflicting emotions. He walked to the opposite corner from the window, drawing his knees up next to his chest in a huddled form, as the weight of taking a life washed over him. Silence settled around Blayne, broken only by his heavy breaths. A wave of raw emotion crashed, and he turned his head and vomited on the ground. His chest tightened, and tears welled in his eyes as he grappled with the realization that he had ended another person's life. Even at that moment, Blayne realized some would call him a hero, but in the depth of his soul, something broke.

"Blayne, Blayne!" a voice yelled from inside the bell tower. He registered the voice screaming his name but not loud enough to move him to action. Seconds later, someone threw their arms around his neck. Blayne was still crying as he looked at Ethan and held onto him like a life preserver tossed to a man who went overboard in a roaring sea.

Amid a flurry of voices and bodies, Blayne was helped to his feet. Then he descended the tower stairs in a haze. By the time his feet hit the bottom landing, he was getting his wits about him. He still shook, and the tears wouldn't stop streaming down the side of his face.

Ethan sat Blayne outside, and someone handed him a bottle of water. Ethan kneeled next to Blayne and placed a gentle kiss on his forehead.

"I've got ya." Blayne reached out, and Ethan curled into Blayne's lap and clearly wouldn't let his boyfriend go.

Ethan grabbed both sides of Blayne's face. "We'll get through this together," he whispered before kissing Blayne. "I promise."

Blayne looked at Ethan. "Sorry. I think I may have vomited in there"

Ethan threw his head back and laughed. "God, I love you, Blayne." He kissed his boyfriend again.

* * * *

Agent Murphy

When the day's smoke finally cleared, there were over a dozen fatalities, twenty people who sustained non-life-threatening injuries, whether by one of the gunmen or the crowd, and five dead assailants. William Johnson was the sniper killed in the dorm. They were still waiting for the fingerprints of the three gunmen in the crowd. Thankfully, FBI agents and the ZERO security team had taken the gunmen out reasonably quickly, though Murphy promised to keep their names out of the press. In the melee, no one knew who shot whom. Then there was Benjamin Jackson, who had been shoved out of the bell tower by Blayne Dickenson.

Murphy had been informed of what had transpired. She told the first agents on the scene to secure the tower for evidence. They'd told them Blayne was just sitting outside the museum door against the wall with his boyfriend, who was overprotective.

It took Murphy thirty minutes to make her way over to where Blayne was sitting on the ground with Ethan. With his arm around his shoulder, Ethan sat beside him, and Blayne leaned into Ethan.

She said hello to an agent who let her by. The ZERO security team and band hovered nearby, watching over both Blayne and Ethan. Sarah slid down onto the ground next to Blayne.

"Well, we find ourselves amid a war zone again," she said, letting out a breath. The evening lights caught a hint of her breath. "We've got to stop meeting like this."

Blayne turned and looked at Murphy. He took a deep breath, closed his eyes and asked, "How do you get them out of your head?"

"You will. It won't happen overnight. Keep seeing Esperanza Secada. You're going to need her guidance as a psychologist more than ever after today. Blayne" — she cupped his chin gently in her hand — "don't do this alone. You have Ethan, you have Kira, you have your Pennington family and you have me." The words barely escaped her lips as the tears welled.

"What now?" Blayne asked. "I killed someone."

"Yes," Murphy said, "but you didn't murder him. If you hadn't killed him, he would have killed more people. And while I know this doesn't make it easier, you made the right call. You made the call any of us would have made if we had the chance. I wish it could have been me in that tower. I wish more than anything you didn't have to be the one in that position. But you are a hero — and I know you won't feel like one, even though everyone will laud you with praise. But what you did was heroic. You risked your own life to save others."

"He was going to kill Ethan. He recognized him and tried to kill him. I just lost it when I realized what he was up to," Blayne admitted.

"Whoa, you hadn't even told me that," Ethan said from the other side of him. "Blayne…" Ethan turned Blayne toward him and kissed him.

"I love you," Blayne said, the words catching in his throat. "I want to go home."

Ethan looked at Murphy, who said, "I can get his formal statement tomorrow or later this week."

"Come on, baby," Ethan said as he pushed himself off the ground. "Let's get out of here. I think we've done enough for today."

Ethan reached out his hand to Blayne, who grabbed it and let himself be pulled up. Ethan threw his arm around Blayne's waist. Murphy stared after them as they walked toward the ZERO family, who enveloped both in a giant group hug.

Dr. Hennigan

Hennigan watched as Murphy talked to Blayne and Ethan. Hennigan wasn't the right person to have this conversation with Blayne. She rarely felt anything when she had to kill someone. It was built into her DNA, but she knew that not everyone reacted to death as she did.

After Blayne and Ethan left, she approached Murphy, who was still sitting on the ground.

"That was very nice what you did right there," Hennigan said. "I'm not what I would call the motherly type. My speech would have been more like, '*Congrats on killing the fucker. He deserved to die. Go celebrate.*'"

"Are you actually that heartless?" Murphy asked, pushing herself off the ground.

"Not at all. I just don't lose sleep over killing someone who needed to stop existing on this planet."

"You realize that makes you sound like a sociopath?"

"As a board-certified psychiatrist, I would probably agree with you. However, that would imply that every individual in the US military is a sociopath. Special forces have frequently been likened to high-functioning psychopaths. Many sociopaths find the military a welcoming environment, once they've ranked up." Hennigan turned and looked at Murphy. "Join me for a walk."

"I should be arresting you," Murphy said.

"You could try, but we both know how that would go. My agents would stop you before you had a chance. Then there would be more bloodshed and bureaucratic nonsense. Take the win."

"I don't know what to make of you, Dr. Hennigan."

"Don't even bother, Agent Murphy. The more you dwell on me, the more your head will ache. Just know that I'm on your side. Although our methods may occasionally be more extreme, our objectives align."

"I seriously doubt that."

"Well, the President, the Director of the FBI and the Joint Chiefs of Staff, among others, believe it's true. Trust me, numerous male politicians have attempted to dismantle The Foundation, yet it still stands firm."

"How did things turn out for your people today?"

"We took back The Complex. There were approximately twenty deaths."

"When we will get those bodies back so we can notify their families and perform follow-up investigations."

"You won't. Sadly, those families will think their loved ones ran off. So many people disappear across this country every day. What's twenty more? But I emailed you a list of the bodies we identified. You can do with that list as you wish."

"I should put you in handcuffs right now," Murphy said.

"But you won't," Dr. Hennigan stated as she turned and walked away.

Chapter Nineteen

Ethan

The brief ride home in the SUV was faster and significantly quieter compared to their earlier journey that morning. Mr. J. sat in the driver's seat and Ms. Z. sat on the passenger side. Zach, Ric and Orr had returned to the hotel in the other SUV to give Blayne and Ethan some space. Ethan sat on one side, staring out of the window, and Blayne sat on the other side doing the same. Ethan watched Blayne's reflection through his window as the nighttime lights drifted by. Distance may have physically separated them, but they kept their hands clasped in the middle.

The SUV pulled into the parking lot at Blayne's place and parked out in front. One sight wasn't expected. Kira stood leaning against her car. Ethan opened the door and helped Blayne out. Blayne was looking better, but he still had this shell-shocked look that worried Ethan.

"I brought Chinese," Kira said, gesturing toward the bags on the roof of her car. "And I couldn't care less if you want to eat or not. If I have to shove an egg roll down your throat, I'll do it."

"We're going to search Blayne's apartment," Mr. J. stated. "And we won't accept 'no' as an answer. We'll also upgrade the security system. Agent Murphy mentioned that the current provider has been underperforming. Apparently, anyone can easily gain access." Mr. J. fixed his gaze on Ethan. You know, security only works when it keeps you secure."

Blayne didn't even protest. He reached into his pocket, pulled out his keys and handed them to Mr. J., who tossed them to Ms. Z., who walked to the front door.

"What's the alarm code?" she asked.

"9, 2, 2, 4, 3, 8, 4, 2, 6, 7, 4, 2, 6, 7, 7," Ethan said.

"Zach, Ethan, Ric, Orr... Cute," Ms. Z. said. "Predictable, but cute."

"It was easy to remember," Blayne said. Blayne leaned against the bumper and stared up at the stars.

Ethan walked over to Kira. "How's he really doing?" she asked, leaning once more against her car.

"He took a life today. I think that shook him more than he expected it to. Everyone keeps reassuring him he did the right thing—"

"Fucking right he did."

"How'd you know?" was almost out of his mouth before he said, "Murphy. You talked to Murphy."

"I was in a meeting at work and couldn't get out of it on short notice. I wish I had been there with her...with you."

"What would you have done?" Ethan asked.

"I'm at least armed," Kira said.

"The last thing that place needed was additional firearms," Mr. J. said, and Ethan glanced over in surprise. Mr. J. was not known for interrupting or speaking up. He was like a fly on the wall, observing everything but refraining from taking action. It was one of the reasons he excelled at his job. He knew when to remain silent. "That place had too many guns. Why they let college students open carry on a college campus is beyond me. Most professionals wouldn't react well in today's situation. Anyone who thinks a 'good guy with a gun' would help today is a moron. When the dust settles, we'll probably learn at least a couple of the victims were shot by people with guns playing hero."

"You took one down," Kira said.

"Yes. And I turned over my weapon to the FBI for testing at the scene. I'm a professional with decades of experience and training. Any idiot in Texas can get a concealed carry permit."

"It's true," Blayne said. "Even my parents have concealed weapons permits. They got them so they could protect themselves at church. Hell, their church even has a mini-militia that's been 'trained' in case of an active shooter there. When they told me this, I thought it was the most imbecilic thing I'd ever heard. One church in Texas was targeted, and now every congregation has created its own police force. Seems like they're worshiping guns more than God."

"It's clear," Ms. Z. said, exiting Blayne's apartment.

Blayne pushed himself off the SUV and made to enter his apartment. As he walked by Ms. Z., she handed him the keys. Ms. Z. said something to Blayne and patted him on the shoulder. Seconds later, Mr. J. did the same thing. Ethan picked the bags off the roof of Kira's car.

"I'm starved," he said. He gestured with his head toward the open door. Kira gave him a weak smile and followed.

"Ethan," Mr. J. said as he entered the SUV. "Call us in the morning. I'm certain Rawlings and Hightower will want to meet with you."

"Great," Ethan said under his breath. He turned his head around and heard the SUV door close as he walked into Blayne's apartment.

He headed straight for the kitchen table. Blayne was already getting plates from the cabinets.

"I need a shower," Blayne said.

"I'm sure we both could use one," Ethan said. He turned and looked at Kira. "Do you mind?"

"Take all the time you need. I'll throw the food in the oven and watch TV while you two get scrubbed up."

"Thanks." Ethan turned to Blayne. "Let's go get clean."

Blayne seemed to come out of his fog as he said, "Together?"

"Of course together. I'm an environmentalist and want to conserve water."

"Likely story," Kira said as she opened the fridge. "Thank God, there's still beer in here."

Ethan reached out and grabbed Blayne's hand. "Let's go."

Blayne

Blayne allowed himself to be led away from the kitchen toward the bedroom. He just kind of stood there in the middle of the room, unsure what to do with himself. It was one thing when they were playing spies. There was a certain thrill to everything, but he'd never even imagined what killing another person would be like. The enormity of taking someone's life...even if that life needed to be taken.

"I love you," Ethan said as he reached up and undid the buttons on Blayne's shirt. Ethan untucked it and Blayne's undershirt before undoing the buttons on the shirt's cuffs. Blayne let Ethan completely slip him out of the shirt, throwing the discarded clothing into the hamper. Next, Ethan unbuckled Blayne's belt and tossed it on the bed. Blayne stood there, shirtless. "We'll get through this…together."

Blayne looked down at Ethan and smiled. "I know we will." He reached his arms around Ethan. "I just… I just…" Blayne was at a loss for words.

"Shh…" Ethan replied. He leaned up, put his arms around Blayne's neck, pulled Blayne's head down toward his and kissed him. After a few seconds, Ethan pulled away. "Yeah, we still need to do something about that breath of yours."

Blayne laughed. Only then did he taste the still sour taste from his stomach acid. "Yeah, I need to brush my teeth. I'm going to go do that." Blayne kicked off his shoes, unbuttoned his pants and shoved them and his boxers down to the floor, stepping out of them. "Hurry up and join me." He walked across the bedroom butt-ass-naked except for his white tube socks. Entering the bathroom, he flipped on the light and immediately went for his toothbrush and toothpaste. He scrubbed his teeth then gargled with mouthwash, because he didn't want that flavor in his mouth anymore.

Ethan entered the bathroom and threw his arms around Blayne's torso. Blayne was just spitting out his mouthwash as he did.

"Now, this should be the photo for our Christmas card this year," Blayne said as he looked at his naked body in the bathroom mirror as Ethan leaned to the side.

"Well, if anyone got a glimpse of that thing," Ethan said as he raked his eyes in the mirror down to Blayne's dick, "they'd know what you bring to this relationship."

"I am more than my dick, I'll have you know," Blayne mock complained as he spun around in Ethan's arms.

"True, you're a big-ass dick...and it's all mine." Blayne was taken aback when Ethan fell to his knees and took all of him into his mouth. Blayne leaned back against the sink, the cool marble feeling chilly against his ass. He looked straight into Ethan's eyes as he started trying to take more and more of Blayne down his throat. Blayne's dick was big and challenging for even the most talented cocksuckers. Still, he appreciated the sheer amount of will and effort Ethan made as he tried to relax his throat and take more of Blayne.

Blayne leaned over and pulled on Ethan's chin, bringing their mouths together. He then repositioned Ethan so his legs were fully on the memory foam bathmat in front of the sink. This served two purposes. It took some of the pressure off Ethan's knees. Blayne knew from experience that having your knees on that tiled floor was not fun. It also meant Blayne could watch himself in the mirror as he entered Ethan. He reached his hand farthest from the mirror and gently placed it on the back of Ethan's head as he lifted the other hand over his head, grabbing the back of his neck with his hand. This way, the entire side of his body was opened up to the mirror, and he could watch as Ethan took his dick as far as he could and fisted the rest of him. Blayne let his eyes slip between staring at himself in the mirror and looking down at Ethan, who was not stroking himself as he sucked on him.

"Fuck, I'm getting close," Blayne said and tried to pull back from Ethan. Ethan wrapped his arms around tighter and wasn't about to let go. Blayne took the hint and sped up the face fucking of Ethan until Blayne exploded down his throat. He pumped out squirt over squirt and audibly heard Ethan as he swallowed it all. When the last spasm erupted from him, his whole body shuddered. "Whoa, I didn't even realize I needed that," Blayne said as he reached down and helped Ethan up, then kissed him.

"Hmm…" Ethan said. "The mix tastes of toothpaste and cum." Blayne shook his head and laughed. "Now I need to brush my teeth and gargle with mouthwash."

While Blayne got the shower ready, Ethan brushed his teeth.

Ethan

The impromptu blowjob hadn't been planned, but it had been amazing. Feeling Blayne erupt down his throat after everything today just felt right. Ethan finished brushing his teeth and gargled with mouthwash. Blayne was already in the shower. At some point, Blayne had finally gotten out of his tube socks. They were folded in half and sitting on top of the toilet.

Ethan walked over to the shower and slid inside behind Blayne. When Ethan entered, Blayne was rinsing the shampoo out of his hair, so he didn't open his eyes. The sight of Blayne's long body under the flow of the stream of hot water caused Ethan to stiffen. He should have finished jerking off while blowing Blayne, but he didn't want to get cum on the bath rug. *Does cum even come out of memory foam?* Blayne finally finished rinsing his hair and said, "Someone's happy to see me."

"You know him," Ethan said. "He has a mind of his own."

Blayne reached out and pulled Ethan into the streaming water. Blayne lowered his mouth to Ethan's. They let their lips touch, then they slipped their tongues in and out of each other's mouths, exchanging their fresh minty breaths. Blayne started showering Ethan with kisses. Ethan let his head dip back out of the water as Blayne kissed the side of his neck. Blayne lowered himself to Ethan's nipples and started nibbling on them gently. Ethan looked down and noticed Blayne was already getting hard again, so Ethan reached out and started stroking Blayne's cock with his hand.

"I want to feel you in me," Blayne whispered into his ear. Blayne spun around in the shower, and leaned against the front wall, just underneath the shower head, showing Ethan where he wanted to be entered.

Ethan didn't need to be told twice. The couple had regularly enjoyed shower sex, so they had the routine down. Blayne handed the bottle of silicone-based lube they kept in the shower caddy next to the shampoo, conditioner and body wash. Ethan put some lube on his hand and pumped it over his dick before taking some of that lube and smearing it down Blayne's crack. To help, Ethan took one of his fingers and worked it into Blayne's hole. He wrapped his other arm around Blayne's midsection. Blayne let out a sharp breath as Ethan's knuckle entered — one knuckle, then two, one finger, then two. All the while, he showered Blayne's back with tiny kisses.

"I need you…" Blayne whispered.

Ethan angled his cock and slowly inserted himself into Blayne. He didn't push forward, he let Blayne back himself onto Ethan. A moan escaped Ethan's mouth when Blayne's firm ass hit his pelvis. He left his dick to sit inside Blayne for a second as he adjusted to him. Ethan then slowly withdrew his dick about three-fourths of the way before sliding himself back into Blayne. Blayne groaned his encouragement, so Ethan picked up speed. Soon, Ethan's speed of entering and exiting Blayne's ass was matched by Blayne's speed on his own cock as he jerked himself off. Ethan was going to have none of that. "Let me," he whispered as he exchanged Blayne's hand for his own. Blayne leaned his now-free arm against the wall and let his head rest there as Ethan edged closer to climax.

Ethan heard a short whimper from Blayne seconds before he ejaculated, coating the wall of the shower with his cum. Blayne's cum mixed with the shower water, swirled around their feet and went down the drain. "I love you," Ethan whispered as he erupted inside Blayne. Blayne moaned. Ethan felt his cum mix with the lubrication inside Blayne as Ethan's cock spasmed with each new release. When he was finally spent, he pulled out slowly then they finished showering.

They were toweled off, lounging around in house clothes and exited the bedroom with guilty looks as they headed into the living room.

* * * *

Blayne

Kira sat on the couch eating Chinese. "I stopped waiting," she said as she eyed them. She picked up the remote and muted the television. "Dear God, you look like puppy dogs expecting to get scolded. You fucked in the shower. No biggie."

Ethan looked at her, "How'd you—?"

"Please, half the apartment building heard that brief bout of lovemaking. I was half expecting the police to show up because of a noise complaint."

"We were *not* that loud," Blayne said. Then he thought about it. "Were we?"

Kira chuckled. "No. And honestly, until I saw the looks on your faces, I wasn't even sure if that's what you two were doing. I know one thing, though. You were *not* conserving water."

Blayne shook his head. "Bitch!"

"Are you just now realizing that?" Kira responded, shoveling some lo mein into her mouth.

"I'm starved," Ethan said.

"It's in the oven waiting for you," Kira said, gesturing toward the kitchen with her now-empty fork. "Hope you two worked up an appetite. I may have ordered enough to feed an army. The way things have been going around this apartment lately, I didn't know how many people to expect."

Blayne headed to the kitchen. He filled his plate and went to sit at the table next to Ethan, who had already bitten into an egg roll.

"What were you watching?" Blayne asked.

"Nothing," Kira said as she clicked off the television.

Blayne looked at her, narrowed his eyes, and said, "Kira, don't. Don't think you're protecting me. Just tell me."

"Are you sure?" she asked. Blayne nodded, so she turned the television back on.

The first thing on the screen was the flashy headline that read '*The Pennington Massacre*', images from that afternoon with what sounded like stock horror movie audio filled the screen.

"Are you fucking kidding me?" Blayne said. "It was bad enough being there live. Did they have to add the extra theatrics?"

"It's RTN," Ethan said as he speared a piece of shrimp into his mouth. "Of course, they must make it more dramatic. It's what they do."

"Tonight, we have a special edition of *In Touch with America*, hosted by Tom Dulce," an announcer said. Tom Dulce filled the screen. He was sitting outside. Heater lamps were placed around Dulce and his guests, who were lit in the night sky.

"Good evening, America," Tom said. *"I'm Tom Dulce. Tonight, I stand before you with a heavy heart, for we find ourselves confronted with a story touching the depths of our collective soul. Over the next hour, we will delve into the tragic events unfolding this afternoon on this campus. The tragic events of the Pennington Massacre have left scars on this campus, the city and the conscience of our nation."*

"Oh dear God," Ethan said. "Could he be more melodramatic?"

"Faced with darkness, we have witnessed the indomitable spirit of humanity. Over the next hour, we will remember the lost lives and celebrate the heroes who put their lives in harm's way to stop this massacre from becoming much worse. Even amid sorrow, we must find solace in our collective humanity. Tonight, we start the long road of drawing strength from our shared experiences and our collective determination to heal and rebuild."

"Wow," Ethan said. "He makes it sound like he was there."

"How did they even get him to Houston this fast?" Blayne asked.

"Oh, he said that in the previous show, which was all about the arena."

"Wait! This is the second show of the evening?" Blayne asked incredulously.

"Of course, it is. You know the old saying, 'if it bleeds, it leads' — and RTN got a twofer with this."

"*I now turn it over to Stephen McNeil.*" The camera feed changed to the internal studio of an RTN affiliate in Houston, the city's skyline visible behind McNeil.

"*Thank you, Tom. With me in the studio tonight is one of the brave souls who witnessed the tragedy at Pennington University today firsthand. The camera zoomed out, and a shot of a blonde woman sitting beside Stephen filled the screen. "Emma, how are you feeling?*" The name '*Emma Davis, Pennington University Student*' scrolled across the screen.

"She's one of my students," Blayne said.

"Isn't she the influencer?" Ethan asked.

"That's her."

"*Emma,*" Stephen began, his voice rich and soothing, "*you were in the right place at the right time to capture something few could have imagined. Tell us about today.*"

"*Well,*" Emma began, her voice shaky but quickly growing confident. "*I was taking selfies and live streaming from the rally, you know. Then, well…everything just happened.*"

"Where were you when it all started?" McNeil asked.

Emma spent a few minutes talking about how she had run, where she'd hidden and how she'd watched someone die right before her. RTN played the footage.

"That's disgusting," Kira said. "They didn't even bother to blur anything."

Blayne looked at Ethan. Neither of them needed a reminder of what the carnage had looked like at the rally.

"*Then what happened?*"

"*I figured out where the guy in the belltower was with the gun, so I started live streaming that. I hoped the police could use the footage as evidence,*" Emma said.

"More like she was hoping to get more views," Blayne said under his breath. Ethan shot Blane a look. "She's a nice enough young woman, but the whole 'influencer' thing is going to her head."

"*Then there was this scream, and a man plummeted from the tower. I was in total shock. I almost didn't look up to find Blayne Dickenson, one of my English professors, peering out of the campus bell tower at the body below.*"

The camera zoomed in on McNeil. "*RTN can confirm exclusively that Blayne Dickenson, a graduate teaching assistant at Pennington University, is being credited with single-handedly stopping the massacre. This young man*" — a closeup of Blayne in the tower filled the screen—"*is an American hero.*"

Blayne groaned, putting the heels of his hands into his eyes, hoping the pressure would make the television screen go away.

"*And more than that, he's a* gay *American hero.*"

That caught Blayne's attention, making him quickly look back at the screen.

The video shifted to the aftermath. There was chaos and panic, but amid it all, Blayne was sitting outside the tower on the ground, comforted by Ethan as they kissed.

"*Yes, America. The other man in the video is Ethan Bond from the boy band ZERO. According to other eyewitnesses, all four members of ZERO attended the rally.*"

Blayne stared at the screen as he watched the intimate moment between him and Ethan that was captured on film play for the world to see. It didn't take a genius to see they were in a relationship.

"*This footage is incredible, Emma,*" Stephen said. "*You've captured a shocking tragedy and a touching love story, all in one. The world thanks you for sharing.*" McNeil turned back to the screen. "*Tom, there you have it. We have a real gay American hero and his boy-band boyfriend.*"

The screen turned back to Tom, who now had several faces Blayne recognized from campus, but he didn't care what they had to say. He turned to Ethan to see how he was doing.

"Well," Ethan said, "that just happened. *Fuck.*"

Chapter Twenty

Dr. Hennigan

She sat in her mother's personal quarters, making the meeting almost a private family affair. Five women sat in the room. All looked like they could be having tea with the king and queen of England. Naturally, the thirteenth-century silver tea set on the seventeenth-century coffee table, once part of a lady's sitting room in the Palace of Versailles, added to the ambiance.

Dr. Hennigan looked at her grandmother, who was sipping tea. Hennigan remembered her first tea-drinking lesson.

"*You hold the cup and saucer at your waist,*" the instructor had told her. "*You raise the cup to your lips. First, you inhale the scent of the tea, then you can take a sip. Let it sit for just a second before you swallow. Last, you exhale through the mouth as you set the cup back on the saucer.*" Of course, you kept your knees together and crossed your legs at the ankles. There were so many etiquette rules. Dr. Hennigan did not know how many of these little tea parties she'd be forced to endure in her lifetime.

"How did this happen?" Sara Hennigan finally asked. The matriarch of the family and Chair of the Foundation was visibly composed. Still, Dr. Hennigan could tell her grandmother was seething just below the surface.

Deborah, Dr. Hennigan's mother, arched an eyebrow in her direction. Anytime she was forced into one of these meetings, she felt like a little girl being scolded. The only difference now was that she had Ms. Wilson and, oddly enough, Ms. Brighton at her side.

"Well, Grandmother." Dr. Hennigan paused as she put her thoughts together.

"Spit it out, Phillipa," Sara said. "I do not have all day. I have a busy schedule."

Dr. Hennigan took a deep breath, maintaining her smile. "Grandmother, the story begins approximately twenty years ago. An agent was deemed inappropriate after training, and the decision to liquidate our losses and move on was made."

"Yes, yes," Sara said with a dismissive wave. "This is the part I already know. What *don't* I know?"

"Cleo Barnes and I escorted Elizabeth Cleburne to an old facility in rural Appalachia where she was disposed of and buried. And that was the last we ever heard of her until this week."

"And we're sure it's really this ghost back from the grave?" Deborah asked.

"Yes, Mother. Ms. Wilson confirmed the facial recognition when our systems were restored," Dr. Hennigan said, gesturing to Ms. Wilson to take her turn.

282

"Although Operative Cleburne has had some cosmetic work done over the years and now has a bad red dye job, the basic biometrics identified her with over a ninety-nine percent certainty."

"How did this happen?" Sara said a little louder.

"We don't know, Mother," Deborah said. "I know you want to blame someone here, but we don't know. The operation to liquidate Operative Cleburne was textbook."

"Three shots, center back with the body dumped in a shallow grave," Dr. Hennigan said.

"As strange as it is," Ms. Brighton said, ignoring the standard protocol for these interactions, "we all know of cases where people survive being shot multiple times, even when they shouldn't. I could list the documented cases from the medical literature, but that wouldn't get us any closer to dealing with the more urgent problem."

"Which is?" Sara said, turning her focus on Ms. Brighton.

"What does she want? And more important, what will she do now? Her ruse is up, and her husband is dead. I think she's more dangerous now than ever."

"I share the same fear," Sara said, placing her tea on the table. "Threat assessment?" This time, Sarah turned to Ms. Wilson.

"We've already put all our facilities on high alert. However, we don't think she has more than eight to ten radicalized followers now."

"On what intelligence is this based?" Deborah asked.

"Dr. Hennigan and Ms. Brighton interviewed the three remaining infiltrators to gain any actionable information."

"And?" Sara asked, turning her attention back to her granddaughter.

"Well, we raided the three other compounds we found out about this morning at six a.m. They were all empty. One was just southeast of Beaumont, TX, on the highway to Louisiana. That one looked like it had been the staging area for the assault yesterday. We suspect Lizzy Cleburne fled there after Pennington. From there, she has easy access to most of the South. Depending on her means, she could have access to almost anywhere in the world."

"Do we think she's still in the US?" Sara asked.

"We cannot be sure, but she seems set on vengeance, so the odds are pretty good that she's in the US and preparing for what she'll do next."

"What do you think she'll do?" Sara asked, staring Ms. Wilson down.

"I do not know, ma'am. We've run several scenarios, and the probability of each is unfortunately similar."

"Cleo Barnes," Dr. Hennigan said. "She'll go after Cleo Barnes." Dr. Hennigan paused until everyone was focused on her. "Cleo was the operative tasked with liquidating her. She seems the most likely target."

"Or her husband," Sara replied. "Killing the President would definitely put a fissure between our organization and the federal government at a time when watchdogs are on the hunt."

"True," Deborah chimed in. "If someone wanted to harm The Foundation, attacking the President and implicating us would do it."

"Until we get more actionable intelligence, I want all of you to pursue this line of inquiry," Sarah said, tapping the marble tabletop with one of her white French-manicured nails. "And, Phillipa?"

"Yes, Grandmother?"

"I think it's time for you and your team to take a trip to Washington, DC."

* * * *

Blayne

The following day Blayne dragged himself out of bed. Ethan had risen earlier and gone for a run. It was something he enjoyed doing whenever he needed to think or just burn off excess energy. Although both men ran, they rarely did it together. When Ethan returned to the apartment, Blayne had just gotten out of the shower and was making coffee.

"How was your run?" Blayne asked as Ethan came in.

"It was a fun game of dodge the paparazzi," he said. "Heads up. There are a few photogs camped across the street. I just smiled and waved. There was no point in pretending. One tried to follow me, but I went down an alley and lost him."

"Ugh. Not this game again," Blayne groused. He'd had enough paparazzi the previous month when he'd pretended to be Ethan to throw off their scent for the day.

"For their sake, I hope not. I seriously doubt our friends at The Foundation would let them, anyway." Ethan walked over and kissed Blayne on the cheek. "I need to run through the shower. The band will meet up at some point today. I already have texts from my publicist. And, of course, I'm avoiding messages from Lucas."

"Don't forget, we have therapy with Dr. Secada this morning."

"Ah shit, I totally forgot about that," Ethan admitted. "How dead would we be if we tried to cancel?"

"After yesterday? I would run to The Foundation to hide from Dr. Secada," Blayne joked. "Besides, we probably need to talk through some things."

"You make it sound so ominous," Ethan said as he pulled a mug from the cabinet and poured himself a cup.

"Aren't you supposed to hydrate after a run?" Blayne said, raising a questioning eyebrow.

"Yes, Mother. But isn't coffee a liquid? That counts as hydration."

Blayne didn't contradict Ethan, because he knew his boyfriend was pushing his buttons. Besides, Blayne hadn't had enough coffee yet to deal with any of Ethan's jokes.

"Go. Shower," Blayne said, pointing toward the bedroom. "We'll run by the Dream Bean for breakfast."

"Sure thing, Mr. Bossy," Ethan said as he turned and headed to the bedroom.

"And you like it when I'm bossy," Blayne called after him.

Blayne sat down at the table and picked up his cell phone. He'd avoided looking at his messages last night because there would be a flurry of texts. Sure enough, he had texts from friends he hadn't talked to in years. He had a text from Dr. Reich he responded to immediately.

Ethan and I are fine. I'm glad you and Jamie weren't at the rally yesterday. Talk soon.

Next, he read a text from Jamie Reich.

Saw your coming out video! Congratulations. Next time, don't cry… It ages you.

Blayne laughed and shook his head. He thought about it for a second and responded.

Cheeky. You're just jealous because I'm dating the hottest member of ZERO.

Almost immediately, his cell phone signaled a response from Jamie.

When did you start dating Orr?

Blayne laughed. He finally wrote back.

Shouldn't you be learning right now? Your mother will kill you if you have your phone confiscated in class again.

This time, he didn't get a response from Jamie. He scrolled through the rest of his messages. Of course, the one he was surprised he didn't see was from his parents. Blayne loved his parents, but they had made it clear that they disapproved of his 'lifestyle'. Unfortunately, that put a lot of strain on their relationship.

Then he pulled up his email. "Holy fuck," Blayne said as he scrolled through his inbox. "Geez, Louise."

"What's up, babe?" Ethan said, coming back into the kitchen.

"I have a ton of emails." Blayne started scrolling through, just looking at the subject lines. "It looks like I have everything from '*thanks for saving our lives*' to '*die, you satanic abomination.*' People sure say the nicest things."

"Unfortunately, you're going to be in the spotlight now," Ethan said. "We kept you out of it last time, but you'll be the hero of the hour. People will come out of the woodwork...both good and bad."

"Combine that with our relationship going public, and we're going to have a lot of scrutiny."

"I'm just hoping people will think of me as *your* boyfriend, and you can take the pressure off me. I won't be Ethan Bond, an international singing sensation—just that hero's hot boyfriend." Ethan threw his arms around Blayne's neck and kissed him on the cheek. "So, my superhero, ready to go face the day?"

"Superhero?" Blayne said as he wrinkled his forehead. "Do I look faster than a bullet or like I can leap tall buildings? I think not. I'm just an above-average gay sex God with a giant dick."

"And that's exactly what you should say anytime someone thrusts a microphone in your face?"

"I'll put something in your face," Blayne quipped as he pushed himself up from the kitchen table.

"We don't have time for that now," Ethan replied with a wink. "But I'm sure I can help you with that later."

Ethan

Ethan was doing his best to hold it together for Blayne. Maintaining his cheerful facade after his run wasn't easy. Ethan had been up early because he hadn't really slept. Every time he had closed his eyes, he had seen the faces of the people shot in front of him the day before. Those faces had been combined with Danny and everyone who had died on the Peregrine flight. Ethan had begun to worry that he was a death magnet.

He had gone for a run because it was one of the rare moments when he wasn't performing or being intimate that he could focus on his body moving. He could concentrate on each pound of his shoe against the pavement and each breath he took. If any of those other thoughts crept inside his head, he just ran faster. He almost wished he could just run away from himself, but he couldn't.

After the shower, he plastered on his happy face, walked into the kitchen and found Blayne engrossed in his phone. They'd joked about Blayne's newfound celebrity and had tossed out a few sexual innuendos, but Ethan turned serious for just a second.

"People often think they're ready for the spotlight, ready for celebrity, but no one is. Well, no one sane is," Ethan said. "Just don't become one of those people who craves it. If you ever desire a camera shoved in your face, step back. Reevaluate who you are and what you want to be."

Blayne looked at him, his laughter fading as he took in Ethan's words. *Did I just cross a line?* The silence felt heavy.

"Ethan…" Blayne began, his phone abandoned on the table as he rose, walked over to Ethan and wrapped him in his arms again. "I appreciate your concern. Really, I do." Blayne stared into Ethan's eyes, and his voice softened. "But you don't have to worry about me. I don't want fame. I have no desire to be in the limelight. And if a few people want to snap a photo of me for the next week, let them. I will not let this change me. My goal in life hasn't changed. I want to finish my doctorate and find a nice teaching job somewhere. If, by some miracle, I use whatever this is to help me do that, great. If I become a nobody tomorrow, that's great, too. I'm *your* someone to fall back on."

A wave of relief swept over Ethan. He held Blayne's gaze, the corners of his mouth tugging upward into a small smile. "Promise me, Blayne," he implored in a low and steady voice. "Promise me you'll remember who you are and what truly matters, no matter how crazy this gets."

"I promise, Ethan." Blayne's smile was genuine, comforting. "We'll be a front-page story for maybe two days. Then, something else will happen, and all this will blow over—because we're not that interesting."

Ethan looked at Blayne, assured that no matter how chaotic things might get, they would tackle it together. They were in this together. And, for the first time in a long time, Ethan didn't feel the urge to run.

* * * *

Blayne

The walk to campus had been a bit more eventful than Blayne had expected. Sure enough, there were paparazzi outside the apartment. The Dream Bean was surrounded by paparazzi. Blayne felt like he had more photographs taken on his way to school that morning than his mother had taken of him on the first day of kindergarten—and that women had documented everything. Once they got to campus, the paparazzi at least seemed to stay back. When Blayne led Ethan to the Felix Tijerina Student Union Building, he was glad not to have a camera pointed at his back. He let out an audible breath as the door closed behind them.

"Is it always like this?" Blayne asked.

"And you wonder why I wear oversized clothes, a baseball cap and sunglasses that cover half my face."

Blayne looked around the student union and noticed pockets of students were doing their best not to stare. Ethan reached out and grabbed Blayne's hand.

"Thanks," Blayne said. "I'm not used to being the center of attention. Well, outside of my classroom."

"Yeah, it's weird. You won't get used to it. You learn to live with it. Most people are just curious."

"I hadn't fully realized this is your everyday life," Blayne said.

"I've done my best to shield you from most of this over the past month."

"Well, you spent most of your time rehearsing or at my place. We weren't exactly hanging out in public that often," Blayne said as he started walking through the building toward Dr. Secada's office.

"True, but when we went out in public, people weren't looking for us, either. And no offense, big boy," Ethan said, "but you're not exactly inconspicuous."

"Would hunching help?" Blayne tried to hunch over and shorten his stride.

Ethan laughed. "Please, don't. That makes it worse."

They got to the door of the counseling center and knocked. The secretary let them into the office a moment later and told them Dr. Secada was wrapping up a meeting and was on her way. The secretary did her best not to stare at them. Finally, she looked at them and said, "I know this is so inappropriate, but can I take a quick selfie with you? My grandson is gay and fourteen. He's a huge fan," she said to Ethan, then turned to Blayne. "And after what you did yesterday…

saving all those lives. It's incredible that he has role models like you." The woman teared up.

Blayne was about to say something when Ethan gently squeezed his hand. "Quick, we better do this before Dr. Secada gets here," Ethan said with a sly smile. The woman came out from behind her desk, and Blayne and Ethan stood. Blayne crouched as much as he could to get in the picture. "Say cheese," the woman said as she snapped the picture. "Thank you. You don't know how much this will mean to him. He's always been bullied. And we tell him it gets better, but it's hard for him to believe that at his age."

Blayne smiled, not sure what to say. He wanted to have some piece of wisdom to impart to the woman, but all he could do was smile politely. The woman pulled a tissue from a box on her desk and dabbed at it. Blayne had seen the woman several times over the past month but had never really talked to her.

"Well, he's already texted me back," she said. She turned the phone to see a teenager waving at the phone with a giant smile. "You totally just made his day."

"Who made whose day?" Secada said as she walked into the office.

"We're here to make your day," Ethan said quickly as the woman put away her phone. Secada knew Ethan was lying, but she said, "Why don't you two come on back?"

Blayne and Ethan stood and followed Dr. Secada through the hall and into her office. She opened the door and pointed to the couch. "Take a seat. Just give me a second." Blayne slipped out of his jacket and laid it over the back of the couch. Ethan did the same thing before sitting down. Secada hung her coat and scarf behind the door before setting her briefcase beside her desk. She grabbed a yellow legal pad and pen and came and sat down in the chair opposite the couch. She crossed her legs, put the legal pad in her lap and readied her pen before asking, "So, what's been going on in your lives?"

Blayne glanced at Ethan as a laugh bubbled up with him, leading to a string of giggles that shook his entire frame. He could barely keep himself upright. His body convulsed with the force of his laughter. From the corner of Blayne's eye, Ethan stared at him in shock before a deep, hearty laugh escaped Ethan. Their laughter echoed around them. They tried to stop, but that led to another round of laughter. Gradually, they gasped in gulps of much-needed air, the laughter dying down.

"That good?" Dr. Secada said.

"Oh, you know," Blayne said, "just an average week." Ethan tried not to laugh again, but his shoulders kept shaking, causing the whole couch to vibrate.

Once Ethan was back under control, Dr. Secada looked at them and asked, "How did that feel?"

"Amazing," Blayne admitted.

"God, I needed that," Ethan agreed.

"Everything has just been…well, insane," Blayne admitted. "I'm sorry. I know we're not supposed to use that word anymore since it's inherently ableist. And the last thing I want to do is make light of mental health, but I don't know how else to describe this week."

"What do you know?" Ethan asked.

"I know more than you think I do — and probably less at the same time. So, let's pretend I know nothing for the sake of this conversation. Let's start there."

So, they did. Thankfully, the client immediately after Blayne and Ethan had canceled, so they had a two-hour conversation that covered the previous week. They left out the parts they weren't sure they could share, but they included enough that Dr. Secada got a pretty good idea of everything that had happened.

"I'd heard a rumor through an FBI contact, who isn't Agent Murphy, that civilian assets were involved in the intelligence aspects of this case. I'm guessing you're those assets from what you just told me," Dr. Secada said matter-of-factly.

"That would be us," Blayne said.

"And you really performed surgery on someone on your kitchen table?"

Blayne thought he'd glossed over that part of the story, but apparently, Dr. Secada had latched onto that little detail. "We just assisted," Blayne said.

"I donated blood," Ethan added.

"And all this led to yesterday?"

"It's been a crazy week."

"Now, Blayne, did you notice you ran *toward* danger every time something happened this week?"

Blayne considered it for a moment. "I did, didn't I?"

"Why?"

Blayne sat there momentarily before saying, "I wanted to be strong for Ethan."

"Honey," Ethan said, turning to look at Blayne, "you are strong enough. You're one of the strongest men I know."

"But I ran. You had a gun to your head, and I ran." The words were out of Blayne before he even had them formulated in his brain.

"No," Ethan said. He reached up, grabbed Blayne's chin and turned it to look at him. "I told you to run."

"You were helpless on the ground because I tripped you — and I ran."

"Guns were going off all around us. You stumbled, and I tried to help you. I took a nosedive because I tried to steady you when you didn't need it. So, yes, I told you to run."

"How long have you been holding on to that?" Dr. Secada asked.

"I don't even know if I was aware I'd been holding that one in," Blayne admitted. "In retrospect, I feel like everything I did this week was to somehow make up for leaving Ethan on the ground when he needed me most."

"And I didn't want you to get involved in any of this, because I feel responsible for turning your life upside down. If you hadn't met me…" Ethan let the words hang in the air.

"I don't want to be the person I was before I knew you," Blayne said. "Sure, our lives have not been exactly conventional, but I only think I could have gotten through this because I've had you at my side."

"Well, I'm not going anywhere," Ethan said plainly.

"Good, because I don't want you to go anywhere." Blayne looked Ethan in the eyes and said, "You're stuck with me, Ethan Bond."

"No, you're stuck with me, Blayne Dickenson."

There was a moment when Blayne wanted to grab Ethan in his arms and do all kinds of unsavory things with him on the couch. The sight of Dr. Secada brought him back to reality.

"And what about you, Mr. Bond?"

"What about me?" Ethan asked.

"In previous sessions, you'd admitted you were scared to death of being outed. How are you doing after last night?"

"I had a sniper trying to blow my brains out yesterday. A viral video showing me making out with the man who stopped that from happening just doesn't seem as important today."

Dr. Secada raised an eyebrow at Ethan. Blayne squeezed Ethan's hand as the room filled with silence.

"Okay," Ethan said, a little exasperated. "It still hasn't hit me yet."

"Have you heard from your parents?"

"Maybe..."

Dr. Secada cocked her head to the side. She didn't ask a question, but the question was heard.

"Okay, I haven't even looked at my cell phone today. I'm unsure if I'm ready to deal with that drama yet."

"Drama?"

"My family. The ZERO team. My fans. The *drama*!"

"Well, ZERO is gonna be cool about it. They've known," Blayne said.

"The guys have known. But Hightower and Rawlins, not to mention everyone else...?"

Blayne let out a sigh. "They've known. I know they've known. Everyone has talked about it. They just haven't talked about it with you."

"How do you know?" Ethan asked, almost a little defensive.

"How do you think I know?" Blayne asked back.

Blayne and Ethan answered at the same time, "Ric."

"He can't keep his mouth shut," Blayne admitted.

"He never could," Ethan agreed.

"I know you've been worried about coming out to them, but they've always been your biggest support team, and they will continue to be."

"What's the worst that could happen?" Dr. Secada asked.

"I could lose my job, my livelihood."

"And I would beat them up. Remember, I'm *'a real gay American hero'* and you're just my *'boy-band boyfriend.'* I'll protect you."

Ethan stared at Blayne and couldn't help but smile.

"I'm missing something," Dr. Secada said.

"Last night on television, RTN had a special about what happened yesterday. Stephen McNeil used those words to describe us. I knew you wouldn't let me forget them," Ethan said with a playful pout.

"Never. I will have those words etched on our tombstone when we are old and gone. *'Here lies the gay American hero and his boy-band boyfriend.'*"

Ethan

Ethan didn't know much about therapy, but he believed they had made progress during their two-hour marathon session with Dr. Secada.

"When do we need to see you again?" Ethan asked as he stood from the couch at the end of the session.

"Anytime you need me, I'm here for you. The FBI understands that victim trauma comes in waves. You may feel excellent today and have a setback tomorrow. Let's face it. If we had talked yesterday, I would have showed up at your house today, knowing what had happened. I'm not going anywhere. But do we need to see each other every week? Probably not. But I'm still available if you need me."

"And we promise to come to see you if we do," Blayne said as he reached down and picked up his coat from the couch. Blayne then grabbed Ethan's and helped him into it without asking.

Dr. Secada opened the door to her office and started walking down the hallway toward the small reception area in the front.

"Agent Murphy?" Secada said. "Well, this is a surprise."

Ethan pulled up behind Dr. Secada, and there was another person in the office he hadn't expected to see. "Mr. J., what are you two doing here?"

"How did you get to campus this morning?" Mr. J. asked.

"We walked," Ethan said. Ethan looked at Mr. J.'s face as it tightened into a stern grimace, as deep-set frown lines creased further into a scowl.

"You probably shouldn't tell him you went for a jog this morning," Blayne said. Mr. J.'s sharp, hawk-like eyes, flashing with frustration, narrowed even farther.

"Thanks, Blayne," Ethan said sarcastically. "You're the kid who used to tell on the other kids in class."

"Pretty much."

"How can I keep you safe when you keep doing stuff like that?" Mr. J. said in a low growl.

"Whoa," Ethan said, holding up his hand. "I do this stuff all the time. What's happened?"

"There's been a credible threat against your lives," Agent Murphy said.

"Just tell them straight," Dr. Secada offered. "It's best to just be honest with them." She turned to Mr. J. and said, "I'm Dr. Esperanza Secada. I've worked with the Veterans Administration treating post-traumatic stress disorder before I came to work here at Pennington. I still see clients on the VA side, so I maintain my security clearance. When Agent Murphy sought someone local to work with Blayne and Ethan, she connected with me."

"It's nice to meet you, Doctor," Mr. J. said, extending his hand. "I'm Jameson Johnson, head of ZERO's security. Not that I can head their security when I don't know what's happening."

"Ex-Marine?" Dr. Secada asked.

"Something like that. Been mostly in private security for a couple of decades now."

"So, what exactly is this threat?" Dr. Secada asked.

"We picked up chatter last night. The ringleader of the organization that planned the attack last night escaped. She vowed vengeance against the man who killed her husband and, by extension, also threatened Ethan."

"What did she really say?" Ethan asked.

"She said she wanted to kill the murderous pervert and his homosexual lover," Murphy said. "We're taking this threat seriously. This woman is clearly unhinged, and we think losing her husband may be the tipping point. She's going to do something — "

"Which is why we don't want either of you going anywhere without a security detail," Mr. J. added.

"I can't exactly have a security detail around while I'm teaching," Blayne said. "It would be awkward. Besides, how would I explain that to my students?"

Murphy turned and looked at Blayne. Ethan looked at Murphy's face and didn't like what he saw there. There was a look of sadness and pity. "Unfortunately, I've been in meetings with Pennington University officials today, and they ask you to take a leave of absence. You'll be paid for the rest of the semester, and you can continue your coursework, but you'll need to do it away from campus until this is straightened out."

"I won't take the leave," Blayne said, looking at Dr. Secada. "They can't do this, can they?"

"*Should* they be able to do this? No. *Can* they do this? Yes."

Murphy said, "They can bar anyone from the campus if that person is a perceived threat. And like it or not, *you're* a perceived threat."

"This is so fucked up," Blayne said.

"We'll get through this…together," Ethan said as he wrapped his arm around Blayne's hips.

Ethan's phone started buzzing. He pulled it out and saw it was from a two-o-two area code. "Does anyone know where the two-o-two area code is located?" Ethan asked.

"It's Washington, DC," Murphy said, her eyes taking on a serious look. "Answer it but put it on speaker."

Ethan did as he'd been told. "Hello?" he said, stretching out the word into a question.

"Please hold for the White House," a voice said.

A second later, a click came, and someone said, "Is this Ethan Bond?"

"Yes," Ethan said hesitantly.

"Hi, this Sepi Amin, the White House Chief of Staff. We've been trying to call both you and Mr. Blayne Dickenson. Do you know how we can get ahold of Mr. Dickenson?"

"He's here, beside me. You're on speakerphone."

"Perfect. Good afternoon, Mr. Bond and Mr. Dickenson. The President would like to award you both the Presidential Citizens Medal for your heroic action yesterday and last month. We are aware of the sacrifices you have made for our country. This award is a small token of the President's and your country's thanks. We'd like to get you to Washington, DC, for a ceremony in the Rose Garden."

"Uh-huh," was all Blayne got out of his mouth. Ethan looked at Blayne, who clearly didn't know what to think. Thankfully, Agent Murphy stepped in.

"Sepi, it's Special Agent Sarah Murphy. I'm with Blayne and Ethan right now. They're a little taken aback by the President's generous offer. Can we call you back later?"

"Hello, Agent Murphy. You sure seem to be everywhere these days," Sepi Amin replied. "That would be fine. Please have someone from Mr. Bond's and Mr. Dickenson's teams contact the First Lady's office to make the arrangements."

With that, Murphy motioned for Ethan to hang up the phone.

"Well," Ethan said, "that just happened."

Chapter Twenty-One

Blayne

It had been a while since Blayne had been on a plane, and he'd never flown first class. The Peregrine Airline crew had been top-notch. The flying time had been just over three hours. Besides having large, overstuffed chairs on the plane, the experience hadn't changed radically. He'd always imagined life in first class was a mysterious affair. Still, he honestly questioned whether the cost was worth it. The same drinks that were served in economy class were also served in first class. Since it was a short-haul flight by aviation standards, their snack choices resembled anything they could have picked up for a couple of bucks at one of the airport convenience stores.

The real first-class experience for Blayne was the handling of the band by the airline. From the moment they'd arrived at the airport, the band was swiftly ushered through back corridors to bypass the traditional boarding process. There was even a special TSA gate that celebrities and dignitaries went through. Blayne questioned whether the aim was to expedite their progression through the airport or to prevent them from obstructing the regular flow of other airline passengers.

"Have you ever been to DC?" Ethan asked.

Blayne had chosen a window seat and kept pointing out monuments from the air as they landed at Reagan International Airport. "I went on a field trip in middle school, but that trip was crazy fast. It was all about getting on a bus, getting off a bus, seeing a monument for two minutes, taking a picture and getting back on the bus. The only part I remember was meeting my congresswoman. She led us on the tour of the Capitol Building. She showed up for the photo-op, and one of her staffers led the tour. What about you?"

"My parents brought me when I was a kid, and we've been through here a few times over the years. But honestly, I haven't played tourist here since I was a youngster. If my parents didn't have a picture of me standing before the Lincoln Memorial, I wouldn't even know I'd been here."

"Speaking of memorials," Blayne said, "I can see the Washington Monument." Blayne stared at the white obelisk.

"Do you know it was almost not finished?" Ethan asked. Blayne gave him a questioning look. "It's true. The short and not nearly sordid version of the story is that construction started in the mid-1800s, and when it was something like one hundred and fifty feet tall, they ran out of money. The whole thing had been started from donations. When those ran dry, construction stopped. Then there was the Civil War, so nothing happened then. When they finally got funded again, they couldn't find the same marble, so the top part is a different color."

"And why do you know that?"

"I know things," Ethan said. Blayne cocked his head to the side, questioning Ethan. "I watched a documentary one night when I couldn't sleep."

The first bounce of the back wheels hitting the tarmac jolted them out of their conversation. The pilot hit the brakes hard and fast. Soon the plane was veering off the runway and taxiing toward their gate. The aircraft was parked in just a few minutes, and the group exited the plane.

A Peregrine representative met the group with a big smile as they hit the top of the jetway. "Welcome to Reagan International. If you'll follow me," the woman said. She turned and headed for a security door. Within a few seconds, the group was once again navigating through back passages. They were led out into a small car park area where three SUVs were lined up and ready to whisk the group away to their hotel.

The team had hired local drivers for their stay, hence, introductions were made before Blayne, Ethan, Hightower and Rawlins climbed into the back of an SUV. The men didn't talk as much as they hovered over their respective smartphones and conducted business as they left the area.

Blayne couldn't tear his gaze away from the windows. He shifted his head back and forth as he tried to watch everything whisking by. On the left, he read a sign for the Jefferson Memorial as they crossed a bridge and headed into the district. On every corner was a sign for a museum or historic landmark. While struggling to absorb everything zipping past, it felt like constant whiplash as he swiveled his focus from one side of the vehicle to the other. Up on the left, he could again see the Washington Monument. Then they pulled into the drop-off area of the Waldorf Astoria. The building looked like it should be in London, with its giant clock tower.

"Welcome to the Waldorf Astoria, Washington, DC," a valet said as he opened the door to the SUV. "Checking in?"

"Yes," Hightower said.

"Great. I'll gladly help you with your luggage," the valet responded.

"We have about twenty rooms, so you might need some assistance," Hightower replied.

"Of course, sir."

Blayne looked at the smile on the valet's face. In Blayne's mind, he envisioned an entire conversation concluding with the valet retorting, '*I think I know how to do my job*.'

Thankfully, the valet had a series of bellmen out there quickly, and their luggage was sorted onto various carts and sped away into the hotel.

"Is it always this complicated?" Blayne asked when they finally entered the hotel. Blayne couldn't help but take in the place's opulence, everything from the marble flooring to the giant glass ceiling overhead. "Wow, this place is beautiful."

"That it is," Ethan replied. "I always love staying here. Wait until you see the rooms."

The group waited while Rawlins and Hightower checked them into the hotel. A few minutes later, they returned and started handing out cards.

"Ethan and Blayne, you're staying in the Post Office Suite," Hightower said, handing them keys. "Everyone is free for the rest of the evening. Just make sure you're down here at nine a.m. tomorrow. We have the ceremony at the White House at eleven, but they want us there no later than nine-thirty."

On that note, the group headed to the elevators. Ethan took out his keycard and opened the door to the Post Office Suite. Their bags were already in the room. Blayne pulled out his phone and started sending pictures to Kira. Everything was just so over-the-top. He was living it up as a king. In fact, the one word Blayne could use to describe the suite was 'regal'. The Romanesque style of interior design, featuring cream-colored walls, royal-blue furnishings and gold accents, exuded elegance. "Wow," Blayne said, turning to Ethan. "I feel like royalty in here."

"Well, you are my prince, so I guess it's fitting," Ethan said.

"How big is this place?" Blayne asked, taking pictures of the large living area, dining table for eight, separate bedroom and enormous bathroom. "Geez! This bathroom is larger than my dorm room at Tech."

"This suite is larger than some people's houses," Ethan admitted. "I always love it and feel a little uncomfortable in these places. It's just so gaudy to me. You know, so over-the-top that I always question, 'Who actually lives like this?' Then I realize, I do. I don't think I'll ever be truly comfortable in a place like this."

Blayne walked over and enveloped Ethan in his arms before kissing the man. "Don't worry. I'll keep you grounded."

"Shall we try out that walk-in shower?" Ethan asked with a grin.

"Time to break in the Post Office Suite, *officially*," Blayne said in his best Detox Icunt impersonation.

* * * *

Ethan

Ethan was worn out after making love in the shower, then on the bed then on the dining table. He toweled off from his second shower of the afternoon.

"If we keep this up, we're going to need more towels," Blayne joked as he popped Ethan in the ass with his wet towel.

"Ouch!" Ethan yelped as he shot Blayne a glare. "Do that again, and you're not going near my ass for a week."

Blayne got a devilish smile and spun the towel as if he was going to flick it at Ethan's ass again before he broke out into laughter.

"I'm starved," Ethan said. "I think it's time to order room service."

"I can't believe we're in DC, and we're going to order room service. This city has amazing food options, and we're just too lazy to leave our bedroom."

"Not lazy, exhausted. Besides, the hotel restaurant is one of the best in the city. People clamor to get reservations downstairs, and we can have them just bring it to us. I call that a win."

Ethan walked over to the desk and found the leather folio containing the extensive room service menu. Blayne ordered the pan-seared Alaskan halibut, and Ethan ordered the half chicken, roasted. They also ordered the most expensive bottle of wine on the menu.

While they waited, Ethan pulled up his email and went through his business while Blayne lay on the bed reading a book he'd picked up at the airport that morning. A knock sounded on the door.

"Room service," a voice said.

Ethan approached the door and looked through the peephole. Someone standing in a Waldorf Astoria uniform with a cart topped with covered dishes waited on the other side of the door, so he opened it.

"Hello, Ethan," the woman said as she pushed the cart into the room.

"Richardson!" Immediately, two other women followed her into the suite.

"Nice digs," Denzili commented as she closed the door behind them.

"Sorry to intrude like this," Dr. Hennigan apologized, "but such is the nature of our lives."

"What are you doing here?" Blayne asked, entering the living area from the bedroom.

"Is that any way to greet an old friend?" Dr. Hennigan asked. Blayne stood there silently. "I'm joking. We have received intelligence about a credible threat against the White House. We've tried going through our usual channels but haven't been able to get through to anyone. And by happenstance, you're going to be there tomorrow."

"You've gotta be fucking kidding me," Ethan complained. "Can't we just have a nice day at the White House with no credible threats?"

"Yeah, we're over the whole 'credible threat' thing. It's beginning to feel like our lives are a credible threat," Blayne added.

"I take it this means you know about the threats against your lives?" Hennigan asked.

"Yep," Ethan replied. "And we haven't been able to sneeze without security immediately handing us a tissue."

"I'm actually surprised you got in here," Blayne admitted. "How did you get in here?"

"We paid the porter to let us deliver your meal. It wasn't that difficult," Richardson explained. "You two should be more careful about who you open your door for."

"That's good advice," Ethan said. "So, what is this threat?"

"We don't know," Dr. Hennigan admitted. "We just need you to let Cleo Barnes know something is happening. And, more importantly, we need you to give her my cell phone number and ask her — no, tell her — she needs to check in."

"And why would we do that?" Ethan asked.

"Because we're asking you nicely," Denzili said. "And you know we don't always do that."

"Denzili!" Dr. Hennigan chastised, throwing the woman a side glance. "We're afraid that Cleo Barnes, or her husband, is being targeted by the same woman who is targeting you."

"Why?" Blayne asked. "I mean besides the obvious, them being the President and First Lady and all."

"As you already know, Laura Lee Jackson, originally known as Elizabeth Cleburne, was liquidated. Somehow, she survived. The operative who performed the liquidation was Cleo Barnes."

"Holy fuck!" Blayne said.

"As you can see," Dr. Hennigan said, "our interests, your interests and the interests of the United States all align right now, which is why we need you to get a message to Cleo Barnes."

"Just as long as there are no earpieces this time," Blayne said. "I'm sorry. I couldn't take all the chatter last time."

"This is very simple and straightforward." Dr. Hennigan walked over to the desk in the room's corner. She grabbed the pen and pad of paper. She quickly wrote on some of the paper then ripped it off the pad before walking over and handing it to Ethan.

"This is my cell phone number…for now. Simply give it to Cleo and instruct her to call me. It's that straightforward."

"Uh-huh," Ethan responded skeptically. "No offense, but nothing involving you is ever that simple."

* * * *

Blayne

The SUVs pulled up to the east side of the White House, where they were quickly ushered past the security detail. Sepi Amin greeted them when they entered the East Wing of the White House lobby.

"Good morning," Amin said after everyone was cleared through security.

Unfortunately, the ZERO security team wasn't with them at the White House. However, Blayne figured they were about as safe and secure there as they would be anywhere else.

"If you'll follow me," Amin said. She led the group through the Garden room and down the East Colonnade. "To your right is the Family Theater. On those rare occasions when the President and First Lady get to kick back and watch a movie, this is where they do it." Up next was the Visitors Foyer. "I will hand you off to one of our interns, who will take you to the Palm Room. If you need anything, Clarissa can answer your questions or get you anything you need."

Amin didn't even wait for a goodbye. She entered the doors to the central part of the White House.

"Okay, if you'll follow me. We are currently standing in the Visitors Foyer, which is the entrance to the Executive Residence," Clarissa said as she opened the door and waited for the group to enter before she said, "The hall that we are now in is Center Hall. It connects the Visitor's Foyer with the Palm Room. On the right is the library, and on the left is the Vermeil Room, added to the White House in 1902 as a formal sitting room used by the First Lady. Next to it is the China Room, created by Woodrow Wilson's second wife, Edith, to house the ever-growing china collection. The china sets of each President, either state or from their personal family collection, are showcased in chronological order."

The young intern provided historical tidbits as she walked them down the center hall. They saw everything from the Map Room to the kitchen along the way. Finally, the woman opened a door and led them into the Palm Room. "Sorry to disappoint you if you were expecting palm trees," the intern joked as she ushered them in. "The Palm Room primarily gets its name from the conservatory look. There was a time during the Coolidge administration when the First Lady decorated the room with palms and even had a porch swing brought in here. Now, it's primarily the staging area for any events in the Rose Garden."

Blayne and Ethan walked around the little room before sitting between two giant potted ferns on a blue, rustic-looking bench.

"You ready for this?" Ethan asked. He reached up and straightened Blayne's tie before gently pressing down the pocket square on his chest.

"God, I hate ties," Blayne said. "I always feel like I have a noose around my neck."

After the invitation to the White House, Blayne and Ethan had gone shopping to find suits.

"Trust me... I don't feel comfortable in a suit and tie, either. But it's better than wearing a tuxedo or some clothes my stylist picks out for me. I'm constantly vetoing what they want me to wear."

"That sounds familiar," Blayne said with a smirk. "Only you're my personal stylist."

"And I've never steered you wrong," Ethan said. "We both look hot. We'll look amazing in all the photos. Who knows? Maybe we'll land a magazine cover or two."

Blayne looked to the left. He could see the reporters milling around in the Rose Garden through the glass doors.

"This is all still surreal," Blayne said. "I can't believe we're about to get medals from the President of the United States in a Rose Garden ceremony. None of this makes sense to me."

"Where are my heroes?" a chipper voice said, her voice reverberating off the marble floor. Blayne turned to see Cleo Barnes strolling into the Palm Room, followed by her husband.

Blayne immediately jumped to his feet and practically dragged Ethan with him as the First Lady approached. Much to Blayne's surprise, she dove right in for a hug and a kiss on each cheek.

"Let me introduce you to my husband, Jeffrey." Cleo looked around the room briefly and found that the President was talking to Sepi Amin. "Jeffrey!"

The President turned and looked at his wife. "Yes, dear?"

"I want you to meet the boys," Cleo said.

"They're young men, dear," Barnes said as he strolled over and extended his hand.

"It's…an honor, Mr. President," Blayne said as he shook the man's hand.

Ethan just looked starstruck as he shook the President's hand. "Thank you for having us," Ethan finally said.

"Thank you for being the heroic young men you've been," the President said.

"Mr. President," Amin interjected.

"If you'll excuse me," the President said before returning to his Chief of Staff.

"That's how it usually goes," Cleo admitted. "I'm amazed at how busy that woman keeps my husband. But she's been the captain of this ship, and I wouldn't have it any other way."

"Umm…" Ethan began, reaching into his pocket and pulling out a folded piece of paper. "We have a note from our mutual friend."

Cleo tilted her head slightly. She grabbed Ethan's hand. "Let's get some photos before we head into the Rose Garden." When she let go, the piece of paper was gone.

She dragged them over to the White House photographer, who started snapping shots of everyone.

"Sepi, how long do we have?" Cleo asked, once the round of pictures had been taken.

"You have about fifteen minutes."

"Perfect," Cleo said. "I'm going to show the boys — or rather, the young men — my favorite painting." She grabbed Blayne by one hand and Ethan by the other and dragged them to a door heading west. "Welcome to the West Wing," she said as they passed a couple of staffers. "We're walking through the Western Colonnade. You'll see the press offices on the right, and here's the Briefing Room. It's the one you see on TV all the time. And up ahead is the Cabinet Room. Let's look inside." She knocked and poked her head in. "Empty." She gestured for Blayne and Ethan to follow. She shut the door behind them, perched on the giant executive table in the room, and her facade immediately changed. "What did Phillipa tell you?"

"She's been trying to reach you through normal channels but hasn't gotten through to you in about forty-eight hours," Blayne explained.

"That worries me. That means someone at the White House switchboard has been messing with my calls for almost two days." Cleo strummed her nails against the wooden table as she looked distant for a second, deep in thought. "Any actionable intel?"

"Only that she's worried you're a target," Ethan said.

"I figured as much," Cleo admitted. "I've also seen the threat reports against you. How are you holding up?"

"As best as can be expected," Blayne admitted. "It's all been a whirlwind."

"I am sorry that civilians, such as yourselves, have gotten dragged into all this cloak-and-dagger shit. You're neither trained nor prepared for this life. I chose it. Dr. Hennigan sort of chose it."

"Are you two close?" Ethan asked.

"No one's really *that* close with Phillipa. Well, maybe Ms. Wilson, but I'm unsure about that. I don't know how Phillipa does what she does. She never had a choice. She was born into this life. I...I at least made decisions long ago that set me on this trajectory. I play the dutiful, albeit slightly ditzy wife for the press and keep the ship running behind closed doors."

"Does the President know about this?"

"Jeffrey? No, he's clueless. Probably the only one who has any suspicion is his Chief of Staff. She at least sees through the public veneer I've created." She reached over to a pad of paper and grabbed a pen off the table and scratched out something on the paper before handing it to Ethan. "Give this to Phillipa. It's my personal cell phone number. It's a secure line and not one controlled by the Secret Service."

"We'll pass it along when we see her," Ethan said, pocketing the slip of paper.

"Okay," Cleo declared, "let's start this show." Immediately, her relaxed posture stiffened, and the fake smile plastered as she pushed herself off the table, opened the Cabinet Room door and led them back down the hall.

Ethan

They walked back into the Palm Room. The Chief of Staff stood huddled in the corner with the President. Ethan wished he could be a fly on that wall. Cleo Barnes had the full hostess-with-the-mostest routine down as she flitted around the room, ensuring everyone was okay.

"The ceremony starts in five minutes," Sepi Amin said.

Cleo had returned to Blayne and Ethan and clapped her hands twice. "Excuse me. Before this starts, I just want to thank everyone for being here today." Suddenly, she tilted her head to the side and put on a confused look. "Something's missing."

The door to the West Wing opened. Ethan turned his head and almost fell over. In walked both of their best friends. Stephanie wore a navy dress, and Kira was clad in a burgundy business suit. Ethan heard himself squeal. He and Blayne ran to their friends and enveloped them in their arms.

"I thought you said you couldn't make it?" Blayne asked Kira. "Something about. '*I can't get time off work.*'"

"And you," Ethan said, looking at Stephanie. "Aren't you a sight for sore eyes? I've missed you."

"When did you get here? Where are you staying? How did you do this without us knowing?" The questions flew out of Ethan's mouth.

"You'll have plenty of time to talk after the ceremony," Cleo said.

"Thank you, Madam First Lady, your highness." The awkward words stumbled out of Stephanie's mouth like she realized who was standing in the room. She looked to the side and said, "Oh my God, it's the President!"

Jeffrey Barnes looked around the room and asked conspiratorially, "Where?" garnering a giggle fit from Stephanie.

"Jeffrey," Cleo said, swatting him on the shoulder, "play nice. He's been playing that game since he got elected. And please, just call me Cleo." Cleo extended her hands to the women.

"And I'm Jeffrey or Mr. President." He shook their hands as well.

There was something genuinely folksy about Jeffrey Barnes. Ethan had to remind himself that he hated the man's political stances on almost everything.

"Well, now that the entire party is here," Sepi Amin announced, "the White House press corps is waiting.

First, we'll take your family and friends out and seat them in the first row in front of the attending dignitaries. Once they're settled, the official ceremony will begin. Mr. President and Madam First Lady will walk out first. They'll wave. The President will walk to the podium to deliver his remarks. He will announce you to the press. You'll go out and wave. Don't forget to smile. Are we ready? Good." She nodded to the intern, who'd suddenly appeared.

Blayne's pocket vibrated. He was mortified. "I swear, I thought I turned that off," he said. He pulled it out. "*Sniper… Save the President.*"

"If you'll follow me," Clarice said, gesturing to the door. She reached out and opened it.

Blayne looked and saw that President Barnes was in the way of the open doorway. He took two steps, throwing his body at the President. Ethan wasn't sure what was happening. A potted plant in the back of the Palm Room exploded. Ethan threw himself at Cleo Barnes, throwing the First Lady to the ground and covering her with his body. There was a scream, then there was yelling. Hands started to yank him off the First Lady.

There was gunfire from somewhere. A brilliant, blinding light turned the world white. The shockwave followed. A thunderous boom shook the building, rattling windows in their frames. Ethan looked around, but the Palm Room seemed intact. The First Lady was huddled under his body, protecting her head. He yelled something into her ear, but he was unsure if she heard it.

He was pulled off the First Lady then shoved to the ground by the Secret Service. He turned his head to find Blayne being pulled off the President. Just outside,

Ethan glimpsed the Rose Garden. What had been a serene and picturesque garden seconds before had transformed into a maelstrom of chaos and confusion. Roses and other floral beauties were torn and thrown asunder by the blast. The people caught in the vicinity were on the ground, dazed and disoriented, their clothes dirtied and singed. Some scrambled to their feet, while others remained lying amid the ruined garden.

Ethan was yanked to his feet while Cleo Barnes yelled at a man in a black suit. "Get your hands off of them," her voice rang out. "Agent Malone, they just saved our lives."

Ethan was dragged from the room, the tips of his toes scraping the red carpet of the West Wing as they left the Palm Room. Everything happened so fast that he barely registered what was going on. He looked down at his suit and noticed that he'd lost the pocket square from his suit coat.

"Unhand them," Cleo Barnes yelled.

"How do you know they weren't involved in this attempt on yours and the President's lives?"

"I just do," Cleo screamed. Everyone was screaming. Ethan's ears rang, but his hearing was slowly coming back. He must not have been too close to the explosion. The agents dragging him let him get his feet beneath himself so he could stand on his own. Dazed, Ethan looked around the hall as people ran in a dozen directions.

"Ma'am, that's not good enough. Let's get them to a secure location and question them."

"I'm coming with you."

"You need to go with Chesapeake to PEOC."

"No, take them to the Cabinet Room. You can talk with them there."

"Fuck!" the agent said, before speaking into his wrist. "Chesapeake is heading to PEOC. Cumberland is staying in the West Wing. Has anyone contacted Patuxent's or Anacostia's details?"

"Delta is meeting Chesapeake in PEOC. The building is in lockdown," Ethan heard.

They were ushered to the end of the corridor. He looked to the right. The Press Secretary was already standing behind the podium, briefing the public. A door opened, and Ethan was shoved into a chair, his hands handcuffed behind his back. Across from him, a disheveled Blayne was pushed down in a chair. Two guards hovered over them. He looked and noticed that Cleo and the one agent hadn't entered the room with them. They sat there like that.

"Are you — ?" Blayne tried to ask.

"No talking," the agent next to him said.

Ethan mouthed, "I'm okay."

At least an hour passed before a man in a black suit with silver hair entered the room, followed by Cleo Barnes. The man sat at the end of the table. Cleo positioned herself against the wall behind Ethan. The man said nothing. He just eyed them both.

"Are you members of the Constitutional Liberation Army?"

"Of course not," Ethan said.

"No," Blayne replied at the same time.

"Did you try to assassinate the President and the First Lady?"

Cleo let out a stupefied snort behind Ethan. "They saved us from a sniper. Why would they do that if they wanted us dead?"

"Madam First Lady, please let me do my job." The man turned back and looked at them. "Mr. Dickenson, you attacked the President. Why?"

"I didn't attack anyone. The door opened. I turned my head to look at the President, and there was a red dot on his chest. I just reacted."

"Why would you react when you saw a red dot?"

"Because I've seen a lot of movies. I know when the shiny red dot appears on someone, that rarely ends well. I just reacted."

"Why were you the only one who saw—?"

"He wasn't," Cleo said. "Agent Malone, I saw it, too. I just didn't... My body just stood there." From the sounds of the performance behind him, Ethan was sure Cleo Barnes was crying. The Secret Service agent—at least that's who Ethan assumed the man was because he hadn't precisely introduced himself to the group—shot Cleo a glare. "That's why I know they're not involved in this."

"And you, Mr. Bond, did you see the dot?"

Ethan hesitated momentarily, then said, "From the direction I was standing, I didn't see it. I saw Blayne react and follow suit to protect the First Lady."

"You realize that makes little sense," the agent said. "Why would you just react when Mr. Dickenson moved?"

"Because he wouldn't move like that unless something was wrong. After what we've been through, we've both been hypervigilant."

"Oh dear, that's totally understandable," Cleo said, coming to sit down at the table. She put her arm around Ethan's shoulders and shot the agent a death glare. "Now, can we get these off them?"

Ethan could tell the agent wanted to object but acquiesced. The agent behind Ethan said, "Please stand." Ethan stood. Another agent removed Blayne's cuffs. Ethan rubbed his wrists.

He turned to Cleo. "Is everyone okay? I saw a…" His voice trailed off because he couldn't finish the sentence.

"An intern was shot," Agent Malone said. "There were also several people in the press corps that were shot. And the Secret Service stopped a van carrying explosives that was attempting to crash into the White House."

"And the sniper?" Blayne asked. His face had gone white. "Did you catch the sniper?"

The agent looked at Blayne. "How do you know it was a sniper?"

Cleo looked at the agent. "Are you that dense? Do you even know why these men are here today?"

"No, ma'am."

"Mr. Dickenson single-handedly stopped a sniper from killing people in Houston."

"I heard something about that on the news," Agent Malone admitted.

"Well, this man risked his own life to confront the sniper in Houston. And today, he risked his life to save my husband. And you" — she turned to Ethan — "you risked your life to save me." A tear welled in her eye. "These are true American heroes."

Ethan looked across the table at Blayne, whose face fell into a weary grimace, his eyes rolling upward as if to say, '*Not again.*'

"We just reacted," Ethan said, "like anyone would. If Blayne hadn't been standing and looking at the President at the right time…" He didn't need to spell out what could have happened.

"Just be glad, by some trick of fate, they were looking in the right direction. Now, go check on my husband. I'm sure he needs you more than I do. And get these two men their family and friends back in here. I'm sure they're worried sick—the way you and your men overreacted."

"They didn't overreact," Blayne said. "Given what they knew, their reaction seemed perfectly justified. I was lucky. It's the second time I've been in the right place at the right time. They took immediate action to save everyone. They're the genuine heroes here." Blayne looked at the agent and said, "Thank you."

Agent Malone looked uncomfortable briefly before saying, "You're welcome. Just doing our jobs." He stood and motioned for the other two agents to leave with him.

"I'm going to stay with our guests," Cleo said, resting her hand on Ethan's shoulder. "Can you have the kitchen send something over?"

The agent grumbled something as he shut the door.

Cleo let out a groan. "Was asking for food and drink a bit over-the-top?"

"Probably," Blayne said.

"Well, you're the one who blew so much smoke up Agent Malone's ass, he was practically a chimney. I guess neither of us is that great at being subtle." She walked around the table and slumped into the chair where the agent had been sitting moments before.

"So, what really happened?" Cleo asked, turning to look at Blayne.

"I got a text." Blayne patted his suit jacket. "Fuck, I don't know where my phone went."

"This one?" Cleo asked, pulling a cell phone from her cleavage. "Sorry. Women's suits aren't usually made with pockets. I saw it when they pulled you off the President. My bra was the first place I thought to hide it." She slid it across the table.

Blayne unlocked his phone and slid it back. Cleo read the text. "Dr. Hennigan?" she asked.

"Could have been Denzili or Richardson?"

"Still," Cleo started, "your reaction time there was impeccable. If you had hesitated even a second, we'd have lost our President."

"And you?" Ethan asked.

"Maybe." Cleo shrugged. "I would like to think my reaction time after seeing the President go down would have been faster than that of a sniper's, but I can't say."

"The explosion?" Ethan asked. "What happened?"

"A van crashed through the Northwest Appointment Gate and was headed to the Rose Garden. Our security took it out before it got too close, but the van had explosives on board."

"What about the people in the garden?" Blayne asked.

"I don't know yet. I think there may be some casualties. But honestly, I really do thank you. You saved my husband's and my life today. I won't forget it," she said. "I can see why Phillipa likes you. I'm just sorry you got tangled up in our world."

The doors flung open. Cleo's demeanor changed instantly. Ethan wondered how she turned it on and off like a light switch. It seemed exhausting.

"You're okay," Stephanie cried as she entered the room and practically threw herself at Ethan. "When they carried you off, I thought you'd been hit. What happened?"

"Your boys were heroes again," Cleo said. "Oops, I did it again. Your *men* were heroes." She turned to Blayne and Ethan and said, "We'll be in touch."

* * * *

Blayne

The drive back to the Waldorf Astoria was more subdued than the trip to the White House a few short hours before. The entire city seemed transformed. Everything was quiet. People weren't out walking around. The news crews were all gathered outside, broadcasting from the fence of the White House. The smoke from the exploded van could still be seen in the sky when their group was ushered back out of the East Wing of the White House into their caravan of SUVs.

When they arrived at the Waldorf Astoria, ZERO's security, the added drivers and the hotel security team formed a circle around them. Blayne stood just tall enough above everyone else to catch guests' looks as the group entered. He could only imagine what their ragtag group looked like, having survived another attack.

"Where are you staying?" he asked Kira.

"We're one floor up. I have a two-floor suite. The king-sized bed is on the first floor, and this spiral staircase leads up to a small library and desk. I don't think I've ever seen a hotel room with its own wraparound loft," Kira said.

"What about you, Stephanie? Where did they put you in this place?"

"I have a suite overlooking Pennsylvania Avenue. Trust me. As a schoolteacher, I could never afford these prices. It's almost five grand a night," she explained. "And it's three times larger than my first apartment was in New Orleans."

"Welcome to how the other half live," Blayne said.

"And by the other half, he means me," Ethan joked, throwing his arm around Blayne. "I'm determined to get this man used to the finer things in life."

"It's not all bad," Blayne admitted. "Some of it is just overkill. But, Stephanie, as a graduate student, I couldn't afford any of this, either. I have a two-bedroom apartment and barely squeeze by, so I'm with you." Ethan shot him a worried look. "Don't worry about me. Graduate students are notoriously overworked and under-funded. Yet thousands of us graduate across the country every year with piles of school loans and credit card debt. It's the American way."

"What are you two doing for the rest of the evening?" Stephanie asked.

"Getting cleaned up," Blayne said. "Probably take a nap. Then, who knows?"

"Let's plan on eating in the hotel at seven-ish?" Kira said.

"Sounds like a plan," Ethan agreed. "Just the four of us."

Kira and Stephanie exited their floor, and Blayne and Ethan went up to their floor. Somehow, Ms. Z. had beaten them to the floor and was already standing outside their door.

Before Ethan could say anything, Ms. Z. informed them, "Until further notice, you will have around-the-clock security. It will either be us, the Metro Police, the FBI or Secret Service. We've agreed to rotate. This is not an option, and it came down from Hightower, Rawlins and the President of the United States, so you're stuck with us for the time being."

"Have you seen the news?" Ethan asked.

"Yes," Ms. Z. admitted. "The White House has not released your involvement in saving the President's and First Lady's lives. We're unsure if the Secret Service will keep that under wraps."

"How many...?" Blayne started, then appeared to hesitate.

Ms. Z. knew what he was asking. "Nothing has been released to the public."

Something in her voice made Blayne pry. "But?"

"Through back channels, we know the intern who was shot died before they got her to the hospital."

Blayne sucked in a breath and leaned against the door for support. "She was so young and excited to work in the White House."

"There are at least two or three more confirmed deaths." Ms. Z. paused. There was something she clearly wasn't saying.

"Out with it," Blayne said, steeling himself for whatever would come next.

Ms. Z. turned and looked at Ethan. "There was a small group of ZERO fans waving signs outside the gate where the van rammed through. At least two of those killed were young fans."

Ethan's face went slack. Blayne then turned to his boyfriend and wrapped his arms around him. Ms. Z. pulled out her security card and let them into their room.

"Thanks," Blayne said as he closed the door behind them.

They headed to the bathroom. Blayne helped Ethan with his suit and folded the clothing into a neat pile.

The bathroom had a large walk-in luxury spa tub. Blayne turned on the water and let it fill while removing his suit. Blayne looked through the hotel amenities and found a box of scented bath salts he dumped into the water.

He lowered his body into the tub and coaxed Ethan to join him, sitting between his legs. Blayne leaned against the back of the tub, and Ethan leaned against him. Blayne wasn't sure how long they lay like that. They didn't talk. They just sat there holding on to each other. Occasionally, one of them would have a moment when the tears came. The longer Blayne sat in the tub, the more he realized that whatever was happening to them wasn't over.

Chapter Twenty-Two

Ethan

Ethan felt like a prune leaning against Blayne's wet torso. The water had lost its warmth long ago, but they had just stayed wrapped in each other's arms. Time had slipped by, and the sky had gone black. The bathroom had been enfolded in darkness.

"We probably should see what time it is. We're supposed to meet Stephanie and Kira at seven," he said.

The light switch flipped on. "You have about forty minutes. That gives us twenty minutes to talk, then you'll have twenty minutes to get ready," Dr. Hennigan said as she walked into the bathroom and leaned against the counter on the other side. "Don't worry. I can't see anything," she said, gesturing to them.

"I would ask how you got in here," Blayne said, "but I wonder why I'm ever surprised."

Dr. Hennigan smiled. "First, I am sorry about today. We didn't know there were CLA members in DC. The last intelligence we had placed Laura Lee Jackson or Lizzy Cleburne... Well, you know whom I'm talking about. Anyway, she isn't near DC. We think she's heading this way, but we had no reason to believe she would carry out this attack." Hennigan looked at them for a second. "I don't know if you know much about the history of terrorism. But in 1984, the Irish Republican Army planted a bomb in a hotel where Margaret Thatcher was supposed to stay. Their plan was thwarted. But they released a statement that read, '*You have to be lucky all the time. We only have to be lucky once.*' Sadly, it's a game of odds. We will never win all the time. We can't. We cannot prevent every terrorist attack from happening. We do our best to try, and we learn from our mistakes. That's all any of us can do." She laughed a second to herself. "Trust me. Since I met you, all I've been doing is learning from new mistakes." She shook her head. "Anyway, I wish we could have given you more of a heads up than we did, but we saw the sniper's nest seconds before he took his first shot. Honestly, we were all fortunate things panned out the way they did today. I don't like luck. And I never want the CLA to get lucky again."

"From your mouth to God's ears," Blayne replied.

"Amen," Ethan whispered. "So, what are our next steps?"

Hennigan chuckled and shook her head. "Your next steps are to live your life. This isn't your fight. My goal is to keep you safe, and we're coordinating efforts with a range of agencies, some you've never heard of, to ensure that happens."

"Do you think she would try something now?" Blayne asked. "The heat has to be on her."

"I think a sane person would avoid doing something right now, but I don't think that's what we're dealing with here. Unfortunately, we don't know what she's thinking. To answer the question, we don't know. She could do it today, tomorrow or a year from now. She wants revenge and has targeted The Foundation and the First Lady for previous grievances. And now, she's coming after Blayne for killing her husband." Blayne started to say something, but Dr. Hennigan cut him off. "You know, and I know, that you did nothing wrong. You saved lives. You were a hero then, and you were a hero today. But to Jackson or Cleburne or whatever name she changes to tomorrow, you are guilty in her eyes. After tonight, you shouldn't see me again. But I want you to know that until she's caught, we are watching out for both of you." She looked at her watch. "I took up an extra minute. You now have only nineteen minutes to get downstairs for dinner."

She didn't wait for a response but turned and left.

Blayne

Blayne and Ethan showered and made it down to the premier restaurant in the hotel atrium in record time. Ms. Z. had gone off duty and was replaced by a polite FBI agent who didn't completely understand why she'd been tasked with guarding a pop star and his boyfriend. Blayne didn't mind being the arm candy of the pop star.

They had just arrived at the restaurant when Blayne received a text from Kira telling him they were running behind. Stephanie and Kira were also running late, so

Blayne and Ethan caught their breath as they waited. The FBI agent stood a polite distance away from them as they huddled near the restaurant entrance. A sign requested guests not to be seated until their entire party arrived. Blayne didn't mind waiting. It felt good to stand after the long bath.

"Sorry we're late." Kira's voice boomed through the lobby. "Geez, I didn't mean to yell that loudly."

"This place has some pretty impressive acoustics," Ethan said. He reached out and grabbed Stephanie's arm, and said, "Shall we?"

"Yes, I'm starved. I just realized on the way down that I had eaten nothing since breakfast."

Blayne's stomach took that time to rumble. "I guess that makes two of us."

The group walked to the maître d'. "Kira Strickland, party for four."

"Right this way, madam," the man said as he grabbed four menus and a wine list and motioned for them to follow.

As the group moved, it was then that he realized the women had their own security detail. The security guards followed them into the restaurant. The maître d' stopped and said, "Excuse me? We had this as a party of four, not six."

Kira and Stephanie's security reached into her pocket, pulled out a wallet and flashed her credentials. "FBI. We're just ensuring the safety of your guests. We'll be discreet."

"Well, I can't have you hovering. I'll seat you at a nearby table. I'll also send out our head of security," the maître d' said. The agent nodded, and the group continued through the restaurant to a small alcove that was secluded and off to the side.

After the group was seated, the maître d' handed them their menus, recommended they look at the specials insert and left the group to get settled at the table. Seconds later, a busboy with a water pitcher showed up and asked them, "Do you prefer regular water, bottled water or sparkling water?"

"Regular is fine," Blayne replied. The others nodded their heads. The busboy poured water for them before leaving the table.

"I'm almost amazed they don't send a taste tester to ensure our water is safe," Stephanie said. "I mean, this is a bit much." She nodded toward their security detail.

"You get used to it," Ethan said. "I've had my security shadows for a few years. Admittedly, this is even beyond what I'm used to. If they do their jobs, you don't even realize they're there most of the time."

The server approached the table, reviewed the menu and asked if anyone had specific dietary restrictions. She informed them that the chef would like the chance to cook for them directly and off the menu.

"Of course," Ethan said. "And thank the chef for the opportunity."

"Well, that's a surprise," Stephanie said. "I've never had a chef at a five-star restaurant even know I was there. Admittedly, the only five-star restaurants I've entered were down in the Quarter."

From the moment the first dish was served to Blayne, he knew this would be an unforgettable culinary journey. The amuse-bouche, a delicate wafer topped with vegetable caviar and smoked fish, was not something he had ever tasted in West Texas. The flavors danced on his tongue. This was followed by a smooth lobster velouté, which the server explained was "subtly kissed by saffron so the rich the creaminess will envelop your palate with an embrace from the sea." Blayne wasn't sure if his palate was embraced by the sea, but it was delicious. Course number three was the appetizer, "a ravioli filled with earthy black truffles and rich foie gras, bathed in a light, buttery broth, which will provide a decadent foray into the harmony of land and river."

When the server left the table, Blayne looked at Kira. "Did you understand half of what she just said?"

Kira smiled and said, "Not at all. And honestly, I don't even care. This is amazing."

"I know," Stephanie agreed. "Ethan?"

His mouth was filled with ravioli, so he just nodded enthusiastically.

Next, it was time for their fish course, which Blayne didn't even realize was a thing. The server called it "*dorade royale en croûte de sel de mer*," which translated to sea bream baked in a salt crust, served with a drizzle of citrus-infused olive oil.

"I admit, this is the first time I've ever tried sea bream," Ethan said after finishing three-fourths of the plate. "I need to slow down. We still have three courses to go."

"I'm going to need to purchase an entirely new wardrobe if I keep eating like this," Stephanie agreed. "Not that I mind."

Next, the server showed up with "*carré d'agneau en croûte d'herbes*, which was a tender, herb-encrusted rack of lamb, served with a robust red wine jus."

"I have to ask," Stephanie said. "What's a wine jus?"

With a practiced smile, the server explained, "A wine jus, ma'am, is a light yet flavorful sauce made from the natural juices of the cooked meat, which is enhanced with wine and often other ingredients, then reduced to concentrate its flavors. Here, the chef's wine of choice tonight was the house cabernet sauvignon."

"Thank you," Stephanie said. "I'm definitely getting a culinary education tonight."

The server beamed and left the table for them to enjoy.

"So, what will happen to the shows here in DC?" Kira asked.

Ethan swallowed the bite of lamb in his mouth before saying, "I don't know. I'm sure Rawlings and Hightower are figuring things out. We may cancel. We may postpone. We may go on as planned. I just don't know. And honestly, it's the least of my concerns. Playing a sold-out concert just doesn't seem that important, given everything else that's happening."

"How much do you know about what's been going on, Stephanie?" Blayne asked. "I just don't know how much Ethan has been able to tell you."

"Not that much," Stephanie said slowly. "He's been vague over the phone. I assumed it's because he's assuming someone's listening in on any phone conversations."

"That's a pretty astute observation," Ethan admitted. "I've become a little paranoid. As the adage goes, 'Just because you're paranoid doesn't mean someone isn't watching you.'"

"Kira and I talked a bit when we got back from the White House, so she filled me in on a few of the missing pieces to the story," Stephanie said. "Including that the person who blew up my house may be one of the *good* guys." Her voice rose at the end of the sentence, making it sound more like a question than a statement.

"To say it's confusing is putting it mildly," Blayne admitted.

"I just wish there was something we could do. I feel helpless," Ethan said. "There's just been so much death and destruction. I need to put something positive out into the world."

"What about a benefit?" Kira asked. "My law firm puts them on once or twice yearly to help various causes. I think they do them just so they can dress in formal wear and hobnob with rich people, but it's at least something."

"Here is your next course, *salade d'endives et de Roquefort avec vinaigrette de champagne*," the server said as she approached the table. She handed out salads. "We have a crisp endive and Roquefort salad, served with a champagne vinaigrette."

"Okay, I'm confused," Blayne said. "Why are you serving the salad after the main meal? This just seems backward. And I'll apologize now, but I'm from West Texas, so this is a novel experience."

The server smiled. She leaned in and said, "I'm originally from Alabama, so I get it all too well. When I started working in fancy restaurants, I was a complete idiot. Regarding your question, the salad is served after the meat course in traditional French and European dining. Fresh vegetables aid digestion, and the acidic dressing refreshes your palate. So, it's an ideal transition from the meat course's heartiness before the dessert's sweetness."

"Interesting," Blayne said. "I've never heard that before. It kind of makes sense."

The server raised her eyebrows quickly with a smile. "Enjoy."

"What were we talking about?" Ethan asked.

"Benefits," Kira said.

"Oh yeah," Ethan said, spearing a piece of salad and ushering it to his mouth. "We've performed at a few benefit concerts over the years."

"That's a great idea," Stephanie said. "Why not throw a benefit concert?"

Ethan thought about it for a second. "They're not exactly easy to assemble, but it's possible. I'd have to get everyone on board."

The group spent a few minutes discussing the possibility of a benefit concert before the server appeared with their last course.

"I don't know where it's going to go," Stephanie said as the server approached the table, "but I'm going to figure it out. Those look amazing."

The server explained that the dessert was a rich dark chocolate mousse paired perfectly with a tart raspberry coulis. Blayne didn't know what that meant, but his mouth watered as he took his first bite.

The group devoured their desserts.

"Good evening, I'm Chef Sébastien Leclerc," a middle-aged man said as he approached the table. "Thank you for letting me cook for you this evening."

"No, thank *you* for cooking for us," Ethan said. "That was amazing."

The group spent a few moments gushing over the meal, telling the chef their favorite parts.

"And kudos to your amazing server," Stephanie said. "She explained everything so well. The food was amazing, but she really provided exceptional service."

The chef beamed. "Well, I'll let you get back to our meal," Chef Leclerc said. "I just want to thank you for what you've done. My cousin lives in Houston, so I've been following your story closely. Then today…" The chef let it hang in the air. "When I heard you would eat with me tonight, I jumped at the opportunity to return the favor you've performed for our country."

"Thank you for the compliment," Blayne said sheepishly. "I'm still getting used to being recognized, so all this is overwhelming."

"Well, I'll let you get back to your evening. Oh, and the meal is on me."

Chef Leclerc left the table before the group could attempt to protest his generosity.

The group stayed for another thirty minutes as they were brought after-dinner drinks. By the time Blayne left the restaurant, he was stuffed beyond belief and ready to collapse into bed.

* * * *

Ethan

Ethan woke up the following day to the sound of his phone ringing. He grumbled, and Blayne made some kind of unintelligible sound. He pulled the phone from its charging cable and rolled over to see who was calling.

"Ethan," he said into the phone.

"We're meeting in one hour in my suite. I'm up in the Presidential One suite. Your security detail will know how to get here," Rawlins said. "This is an all-hands-on-deck meeting, so bring Blayne with you."

"See you in an hour," Ethan said.

"Who was that?" Blayne asked.

"Rawlins. We're meeting up in his suite in an hour. He said I needed to drag your ass out of bed with me."

"I don't wanna get up," Blayne said in a whiny voice.

"Someone needs their morning coffee. We have an instant coffee machine in the room. I'll make you a cup while you shower," Ethan said as he inched the duvet from Blayne's torso. Blayne rolled over and gave Ethan some stink eye.

"I'm cold now," Blayne said. "I need a new cover." He reached out and grabbed Ethan, rolling him onto his chest, wrapping his arms around Ethan like a child clinging to a teddy bear. And he tickled Ethan.

Ethan howled with laughter. His ribs were incredibly ticklish, and Blayne knew it. "Stop. You're going to make me wet the bed," Ethan said between breaths and laughter.

"Maybe I'm into water sports," Blayne said before tickling Ethan again.

"Eww," Ethan said. "Unless I'm stung by a jellyfish at the beach and we're the only two people around for miles, please do not pee on me…ever."

"Noted," Blayne said, clearly more awake than before he had engaged in his tickle offensive against Ethan. "I guess we should get going."

"Go shower," Ethan said, shooing Blayne toward the bathroom. "We could do it together, but we don't have time for that."

"Yeah, our showers together are notorious for being a little too long because of everything we do in the shower that doesn't involve scrubbing each other's backs."

"Bingo. Now, go."

"Why do I have to go first?" Blayne complained.

"Because if you don't go shower now, I'm going to come out and find a lump buried back in the duvet. Now march, mister."

Blayne gave a little salute but pulled himself off the bed and headed toward the bathroom. Ethan propped himself up against some pillows and started scrolling through his emails. He was halfway through the list when he received a text from Stephanie.

Turn on RTN.

It took him a second to find the television remote. After looking around the room, he found it on the desk and turned on the TV. He scrolled through the channels until he saw RTN in the screen's right-hand corner. It was a commercial, so he headed back to bed.

"*Good morning, America. This is Tika Downs. I have breaking information about yesterday's terrorist attack on the White House. RTN has confirmed that the people responsible for the terrorist attack yesterday are the same domestic terrorist group responsible for the attack in Houston last week. We go now to Stephen McNeil, who is at the White House.*"

Ethan groaned at the mention of McNeil. A closeup shot of the redheaded man with his close-cropped beard appeared on the screen. "*Yesterday was a horrific day in the history of the United States. There has not been a more heroic deed since 1981 when James Brady intervened to shield then-President Ronald Reagan when John Hinckley Junior tried to assassinate the late president. RTN has corroborated from several sources that the sniper who attempted to kill President Barnes was thwarted by Mr. Blayne Dickenson. You may recall that Blayne Dickenson was caught on camera throwing one of the active shooters out of a bell tower during the Pennington Massacre.*" The video played of the body flying out of the window, followed by Blayne sticking his head out. "*We have also confirmed with sources close to the President that Mr. Dickenson and his boy-band boyfriend"* — Ethan groaned at the phrase — *"Ethan Bond were at the White House to receive the Presidential Citizens Medal at the time of the attack."* The video of Ethan and Blayne kissing played. *"During the attempt on the President's life, Blayne Dickenson put himself in harm's way again. Furthermore, Ethan Bond did the same for First Lady Cleo Barnes."* A video shot from someone in the Rose Garden showed the door being opened. You couldn't see that Blayne tackled the President clearly, but his tall body took the President to the ground.

"Stephen, have you contacted Dickenson or Bond's representatives for comment?" Tika asked.

"Unfortunately, our attempts to reach out have not been returned," Stephen said. Ethan looked at his phone. There were no texts or email messages from RTN, so their crack team of investigators hadn't been trying to get hold of him that hard.

"Any word from the White House?" Tika asked.

Footage of Sepi Amin was shown entering the staff entrance at the White House as a camera was thrust in her face. She turned and looked at Stephen with a look of abject disdain. *"Can I help you?"*

"Yes. Can you confirm that Blayne Dickenson threw himself in front of a bullet intended for the President yesterday?"

She looked shocked, followed by, *"How did you hear about that?"* She paused briefly and said, *"No comment,"* before turning around and heading through the White House security gate.

"As you can see, the Chief of Staff of the White didn't exactly confirm the question, but her response is definitely not a denial."

The television went back to Tika in the studio. *"We'll have more on this breaking story as information becomes available*." She turned to a different camera. "*In other news, could your cat be secretly trying to kill you at night?*" Ethan turned the television off.

"Well…" Blayne's voice said. Ethan looked over to find Blayne standing in the bathroom doorframe. He had a towel tightened around his hips and used another to dry his hair. "We shouldn't be too surprised that we couldn't keep the story under wraps for long."

Ethan's phone buzzed. He had a news alert. "It's on the RTN website now. The headline is, '*From ZERO to Hero*?'" Then Ethan started getting a dozen text alerts. "Well, it's out there." He silenced the phone.

"The shower's all yours," Blayne said.

Blayne

Blayne threw on a pair of jeans and a long-sleeved polo shirt. It may not be the new designer clothes Ethan had bought him, but it was what he was most comfortable in. And for some reason, he just wanted to be his old self for a while.

He had texts from family and friends asking about the latest news story. He only responded to Dr. Reich because he knew she'd worry if he didn't respond quickly. There was a cheeky message from Jamie. He just sent back a poo emoji. There was a message from Dr. Secada. Blayne wanted to skip that one, but figured it was best to let her know it was nothing and that he and Ethan were fine. He looked toward the bathroom and heard the shower still running, so he went to the RTN website, read the story and watched the video of him throwing himself in front of the President. He had to admit, the video made him look like a badass superspy.

"Dickenson, Blayne Dickenson," he said in his best fake British accent. "Yeah, doesn't work."

A ping sounded. He had a new text message. He pulled up his notices and found a new message from Kira.

Just saw the news. Your fat ass was in the way of the world seeing my arm. What gives?

Blayne chuckled. He thought about what he wanted to say and typed back.

I'm sorry if my perfectly sculpted runner's ass impeded your arm's big moment. Next time I try to save the President's life, I'll watch my camera angles.

See you in a few. We received an invite to the meeting in a few minutes. Heading up.

Still waiting for Ethan to get out of the shower. Be there soon.

The water in the shower turned off, and Blayne waited for Ethan to emerge. "Well, this should be an interesting day."

"Anything new?" Ethan asked as he walked to his suitcase and pulled out his clothes. Blayne noticed that Ethan also wore comfy clothes, jeans, a T-shirt, a pullover hoodie and his tennis shoes.

"Kira is pissed that my ass got in the way of the camera showing her arm when I was saving the President's life," Blayne said in his most serious tone before smiling.

"No offense to Kira, but I'd rather see your ass any day over looking at her arm."

Ethan bent over to finish tying his shoes. When he sat back up, he said, "Ready?"

"As I'll ever be."

Blayne pocketed his wallet and cell phone before strapping on his smartwatch. "Let's do this." He walked over to the door and opened it to find two security guards outside. Blayne just smiled and nodded his head.

"We were told you knew how to get to where we're going?" Ethan said.

"We do," the shorter of the guards said.

"Lead the way," Blayne said.

And that's precisely how it worked. One guard led the way, while Blayne and Ethan walked together, and the second guard followed them. Blayne was not used to being around security, but Ethan seemed oblivious. As they walked, Blayne wondered at what point in Ethan's career did being surrounded by security become just part of life. He'd have to remember to ask. Their escorts led them to the elevator. The elevator opened, and it had three people inside.

"We'll wait for the next one," the guard said.

The people in the elevator got saucer-eyed looks. One woman looked around the security personnel to see who he was protecting, so Blayne smiled and waved at the obviously disappointed-looking woman.

The next elevator was empty, so the group piled in and one of the security guards inserted a keycard into a slot above the rest of the elevator buttons. The floor where Rawlins was staying could only be accessed by a keycard.

During the quick trip up, no one said a word. The first security guard left the elevator and motioned for Blayne and Ethan to follow. The hall looked like a security convention. Blayne and Ethan walked through the security line to the door that was propped open. Ethan knocked twice and walked right in.

"Good morning," Rawlins said as Blayne and Ethan entered. A buffet was set up, and Rawlins gestured. "Breakfast?"

The smell of coffee filled Blayne's nose, and he looked to find a fancy silver coffee chafer urn. "Thanks," he said to Rawlins and went right to the urn. Ethan was right behind him. Blayne turned and looked at Ethan. "What happened to that cup of coffee you were going to brew me?"

"Uh…I got a text from Stephanie to turn on RTN."

"That would do it."

"How'd you two sleep?" Stephanie asked. He hadn't even seen Kira and Stephanie standing in the room because of his coffee tunnel vision.

"Fine. We both slept well."

"You?" Ethan asked.

"I think I spooked at every noise. I ended up tossing and turning half the night," Stephanie admitted.

"And you?" Ethan turned to Kira, who had joined them. "You sleep, okay?"

"After dinner, I responded to some work emails. By the time my head hit the pillow, I was out like a light."

"If everyone can finish getting their breakfasts and take a seat," Hightower said loudly over the conversations in the room.

Blayne went over to the buffet, dished out some scrambled eggs and grabbed a couple of biscuits and three slices of bacon. Ethan had opted for a yogurt parfait. Blayne shot him a questioning look.

"How can you eat anything after last night's dinner?" Ethan asked.

"I'm a growing boy," Blayne joked.

Ethan led Blayne over to the table, and they sat in the empty seats next to each other. Blayne doubted this seating arrangement had been an accident.

"Thank you for coming," Rawlins said. "As you know, someone filmed the attack at the White House yesterday, so inquiries are flowing in from around the globe. Mr. Dickenson," Rawlins said, turning to look at Blayne, "with your permission, we'd like to filter all media inquiries for you to the same team that handles Ethan."

"Do I really need — ?" Blayne asked.

"Yes," Hightower, who sat at the other end of the table, confirmed. "For one, you're part of our family now. We want to make sure everyone around this table is protected. And two, you will be inundated with media requests. And unless you want to be dodging the press left and right, it's best to have someone you can direct them to."

Blayne turned and looked at Ethan, who gave him a reassuring smile and a nod. "Okay."

"Great," Rawlins said. "You've been asked to return to the White House this morning."

"What?" Ethan asked. "Why?"

Rawlins looked to Hightower. "I took that phone call. The White House wants everything to be business as usual. Obviously, they cannot have the fancy reception they were hoping for. However, they still want to give you your awards in a much smaller, more controlled environment. They want to keep it very small. Just you, the President and the First Lady. Mr. J.

will drive you to the White House. He will hand you off to the Secret Service, who will take you into the East Wing to the First Lady's personal offices. The White House's social media team will broadcast the ceremony live. It will be more subdued than yesterday...given everything that happened."

"Okay," Ethan said.

"We can't exactly wear what we did yesterday. And I didn't bring another dress outfit," Blayne admitted.

"Actually," Rawlins said, "I think what you're both wearing right now is perfect. The boy-next-door look is exactly what the White House wants. It's all about optics. Despite what happened yesterday, everyone is still working. Our country is still running."

Blayne would never get used to the world of public relations. He just nodded. Ethan reached under the table and gave him a reassuring squeeze on the knee.

Rawlins and Hightower then discussed the security changes that would happen at their concert venue. Toward the end of the conversation, Ethan jumped into the conversation.

"We had an idea last night," he said.

"Oh?" Hightower asked.

"And we don't know if this is workable, but we want to throw a benefit concert. Between the people injured at Pennington, our fans outside the White House and those injured in the Rose Garden, we just feel like we want to do something. Take the proceeds and donate them to the victims and their families."

"If you raise more than necessary, you could set up a charitable fund to help future victims of domestic terrorism in the US," Kira suggested. The table shot her a look. "I talked to one of my partners about managing benefits last night. This was a suggestion he made."

"Interesting," Rawlins said. "The press would love this."

"It's not about the press," Ethan said. "I just feel... *We* feel," he said, looking at Blayne, "that we need to do something."

"I'm in," Ric said. "Just tell me when and where."

The other guys agreed instantly.

"I'm betting we can even get some other groups, depending on when we can organize this."

"We'll have to find a venue," Hightower said. "I'll put our people on it."

The group spent the next bit of time discussing their rehearsal schedule and what the next few days would be like as things calmed down. Before they knew it was time for Blayne and Ethan to head to the White House. They left the suite, and everyone promised to tune into the live stream from the White House.

Mr. S. and Ms. Z. were waiting in the hall outside the suite to escort them to the SUV in front of the hotel. The stroll through the lobby was surreal. People stopped to look at Blayne and Ethan. Blayne felt like a guppie in a bowl from all the stares they were getting.

"I don't know if I'll get used to this?" Blayne said. He realized he was sounding like a broken record, even as he said it.

"Just know you don't have to get used to this alone. I'm going to be at your side every step of the way," Ethan said, grabbing his hand.

* * * *

Ethan

The plans went precisely as they had been described. Mr. J. pulled up to the White House, and

Secret Service agents greeted them on the sidewalk. They opened the doors, Ethan and Blayne exited and were seen through the East Appointment Gate. They walked through the magnetometers and entered the East Wing of the White House. An older woman was there, introduced herself as the White House Social Secretary and escorted them to the First Lady's office on the second floor of the East Wing. Things were quieter than they had been the day before.

"So, what exactly is a social secretary?" Ethan asked.

"My job is to plan, coordinate and execute any social event under the White House umbrella — everything from state dinners to medal ceremonies, like the one we had yesterday..." She paused as she realized what she'd said, "I'm so sorry. I didn't mean to —"

"It's okay," Blayne reassured her. "We're all struggling to come to grips with yesterday." The woman nodded. "So, beyond the First Lady, what other offices are in this building?" Blayne asked.

"Great question. We have the Office of Correspondence. They handle any mail that comes to the White House and write back or ensure the most appropriate person writes back. We have the Graphics and Calligraphy Office, which technically falls under the Social Office of the White House."

From the look on Blayne's face, he regretted asking the question. Ethan tuned the woman out until she offhandedly mentioned that the East Building was built by Theodore Roosevelt.

"The building was built in 1942 to cover the Presidential Emergency Operations Center — PEOC — construction. It's called 'pee-ock' around here," she said, giving the phonetic pronunciation. "Anytime there's a threat, the President, Vice-President and anyone else deemed necessary are evacuated to PEOC."

"So, that's where Barnes was taken yesterday after…?" Ethan didn't finish the sentence.

"I would assume so, but I officially do not know. There are other secured rooms in the White House, but PEOC is the one people are most familiar with. And here we are," she said, leading them into an ornate inner office. "I'm going to let the President's office know you're here."

"How are my boys doing today?" Cleo asked, exiting her office. She paused for a second. "Sorry about that. I keep calling you boys. I know you're young men. But I look at you, and you're not even as old as my children. My oldest, she's almost thirty, heaven help me. My youngest? He is just a few years older than you, which is probably why I keep thinking of you as children."

"I take it you had her when you were ten?" Blayne said.

"You're definitely a charmer, that you are," Cleo said.

The door shut behind them, and Cleo's pretense once again disappeared. "But really, how are you two doing? Phillipa told me she dropped by to check on you last night."

"That's one way to put it," Ethan said.

"What did she do?" Cleo asked.

"Let's just say that Blayne and I were alone in the bathtub when she visited."

Cleo bit her lower lip as she tried not to laugh. "Phillipa does like letting people know she can always get to them when they're most vulnerable." Cleo leaned against the sizable ornate desk and crossed her legs and arms in front of her. She wore a navy sleeveless fitted dress. "So, I hear you're thinking about a benefit concert?"

"How do you—?" Ethan asked. Cleo tutted and tilted her head slightly, giving him a small smile. "I need to stop asking that question."

"Now you're learning," Cleo joked. "Actually, your people called my people while you were coming over. I heard you were looking for a venue, and I thought the West Lawn of the US Capitol Building would make a great place. Plus, it's a facility we're used to securing because of the other events there."

"Wow, this is moving fast," Ethan admitted.

"That's how we do things around here. The only thing is that it will have to be funded through private donations, which won't be a problem. We can pull the concert off for less than twenty million."

"Why not skip the concert and use the twenty million to help people?" Blayne asked, the comment coming out more snidely than he had intended.

"Because that's not how rich people think," Cleo admitted. "Give a couple thousand dollars to help cover the costs of an intern's funeral? Never. Give five million to have your name listed on a banner for a benefit concert? They'll pull out their checkbooks and ask who to make it out to."

The door opened, and the social secretary walked in with the President. The President wore casual suit pants and a cardigan sweater with the Presidential seal on the chest.

"Good, we all got the memo to dress casually," Barnes said. "Well, except for my wife. This is about as casual as she gets. I swear, she'd wear a pantsuit to bed if I'd let her get away with it." He then laughed at his own joke.

"Mr. President." Sepi Amin stood in the door and tapped her watch.

"Oh yes, I have a phone call in twenty minutes. I've prepared a few remarks. Then I'll give you your medals, and that will be it."

"We're going to start the live broadcast in sixty seconds. It will go out to our social media channels, and we'll simulcast it to the press corps, who don't know we're doing this," a frenzied-looking young man informed the group. "Oh yeah, hi. I'm in charge of the White House's social media team," the man said before getting his camera and lights in position. Everything was very professional and designed to look like it *wasn't* done professionally.

Cleo looked at them and winked.

"In five, four, three, two." The man holding the camera pointed to the President.

"My fellow Americans… Today, the First Lady and I gather to honor two extraordinary individuals who exemplify courage, selflessness and dedication to our nation. Blayne Dickenson and Ethan Bond, your actions before and during yesterday's attack on the White House serve as a beacon of hope and a testament to the strength of our democracy."

"Blayne," the cameraman turned the camera to focus on Blayne. From the corner of his eye, Blayne did his best not to look at the camera and stared at the President. "Your bravery in the face of unimaginable danger and your unwavering commitment to defending our democracy inspire us all. Ethan," — Ethan stood a little taller hearing his name called — "your quick thinking and decisive actions ensured the safety of the First Lady, demonstrating your unwavering dedication to the well-being of our nation's leaders."

The camera panned back to the President. "In recognition of your exceptional contributions yesterday and on that fateful day in Houston, Texas, it is with immense pride and gratitude that I present you both with the Presidential Citizen's Medal. This distinction is a lasting tribute to your unwavering dedication to our nation." Cleo opened a box and tilted the medal just enough so the camera could catch it on social media. *She's good,* Ethan thought.

Cleo handed the President the first box, and he handed it to Blayne, shaking his hand while saying, "May your actions continue to inspire us to stand tall in the face of adversity, to protect the sanctity of our democracy." He handed Ethan the second medal and shook his hand. "And to embody the principles that define us as a nation that will not bow down to terrorism, domestically or abroad."

"Thank you, Blayne and Ethan, for etching your names into the annals of our nation's history and reminding us of the power within each of us to shape a brighter future. Your country owes you a debt of gratitude. God bless you both, and may God bless the United States of America." There was a pause, as nothing was happening.

"And we've stopped broadcasting," the social media guy said.

"Again, Blayne, Ethan, thank you for saving mine and my wife's lives. I wish I could stay longer, but I must make this conference call."

"It was nice seeing you again, Mr. President," Ethan said.

"Yes, Mr. President," Blayne added. "Glad we could be of service."

As soon as the President was out of the office, Cleo looked at him and said, "*Glad we could be of service*?"

"It was the first thing that popped into my head," Blayne admitted. Cleo let out a low chuckle.

"Thanks for coming in so quickly. I know this may seem a little cheesy. Still, these videos help settle the country, let them see that things are back to normal and understand their country is working for them, even after what happened yesterday. The people of this country need to know we're still here."

"It makes sense," Blayne says. "It's weird being on this side of everything."

"I honestly forget what it was like before I became a political spouse. It's just part of who I am now." She gave them a small smile. She approached the door and said, "Let me show you out."

"One thing before we go," Ethan said. Cleo turned to look at him and gestured for him to continue. "Do you agree with his politics? I mean, his political stances are cringeworthy on a good day."

Cleo looked at Ethan with a faint smile, as if she had anticipated this inquiry. She adjusted her posture, maintaining an air of grace and composure. "Ethan, let me be clear. My role as the First Lady is not about personal opinions or political ideologies." She paused, her eyes momentarily scanning Ethan's face. "I'm here to safeguard the welfare and security of this nation on behalf of The Foundation. Politics, as you might imagine, is an arena of differing opinions and ideologies. I must focus on the bigger picture, our citizens' wellbeing and our nation's stability. I stay out of the petty squabbles of politicians."

Ethan nodded, intrigued by her response. "So, you don't align with your husband's conservative stance?"

Cleo chuckled softly. "Oh, Ethan, my husband is a complex man. He's not driven by any strong ideological convictions. Jeffrey's generally a nice guy, a people pleaser. Unfortunately, that means he never questions the party platform. It's the bedrock of his political identity." She took a moment to gather her thoughts before continuing. "In that regard, the President is more of a follower than a leader. It's precisely what made him electable. He possesses a certain charm and affability that resonates, but it also means he's susceptible to influence from various factions within the party."

Cleo leaned in, her voice dropping slightly. "Believe me when I say that I regularly put a stop to some of the more extreme proposals that arise from the hardline whackados of the extreme right. I keep him grounded, reminding him of the needs and values of the American people. It's a delicate balance, Ethan, but someone has to do it." With that, she turned, opened the door to her office and gestured for Ethan and Blayne to follow.

They took a faster, less touristy route to the entrance of the East Wing. She opened the visitor's door. "We'll be talking soon," Cleo said as she shook hands while slipping each a business card. "My cell is on the back if you need to get a hold of me directly." She didn't wait for a reply. She turned and headed back into the White House.

"If you'll follow us," a Secret Service agent said.

Up ahead, a black SUV was pulling up to the curb. Ms. Z. was getting out and opening the door as Blayne and Ethan exited the White House proper.

Chapter Twenty-Three

Dr. Hennigan

The limo drove down the gravel roadway toward the towering mansion. Dr. Hennigan checked her makeup one last time. The torch-lit driveway curved in front of the ornate columned entryway. There was a line of cars. Each got their turn pulling up to the red carpet that led into the exclusive event. The car pulled up, and the door was immediately opened by a handsome man in uniform. She handed him her invitation then her hand as she stepped out of the limo and onto the carpet before heading up the stairs.

"Dr. Phillipa Courtenay," a man yelled when she reached the top stair and entered the atrium. Not that anyone was listening to all the attendees being named. A server passed by, and she grabbed a flute of champagne. She never enjoyed having her hands too empty at these events, so she had her clutch in one and the champagne in the other. Several eyes turned in her direction. Her pale skin almost glowed against the red-and-black Gothic-inspired gown she wore. The satin bodice was decorated with intricate black lace leading to a high collar. A crimson skirt billowed out around her. It was gorgeous, even though it was far from practical, but tonight wasn't about practicality. She wore a ruby necklace around her neck and two black diamond earrings.

And there she was... Dr. Hennigan observed the other woman for a moment. She was dressed in a blue ballgown also dripping in diamonds. When the woman looked her way, Hennigan tipped her crystal flute and nodded. The woman mimicked the action. She had ten to fifteen minutes before their clandestine meeting. Around them, couples mingled—men in tuxes and women in ballgowns. The ostentatiousness of it all almost sickened her. She was surrounded by old money. Not that her family didn't have its own minor fortune, but these were the people who didn't work a day in their lives and assumed everyone else on the planet was there simply to serve them. They had done nothing to earn their fortunes, besides having the right genetic composition at birth. But these people had the money to move mountains. She looked at one woman wearing a green gown who had recently had a mountain removed from her property because it was in the way of her view of the sunset.

Hennigan drifted in and out of the crowd, listening to bits and pieces of conversations.

"Phillipa," a woman said, next to her, "I'm amazed to see you here. This isn't your usual haunt."

"Amara," Hennigan responded, giving the woman a once-over. "I'm amazed customs let you into the country."

Amara Conti was born into Italian aristocracy. She at least leveraged her family's fortune and influence to become a dominant businesswoman with her fingers in finance, real estate and media, predominantly in Western Europe and the Mediterranean. Some of her dealings were with less-than-savory characters. The Foundation had long known that she was laundering money for various criminal enterprises. Unfortunately, their best forensic accountants could not trace the money back to her.

"I heard about that horrible affair in your family's business. I hope your mother and grandmother are okay," Amara said as she smiled.

"I will send them your regards," Hennigan said. "Now, really, I must talk to someone whom I actually like."

Without waiting for a word, Hennigan walked away.

"I don't trust that woman," Ms. Wilson's voice said in Hennigan's ear. "She knows more about what's going on in the world than she ever lets on."

Hennigan was surrounded by people, so she couldn't respond. A few moments later, she entered the powder chamber filled with couches. This was where all the women conducting business or looking for the latest gossip would eventually end up.

Hennigan found the woman she needed to talk to sitting on a bench, touching up her makeup. She walked over and sat down next to her.

"Cleo, it's good to see you," Hennigan said without looking at the First Lady.

"Phillipa, what a delight." Hennigan set down her champagne flute, pulled out a tube of dark red lipstick from her clutch and acted like she was touching it up. "Going for the modern vampire look, I see?"

"Black and red look good on me," Hennigan said. "Just like navy seems to be your color."

Cleo let out a polite laugh. "We both know I prefer black, but we all wear costumes for our roles."

"That we do." Hennigan placed the lipstick back in her clutch before picking up her champagne flute then looked around the room. She sipped and asked, "Shall we go for a walk in the gardens?"

"I only have a few minutes. My security detail will see that I'm gone," Cleo said.

"That's all that I need."

They left the powder room and took a series of doors until they walked outside into an expansive garden. A neoclassical carved stone bench was ahead, designed to look like peacock feathers. Phillipa sat down, and Cleo followed suit.

"I always loved it here when I was growing up," Hennigan said. "Do you remember the first time I brought you here?"

"It was just after my training. I was still figuring out my place in the world, and you thought being in this environment would help me learn to be a *lady*," Cleo said, exaggerating the last word.

"You were a diamond in the rough. I saw it, Mom saw it and even my grandmother saw it. You may not have had the same background as some of our recruits, but we knew you'd be better suited for this line of work than most."

"And I have been," Cleo said. "What do you need from me?"

"Nothing now, but be careful with my two pets. I've grown fond of them. If anything were to happen to them, I would be very disappointed."

"Don't worry, Phillipa. I've grown fond of them, too. There aren't many people who will throw themselves in front of a bullet for you. They're just so...genuine. You almost forget what that looks like in our line of work."

"We have very few genuine friends," Cleo agreed. "And while I consider you one, I also know that you would bury me if you were ordered by the Chairwoman to do so."

"You can at least take solace in knowing I wouldn't enjoy it," Hennigan agreed.

"When are you going to retire to a desk job? Your mother must be getting antsy for you to find someone, so you can continue the familial line."

"I just need to find the right man for my donation. I'll be using modern medicine to get pregnant."

"I wouldn't expect anything less. Do you have your sights set on someone?"

"Not yet," Hennigan said. "He'll have to be the right combination of genetics." She didn't tell Cleo that Deborah Hennigan thought the Barnes' son would make an excellent donor.

"Well, we should get back to the party," Cleo said.

"We should," Hennigan agreed. "Just watch your back. You know Lizzy is coming for you."

"I do," Cleo said. "But we always feared this day would come."

"That we did."

"Does your mother or grandmother know?"

"What you did? Of course not," Hennigan said, sipping her champagne. "And it will stay that way. You gave a friend a chance to disappear and become someone new. She wasted it."

"I was young, naïve and believed in the goodness of humanity," Cleo said. "Now, we're two middle-aged, jaded women who know better."

"I'll drink to that," Hennigan said as she lifted her flute and sipped.

"I'll see you inside."

Hennigan nodded as her one loyal friend walked away. She took a deep breath and enjoyed the fresh air.

"She doesn't know how much I know," Ms. Wilson said in her earpiece.

"No. And just like my mother and grandmother will never know about Lizzy, Cleo will never know about you. Sadly, that's just the way our world works."

"Do you think you can trust her?" Ms. Wilson asked.

"More than most, but that doesn't mean much. Please save that audio to a USB and lock it in my safe. I hope I'll never need to use it, but one never knows in our line of work." She pushed herself off the bench and headed back inside. "I'm going back in. I won't need you for the rest of the night. Good night, Ms. Wilson."

"Good night, Dr. Hennigan."

Phillipa reached into her ear, pulled out the earpiece and slipped it into her small clutch. She took one last breath before heading into the house.

She was barely in the door when a man yelled her name.

"Phillipa, you came." An older, distinguished gentleman in a tux came over and hugged her.

"Of course I did, Daddy. I wouldn't miss this for the world."

* * * *

Ethan

The next few days were a whirlwind of preparations. When Cleo Barnes said she would throw a concert, she put those wheels in motion and went full steam ahead. The concert was scheduled for Saturday night. And true to her word, she worked to get the National Park Service to relent and let them use the West Lawn of the US Capitol. They had sold over one hundred thousand tickets. Tickets were by donation only, since the expenses of the concert were being paid for by private donors. The First Lady had also secured plenty of funding to cover all the show's costs. The Park Service said they could fit up to five-hundred thousand people in that area if necessary. But unlike the Fourth-of-July concert, this one wouldn't appeal to everyone, which was perfectly fine with him. The organizing team secured Echoed Harmony, Melodic Mirage, Stella Starling, Midnight Riot and Riley Neon to come play the concert for free, so it was shaping up to be a full night. This would still be the largest concert ZERO had ever played.

And through it all, Ethan and Blayne kept their security tails, and no one would tell them anything about the status of Laura Lee Jackson and the CLA. Ethan kept expecting Dr. Hennigan, Denzili or Richardson to appear out of nowhere and whisk him and Blayne away for some secret mission that would somehow turn deadly, but everything remained boringly quiet. Never in a million years would Ethan think he'd be disappointed for a day when there wasn't any action, and he'd been the one blaming Blayne for enjoying the cloak-and-dagger stuff too much. But then, Ethan had always been a bit of an adrenaline junkie. He got it through sports then being on stage.

By the time the evening of the concert rolled around, the world was back to normal. They had afternoon soundchecks that were closed off from the public and media. RTN had agreed to broadcast the benefit live, but they could not film the soundcheck. They could interview backstage, but Ethan had avoided Stephen McNeil by hiding in a port-a-potty for twenty minutes. Not his most glamorous moment, but he was okay with that. When he'd told Blayne about this back at the Waldorf, Blayne had a good laugh at his expense.

"Well, what would you have done?" Ethan asked when Blayne finally stopped laughing.

"I would have used my muscle to kindly let him know that he's a perceived enemy combatant and had him shipped to a black-site prison in the Baltic Sea."

"Why the Baltic Sea?"

"Just sounds more ominous," Blayne admitted.

They showered together. Blayne let Ethan fuck him while they got ready for the show. It wasn't their most romantic tryst in the shower, but it was the relief they both needed — something simple, something routine and something fast.

* * * *

Dr. Hennigan

After the party, Dr. Hennigan made her way to DC. The short trip had given her time to catch up on intelligence. Unfortunately, they still weren't close to figuring out where Lizzy Cleburne was heading. Well, they knew where she would end up. They just didn't know how she'd get here. By the following afternoon, Dr. Hennigan was getting antsy. She always got that way after spending time with her father. She loved him, but he didn't really play a significant role in her life. He was money...ancient money. Her grandfather hadn't required her dad to get a job. He was told he must go to college and find an avocation once he had a degree. Grandfather hadn't cared what her father did. He just wanted to make sure her father did *something* with his life. Her father had given her the same talk, and was then surprised when she went further and earned a master's degree, a medical degree and a PhD. He often referred to those as her hobbies. Of course, he did not know what she did for a living. For her, the family wealth made it easy to slip in and out of society, granting her access to a world she wouldn't have otherwise. The same was true for her mother and grandmother. Hennigan women learned long ago that they needed to marry the rich and powerful.

The buzzing of her cell phone brought her out of her trip down memory lane. "Hennigan," she said as she answered.

"Dr. Hennigan," Ms. Wilson replied, "we just got a hit. Last night while you were at the party, I altered Homeland Security's database to ensure all the known aliases of Lizzy Cleburne would be flagged by the airports or the TSA. One name just popped up. I'm pulling up airport security as we speak."

"Why did you call?" Hennigan asked.

"I realized you'd be bored and in a mood after last night, so I'm hoping to do my part as fast as possible so we can get you back out there. Now, give me a second."

Hennigan smiled. Ms. Wilson knew her too well. It was possible that this safe house was rigged with cameras, and she might be under surveillance now. How Ms. Wilson coordinated this without leaving The Complex still amazed Hennigan. Ms. Wilson was not one to give up her sources or the names of the minions she employed to keep her part of the operation running. And if there weren't financial discrepancies, no one cared to ask Ms. Wilson how she did what she did.

"Got her," Ms. Wilson said. "She flew in early this morning to Stewart International Airport."

"Where the hell is that?"

"It's a smaller, regional airport that's part of the Port Authority of New York and New Jersey. It's a town sixty-plus minutes north of New York City. The airport is smaller, but several air carriers fly in and out." There was more typing. "It looks like she rented a mid-sized gray sedan from AutoPilot Rent-A-Car, license plate YKG-2087." There was more typing. She parked the vehicle in Midtown Manhattan, which was towed to the NYPD Tow Pound in Hell's Kitchen a little after noon."

"Well, it's nice to know the NYPD is efficient at something," Hennigan said.

"Then, nothing. Where was the car illegally parked?"

"It was left in the fire lane next to the Port Authority Bus Terminal."

"Well, I seriously doubt she grabbed a bus. From what I remember, taking a bus with others wouldn't be her style. I haven't been to that area. Are there car rental agencies there?"

More typing. "Yes and no. None of them have car lots there, but there are several within walking distance. Plus, there is long-term parking at the Port Authority. She could just as easily steal one of them."

"Keep looking. Once you have information on her next location, let me know immediately."

* * * *

Ethan

The group got to the Washington Mall with relative ease. They had access to a green room tent and various trailers for dressing rooms. Ethan had a small trailer where he could get ready. His hair and makeup team had already ensured all the concert costumes were steam cleaned and prepared for him. During the show, they would have a runner grab the next costume from the trailer and help him make quick changes in the wings.

When they got to the trailer city, everyone was paired with their personal chaperone for the evening's event. Thankfully, Ms. Z. had been assigned to him, so he knew who would be looking after him. At precisely six p.m., Riley Moon started into her set. This audience was more enthusiastic about Riley's return to the musical world after a hiatus than those in Houston. Ethan had only met Riley several times in passing, but she seemed like a nice older woman. He could only imagine how hard that must be to return to touring after having disappeared and had children to be virtually forgotten. At one point, Riley had toured malls across the United States and broke several concert attendance records of her own. Now, she was a footnote and relegated to an opening act.

A knock on his door interrupted him, causing him to look up from his phone. "Enter."

Blayne walked in with Stephanie and Kira. "How are things back here?"

"Just waiting," Ethan said. "Half of tonight is just waiting to go on. How are things looking up front?"

"Well," Stephanie said, "Blayne tried to go out front, was spotted by a teenage boy who pointed, screamed and practically fainted at seeing him."

Blayne pouted. "I thought we agreed not to tell that story."

"No, you begged us not to tell the story," Kira said. "We never agreed to that at all."

Ethan turned to Blayne. "What did you do?"

"I turned and ran. The poor guy from the Metro Police Department chastised me for taking off without warning him."

Ethan gestured to the couch and one empty chair. "Take a seat. It's going to be a while."

"But back to your first question. It's filling up out there. Lots of people were out on the grass with blankets. I'm sure the food vendors are doing bang-up business," Kira said. "There will be a lot of money going to charity tonight. You should feel proud of yourself. You've done a good thing here."

"*We've* done a good thing," Ethan said, being sure to emphasize the word 'we'. "It was your idea, after all."

Another knock on the door. "Enter."

The door slowly opened. "I'm just checking… Hey, babe."

Kira whipped her head toward the door. "Sarah?"

"In the flesh," Agent Murphy replied. "I got the call this morning to fly to DC and help coordinate the interagency task force tonight. Lots of moving parts."

"Why you?" Blayne asked. "I mean, not that you're not qualified, but it seems strange to fly someone in from Houston to do this?"

"Trust me," Agent Murphy admitted. "I had the same reaction. But I was asked specifically by the President to head this up tonight."

"The President called you?" Kira asked.

"Well, no. The President called Director Steele, and Director Steele called me. I didn't even have time to pack a bag. I was told a jet was at the private airport we use, and I was whisked away."

"You'll have to stay with me tonight," Kira said. "You should see the amazing suite they've put me up in. It has a library on the second floor of the suite!"

Agent Murphy looked down at Kira and sighed. "Sadly, they have me taking the redeye home. Besides, the security part of this will take hours after the concert is over. It will be a long night then a long flight back to Houston."

"Why are you going back to Houston?"

"There's a meeting at the Johnson Space Center tomorrow afternoon. Agency heads from NASA, the FBI and the Department of Energy will be there. Should be fun," Sarah said sarcastically. "But then, I'm off on Monday." She looked at Kira. "You going to be back in Houston by then?"

"I'm flying back tomorrow afternoon. I have meetings during the day on Monday, but I have no plans on Monday evening."

"Date night?" Murphy said hopefully.

"Definitely," Kira said.

"Well, I'd best be finishing my rounds," Agent Murphy said.

Kira stood and kissed Sarah.

"Stay safe," Murphy said while exiting the trailer.

"I feel safer already, knowing you're here," Ethan admitted. Murphy nodded, then she shut the door.

Agent Murphy

The sun set and the music blared as she left the small trailer. She pulled her walkie-talkie off her belt loop.

"This is Murphy. Checking in."

"Agent Murphy," a male's voice she didn't recognize said, "so far, everything looks good. Just got a report from the Capitol Police. The four entrances are flowing smoothly. No major hiccups."

"Thanks." There were two major pinch points onto the Western Lawn. They had set up security points on the north or the Senate side of Capitol Square at First and Constitution and Third and Pennsylvania. They then had entrances on the south or the House side of Capitol Square at First and Independence and Third and Maryland. All attendees were subjected to search. It was a massive security undertaking. And most of this was in place long before Murphy landed on the ground this afternoon.

"Agent Murphy," her walkie-talkie chirped.

"This is Murphy."

"Good evening, Agent Murphy," Dr. Hennigan said.

"You," Murphy blurted.

"Is that any way to greet an old friend?"

"What do you want?" Murphy said. "And how are you even talking to me?"

"Well, I'll start with the first question but won't answer the second. As for the first question, we have actionable intelligence that Laura Lee Jackson landed north of New York City this morning, rented a vehicle and drove into Manhattan. She then ditched her rental car and stole a different one from the Port Authority. We tracked that vehicle just south of Philadelphia to a mall where it had been torched." Murphy took a quick breath. "Based on your reaction, I assume you understand what this means?"

"She's heading here."

"That's our assessment as well."

"How do you know this when no one else seems to have heard anything?"

"That relates to that second question I promised I wouldn't answer. Besides, you probably don't want to know our methods."

"Who the fuck are you people?" Murphy exclaimed into the walkie-talkie.

"Excuse me? Who is this? This is the Capitol Police. Identify yourself," a voice said in rapid succession.

Murphy chose to ignore the question and continued walking through the maze behind the stage. She spotted a rocker from a group she'd listened to as a teenager smoking a joint. Technically, DC had legalized small amounts of pot, but smoking in public was still not allowed. Moreover, these were federal grounds and not part of the Washington, Douglass Commonwealth, so the legality was unclear. At worst, the pot was a minor offense.

"Take it inside, please," she said as she passed the man. "I don't want someone to decide to arrest you. The next member of law enforcement to walk by may not be a fan."

She didn't wait for the man's response. She had places to be.

"Agent Murphy," her walkie-talkie squawked.

"POTUS and FLOTUS just arrived with their grandchildren and are heading to the ZERO greenroom tent."

"What the fuck?" Murphy cursed, grateful she hadn't pressed the button when she said it. "Can you please get the Secret Service on the line for me?"

"One second," a voice responded.

Murphy looked around, didn't see anyone, so she kicked the tire of a trailer repeatedly until someone poked their head out.

"Sorry," Murphy said and moved along.

"Agent Murphy, this is Agent Malone. You asked to speak with me?"

"Are you in charge of the POTUS detail?"

"I am."

"Why weren't we informed that POTUS and FLOTUS were coming tonight? We aren't set up for their security?"

"It was deemed 'need to know.' It was also a…last-minute decision," the man said, lowering his voice.

"I see." Ahh, the whims of the President and his wife. "Do you need extra security?" she asked.

"I think the Secret Service is perfectly capable of handling their security," the man replied.

Murphy didn't appreciate the smarmy tone of the man, but she didn't want to push her luck. "If you need anything, let me know."

She was about to disconnect the conversation but thought she should at least let them know. "Agent Malone, we received actionable intel that the leader of the CLA appears to be making her way toward DC."

"Why haven't we heard this?" Agent Malone asked.

"I just found out myself."

"From whom?"

370

She paused, trying to figure out how to describe Dr. Hennigan. She went with, "A security agency outside of the US. They wouldn't explain their methods."

"Interpol?

"It's an extra-governmental security agency. Think more like private contractors."

"Well, until one of our security agencies raises a red flag, I wouldn't trust those private contractors. They're always trying to make a name for themselves. And if you want to maintain your career, I suggest you keep that intelligence to yourself. You don't want to be known as 'the little girl agent who cried wolf.'"

The patronizing tone in the man's voice made Murphy want to stalk him down and punch him in the face, but she kept her temper together. "You can do whatever you want with the intelligence. But if I were you, I'd inform the President and his wife."

"Don't tell me how to do my job, young lady." He continued talking, but Murphy switched off the walkie-talkie. She was tempted to go back and join the pot-smoking rocker.

Chapter Twenty-Four

Dr. Hennigan

Her team came in on three different buses. It was easier to separate and enter the grounds that way. She dressed like countless other tourists, planning on being outside in the autumn cool. Thankfully, it wasn't raining, so she was at least glad she wouldn't be wet on top of the cold.

"We are approaching the US Botanic Garden," a voice said over the intercom. *"Buses leave from this location every twenty minutes. The last bus will depart approximately two hours after tonight's concert. I recommend being at the bus stop at least thirty minutes before the last bus to ensure you secure a seat."*

The squealing of the bus's brakes was followed by the sound of the doors opening as the back part lowered to let someone off in a wheelchair. Hennigan took a deep breath of the evening air as she stepped off. She walked back up the street to the entrance she was using. She wore a long overcoat that concealed several pockets that wouldn't reveal their contents.

"Have your tickets and driver's license ready," a gate attendant said as they formed people into queues to head through security.

She retrieved her driver's license and the ticket she had purchased online, handing them over to the security agent, who examined the ID then her face. "Name?"

"Phillipa Courtenay," she said, using her father's last name.

"Reason for your visit?"

"The concert. I just love ZERO."

The guard handed her back her ID and kept the printed ticket. Phillipa walked away to head through the metal detectors. She'd already checked that day to see they weren't using full-body screeners, only magnetometers. She immediately recognized the make and model, so she knew the best way to bypass its security.

She pulled out her phone and made it look like she was answering her phone. "Ms. Wilson, I have a walkthrough TitanScan Metal Detectors Model 3000 in front of me."

"I understand. Walk with the phone toward the machine. I just need it to detect its signal near the machine for a few seconds."

Phillipa walked forward. "Please take off your coat and put everything in the bin beside the scanner," a security officer said.

Phillipa removed her coat and kept her phone in her front right pocket. Her jacket was about to go through the scanner. She started planning escape options if her coat entered the machine and its interior pockets were detected. She was beckoned forward.

The alarm above her went off.

"Ma'am, is there anything in your pocket?"

Phillipa reached into her pockets and pulled out her cell phone.

"Ma'am, everything must be scanned. Please put it on the conveyor belt and come back through the scanner."

Phillipa walked over, picked up a round dish and placed her cell phone inside. She then walked through the metal detector with nothing going off.

She turned to the guard and said, "I'm so sorry about that. I totally forgot."

"It happens a lot." The guard glanced at her and said, "Enjoy the concert."

She collected her coat, purse and phone and proceeded onto the grounds of the Capitol Building. The lights and music beckoned ahead.

"Let Denzili and Richardson know that we have infiltrated the security system," Hennigan said. "Have them meet me at the James Garfield Monument in thirty minutes. Also, patch me into the police chatter. I want to hear what's going on here."

"Honey, come back to bed." Through her earpiece, Dr. Hennigan caught a distant voice in Ms. Wilson's background.

"Huh?"

"I'm running an op," Ms. Wilson replied. "I'll be back when this is over. It could be a while."

Then it hit Hennigan. "Was that…?"

"Yes," Ms. Wilson responded. "Ms. Brighton and I are giving it another go around. Maybe she'll even coax me outside for a picnic."

"Are you sure you won't burst into flames?" Hennigan joked.

"Despite the rumors — some of them I know you've started — I'm not a vampire." Hennigan could hear the door slide shut on Ms. Wilson's side. "Ms. Brighton and I had a strenuous workout."

"That's what the kids are calling it these days?"

"Phillipa! We were training," Ms. Wilson replied defensively.

Hennigan wanted to laugh and could almost see the horror on Ms. Wilson's face in her mind, so she stopped herself. Even she knew better than to test Ms. Hennigan's patience and generous spirit.

"Well, that's peculiar."

"What is?" Hennigan asked.

"I'm not the only one piggybacking around in their security system. They're being actively hacked."

"Can you stop whoever it is?"

"Do you even need to ask?"

Hennigan made her way to the James A. Garfield Monument. She looked up at the President, who had lasted only four months before being gunned down by Charles J. Guiteau. The statesman stood up top looking completely grandiose. Three men clad in what looked like Greek togas allegedly represented the three parts of Garfield's life — student, warrior and statesman. None of the three allegorical figures spread around the base looked like Garfield. They seemed more like a gay man's fantasy at a frat party, all half-dressed and perfectly sculpted physiques.

"They're out," Ms. Wilson said. "I closed the backdoor. I'll continue monitoring, but they shouldn't be able to regain access. If they attempt to, I'll receive a security alert."

"I should let Agent Murphy know," Hennigan said. "Patch me through to her communications channel."

"Finding her signal."

Suddenly, she heard Murphy say, "Whoever arrested the lead singer for Midnight Riot for smoking pot in his trailer, please know I will find you and make your life miserable. And that's not from me, that's from the White House Chief of Staff. Apparently, Midnight Riot was invited tonight by the President."

"Tough night?" Phillipa asked.

"Oh, for fuck's sake," Agent Murphy said. "The last thing I need is you fucking with me, too."

"I promise I'm not here to fuck with you. You think we're on opposite teams, but we aren't. Anyway, I just wanted to inform you that someone had hacked into the external security systems protocols. It's entirely possible someone got in with something they shouldn't have."

"Fuck!" she heard Murphy scream. "How do you know this?"

"Because *we* were hacking into those external security system protocols and found them."

"Why are you telling me this? You just broke—I don't know—how many federal laws?"

"And you should know by now that I don't care how many of your laws I break to get the job done. That's what I'm for."

"Dr. Hennigan," Ms. Wilson interjected.

"Who's that?" Murphy asked.

"You don't need to know," Hennigan responded.

"Something is seriously wrong," Ms. Wilson said. "We just lost both drones keeping eyes on the gates."

"Agent Murphy, keep your eyes open," Hennigan warned. "Whatever is about to happen is going down soon."

* * * *

Ethan

The concert was going precisely as planned. When an assistant stage manager came to give him his ten-minute heads up, he was dressed and ready for their first set. The group was to perform a pared-down version of their full concert, just three of the five sets. That meant only three costume changes, but the show was anticipated to end by eleven-thirty, provided no unforeseen issues arose.

"Break a leg," Blayne whispered in his ear before he kissed him goodbye. "We'll be in the greenroom tent. Well, I may let my security detail secret me onto the grass if I can do it without causing too much of a scene."

"You better not steal the limelight away from me, buddy," Ethan yelled as Blayne, Kira and Ethan walked away.

"Dude," Ric said, coming up from the side of his trailer, "you've got it *so* bad."

"Yep," Orr said, popping up on his other side. "You'll be next to perform the post-engagement press tour."

"We've barely started dating. We're not even talking about marriage yet," Ethan said. "It's way too soon to have that discussion."

"Uh-huh," Rick said. "I give it less than two months before you're engaged."

"I'll give them six," Orr said. "Let them take things a little slow."

Suddenly, Zach appeared, having been eavesdropping on their conversation from the shadows. "I doubt they'll last the month. Our two are practically honeymooners, as it is. And they've already gone through more than most married couples do in their entire marriages."

"True," Ric agreed. "Three assassination attempts?"

"Four," Zach said. "Plane, Blayne, Pennington and Rose Garden." Zach turned to Ethan and asked, "Am I missing any?"

"Well, there was the ambush with the missile, but I've been assured that wasn't an actual attempt on my life."

"All joking aside, it's been a hell of six weeks, but you two seem to fit together well," Ric said.

"Okay, let's cut it with the touchy-feely crap," Ethan said. "You're gonna make me cry, and I just put on my makeup." He had cracked the joke to stop himself from tearing up.

"Let's do this." The four guys placed their hands in the center of their circle and together they yelled, "Three, two, one, ZERO!"

They jumped, slapped each other on the backs and made their way to the stage. ZERO found their positions underneath the set for their launches onto the stage for Act One. They got there just as the voiceover for their concert was beginning.

"*This concert is being filmed and broadcast worldwide on the Real Time News Network. We want to thank the corporate sponsors for making this concert possible. You can see their logos around the venue and now scrolling across the television. Please, keep those donations coming in for the Domestic Terrorist Victims Fund. All proceeds raised tonight will support the victims and the families of victims injured or killed by homegrown extremists. Using personal photography, videography and cell phones to capture any part of this event is strictly prohibited by law. Violators will be removed from the concert and could be banned from the venue permanently. Get on your feet, put your hands together, and let's hear some noise for Zach, Ethan, Ric and Orr…ZERO, live in concert!"*

Ethan stood on the counterweight platform below his star trap. The beginning orchestration was a remix of ZERO's hit songs. He took a calm, centering breath, double-checked his headset and mic bag were secure and said a quick prayer. He recognized the crescendo as it started. He heard, "Cue Zach in three, two, one," in his earpiece. Ethan heard the mechanism next to him shoot Zach up through the trapdoor onstage, where the crowd erupted. "Cue Ethan in three, two" — he took a deep breath — "one." Ethan was launched up through the underside of the stage, floated for a second over the trapdoor as it closed below him, landed and posed. The crowd noise soared, and Ethan took his first deep breath of the night. "Cue Ric, in three, two, one…" More screaming as Ric landed on stage. "Cue Orr, in three, two, one…" The crowd lost its minds as Orr hit the stage, paused, and all the stage lights zeroed in on the four men, taking them away from just shadows.

"Break a leg, guys." Ji Chu-young's voice came through his earpiece. "Switching you to track audio in three, two, one." The guys let out their first notes as they dove into the high energy of *Desire's Dance*.

"*Hit the streets, we're feeling alive,*" Zach sang.

Ethan followed with, "*A night of freedom, ready to dive.*"

Ric then sang, "*Pulsating lights, and the bass so loud.*"

"*Desire's dance, we're lost in the crowd,*" Orr sang. There was a slight hesitation in the song before everyone jumped in on the chorus, and the entire team of backup dancers seemed to come out of nowhere all over the stage.

Three minutes and twenty-three seconds later, the song ended. All four men were right on the front of the stage, catching their breaths.

Ji Chu-young suddenly cut in, "Slight change of plan, guys. Hold your position. Turn and look at the monitor to your right."

Ethan was confused but turned to look at the video screen off to stage right.

"Good evening, my fellow Americans. My wife and I want to welcome you to the West Lawn of the United States Capitol for this benefit concert. As the world knows, earlier this week, there were attempts on our lives. Thanks to the quick actions of Blayne Dickenson and Ethan Bond" — the photo with the President during the awards ceremony flashed on the screen — *"the First Lady and I were saved from a would-be assassin. They may have saved us, but they saved democracy from the hands of extremists bent on destroying our way of life. I stand before you as your President, filled with gratitude and humbled by the unwavering courage of two extraordinary individuals. Today, as we enjoy ZERO's captivating music, let their melodies remind us of the triumph of the human spirit over adversity. Their performance symbolizes unity, resilience and the healing power of art."*

He looked down at his grandchildren standing before them and said, *"Tonight, I am alive to watch my grandchildren's smiling faces as we are reminded of our duty to safeguard their dreams. Let us cherish our heroes, celebrate our collective strength, and work toward a world where compassion and valor prevail over hatred and violence. Thank you, and may God bless the United States of America."*

"*Please rise*," a voice urged, "*for the singing of the national anthem.*" A quick, nervous look was exchanged among the guys before they heard, "*Sung by Heartland Melodies Hall of Fame inductee, Tammy-Lynn Maybelline.*"

"Sorry about this, guys," Chu-young said. "No one told us this was happening until we were in the middle of the first song. You can move to your spots for *Love Sync.*"

While the group started moving, Ethan looked over and a diminutive woman stood on a stage with a guitar as she strummed out the *Star Spangled Banner*. She was fully decked out in red, white and blue sequins and jewels. Her giant bouffant hairdo was almost as tall as she was.

"Heads up. We were just told by the network that they plan on showing the stage at 'our flag was still there.' Please do your best to sing and look patriotic," Chu-young said.

The anthem was suddenly drowned out. There was a blinding flash of light and an explosion tore through the air like a primal force unleashed as a concussive shockwave engulfed Ethan. An invisible hand seized him, yanked him off his feet and propelled him into a disorienting ascent. Time slowed as his body was launched skyward and backward toward the back of the stage. He slammed back to the ground as if time had suddenly caught up. Ethan's head hit the stage, and his world went black.

* * * *

Blayne

Tammy-Lynn Maybelline strummed through the song. She was going through the music when the area was filled with a white light, followed by the concussive roar that whipped through the tent.

"What the hell?" Blayne yelled. His eyes darted to the Secret Service agents in the room, who immediately encircled the President and his family.

One monitor finally started showing what was going on. The part of the stage where ZERO had been standing just moments before was gone. Blayne tried to run, but enormous arms enveloped around his torso.

"I'm not letting you go out there," Mr. S. said. Blayne tried to fight the ex-Navy Seal, but there wasn't any chance of getting away from the man whose biceps were as big as Blayne's head.

"I need to get to him," Blayne attempted to explain.

"We have three people out there right now," Mr. S. said. "Let them do their jobs. My job, right now, is to protect you three. If you leave here, you're not letting me do my job."

Blayne was compelled to kick and claw at the man to make him let go.

"Blayne," Kira's voice cut through the noise, "trust them. They're professionals."

A second explosion cut through the air with a bone-rattling roar.

* * * *

Dr. Hennigan

Hennigan was already trying to determine what happened when the second suicide bomber exploded. The first two had been near the stage. She glanced at the stage, the ZERO security team handling the situation. Mr. J. motioned for one of the guards to pick up Ethan, who wasn't getting up. Mr. J. walked over to the other security guard, who wasn't moving. He crouched down next to the body, and his hands trembled slightly as he reached out to check for the body for a pulse. There was a fraction of silence, a brief pause filled with anticipation and hope. Even from her distant vantage point, Hennigan could see the dreadful realization ripple across Mr. J.'s face. His scream, raw and guttural, echoed through the chaos.

She wanted to take charge of the stage but knew her talents were needed elsewhere.

"Ms. Wilson?" she yelled through the chaos. A group of women were jostling to get past her. She finally pushed one out of the way. The massive throngs of people trying to flee but not knowing where to go was dizzying. "What can you tell me?" Dr. Hennigan momentarily spun for a second in a circle as she tried to orient herself.

"I'm tracking security cameras as we speak. It looks like both people were wearing the same brand of jacket and a ZERO concert T-shirt."

"Can you see if they entered with anyone else?" The words weren't even out of her mouth when gunshots started piercing the night. She dropped to the ground. "Gunfire. Denzili?" she said.

"On it, boss. Looks like three shooters are making their way from the back of the park, heading northwest toward the stage. They appear to be carrying assault rifles and are shooting indiscriminately."

"Take 'em down," Hennigan barked. "Ms. Wilson?"

"Two more people with similar outfits are still navigating their way through the crowd."

"Phillipa!"

A violent percussion tore through the night, throwing her to the ground as a splintering sound erupted nearby.

Hennigan lay in the dirt, dazed. There was distant screaming of her name over and over again. She pulled herself up to her knees and shook her head. A wall of people moved in her direction. The first woman to make it near her didn't see her on the ground and almost stepped on her. Phillipa lashed out with her leg and connected with the woman's knee. She couldn't hear the cracking sound but she felt the bone give way. Phillipa dragged herself to a standing position and slowly pushed herself away from the mob. Anytime someone got too close, she would shove them into someone else. People quickly started frantically streaming around her. When this swarm passed, she glanced back at the ground. Fifty yards away the lifeless body of the woman she had kicked lay, crumpled on the ground, having been trampled by the horde.

I'm sorry. "Ms. Wilson, report?"

"Thank God!"

"There was a third explosion,"

"I gathered as much," she said dryly.

"I'm looking for the fourth one."

"The shooters?"

"Denzili took down two, and Richardson took down the third."

"Where the hell are the Capitol Police?"

"They're overwhelmed with the fleeing crowd. They weren't prepared. There she is, at two o'clock."

Hennigan turned and found a woman wearing a yellow jacket standing in a daze.

"Richardson, Denzili?"

"We have a visual, boss," Denzili confirmed.

"Approach with caution," Hennigan warned. "I'm going to distract her." She then withdrew her gun and fired twice into the air.

The woman spun in her direction.

"I didn't know," the woman screamed. "We were told these were like those smoke bombs, like the ones they have at gender reveal parties."

"Put the trigger down," Hennigan instructed. "We can help you."

"You don't understand. No one can help me. I don't have control." The woman looked frantic. "We were told we'd be safe if we followed her instructions."

"What's your name?"

"Martha Thompson. My husband, and my children…" The woman fell to her knees and started crying."

"Martha Thompson, her husband Jake and teenage boys James and William were reported carjacked two hours ago on the DC side of Baltimore," Ms. Wilson said.

The other three bombers.

"We were told to walk to the stage and that we'd be okay." The woman tried to stand again but collapsed back to the ground. "She promised we'd be okay. Then Jake…"

"Connect me to the FBI," Hennigan said.

Her ear was met by screaming and yelling. "Agent Murphy, are you there?"

"This isn't the time," Murphy screamed. "I'm a little busy."

"You need to heed my words and listen now. This is a distraction. I repeat, this is a distraction."

More noise came over the speaker from Murphy's side.

"Is that you on the field talking to the bomber?" Murphy asked.

"Yes. Her name is Martha Thompson. Her husband Jake and her teenage boys James and William were carjacked two hours ago. They were forced to wear the suicide vests. They're being remotely detonated from somewhere."

"Why hasn't hers gone off?" Murphy asked.

Because I'm being lured in, Hennigan thought.

She looked up. Richardson was still getting into position, but Denzili was coming in from behind the woman.

"No," she yelled. "Fall back."

A flash of brilliant white and yellow light filled Hennigan's eyes as her body flew. She instinctively braced herself and readied her body for impact. Even as she was propelled through the air, Hennigan's mind raced to grasp the reality of the misstep she had just taken. Her cheek hit the grass with a crunch as she landed, and her body rebounded off the Capitol lawn.

Dazed and disoriented, Hennigan turned her head. She struggled to push herself from the ground. Her shaky body felt like a marionette with its strings severed. Every movement was a battle against vertigo that threatened to pull her back into the abyss of confusion. Suddenly, she felt arms under her. She was being lifted, floating above the ground. Her eyes fluttered open, but all she could see was the ground rushing by. She tried to focus. *Feet running. Being carried. Over someone's shoulders?* The thoughts flooded her mind in a whirl as she tried to make sense of the situation.

Chapter Twenty-Five

Blayne

Saying Blayne was royally furious would be the understatement of the year. He couldn't believe his friends would betray him like that. He needed to run to Ethan, find and protect him. But his friends were more worried about his safety than his needs. There was a part of Blayne who knew his friends were right, but it didn't make him feel any better.

"We need to move Chesapeake, Cumberland and Anacostia's children," a Secret Service agent whispered into his cuff. "Have you secured Anacostia and Delta?" There was a pause in the conversation. Blayne wished he could hear what was happening in the agent's earbud. "Is Delta in PEOC?" Another pause. "Good, keep her there."

The agent saw Blayne staring at him, so he walked farther to keep his conversation private.

"What are you hearing?" Blayne asked, turning to Mr. S.

"There's a lot happening." Mr. S. raised his hand, signaling Blayne to wait a moment. "Three bombers and three gunmen are down. They're still looking for a fourth bomber in the crowd," Mr. S. whispered. A somber veil draped his features as his posture slumped slightly and his usually steady frame faltered.

"What's wrong?" Blayne asked.

"Ms. Z. is down… The second bomber… Dear God."

"What about everyone else?"

Blayne was on the verge of snapping when Mr. S. raised a finger, signaling him to remain silent momentarily.

"The band is okay. They're being brought here now. Ms. A. is carrying Ethan."

"But you said—"

"He's alive. Not responsive, but breathing."

A fourth deafening blast was heard and felt in the tent.

A scream pierced the tent. Blayne looked over to see Cleo Barnes holding her grandchildren to her, doing her best to comfort them.

"What the fuck is going on out there?" Blayne asked.

Just then, Mr. J. entered the tent. A gash on his head covered the right side of his face in a bloody mask. Ms. A. entered a second later, carrying Ethan, who was still out. Blayne ran to the woman and took Ethan from her arms.

"What's wrong?" Blayne asked.

Ms. A. pointed to a lump on the side of Ethan's head. "During the second blast, he hit his head. He's been unconscious ever since."

"First aid… I need first aid."

"I can help," Cleo Barnes offered, startling Blayne by suddenly appearing at his shoulder.

"He's not conscious."

"The second blast threw us," Ric said, coming up on the other side. "Ethan just didn't respond."

"Put him down over there," Cleo said, pointing to a part of the tent that wasn't covered. "Can I get a blanket here?"

Blayne carried Ethan over to the spot Cleo suggested. Cleo crouched down and immediately checked Ethan's pulse. "His pulse is strong. I see nothing wrong with his breathing. I see no outward signs of swelling. Of course, we'll want to get a CT scan as soon as possible to ensure there's no internal bleeding or swelling." She turned and looked at a woman on the other side of the tent and yelled, "Agent Malone, get George Washington University Hospital on the line. As soon as we can move, we have a patient needing emergency care transport. Warn them about possible head trauma and the need for a CT scan."

The sound of a gunshot in the tent caused everyone to flip their heads toward the entrance, where a woman in a ZERO concert T-shirt stood under a red jacket. A Secret Service agent was dead at her feet.

Mr. J. immediately reached for his gun, but she shot him before he could grasp his weapon.

She then clicked her tongue disapprovingly at the group and eyed the other agents in the room, "I wouldn't if I were you. I'm rigged with an explosive device equipped with a dead man's switch."

* * * *

Murphy

Murphy was doing her best to coordinate with all the various law enforcement agencies around the

Capitol. The chatter from various agencies such as the Capitol Police, Metro Police, Secret Service, FBI and emergency services made it impossible to get a clear picture of what was happening.

On the monitor, Murphy watched a group of three people approach someone. "Is that one of our drone feeds?" she asked, pointing to the figures.

"Yes, ma'am," replied the agent at the computer terminal.

"Can you zoom in?"

Dr. Hennigan's voice suddenly came in crystal clear through her earpiece. "Agent Murphy, are you there?"

"This isn't the time," Murphy said. "I'm a little busy."

The FBI agent at the terminal shot her with a confused look. She pointed to her earpiece.

"You need to heed my words and listen now. This is a distraction. I repeat, this is a distraction."

The drone finally got into position as three-armed people surrounded a woman on the ground. The woman was the fourth suicide bomber.

"Is that you on the field talking to the bomber?" Murphy asked.

"Yes," Dr. Hennigan said. "Her name is Martha Thompson. Her husband Jake and her teenage boys James and William were carjacked two hours ago." Murphy grabbed a pad of paper, wrote out their names and handed it to an agent, who immediately started typing away. Murphy didn't catch what Hennigan said, but she heard the words "forced" and "remote."

"Ma'am, the names you provided were victims of a carjacking two hours ago."

"Run them against our images of the bombers," Murphy said. Into her walkie-talkie, she asked, "Why hasn't hers gone off?"

No sooner had she finished her sentence than the woman sitting on the ground detonated.

"Ma'am, facial recognition confirms the carjacking victims were the suicide bombers."

Murphy lowered her head, trying to put all the information together. Then she remembered what Dr. Hennigan had said, "Fuck, this is a distraction. Can you get me eyes on the President?"

"No, ma'am. And the Secret Service isn't responding."

Murphy didn't think twice. She bolted from the mobile command trailer and headed toward the greenroom tent.

* * * *

Dr. Hennigan

Richardson had taken her around the stage and propped her up against a trailer in the back.

"Are you okay?" Richardson asked.

"Will be. Denzili?"

Richardson shook her head once.

"Fuck!" Hennigan cried into the night air. She took a quick breath and centered herself. She'd have time to mourn later.

"Phillipa?" Ms. Wilson's voice said. "Can you hear me?"

"I'm here."

"I'm afraid I have bad news," Ms. Wilson said. "It looks like Lizzy has taken the President hostage."

"On it."

Hennigan turned and started heading toward the tent.

"Also, from my analysis of the videos, I want you to know that Lizzy somehow accessed our weapons cache at a warehouse outside of Philadelphia."

"That would explain the excessive weaponry," she said.

"It also explains how they got past security wearing the vests. They were using an explosive compound *we* created. It's experimental, so meager quantities are available."

"We'll have to deal with the fallout from that later," Hennigan said.

"From my calculations of the blast zones, there was only enough material to make four explosive devices. Unless she supplemented it somehow, she's used what she had."

"Well, that's at least one minor miracle," Hennigan said as she turned the corner.

Agent Murphy stood there, her gun drawn, pointing it at Hennigan.

"Phillipa Hennigan, you're under arrest," Murphy said.

Hennigan rolled her eyes, "We really don't have time for this." She glanced down at the gun in her hand, which was pointed at Murphy's stomach. "How about we holster our weapons and focus on saving the President?"

Murphy hesitated.

"Right now, we're on the same side." Hennigan glanced around and noticed that Richardson wasn't within sight. *She's probably waiting to see how this plays out.* "As soon as this ends, we can play cat and mouse. Agreed?"

"Let's do this," Murphy said. "But I *will* come after you."

"I wouldn't expect anything less," Hennigan said. She smiled at Murphy, even though she knew the other woman wouldn't see it in the night.

They made their way through the maze and quickly approached the tent.

"I wouldn't if I were you," Lizzy's voice cut through the night. "I'm wired with an explosive device with a dead man's switch."

"Fuck," Murphy said next to her.

"She's not," Hennigan said. "She only had a finite amount of the substance she used to make the bombs. From our analysis, there's no way she has anymore."

"But she could have used something like C4," Murphy whispered.

"She's not the type to take the risk of killing herself. She's bluffing."

"Why would she do that?"

"Because it gives anyone in there pause before they contemplate doing anything."

"You there," Lizzy said. "I want all of you to move in front of the entrance."

There was a shuffling of feet within the tent. Seconds later, a small barricade of people blocked the main opening.

Blayne

Blayne shielded Ethan's body in the corner. Cleo crouched next to him as Lizzy grabbed her grandchildren and threw them in with the group she was using as a human wall to cover the entrance.

"That fucking—"

"We won't let anything happen to them," Blayne reassured the First Lady.

"You can be sure of that," Cleo said. She stood, looked at the woman and said, "Hello, Lizzy. It's been a while. What on earth do you think you're doing?"

A hushed silence fell as people in the tent realized that the women knew each other. Blayne admired the First Lady's audacious move.

"Hello, Cleo," Lizzy said, leveling her gun at her. "Long time no see."

"What, twenty years? Give or take."

"Since you abandoned me to die," Lizzy retorted.

Cleo shrugged. "Let bygones be bygones."

"You know this woman?" President Barnes asked.

"We had the same mentors a long, long time ago. As you can see, our lives took very different directions."

Lizzy laughed and said, "You call what they did to us at The Foundation 'mentorship'? It was torture. And as soon as I was no longer useful, they had you get rid of me."

"Well, evidently, that didn't work," Cleo remarked. "And yes, I think The Foundation provided us mentorship that has helped us survive all these years. It's just too bad you forgot the values and lessons they instilled in us so long ago."

Suddenly, Lizzy raised her gun, and the sound of gunfire reverberated throughout the tent.

Dr. Hennigan

Lizzy and Cleo were talking. Taking advantage of Lizzy's distraction, Hennigan and Murphy stealthily maneuvered into position. As soon as Lizzy lifted her weapon, Hennigan did the only thing she could. She leveled her gun at the young man standing with his back to her and pulled the trigger.

As the young man collapsed, Murphy rose from her crouch and fired two rapid shots into the back of the assailant.

The room remained silent for a split second before the tent became a frenzied place of movement.

The Secret Service pointed their weapons at Murphy, who lowered her gun and yelled, "FBI."

Hennigan used the moment of confusion to slip away. She had only taken a few steps when Richardson joined her side.

"Where'd you go?" Hennigan asked.

"I wanted to provide backup in case something went sideways."

* * * *

Ethan

Ethan awoke in a hospital room shortly before noon. The sound of beeping hospital equipment made his head hurt. His first instinct was to yank the wires he was hooked up to, setting off a fresh array of alarms that amplified his headache.

"Hold on," Blayne interjected, seizing his hand. "You're safe now."

"Where am I?" Ethan asked.

"You're at George Washington University Hospital. What do you remember?"

"Nothing really." Ethan attempted to sit up with Blayne assisting him in adjusting the hospital bed to a sitting position. At first, the room spun a bit, but things calmed down in a few seconds. "I remember starting the concert, then everything's hazy."

For the next few minutes, Blayne briefed Ethan on the events that unfolded after he had lost consciousness.

"Wow," Ethan said. "That's intense."

"I have some bad news," Blayne said. "But we can talk about it when you're better."

"Just tell it to me straight," Ethan insisted.

"Mr. J. was shot. Don't worry. He's doing okay and already trying to get checked out of the hospital. But…" Blayne closed his eyes trying to fight back his own tears. "We lost Ms. Z. One of the bombs…"

A choked cry escaped Ethan's lips as tears welled in his eyes. "How bad was it?"

"Ms. Z.?"

"No, everything."

"It was bad. Quite a few people are still in intensive care units across the district. We won't know how bad it will be for a few days, probably. The press is already blaming the President and First Lady for having this concert and allowing the terrorists to attack. The White House is blaming the FBI, who is blaming the Secret Service, who is blaming everyone else. Southern conservatives are blaming leftists, and progressives are blaming right-wing extremists. So, basically, it's business as usual in DC. Thankfully, no one is pointing their fingers at us this time."

"This is all my fault," Ethan said. "If only we hadn't staged that damn concert—"

"No way, absolutely not. I won't allow you to shoulder the blame for any of this. Is that understood? This is all one hundred percent on the shoulders of Elizabeth Cleburne. The news has been pretty sketchy about her biography."

A voice chimed in, "Knock, knock," from the door. Ethan pivoted to see Stephanie standing there. She ran to his bedside and gave him a hug.

Ethan winced.

"Oh my God, I am *so* sorry," Stephanie apologized.

"It's okay," Ethan replied. "I'm just a bit sore, that's all."

"Have the doctors seen him yet?" Stephanie asked Blayne.

"He just woke up. We were conversing." Ethan caught the look Stephanie flashed Blayne. "I wasn't going to keep anything from him. He had a right to know." From the look that crossed Stephanie's face, Ethan could tell this had been a conversation they had previously had.

"Well, I'm going to go find his doctor," Stephanie said, "and tell the guys. They're all out in the waiting room." She looked down at Ethan. "Be prepared. Everyone is going to be fawning all over you. You gave us a fright."

With that, Stephanie left them alone.

"You gave me quite a scare," Blayne confessed. "When Ms. A. carried your body into the VIP tent, my heart shattered."

"It's okay," Ethan said, grabbing Blayne's hand. "I'm fine. We got through this together. I'm guessing it's over now?"

"Yes, any remaining members of the CLA were apprehended. Most of the remaining were low-level ideologues who weren't privy to what their leadership was up to."

"I suppose I should inquire... What about me?"

"Oh, yes, my apologies. You sustained quite a blow to the head. You were unconscious for about twelve hours. Thankfully, there was no internal bleeding or swelling. The doctors say you'll make a full recovery. We were just waiting for your body to heal and decide to wake up."

Ethan let a breath out through his nose. "You know I love you, right?"

"I love you, too."

"Great, make me a promise that we'll never do this again."

"That is a promise I'm more than happy to make. My days of running toward danger are officially over."

Having said that, Blayne leaned in to kiss Ethan.

"Excuse me," a voice piped up from the other side of the curtain, punctuating the room's silence."

Blayne stood up and pulled the curtain back. Lucas lay in the bed next to Ethan.

"What happened to you?" Ethan asked.

"That woman shot me!"

"What woman?" Ethan asked.

"That crazy assassin friend of yours."

"Agent Murphy told me they needed a clear shot at Lizzy Cleburne. Unfortunately, Lucas was being used as a human shield. Dr. Hennigan did what Dr. Hennigan does. She made a decision," Blayne said, then gestured to Lucas.

"Oh, man," Ethan said, "I'm so sorry to hear that. What about the bullet?"

"It went through him with no significant damage," Blayne explained.

"No significant damage?" Lucas retorted. "I'm confined to a hospital bed. How can this not be significant?"

"Trust me," Blayne said. "If Dr. Hennigan had wanted you dead, you'd be dead."

Epilogue

Dr. Hennigan

A week had passed since the incident at the Capitol. The initial shock had faded, replaced by the steely determination that comes with picking up the pieces. Dr. Hennigan was gratified to witness the country finally uniting to seriously address homegrown extremist groups for the first time. Even right-wing politicians, who typically relied on these groups for votes, had put forth only a few of their customary "but what about the left" arguments.

Once again, she found herself having tea in her mother's personal quarters. Her mother and grandmother sat in ornate chairs on the other side of the coffee table while Hennigan sat on the couch, flanked by Ms. Wilson and Ms. Brighton. The room was chilly and quiet, with each woman lost in her own thoughts.

Hennigan cleared her throat, straightened her notes and began the post-operation report. The numbers were daunting. While the casualties were not nearly on the scale of 9/11, they were significant enough to elicit grim expressions around the table.

"Cleo Barnes is safe, and her cover remains secure," Hennigan reported, offering some good news.

"And what about the CLA?" asked the eldest Hennigan.

"Permanently disbanded. The FBI had made quick work of rounding up anyone with connections."

"What about links between Elizabeth Cleburne and The Foundation?" Hennigan's mother, Deborah, asked.

"I've eradicated any records showing any connection between Cleburne and anyone from The Foundation, apart from Cleo Barnes."

"Why didn't you scrub any connection with Cleo?" Deborah Hennigan asked.

"Easy. There were too many witnesses in the VIP tent at the concert to scrub those links. Instead, I constructed a plausible backstory linking Cleo and Laura Lee. It makes it abundantly clear that they parted ways over two decades ago. It makes it look like Cleburne was jealous of Cleo Barnes and hatched this intricate plot out of some form of mental illness."

The senior-most Hennigan steepled her hands under her chin. Everyone waited to hear what she would say. "We were lucky this time. I don't like how close we came to losing everything we've spent generations building." She turned to Ms. Brighton. "In your assessment, what changes should be made?"

Ms. Brighton let out a breath. From the look on her face, Dr. Hennigan could tell the other woman knew this question was coming, but she still wasn't happy to be asked.

"I am concerned that Elizabeth Cleburne survived liquidation. I believe we need to reconsider our protocols for internal asset liquidation to ensure such an incident never reoccurs. I also worry about the exposure this whole incident had on The Foundation. Norms that have lasted the organization for over a hundred years were violated." Before Dr. Hennigan could protest, she added, "But I don't think these were necessarily a bad thing. We've been insular for a long time. The world is changing. I think we must adapt."

Sara Hennigan took in the information. The older woman took a sip of her tea. "I'm afraid I agree with your assessment, Ms. Brighton. The Foundation does not exist in the same world our predecessors created. Being an old woman, I'm not fond of change. However, for The Foundation to maintain its relevance, we must adapt." There was a pause before she asked, "Anything else?"

"I've connected Lizzy to several of The Foundation's previous operations," said Ms. Wilson. "The Houston convoy attack has now been blamed on the CLA."

"And Sarah Murphy?" Hennigan asked, her tone cautious.

"We've provided her with sufficient leads in Houston to keep her busy for a few years," Ms. Wilson replied. "She's not an immediate concern. She's been permanently appointed to the Houston Field Office."

"What about the young men you continuously involve in our affairs?" Deborah asked.

"They are dealing well, considering," Hennigan said. "Their assigned therapist is one of ours. We are keeping tabs on them."

The conversation lulled as the women sat in silence, sipping their tea. Finally, Sara looked at the group. "We can't end this meeting without discussing the elephant in the room. Who funded this? The CLA didn't have the capital to do this alone."

Ms. Wilson cleared her throat. "We cannot confirm, but certain indications are pointing to the Aegis Concorda," Ms. Wilson stated, her voice steady.

Sara Hennigan scoffed, a sharp, almost bitter sound. "They wouldn't dare."

"Chatter suggests otherwise," Ms. Wilson replied, meeting Sara's fierce gaze head-on. "They've set their sights on US territory."

The matriarch's eyes hardened. "Then we shall take the fight to them." The words resonated in the silent room, setting the course for what would come. The battle lines were drawn.

Want to see more from this author? Here's a taster for you to enjoy!

Love and Liquidation: Rhythmic Reclamation
Jason Wrench

Excerpt

Thump. Thump. Thump. The pulsating music from the speakers made the room quiver, each bass note sending a tangible vibration through the club. All around, bodies moved rhythmically, swaying and gyrating in sync with the beat. Some dancers kept their distance from their dancing partners, while others might as well have been fucking on the dance floor. He fell into the latter category. The twink he was dancing with had his legs wrapped around his waist, their sweaty torsos pressed together. He'd long since shoved the T-shirt he wore to the club into his back pocket. Absently, he pulled his hand away for a second to make sure it was still there. As if sensing he was getting distracted, the twink thrust his pelvis against his fully erect cock. The only thing keeping him from entering the twink was the barely existing clothing between them.

Neon beams in shades of cobalt and fuchsia cut through the haze, illuminating the twink's face in brief, vivid flashes. *What was his name again? Connor? Justin? Matthew? Fuck! Does it matter?* The air was thick with a cocktail of aromas—the overpowering smell of sweat mixed with sexual desperation, the sweetness of spilled cocktails and traces of every variety of expensive cologne. If he inhaled deep enough, he could smell the bleach aroma of guys who hadn't waited to take their trysts to the back room.

What time is it? he wondered. He hadn't bothered to wear his watch. The last time he'd worn a watch to the club, the watch hadn't been on his wrist by the end of the night. He'd never know whether it had slipped off his wrist naturally or had been nabbed by a thief.

The twink leaned forward and traced his earlobe with his tongue. "I want you in me," the twink whispered in his ear.

"You think you can handle me?" He gave a quick thrust with his cock into the twink's ass to remind him how large he was.

"I think I'll manage," he said with a grin, unwrapping his legs and dropping to the floor. *God, he really is short.* The twink grabbed him by the belt and dragged him through the dance floor toward the back of the club, where a small labyrinth of darkened rooms existed, illuminated by black lights, ensuring minor visibility of the sexual tableau. Men of all colors, shapes and sizes were in various stages of undress and compromising positions.

He recognized a Senator's aide strapped to a St. Andrew's Cross being whipped. He almost wanted to stand in line and get his own chance at lashing the aide. That particular aide had recently single-handedly blocked legislation to increase funding for low-performing schools with marginalized student populations. He wished he had his cell phone on him so he could snap a couple of pictures and send them to the Senator. He wondered if the family-values-toting conservative Senator had any idea what his aide got up to when he was off the clock.

A pull on his belt reminded him he wasn't there to fuck over the Senator's aide. He was there to fuck the twink. The small guy pulled him past the sling, where a guy lay splayed for the world to see, his legs spread wide. From the looks of the glowing goo coming out of his ass, he'd already been ridden a few times. He looked at the man's face and realized he'd fucked him in the past himself. *Good thing I'm on PrEP.*

The twink pulled him over to a wall that wasn't completely occupied with men fucking. The twink pulled his pants down to his knees then turned around, bracing his forearms to the wall. "Do you have lube?" he asked, looking over his shoulders.

"Yeah, I picked up a few when I walked in." The club had giant jars of one-use lubes and condoms sitting on a table near the main bar. They knew their clientele.

He slipped his belt off and pulled his pants and boxers just below his ass, freeing his nine-inch cock as it slapped against the muscles of his stomach. He reached into his pocket and pulled out one of the lube packets. It had a twist top, so he twisted it off and dropped the plastic container on the floor, figuring someone else could clean it up later. He didn't envy whoever had to clean up this place. *They deserve hazard pay.*

He spread all the contents of the lube packet on his dick, ensuring it would be nice and wet when he entered the twink. He slipped a single, lubed finger into the twink's ass without warning the little guy. The gasp was chased by a releasing sensation around his knuckle as the twink relaxed.

"Warn a guy next time," the twink said as he pulsed his sphincter.

"Fine... Here's your warning." He slipped the finger out as he bent deep at the knees, pointed his dick toward the hole and shoved. He reached around and clamped his hand over the twink's mouth before an audible yelp escaped at the sudden penetration.

He released his hand. "You fucking bastard," the twink grunted.

He pulled out again and shoved again. "Want me to stop?"

The twink went limp against him as he muttered, "No," as he pushed back against his dick, clenching and unclenching his hole.

That's all the consent he needed, so he went full steam ahead and provided the twink the fuck of his life. The twink was like putty in his hands. He reached around and stroked the twink's erect cock in time with his own rhythm. He heard a noise from his left, so he glanced over and saw a small crowd had gathered to watch him rail the twink. Admittedly, the sight of someone his height fucking a guy short enough to fit in his shirt pocket must have looked like a Great Dane fucking a Chihuahua.

He locked eyes with a blond guy standing a few feet away, who was stroking his cock, and he smiled. He never would have considered himself an exhibitionist, but over the past couple of years, he enjoyed having others watch as he fucked some stranger in public. Half the time, those strangers watching became his next prey.

"I'm gonna..." the twink got out of his mouth before his cock spasmed under his hand as the twink coated the wall in sticky cum.

It only took a couple more seconds before he released his load inside the twink. His cock pulsed repeatedly as he felt his cum shoot inside the twink. When he finished his last spasm, he pulled out a wet wipe from his pocket and cleaned himself before handing the used wet wipe to the twink.

"Thanks. Looks like you've got a fan club," he said, reaching out and twisting the twink's head to see the group of men still hovering nearby. "Personally, I'd let the guy with the white hair in you next. I can attest, he's a good time." He was already buckling his belt when the twink turned to stare at him. The twink was already erect again.

"Can I get your number?" the twink asked.

"I don't give it out to strangers." He gently patted the guy on the head. "But look for me." With that, he turned and headed to the exit. Leaving the back labyrinth and entering the main dance floor, he pulled his T-shirt from his back pocket, glad it was still there. He slipped it on over his head as he made his way to the club's front door. Before exiting, he stopped by the doorman to pick up his coat and cell phone.

"Leaving so soon?" the coat checker asked. "That's a record, even for you."

"I'm a hot guy in my twenties with an enormous dick. Bottoms throw themselves at me," he replied, reaching into his front pocket and pulling out his wallet. He slipped out the green ticket and handed it to the coat checker.

With the ticket in hand, the coat checker turned around and shuffled into the back of the room before returning with a light blue bomber jacket.

"You're gonna freeze out there in this thing," the coat checker said, handing him the jacket.

He reached into the jacket and pulled out his cell phone before slipping it into his back pocket. "Trust me. It could be a blizzard out there right now, and I don't think I would freeze," he said with a wink before he slipped into his jacket and pushed open the metal bar holding the door closed, slipping into the cold DC night air.

The sweat chilled quickly against his skin, and his temperature dropped fast. He headed down the alley from the club's entrance onto New Hampshire Avenue, where he took a left and headed toward Dupont Circle. His three-thousand dollar-per-month apartment was just off the Circle. On the other side of the street, he watched a couple of Argentinian Guards milling around their embassy's entrance. He'd fucked one of their guards a year ago. That was one of the nice things about living so close to Embassy Row, a constant rotating pool of international ass—and the occasional dick.

"Hey, hold up!" a voice yelled from behind him. Assuming it was intended for someone else, he ignored it. "Blayne Dickenson?"

He spun around and took in the man in the blue suit, jogging his way.

"Who's asking?"

"I thought I recognized you leaving the club."

Blayne looked at the man in his suit. Wearing that buttoned-up outfit wouldn't have gotten him past the bouncer. The suit was decently fitted, but Blayne could tell in the dim light of the streetlights that it was off the rack.

"And you are?" Blayne asked, taking a suggestive step in the guy's direction.

The man reached out, put his hand on Blayne's chest and pushed him gently away. "Someone who isn't looking to have sex with you, not that I didn't enjoy the show." The man whipped out a cell phone, swiped at the screen and turned it toward Blayne as a video of him fucking the twink played.

Blayne growled and reached for the phone, but the man danced backward, keeping himself and the phone out of Blayne's reach. "I just want to talk."

Blayne clenched his fists at his sides and said through gritted teeth, "And why shouldn't I beat the crap out of you now and take your phone?"

"Cool down, big guy," the man said, putting the phone back in his coat pocket. "Like I said, I only want to talk. You talk to me, and I destroy the video."

"Why should I believe you? You've already broken the law and illegally filmed me having sex."

"I never said I filmed you—"

"Oh, so you had someone else do your dirty work—"

"No, I called in a big favor to get this video. And they weren't filming you." The guy looked at Blayne quizzically. "You have no idea who you were fucking, do you?"

Blayne shrugged. "Should I? He was a random twink who came on to me. Said he'd heard about my big dick and wanted to see if the rumors were true."

"You were just filmed fucking Drew Ellis." The man stared at Blayne, clearly expecting Blayne to know who he was talking about, so Blayne shrugged. "The Speaker of the House's twenty-one-year-old son."

"So? He's legal."

"That's not the point," the man said. "If the video got out, it would be a pretty large political scandal for the Speaker and probably ruin Drew's life."

"And I'm supposed to care…?"

"It would drag you back into the press, which I guess is not something you're looking for."

Blayne looked down at the man and asked, "What do you want?"

"Just to talk. Give me an hour. I'll tell you everything."

"And you are?"

"Todd Rice," the man said, extending his hand. "I write for *The Capital Pride Times*."

The Capital Pride Times was a small independent newspaper focused on gay issues in the district. They had copies in almost every LGBTQIA+ bar, store and restaurant, so it was hard to miss.

"No. God, fuck no!" Blayne said. "You said it yourself. I don't want to have anything to do with the press." He narrowed his eyes and added, "So, you can go fuck yourself."

Blayne turned around and walked away.

"What about the video? I'll post it online!"

"And I'll sue your ass," Blayne called behind him. "Put that thing you call a newspaper out of business while I'm at it."

"What about Drew Ellis? Don't you give a shit what will happen to him if the video goes public?"

"Not especially," Blayne called out in an almost sing-songy voice. "He's a big boy. He can take care of himself." Blayne spun on the sidewalk and stared back at the reporter. He paused briefly and added, "Well, maybe not that big. I've played with dolls larger than him. He may be a pocket-gay, but he sure knew how to take it like a man."

"Wow, you have turned into a fucking asshole. I'd heard the rumors around Dupont Circle." Silence hung between them before the reporter asked, "I wonder what Ethan would say about that?"

Before Blayne knew what he was doing, he took a few quick strides, lifted the guy off the ground and held him even with his eyes. The guy kicked at Blayne, pure terror washing across his face.

"I'm going to say this once and only once," he said, bringing the man inches from his face. Blayne was close enough to smell the breath mint the reporter had been clearly sucking on. "Never say that man's name to me again." Blayne put the reporter down and walked away.

"You don't recognize me, do you?" the man called after him.

"Nope. And I don't give a fuck." Blayne kept walking.

"I liked you better before you met *him*. I totally had a crush on you. God, you're the guy who made me realize I liked men."

Blayne stopped again before slowly turning to stare back at the reporter. "Who are you?" Blayne asked, his face scrunched up in confusion.

"You like your coffee black with a dab of milk. Nothing fancy."

Blayne's eyes grew wide with sudden realization. "The Dream Bean?" Blayne drew out the question as he finally put it together.

"You also taught me freshman composition. God, I fantasized about you. You were so fucking hot. I may have snapped a couple of pictures of you with my cell phone during class then jerked off to them in my dorm room."

"Wow. You're not the young kid I had in class anymore." Blayne paused a beat then added, "Well, you've seen me in action. Hope you enjoyed the show." The anger seethed beneath his words. "Now, run along home and jerk off to your heart's content. But if that video ever comes out, I will end you. I couldn't care less about freedom of the press. I will sue you until you return to whatever tiny farm town in Texas you crawled out of."

Todd barked out a laugh. "Listen to yourself. You sound like someone from a mob movie. I almost expected you to say *'capiche?'* at the end of that sentence." Todd stared up at Blayne, his posture relaxed. "I don't plan on doing anything with the video. The person who shot the video wasn't there for you but saw you fucking Drew Ellis, so he thought it would be a good idea to follow the story. I had him send me the file and delete it off his cell. No one else knows about it. I'm not here to ruin you or Drew Ellis."

"Then why was your camera guy there?"

"To get an incriminating video of one of those homophobic Southern Senators who likes to pass anti-gay legislation by day while getting fisted in public at night."

"That's still sleazy. I mean, there's a reason people aren't allowed cell phones in there."

"It's the hypocrisy of it. That's also why my camera guy shouldn't have shot video of you and Drew. Drew is openly gay, and his mom is a huge gay rights advocate." Todd slipped the phone into the back pocket of his pants.

"Listen to you, all grown up," Blayne said, the anger slipping from his voice. "And I remember you, Todd. I didn't recognize you, but I remember you." Blayne let out a sigh as he smiled. "And, I noticed you," Blayne said, letting his eyes graze down Todd's body. Blayne stepped into Todd's space and leaned in, asking, "How'd you end up in DC?"

Todd blinked rapidly before stammering, "I finished my undergraduate at Pennington, then was accepted to Columbia for my MA in journalism. Took this job right out of graduate school."

"Uh-huh," Blayne said next to Todd's ear. "Do you miss how big things were in Texas?" He pressed himself into Todd, wrapping an arm around his waist. Todd sucked in a breath as Blayne ground himself into him.

Blayne snaked his fingers into Todd's waist, letting his nose graze along Todd's jawline. Blayne ground himself into Todd once more, showing Todd he was ready to go again. Todd let out a whimper as Blayne grabbed Todd's ass and slipped the phone out. Blayne whispered into Todd's ear, "Maybe you'll let me show you that fantasies can come true sometime." Blayne pushed himself away from Todd and smiled down at him before turning and walking away. Blayne played with the phone. *Thank God, the lock screen didn't initiate.* He searched for the video file and deleted it. He also found the work email and deleted the file there.

Blayne leaned against the wall and waited for Todd to realize he'd taken the phone. Sure enough, seconds later, he heard leather soles slapping against the sidewalk heading his way.

He spun around the corner and almost collided with Todd.

"You stole my phone," Todd said, a spark of anger in his eyes.

"Deleted the files that shouldn't have been there in the first place," he said, handing Todd his phone. "I may be jaded. I may have lost my shit. But I won't let someone blackmail me. No matter how nice I thought your ass was…er, is."

Blayne turned to the crosswalk and hurried across the intersection.

"Will you be there tomorrow?" Todd yelled after him.

Blayne held a hand in a wave without turning his back and kept walking.

Climbing two floors, Blayne reached his tiny one-bedroom apartment in the hall's middle. He despised it for the noise from neighbors on both sides. The relentless banging of a headboard against the wall above and the old woman below, who struck her ceiling with her broom handle if he didn't tiptoe, only deepened his hatred. Blayne had a series of noise complaints filed against him by the old woman. From the details of her complaints, you'd think he was Irish stepdancing with a dozen elephants up here. Of course, how she heard anything was beyond him. You had to yell at her to be understood during a conversation.

Upon entering his apartment, Blayne set his wallet and keys on a small table near the door, hung his coat on a bracket behind it and slipped off his shoes. He moved to the kitchen, grabbed a water bottle from the fridge then walked into the living room to collapse on the couch. From there, he could see his alarm clock glowing in the bedroom across the room. His apartment was a stark white box with a few walls and had been his for two years, yet it showed little sign of habitation. The walls were bare, with no artwork or personal touches to signal Blayne's presence. His furnishings were minimal, with just a couch, a wall-mounted TV and a couple of TV trays for dining or laptop work. Despite his intention to buy a desk, he never had. His bedroom was equally sparse. Blayne almost never brought guests back, primarily because his full-sized bed, customized for his height, wasn't inviting for overnight stays. His clothes were either in a dresser or hanging in the closet. Beyond those few personal items, the apartment remained stark. Initially, Blayne's minimalism stemmed from a recent breakup and the belief he wouldn't stay long. Still, eventually, it became his way of life.

He pulled out his iPhone opened his favorite dating app, EndZone, and started aimlessly scrolling through the catalog of men all looking for a quick fuck. Scrolling through the endless sea of dick pics, asses and the occasional smiling face caused his dick to stir again. *What am I in the mood for? Twenty-year-old twink or forty-year-old leather daddy?* He didn't consider himself a bottom, but he'd learned that sometimes it was fun to be blindfolded, tied up in a sling and used like a piece of meat.

Blayne was about to see what DistrictLeatherDad was up to when he noticed he had a voice mail at the bottom of the screen. He sent DistrictLeatherDad a quick message before opening the phone app to listen to the message.

"Dr. Dickenson, this is Sepi Amin, President Barnes' Chief of Staff. I'm calling to remind you the town car will be there at ten a.m. for you...sharp. Please don't keep the driver waiting." There was a pause before she added, "And dress presentably this time." And she hung up.

Blayne closed his eyes, pinched the bridge of his nose and sighed. *Fuck tomorrow!* His phone buzzed with an incoming message on EndZone.

Come on over. I want to play with your ass. Gonna let me fist you this time?

Blayne typed back.

You wish. Be there in twenty. Make that thirty. Should probably shower after my earlier hook-up.

No need. I like the scent of a freshly fucked man.

Be there in ten.

Blayne took another swig of water and headed back into the cool night.

About the Author

Jason Wrench is a professor in the Department of Communication at SUNY New Paltz and has authored/edited 15+ books and over 35 academic research articles. He is also an avid reader and regularly reviews books for publishers in a wide number of genres. This book marks his first full-length work of fiction.

Jason loves to hear from readers. You can find his contact information, website details and author profile page at https://www.firstforromance.com/

PUBLISHING

Sign up for our newsletter and find out about all our romance book releases, eBook sales and promotions, sneak peeks and FREE romance books!